MW01093359

Amplitudes

"Mandelo presents a joyful and impressively varied array of speculative fiction centered on queer resistance and survival in imagined futures. . . . It will give hope to readers who feel the future looks bleak.
—**Publishers Weekly**

"Lee Mandelo makes bold, rewarding choices as editor, and the result is a book that's more than the sum of its parts. These writers aren't just exploring the future. They are the future."
—**Isaac Fellman**, Lambda Literary Award-winning author of *Notes from a Regicide*

"The heraldic moments within *Amplitudes* gloriously reveal the impossible and necessary truths of what a queer and trans foregleam can be; a revelation for those who need a guiding light towards the future and fully embodies the hope, rage, fear, and love that is the beating heart of every queer revolution."
—**Linda H. Codega**, author of *Motheater*

"In these dark times, there's nothing more radical than what *Amplitudes* says just by existing: there is a future, and we are in it."
—**Adam Sass**, award-winning author of *The 99 Boyfriends of Micah Summers*

"*Amplitudes* is a tidal wave of excellent science fiction, brought up from the deep sea of trans and queer talent in our genre. Every story is like a pearl, birthed in grit but shining in perfection, each one strung after the other masterfully by editor Lee Mandelo. Lee knows better than most that our mere existence is resistance, and to look into our future is transcendental."
—**Cecilia Tan**, award-winning author of *Black Feathers*

"*Amplitudes* is a fantastical kaleidoscope of queer futures, encompassing the full spectrum of joy and hardship, resilience and vulnerability. This is the anthology I want with me in the coming years, as a reminder of everything we have to fight for and all the wonderful queer possibilities that await us."

—**Ann LaBlanc**, editor of the anthology *Embodied Exegesis*

"Rooting through a broken, still-breaking world, *Amplitudes* finds amid the danger to trans and queer people real possibilities for resilience, connection, even flourishing. Clear-eyed, breathlessly imaginative, deeply felt, and defiant, this anthology showcases the best of our determination to make a life better than we found it."

—**Theodore McCombs**, author of the
Octavia E. Butler Award finalist *Uranians*

"The stories in *Amplitudes* transport us to the edges of time, space, and possibility as their authors dare us to imagine the future of queerness. Each one offers its own striking vision of how we survive and thrive in these speculative realities, yet they all reflect what has always been true—we will never stop fighting for a brighter tomorrow."

—**Eddy Boudel Tan**, author of *After Elias*

"From a lesbian anarchist knight to a Love Shack circuit party, each story acts as a portal to a new universe, captivating in its own way. A queer and trans anthology that reminds us that as dark as it gets, we will always have each other, and that the future is ours for the taking, if we fight for it."

—**Daniel Zomparelli**, co-editor of *Queer Little Nightmares*

"The stories in *Amplitudes* all crackle with electricity. Editor Lee Mandelo has crafted a set list that sings out with a bold sense of queer rebellion, and he's inviting us all to a raucous dance party."

—**Nathan Tavares**, author of *A Fractured Infinity*
and *Welcome to Forever*

Stories of Queer and Trans Futurity

Edited by Lee Mandelo

EREWHON

an imprint of Kensington Publishing Corp.

erewhonbooks.com

EREWHON BOOKS are published by:

Kensington Publishing Corp.
900 Third Avenue
New York, NY 10022

erewhonbooks.com

All Kensington titles, imprints, and distributed lines are available at special quantity discounts for bulk purchases for sales promotions, premiums, fundraising, educational, or institutional use.

Special book excerpts or customized printings can also be created to fit specific needs. For details, write or phone the office of the Kensington sales manager: Kensington Publishing Corp., 900 Third Avenue, New York, NY 10022, attn: Sales Department; phone 1-800-221-2647.

Erewhon and the Erewhon logo Reg. US Pat. & TM Off.

ISBN 978-1-64566-086-6 (trade paperback)

First Erewhon trade paperback printing: June 2025

10 9 8 7 6 5 4 3 2 1

Printed in the United States of America

Library of Congress Control Number: 2024943941

Electronic edition: ISBN 978-1-64566-087-3 (ebook)

Edited by Diana Pho; interior design by Kelsy Thompson; images courtesy of Shutterstock

The authorized representative in the EU for product safety and compliance
Is eucomply OU, Parnu mnt 139b-14, Apt 123
Tallinn, Berlin 11317, hello@eucompliancepartner.com

Contents

"The future is queerness's domain....

Some will say that all we have are the pleasures of this moment, but we must never settle for that minimal transport; we must dream and enact new and better pleasures, other ways of being in the world, and ultimately new worlds. Queerness is a longing that propels us onward, beyond romances of the negative and toiling in the present. Queerness is that thing that lets us feel that this world is not enough, that indeed something is missing."

—José Esteban Muñoz,
Cruising Utopia: The Then and There of Queer Futurity

Introduction

UNDER MY LEFT COLLARBONE is a tattoo that reads, "not yet here."

What's not yet here is queerness; what's not yet here is the future. I first read these words by queer theorist José Esteban Muñoz in my early twenties, and I've returned to them over and over again since then, because I find their message absolutely electrifying. While the world makes it hard for queer and trans people to survive, let alone thrive, we nonetheless fight our way toward other possibilities—toward the horizon of what Muñoz called queer futurity. Simply but radically, queer futurity argues that *more than this is possible.* Queerness itself rejects the oppressive status quo of the here and now, offering instead endlessly interconnected ways to imagine the "concrete possibility" of another world, another future. Or, many other futures. The same question, of course, underlies some of the most powerful speculative fiction of the last century: *but what if things were different?*

Grounded in the political realities of the present yet imagining alternate possibilities for the future, the twenty-two pieces collected in *Amplitudes: Stories of Queer and Trans Futurity* all answer the question differently... but they share a resistant, critical belief in what we can create together as queer and-or trans people from various backgrounds. There is also a shared sense of hope—though that hope might sometimes be hard-won, complicated, and partial. Queerness and transness themselves move through these stories not as neatly-labelled, concrete identity categories but as dynamic ways of seeing, knowing, and being in the world. After all, what it means to be queer and-or trans depends on our global and local, as well as individual and social, contexts! And there's always going to be a balance of sameness with difference whenever we're aiming for shared solidarity. Relatedly, I see the process of editing an anthology to be more akin to curating a conversation—one which should continue off the page, as well as in future projects by other writers and editors—rather than staking any authoritative claim on representing a given theme.

So, keeping that in mind, my editorial aim with *Amplitudes* was to approach queerness and-or transness expansively: as lived politics, experiences, identities, and cultures; as resistance against oppressive systems of power; as sources of self-making and intense connection with others across time and space; as gateways to pleasure, sex, desire, and intimacy; the list goes on. I was also committed to the goal that *Amplitudes* should gather stories from writers whose approaches varied in genre, content, and style—but also whose perspectives differed across many intersectional experiences of gender, sexuality, race and-or ethnicity, ability, nationality, and so on. Plus, I didn't want the stories to be limited to only those by U.S. American citizens writing in English, because transness and queerness are in so many ways transnational. (This meant, to pull back the process curtain somewhat, setting aside extra budget for stories in translation to fairly compensate *both* the author and translator.) Altogether we received over three hundred and twenty five submissions, an amazing outpouring of queer and trans art. Ultimately, the selected stories gathered here are all in conversation with one another and the broader theme of "queer futurity" in remarkable ways. Some are whimsical, some are tenderly mundane, some are frightening; others are horny, political, provocative, or mournful. Still others consider speculative possibilities around problems like urban planning and climate change, while some might simply set out to cruise you.

What you hold in your hands, *Amplitudes: Stories of Queer and Trans Futurity*, is a collection of possibilities. Other worlds, and other futures. As I'm writing this introduction we find ourselves in a frightening reactionary political moment both in the USA, where I live, and across the globe. Whether it's the growing momentum of right-wing violence, which always oppressively targets gender and sexuality, or the resurgent popularity of "radical" (conservative, essentialist) feminisms destabilizing years of labor by queer, trans, and women of color feminists to create a vision for shared liberation . . . we're stuck in a rough timeline right now. But I need to believe, in a teeth-grit furious sort of way, that as artists and scholars and activists and everyday queers we have futures to strive towards. I need to believe that we'll create better potential futures for those who come after us, exactly how others did *before* us. Stories, I think, help people survive while carrying all our pleasure, and joy, and rage, and grief, and love along with us. Envisioning other and better potentialities, speculating on how our alternate futures might arrive while seeing other peoples' differing imaginaries alongside our own, might help us get closer to the horizon.

And, hopefully, we get there together.

—Lee Mandelo
April 2024

The Republic of Ecstatic Consent

by Sam J. Miller

A song for Samuel R. Delany, in the key
of "Heavenly Breakfast."

i.

We should have been ashamed of ourselves, eighteen of us heading
together to the clinic with the clap, but mostly we found the whole
thing hilarious, laughing out loud from the utter absurd freedom
of being in control of our bodies. Someone came up with an easy
bit of choreo, half stepping and half voguing, "the clap clap," and
we clapped it to Tenth Avenue, startling strangers all the way.

"Let me guess," said the medical provider, when they walked in
and saw how cozy we were with each other, a cuddle puddle that
packed the waiting room, "you're a squat."

"Ding ding ding," one of us said, a loud and silly one.

"We're the Republic of Ecstatic Consent," said a very serious
one, fumbling in their pockets for the business cards we all told
them were ridiculous.

"Two floors of abandoned office space above a Walgreens on the Lower East Side."

"*Someone* wanted to call us the *Empire* of Ecstatic Consent," said another, and glared around the room as if the *someone* might be there, which, maybe they were. "But that's out of keeping with our anti-imperialist mission statement."

"Do you want to be seen one at a time?" asked the provider, uninterested in our history or our praxis.

We laughed. "We spend a lot of time together naked. How do you think we all got the clap?"

"Room's only big enough for five at a time," said the provider, and led the first batch of us back.

Late October; the sun had set by the time we left the clinic and the chill in the air made our body heat more glorious. We walked hand in hand to Broadway and then turned south. Quieter now. Still no shame or regret. We had VD but we also had a script for a seven-day course of antibiotics. Wood smoke and cinnamon tinged the air. We belonged to something beautiful.

We wanted to go home.

We wanted to go to the Piers.

We split into two groups, swallowed up by the city dark in two directions: the black churn of the Hudson River pulling from the west and the cheerful sordid frenzy of Squat Alley calling to the east. More bifurcations would follow, as the night wore on. It didn't matter where we went, whether we were alone or with a group—we carried the Republic of Ecstatic Consent with us everywhere.

The Republic was a squat. A commune. An activist affinity group.

The Republic was a dance club. A revolution. A party.

The Republic was something different for each of us. Our own private way of wanting freedom. When we went out in public we were all expected to have a unique three-to-five-sentence definition of what we were. If you got caught parroting someone else's, you'd get teased. Gently.

A year and a half since the city stopped enforcing eviction orders on unlawful occupants of empty office space, and digital DIY kits started circulating—how to pop a lock and stake a claim and make it stick. At first the priority was homeless folks and migrant families, and, what do you know—those problems were solved with room to spare. Landlords had walked away from tens of millions of square feet of suddenly worthless office space, and that was enough for almost anything. The city, which had been trying and failing to "solve" homelessness by arresting people for decades, realized that this solution actually *did* work to get people out of the public eye and started creating avenues for "adverse possession legitimization." Some squats were total glorious anarchy and some were harsh rigid dictatorships—cults loved squats, as did fundamentalist religious sects—

The door to the Republic was unlocked. It always was. We had very little worth stealing. And anyway the place was never empty; someone was always around to watch out for things, even if they were also partying and/or hooking up and/or working.

"Hail the plague-ridden masses!" someone called out when they heard us climbing the stairs. As always, the ace folks held it down. They'd cooked us two big pots of pity soup; the place smelled like matzo balls and miso and heaven.

The Republic's permanent population was a core group of twenty-seven, but it had almost that many "part-timers"—folks who came through and crashed for a day or a week and then disappeared, moved on, sent us postcards and social media posts from the Pacific Northwest or the Bay or McMurdo. We had a no-creep policy but rarely had to enforce it. The creeps who showed up, lured by stories of easy sex and abundant drugs, got run off pretty quickly by the meetings and strategy sessions that never really ended, just morphed into another meeting.

We were all activists; we were fighting for justice in City Hall and Palestine; we were in all the spaces employing all the tactics; we were chaining ourselves across Fifth Avenue to bring rush hour traffic to a screeching halt; we were triggering cascading failures that slowed the New York Stock Exchange; we were helping run an industrial-grade bioprinter shop that churned out massive amounts of gene-hacked fungus—real good stuff we'd gotten off a Chechen refugee engineer, meaty texture and peppery taste—and we were distributing it to the hundreds of squats where homeless families had set up shop. We were taking part in the hourly coordinated man-in-the-middle attacks that had crippled every extractive venture-capitalist-funded "disruptive" "sharing economy" app.

We were all the things. All the genders; all the ethnicities.

"Not *all*," someone would say, when someone else said that, "let's not practice erasure," and it was true we were a kaleidoscope but not an encyclopedia. But whoever you wanted to fuck, they were probably there.

ii.

We fell in with a police brutality protest arcing east through Chinatown, and we let its manic energy wipe away our other plans and hopes for the evening. Five blocks later and it became clear we were aiming for the Manhattan Bridge, taking over the Brooklyn-bound vehicle lanes on the upper level, thousands of us, no permit but no one to stop us either, a chorus of angry car horns only egging us on.

We chanted. We sang. We shivered in the cold and we loved every second of it.

We argued.

The Republic was not utopia. We were not all friends; we were not all fucking. We critiqued each others' analysis of absolutely everything endlessly.

"It's not like a *problem*," someone was saying, in a tone of voice that implied it was a million percent a problem, "it's just that *some people* act like because they 'have been doing this for a long time' they are smarter and better than us, like it's our fault they're *real real old*."

"Usually it's coming from a place of, *we've tried similar things before and it hasn't worked*," said someone else. "But, yeah, tone and delivery go a long way, sometimes people need to check their privilege."

"Just because *they* failed when they tried it *a hundred years ago* doesn't mean *we'll* fail when we try it now."

We were fighting over tactics that week. And strategy. We fought about those things every week, along with everything else we fought about.

We lived in a bubble of post-capitalist bliss, but the bubble had limits—the gas that heated our home in the winter cost actual money, as did lots of other things we needed or wanted—so lots of us worked at least a little. We sold drugs and we did sex work and freelance graphic design. We had office jobs and we were bike messengers and we reveled in the ruins of the "gig economy," which by then had been dismantled to make way for the collective one. We picked up bottles and cans off the street and ran them through the 3D printer churners to make household items that we sold in the stretch of Second Avenue barricaded with old Department of Corrections buses to make a permanent open-air flea market.

"That trans collective we visited in the Bronx, on the boat off Hunts Point? Been keeping in touch with some of them, and they're definitely a lot less . . . timid."

"Yeaahhhhh," and they stared wistfully out into the darkness below the bridge.

We were not radical enough. We were too radical. Everyone was unhappy, but mostly just a little.

"It's just . . . sometimes it feels like we'd feel more at home in a space that was just for us."

On the far side the police had barricaded Tillary Street, so the leaders of the march just calmly made a U-turn to take over the vehicle lanes going in the opposite direction, heading back to Manhattan to a new symphony of shrieking car horns.

Once there, we retook the streets. And then, at Canal and Centre, we saw the most adorable creature come up from the subway, fully grown but with the kind of wide-eyed excited joy you normally only see on children.

"Cute ears!" one of us hollered, and they blushed extremely adorably, and we all tried our best to look beckoning and welcoming without being creepy about it, because in this city, in this moment, you only have to be homeless until you find your home.

iii.

We got noodles. We nursed them in sullen silence and joyous chatter. The place was packed with protesters, the heat from our bodies and the kitchen fogging the windows and dampening the air around us. Someone shared the news that the wall had come down, and our post-protest euphoria transformed into ecstasy. Some of us stared off into the distance, AR lenses showing us the ceremonies and the celebrations, but most of us wanted to be there, in the noodle shop, in the moment, together.

We were there because we said *yes*.

That's what made us the Republic of Ecstatic Consent.

We said *no* to lots of things.

No is real; *no* is valid. *No* can motivate you just as much as *yes* can.

We fought. Hell yes we fought. Every day, in a billion different ways.

But we were focused on what we said *yes* to, on what we loved. Our consent was expansive, ecstatic. We dreamed. We imagined.

Some of us would move on. Maybe in a month, maybe tomorrow. Some of us would say yes to other things, other families, other ways of being and doing. Some of us would download to the cloud and become part of a different *we*; some of us would hop the first clumsy wormhole-gates and help build the Luna Haven; some of us would burn ourselves alive to shine a light on something monstrous.

Life was very long. The world was so big.

But also.

Life was very short. We were flickering candles in the shape of people, brief players who strutted and fretted on a tiny stage and then were gone.

We ate our noodles. We basked in the heat we made.

iv.

Because:

Because what am I supposed to do with this dull fire, this yawning soaring song inside my chest, this love so strong I'm sometimes afraid it'll crack me like an egg? What do I do in these moments when I scan the crowded subway car or watch the street trees sigh in the wind, and I feel my heart might break from how happy I am, when I wonder how I ever wanted more than this— how could I have wasted those hours I spent staring into my screens, endlessly scrolling or streaming, how could I want any of that when what's real and here and now is so astonishing?

Because what do I do with this rage. This grief. This cease-less howl forever threatening to split me in half. This fury at what humans have wrought, and wreak. Each day's new unending litany of atrocity; history's infinite roll call of cruelty.

Because I came up out of the subway feeling alone and exult-ing in it, this me, this self, this fragile eggshell of a person on its own in the world, no family waiting for me at home, no school or college, I'd come to the big city by myself, I was going to be part of the biggest social transformation in history, I was me, I was I, this thing, this miracle—

—but also I wasn't, I was an atom amid millions of atoms, a cog in a machine three hundred square miles in size, an insignificant piece, a nothing—

"Cute ears!" someone cried, and I turned, blushing, smiling, horrified, exhilarated—and they beckoned—and I followed, down the steps from street level to a tiny gritty restaurant that held summer inside, the sweet smell of cilantro and five-spice powder, the heat and reek of bodies.

Because they cheered when they saw me. They scooted over to make room for me on a bench.

Because I knew then: I is an illusion, a fiction our brains spin to make us keep our bellies full, but we're all born we, we move from we to we throughout our lives—the we of place, of nation, of iden-tity—of couplehood, of family—and when we're truly free, we get to choose which we we are.

Trans World Takeover

By Nat X Ray

THE FIRST GUY WE decided to trans as part of Trans World Takeover was this older lady from San Antonio who was our school's trigonometry teacher slash football coach. Her name was Beryl Shanks. Spider was sus about starting with someone who could be traced back to us that easily, but I pointed out we'd need consistent contact with the target unless she thought we could figure out how to implant one of those testosterone pellets into Beryl's leg without her noticing, which she didn't. We decided to go with gel instead.

At first I thought transing Beryl was gonna work out pretty good, logistics-wise. Our class with her was at the very end of the day, right before she'd head to the field for practice, and she had this giant tube of sunscreen she'd always haul out of her desk drawer and slather all over her face as we were leaving. My plan was to get some of the gel in my hand and like offer to rub the sunscreen in for her, on the back of her neck maybe, and then smear the gel on instead. I didn't think it was that weird. Spider thought it was pretty weird. I was like, People rub each other's sunscreen in all the time, and she was like, Nonsexually? and I was like, I feel like maybe you're the one making this weird, and she was like, You know this is gonna be a repeat thing, man. Like even if it works, you are going to have to offer to rub in Beryl Shanks's sunscreen *every day.*

I said we would cross that bridge. At the end of eighth period I took the gel to the LADIES' ROOM, which they still make me go to, and ripped open the packet and squirted out a little in my hand. It was cold, like lube or one of those moisturizer face masks. But when I went back to the classroom and made my offer to Beryl she just said, That is against several laws, kiddo, and popped her sunscreen shut.

At my side my hand was curled over itself like a clam. I felt the goo ooze down my palm. It's just you missed a spot, I said.

Whatever this is I am not interested, said Beryl. She got up and followed the last of the kids out, leaving me alone with the late-afternoon dust motes. I plopped on my desk and pulled my hoodie off with one hand and smeared the gel on my arms. I'd already done my shot for the week, but what else was I gonna do with it? Plus I was only a few months on T and it hadn't really kicked in yet and I kinda liked the idea of being extra testosteronated, although I heard if you go overboard and take too much it turns back into estrogen. It's why bodybuilders get titties.

I told Spider what had happened and she said, Respectfully, duh. You disposed of the evidence, right?

Yeah, I said. I'm full of man juice, and she was like, No, the packet. The bigass packet it came in that said TESTOPLASM all over it.

I thought the packet was in my pocket but it turned out not to be. This was problematic. Spider was pissed. She asked why didn't I just flush it or something when I was in the bathroom. I didn't wanna tell her it was cause I was saving the dregs for myself, so I was like, Imagine if it clogged and they had to come fish it out.

We went back to the LADIES' ROOM to look for it but guess who was there. Reilley Diis. And her little shitpal Janiss. Doing one of those gas station vapes. We barely got two steps in before Reilley Diis waved away the haze in front of her face, took a gander at us and was like, Oh my GOD, it's LADYSTACHE AND MANHANDS here to WATCH US PEE.

Reilley Diis Nuts, I said, and Reilley Diis said, That's sexual fucking harassment. Janiss took out her phone and started recording us.

This type of shit was exactly why we decided to start Trans World Takeover. Trans people were illegal in our state. If you wanted HRT, you had to either drive twelve hours to the nearest clinic or go on the dark web like we did or else go fuck yourself, and option one only applied if you were eighteen, which we still weren't. If you wanted to be trans at school you could also pretty much go fuck yourself. Once I found a flyer for a secret GSA meeting wadded up behind a shelf in the library and I went without telling anybody. There were two kids there and one of them was the only out gay kid in our grade, Bryan Fargett, yes really, and the other was a closeted trans freshman who said she'd never go on hormones cause she read on our official state health department website that estrogen was an addictive substance. They had to put a sign on the door that said POETRY CLUB so nobody tried to come in, and when I brought up the flyer Bryan Fargett turned bright red and the trans girl said, Dude, I told you don't put anything in writing. I never mentioned it to Spider.

It didn't matter anyway though. After we got done with Trans World Takeover and school, me and Spider were gonna move to Minneapolis and start fresh. We were juniors, so getting close. In

Minneapolis you could do informed consent at eighteen. Spider said Minneapolis was one of the up-and-coming cities of the twenty-first century and plus she always wanted to see that statue that's like the big spoon with the cherry. She said she thought it was sexy.

The next day at school they had an assembly. One of the janitors had found the packet. They made him stand onstage and hold it up the whole time while wearing his rubber gloves, for dramatic effect I guess. The vice principal got all choked up when she told everyone it had been found on the floor of the LADIES' ROOM. She was like, It's tragic enough to find any drug in this school, boys and girls, but a drug of this caliber. Oh it's practically poison to a young woman's body. She was like, Ladies, this stuff is illegal for a reason and that reason is it will make you gross. It will make your butt hairy and your boobies fall off. A couple of the freshman boys started to sniffle too and the teachers passed out paper bookmarks that said SCHEDULE III IS NOT FOR ME with a crossed-out picture of a clip art syringe on it.

Anyhoo, said the vice principal, clearing her throat, we will find the perpetrator, and he or she will be expelled immediately and reported to the authorities. We encourage anyone with information to come forward. Spider looked at me from her row and did a cry-about-it motion and I did a jerk-off motion back.

Okay, new idea, said Spider on the way home. Let's just trans Reilley Diis.

Yeah totally, I said, even though a little part of me was like, What about Beryl Shanks, and another even littler part of me was like, What about jail.

Spider's car was this craptastic hellpit. She said it'd always been a goal of hers to be a shitty car girl but I feel like she took that too far. Fossilized fast food was everywhere. Still, I had an automatic reaction to the car, like the whosits dog drooling at the bell.

Whenever I was in it I got all twitchy and impulsive. I think it's cause it made me feel free, which made me realize how unfree I felt all the rest of the time.

Sorry to drop Beryl already, said Spider, prodding my thigh. I know she was like your white whale. I just think starting with a teacher might be like slightly risky at this juncture.

Not my whale, I said. She wasn't. It was stupid. It was just this one time sophomore year I thought about trying out for football and Beryl Shanks said no cause football was for boys. Even though she got to be the coach. Even though I was a boy. But who cared. It didn't have anything to do with why we picked her. We just needed a cis person who was nearby and sucked and that's what she was.

Okay, said Spider.

It could've been anyone, I said loudly. It still could be anyone. Like why stop at Reilley Diis.

True, said Spider.

Let's trans Janiss while we're at it.

Yeah, fuck Janiss, said Spider. Janiss will make a beautiful man.

And Andrea Fideco, I said, who's this other clown we hate, and Spider said, And vice principal bitchface, and I said, And my mom, and Spider said, And my dad. After that we were just naming people. Crazier and crazier people, like the queen and shit, even though she's dead. The thing was, it felt like every name we said, my video game power bar juiced up. We were vibrating with potential. Whenever we made eye contact it lasted a second too long.

I guess basically where I'm going with this is we went back to my house and bought an objectively insane amount of hormones online and then explored each other's bodies before my parents came back from tennis club. We have this system where we buy credit card numbers for cheap off this one site on the dark web and then we use that to buy HRT off this other site on the dark web. It's very robin hood. Plus the hormone site was having a sale, so also economical. The other thing was sort of new. I mean, not totally, cause a few days before Spider had showed me how she was starting to get a little bit of left boob and let me touch it, and a couple weeks before that I kissed her in a shitty joke way to demo my shitty first kiss with Blake van de Zande in sixth grade, and a month or two before *that* we did one of those love detector arcade games and got IT COULD TECHNICALLY HAPPEN and didn't look at each other for the rest of the day. But this was real intense and kind of slobbery and I don't think anyone was demoing anything.

Me and Spider hated each other when we first met, which was how you knew it was real. Freshman year we had social studies together and got put as debate partners. Our topic was gay people, yes or no. Except our school didn't want to glorify anything woke or crimey so we were only allowed to argue no and it was really more of a presentation. Spider was all pissed about it even though they said the same thing to the kids who got assigned marijuana. She was like, A person is not a debate topic, and I was like, Well let's not do it then, and she was like, No we have to do it, and I was like, This fuckin nerd. I didn't know I was trans then and I didn't know Spider was either. She knew though. She told me later and I was like, Huh.

Anyway, when it was time to do our debate Spider told the teacher she made a powerpoint and when she pulled it up on the projector it was this full-size pornographically HD photoshopped pic of two dudes sucking face. Generous tongues. Also the dudes were the president and the vice president, like, of America. I shrieked and Spider did this small but weirdly elaborate curtsy. She got in-school suspension for two weeks and I snuck her dr pepper every day at lunch, and then she started driving me to school and back, and now she was kind of the only person I could stand.

That Monday Spider never came to pick me up. My parents were already at work by the time I accepted she wasn't coming, which meant I simply did not go to school cause we don't live in the kind of city where you can walk places. I texted her a bunch but she didn't even open the messages. Tuesday I had to get a ride with Bryan Fargett, who lives like two streets down from me, and he was acting real weird and solemn and wouldn't change the radio off dirge indie. When we pulled into the school parking lot I was finally like, Fargett WHAT, and he was like, I just, I'm sorry for your loss.

I made I think this mooing sound like a cow. Like nooooooooooo but less of a word. I couldn't really hear myself so I don't know.

Oh, no, he said. Oh god. Sorry. She's not dead. She just got expelled.

Okay, I said, rubbing my collarbone. Okay. Why would you fucking say it like that though.

I was being hyperbolic, he said. Obviously I thought you knew.

Pretty much everybody knows, said the GSA trans girl from the backseat.

It turned out the GSA trans girl was Bryan Fargett's sister. The two Fargetts. Her name was Gee but it wasn't short for anything yet, and she was wearing cargo shorts and doing one of those crazy rubiks cubes that's like a triangle.

Well great, I said. That's great. The shock of Spider being dead was starting to wear off and the shock of Spider being expelled was setting in. I was like, Can you tell me what happened, and Bryan Fargett looked at my face and was like, I gotta go to class, sorry sorry, and sort of patted me.

Me and Gee Fargett sat in the car in silence except for her rubiks triangle clicking. The air was stale.

Cool thing, I said, and she was like, Yeah thanks. I also do origami.

Neat, I said. She said, And archery.

So how—

Do you guys have hormones? said Gee. Reilley Diis is telling people you tried to poison her with boy hormones.

Suddenly dots connected. I thought of the packet on the floor and the vape clouds and Janiss pointing her phone at Spider. And also at me. Fuck, I thought, am I expelled too, and then I was like, Maybe that would be fine, and then I was like, But why wouldn't they tell me if I was expelled, and then I was like, Reilley Diis is a snitch, Reilley Diis is the devil incarnate. Gee Fargett had stopped rubicking and was staring at me like a gecko.

I thought you were afraid of hormones, I said, and Gee was like, I was just wondering.

I spent pretty much the whole school day waiting for somebody to expel me, but nobody did. In fact pretty much nobody said a word to me. I had to eat lunch by myself behind the bleachers and it was corn dogs, which I hate. The only time I spoke was eighth period when Beryl Shanks called on me to answer a question and my voice cracked like it had never cracked before in my life. It sounded like a piccolo getting assassinated. Beryl Shanks just looked at me for a really long time. I got the question wrong.

A week or so later me and Spider's order arrived on my porch. It was large. Cumbersome, you might say. Like a baby I didn't want anymore. I went to stuff it into one of the duffel bags at the back of my closet and when my dad saw me hauling it backwards up the stairs I told him it was exercise equipment.

Without Spider school got three hundred percent worse. The expulsion had the admin on high alert. They stationed teachers in front of the bathrooms and you had to show your student ID to get in, and they kicked Andrea Fideco off the swim team cause she had polyamorous ovary syndrome so they were paranoid about her testosterone levels. Andrea cried for hours in one of the study cubbies and then Beryl Shanks wouldn't even let her in the LADIES' ROOM to fix her makeup. Reilley Diis had reached unimaginable heights of smugness after Spider left but I think even she felt bad about that one, cause I saw her go up and offer Andrea a poptart after school and Andrea frisbeed it into a tree.

I kept bringing up Trans World Takeover to Spider in hopes some good old-fashioned transing would get her spirits up and also possibly decrease the amount of drugs in my house, but she wouldn't bite. She was lowkey living in her car now. Her parents hadn't handled the expulsion great. On the bright side she had cleaned the place up real nice and had one of those fabric shoe organizer things hanging from the ceiling with all her stuff in the pockets, like her toothbrush and her underwear and everything. You would never know it used to be a whataburger graveyard.

Spider said, You have to understand my priorities have shifted.

Well what are your priorities, I said, and she was like, Maybe, like, fixing my life or whatever. Not living in my car.

I was like, You could use the credit card site to buy a house, but she was like No, I want to fix it for real. Like be in control of it. When I went to give her leg a squeeze she moved it.

I feel like you're not taking this seriously, said Spider.

I'm taking it very seriously, I said, I'm trying to help you, and she was like, I just can't help but notice you're not living in *your* car, which was below the belt cause I don't have one and also can't drive.

It's not my fault they didn't expel me, I said. I don't know why not, okay.

Well I do, said Spider. It's obvious. I was the boy in the fuckin girls' bathroom. You were right where you were supposed to be.

Damn, I said, and she said, In their eyes, I mean.

After that we put on the radio and tried to go down on each

other in the backseat, but I could tell she wasn't that into it and my head kept bumping into the shoe hanger. At home I took out the hormones and scooped handfuls of them and let them crash back into the box like sand. Pills like Spider used, vials and syringes like I used, gel and patches and pellets and some shit I'd honestly never seen before in my life, like this pointy thing called the Arrow. I imagined taking the box down to the river—it was so big I'd have to carry it in something, like my little red wagon from when I was a kid, which I was pretty sure was still in the garage—and standing over the bridge and pouring all of it in.

The next day at school me and Gee Fargett were eating lunch and shivering out back by the bleachers. Gee was a little obsessed with me, I was pretty sure. After Spider left she started hanging around. She maybe thought the expulsion thing was badass. She showed me an origami toad she'd made out of the wax paper from her sandwich and was like, Your face kinda looks like there's a squirrel on it.

Yeah? I said, stroking my lip. Thanks.

The T was starting to kick in by now, I could tell. My pee smelled weird and I had unlocked a new body temperature called sweatycold and half the time when I spoke it was like a secret language for dogs that alternated wildly between grumble and whistle pitch. It was exhilarating. It was terrifying as shit. I felt like everyone was looking at me all the time. To Gee I said, Remember when you asked about hormones.

She kinda twitched her head like no but I saw her eyes widen for a second.

I glanced around. On the field there were some lax bros but they were far away and occupied with grabbing each other's asses, heterosexually. I gripped the edge of the bleacher and tried to say, Well I've got em. For a price, but it came out sort of garbled and Gee was like, Huh?

I will sell you estrogen, I said.

I'd come up with the idea in the Fargetts' car on the way to school, watching Gee put those whiteout strips on her nails and then peel them off and throw them on the floor. I couldn't believe I hadn't thought of it before. Funds, actual real-life non-stolen-credit-card funds, would get Spider hopefully out of her car and definitely back in my good graces. And if I could rope her in it'd keep her occupied so she wouldn't get too depressed. Finding any other customers besides Gee was gonna be a full-time job. I wondered how much we could get away with charging her until that happened.

Gee thought for a minute, squinting at the lax bros. Then she was like, Whatever, okay. Can you sell to my friends too?

Oh uhh, I said. What friends.

Gee snorted and was like, What do you mean what friends, and I was like What do you mean what do I—

I know a lot of people who'd be interested in this, Gee said. Tons actually.

I figured she meant online friends, like discord or whatever, so I was like, I was kinda thinking of keeping it local. Like for shipping cost reasons. Gee was like, This is local. They go here.

You know a ton of trans kids, I said. Here.

Gee was like, Yeah.

Okay, I said. But. Then why was the GSA so lame.

The GSA, no offense, she said, is gay. I just go so Bry won't be lonely. My friends are all inside right now. She raised her eyebrows at me but whatever she was trying to say I didn't get it.

You were scared of hormones, I said, and she was like, Well I hear everyone is at first.

I thought it was slightly cringe Gee would lie about having a bunch of secret friends, but when I remembered I spent the first semester of freshman year telling people I was a werewolf I decided to forgive it. Then the next day two of the lax bros showed up at my locker and were like, Hey man. So uh. Gee said you could help us, acting all shuffly and weird like they had to pee. I was like, Are you guys trying to copy my homework or something cause if you are I did not do it, and they pulled up the cuffs of their jeans to reveal matching trans flag socks.

Oh, I said. Lax sisses.

After gym three chess clubbers and a band kid cornered me by the locker room. Then Gee brought this kid JD from my Spanish class to the car to meet me after school. Then a week or two later I started getting all these texts from unknown numbers. Sometimes it would just be a question mark and sometimes it was more along the lines of Hello this is firstname lastname and I would like to purchase some illegal hormones, but it would've been dumb of me to say no. The cash flow was crazy.

Spider wasn't as interested in helping me as I'd hoped, which as business picked up was getting to be a problem. She was like, I'm telling you I'm taking a break from crime, and I was like, That is so lame, Spider, what else are you gonna do. She was like, I've been asking myself what I'm really interested in and I think maybe art or interior design, and then she showed me this mural she'd done with nail polish on the ceiling of her car that was like the creation of Adam except instead it was muppets fucking. I can't really do it justice.

If you got in on this you could buy real paint, I said, but Spider was like, I might get into making my own pigments. I was just reading about it. Guess what carmine is.

No seriously, I said.

Bugs, said Gee, who was also there. She was in the front seat braiding two friendship bracelets on the console. Spider was like, Bugs as fuck, and they high-fived even though they both had to contort themselves around the seats and it looked kind of stupid.

Your painting's cool, Gee said to Spider, twisting herself back around. Hobbies have been really good for me too. They smiled at each other.

I was hesitant to let Gee get too involved with the new iteration of Trans World Takeover, even though she was good at sourcing customers and I was getting more orders than I could physically deliver and she kept bugging me to let her in on it. I told her it was cause I didn't want her to also get expelled, but honestly who gave a shit. Really it was cause school was still weird without Spider and taking Gee on felt kind of too soon. Like getting a new puppy right after your dog died. Except my dead dog and my puppy might have been hanging out without me.

Also there was the money. I was still like eighty percent sure Spider was gonna come around, once she got bored of making bug paint and stopped randomly turning down my invites to hang out, but until then there was like a slight ethical gray area. I mean just considering the questions of who was earning it versus who got to keep it and all that jazz. It probably made the most sense to wait to give it to her until we teamed back up. Until then I decided not to spend it, except on this sick electric scooter for doing deliveries that counted as a business expense, plus the charging dock and the helmet and the racing suit the scooter store guy made me get. Otherwise I mostly stuck the cash in my secret bank account and let it swell up in there like a toxic algae.

I do think it's pretty cool what Spider did, Gee said to me one day as I was shoving meds into my bag from my locker. I'd started keeping stockpiles of hormones all over the place like squirrel nuts so I'd be ready to fill orders at any time. Zephyr Macleod slid past me with their arm outstretched and I slipped a bottle of E into their sleeve and they slipped some bills into my jeans pocket.

What, get expelled, I said to Gee. Occasionally I still got

surprised by the sound of my own voice. These days it was giving fee fie fo fum vibes. After the mega-order came in I'd decided to try one of the new hormone methods, the Arrow, and it turned out to be like some sci-fi shit. You jabbed it into the back of your neck and it burrowed in like a tick and started pumping you with juice, like the pellet only more potent and you didn't have to get a doctor to stick it in. The box said you only had to replace it once a year. It ruled. I charged a premium for the Arrow and some kids actually paid.

No, said Gee, take the fall. Like it was kinda heroic of her.

What are you talking about, I said. What fall.

Keenan Chowdhury sidled up and reached for a high five and I pressed a vial of T into his palm. Sick fit, he mouthed, I'll venmo you, and vanished into a cloud of theater kids.

Don't forget, I said after him. A couple people turned around.

He was right about the outfit though. The other side effect of the Arrow was it was making me super jacked, which meant yeah, I'd had to get some new shirts. They were of the finest venetian silk and hugged my arm muscles like saran wrap and cost a couple zeros more than my usual six-for-ten pack, but it was mainly to help advertise. Business expense. I was basically a mannequin for testosterone.

I'm just saying she could've snitched on you, Gee said. Everybody knows you were there. So she could've said the T was for Beryl Shanks and it was your idea.

I looked at Gee. She was still wearing her cargo shorts, but her hair was getting longer and kind of curly and her eyes looked bright. I didn't know she knew about Beryl Shanks.

Or you could have, she said.

Huh, I said, slamming my locker shut. Guess I never thought about it.

As the year went on it was getting harder to ignore that half the kids in school were transing their genders. There was even more puberty than normal happening. Everyone was hairy and everyone had boobs and the LADIES' ROOM always smelled like BO. For a while the teachers made a valiant effort, though. I'd rock up to trig with like my stache flowing in the wind and my neck hulking out and my voice two octaves deeper and Beryl Shanks would just be like Hello young lady and hand me a worksheet and a Bic for Her.

But one day, towards the end of spring semester, me and Gee walked into school and there was this gaggle of teachers standing around near the auditorium muttering to each other. It was ominous. You could see some of their heads swivel around when we walked past even though they were trying to be subtle. I said to Gee, Is it just me or are the vibes like especially rancid right now, but she was doing something on her phone and didn't respond.

For the first time in a minute I missed Spider. It had been a few weeks since I last saw her. We'd been hanging out in her car among her increasingly large mass of paintings and sculptures and shit and I'd tried to make out with her, but she just said Maybe we should put a pause on this for a while and went back to drawing something in a sketchbook she wouldn't let me see. I said, Pause means temporary right, and she said, Sure. Afterward I went home and got on ezrealestate dot com and spent all the hormone money on a down payment on this really cute little house with a balcony by the river in Minneapolis. Then I slammed my laptop shut and put it in the closet and didn't look at it again.

At lunch the vice principal announced another mandatory assembly. Really two. The so-called boys were supposed to stay in the cafeteria with her and the so-called girls had the auditorium with Beryl Shanks. Obviously the kids at our school didn't take super kindly to being split up by gender. There were rumblings.

Silence, boys and girls, said the vice principal. This is serious business. Something sinister and transgender is going on at this school and we are going to get to the bottom of it TODAY.

They started trying to get the auditorium group to line up but nobody would do it. The kids all gaggled together in a clump. Some of them held hands. A few started chanting SINISTER AND TRANSGENDER, SINISTER AND TRANSGENDER. I saw Reilley Diis try to push through and get smushed against the wall.

The vice principal was starting to look sweaty. Eventually she waved Beryl Shanks onto the podium next to her and said, If you students are going to refuse to behave, Miss Shanks and I are happy to go ahead and make our announcement right here. Miss Shanks, take it away.

Uh, said Beryl, tapping the mic, howdy.

Only like half the kids in the cafeteria were even sitting down, but out of the corner of my eye I saw Gee slide into a seat at the end of my table. Her cargo pants pockets were bulging and she was fiddling with something stringy. I tried to give her a sneaky wave but she was just staring up at the stage.

At first what Beryl said was pretty much the usual. It was normal to want to trans your gender, and lots of people wanted that, but normal didn't mean okay and it was our responsibility as future citizens of the world to not make illegal freak choices, etc. etc. The vice principal was nodding. Then Beryl was like, So the administration will be implementing weekly blood tests, and any students found to be in violation of the natural order will be dealt with accordingly, and also we are going to make some alterations to the dress code so our eyeballs are no longer subjected to any foolishness such as nail polish on boys.

Then Gee popped up from her chair like she was spring-loaded and whipped a box out of her pocket. In the sunlight coming through the cafeteria window I saw the letters glint: THE ARROW.

She looked at me and saluted and was like, This one's for you, buddy, then heaved back the string on what I realized was a home-made bow.

When Gee shot the cafeteria exploded. Figuratively, I mean, but like barely. It was chaos. People were yelling and climbing all over each other and Beryl had flattened herself to the auditorium floor and some kids jumped over the lunch counter and liberated a vat of spaghetti to hurl at her and the vice principal.

Gee, I yelled, whirling through the crowd, but I couldn't find her anywhere and I kept slipping in puddles of spaghetti sauce. My silk shirt had meaty red smears all over it, which I hoped were drycleanable. Then I saw movement outside the window. Gee was dashing across the front lawn, cargo shorts flapping in the wind, hair flying, bow dangling from her hand, and Spider's car was idling in the pickup zone covered in a fresh coat of colors my eyes couldn't totally comprehend. Spider was hanging out the sunroof pumping her fist. As I watched, Gee threw herself into the passenger seat and they sped away.

Wait, I said too late, slapping my palms against the window. The lawn smeared out of view. On the stage Beryl Shanks unfolded herself from the floor and picked something up. It was the Arrow, clean and pristine.

No weapon formed against me shall prosper, you little shits, she said into the mic, but howling saucy kids were pouring into the halls and I don't think anybody else really heard her.

The Arrow incident was pretty much the end of our school. All students found to have contributed to the disturbance were expelled, which basically only left Reilley Diis and Janiss. I was okay with it cause I was like, Who wants to go to a school that's just Reilley Diis and Janiss, but some of the other kids were pissed. Online there were whispers. A couple people had sent me a link to a group chat I kept meaning to look at but I hadn't yet. Plus everybody being kicked out of school made selling hormones way harder cause I still couldn't drive, and after a while Zephyr Macleod figured out how to get on the dark web and started seriously stepping on my sales. Zephyr had a jeep and a lowest price guarantee or your money back, and I had a mild-to-medium case of depression and a former associate who was now wanted in like three states, so, you know, you do the math.

Seeing as I had literally nothing but free time that summer I spent most of it riding around on my scooter trying to teach myself to do wheelies and stuff. I only went to the chickfila parking lot Spider used to keep her car in cause it had a ramp that was pretty good for tricks and it was huge, plus it was near the river so you'd get the occasional breeze to cut the stink air, but when Spider pulled up behind me she was like, Are you stalking me.

Nuh, I said, slamming on the hand brake and jolting my brain into the backs of my eyeballs.

Spider looked pretty awesome, not gonna lie. She looked fucking crazy. Her hair was bleached to shit and her eye makeup was like when there's a storm coming and the clouds turn green. She wore overalls made out of gutted stuffed animals. Their little legs were the straps. I was wearing a regular shirt.

Spider wouldn't tell me where Gee was hiding out. She was like, Gee is doing wonderfully and sends her best wishes but prefers me to keep her location confidential at this time, and I was like, I kind of feel like I have a right to know, and she was like, Yeah we have a lot of rights in theory. She'd helped me shove the scooter in her trunk and we'd driven to the bridge by my house where I'd thought about dumping the hormones. The smells of fresh soil and garbage water wafted through the cracked windows and I meant to tell Spider she looked pretty but what actually came out was, I bought us a house in Minneapolis.

Spider looked me in my eyes and clapped a hand to my shoulder. A weird feeling slimed through my guts like a fast slug. Respectfully, she said, I am no longer very interested in Minneapolis.

Why not, I said. Gee could come too. We can like harbor her together.

No, said Spider.

It has a balcony, I said, and my idiot voice cracked.

Spider looked out the windshield. You could see a grody slice of our town from the bridge, fast-food signs and shit. She was like, I love you man but don't try to give me any more stuff, and I was like, Well at least I'm trying, and she was like, I think it's okay here. I have a lot of shit to do. But maybe you should go.

I did actually end up moving to Minneapolis later on. It wasn't anything like we thought it would be. For one thing it was cold as shit, and the house turned out to be kind of a shambles. Plus I saw the spoon statue irl and it wasn't sexy at all. But when Spider left me and my scooter by the bridge and drove away I didn't know that yet, obviously. I was thinking about early on when we'd just become friends and we stayed behind after school for no reason and climbed up the back wall of the science wing. It had these bricks that stuck out far enough you could get an okay grip, even though it made your fingers sore and your arms shake, and me and Spider hauled ourselves up to the roof like seals to lay on the baking-hot shingles until the sun went down. We just lay there and looked at the sky.

The Orgasm Doula

by Colin Dean

"IT'S NOT GOING TO happen today," Vincent said. He flopped his head back, clenched muscles relaxing into a frustrated post-coital slackness.

Not with that attitude, I thought, but instead I smiled and snapped off my black rubber glove. "Maybe next time!" I said, forcing optimism into my voice. That was what they paid me for, my optimism. I helped him bring his legs out of the sling's stirrups, brought him a glass of tepid water as he eased himself up.

"Thanks," he said. "We'll try again next week. Maybe try a different video. Lesbians. I don't know."

"I'll make a note," I said. "In the meantime, remember the three Rs: Realize, Relax, Release. You can do it, Vinnie. I believe in you."

He grunted and wiped at his genitals with a fresh towel. I snagged the money from the table near the front door and let myself out.

I checked my watch as I emerged from Vincent's building. Just past eleven. That was good, it meant I had over an hour to do my stretches before the next appointment. Vincent saw me once a week, always in the mornings, because he said that he usually got horniest in the morning. He was a pretty easy client, Vinnie. Some people wanted me to jerk them off for hours, or swore their last orgasm was from DP or TP and hoped recreating that scenario would do the trick. Sometimes I had to wield a vibrator until my hand was numb. But Vinnie was a simple man. He had a moderately thick cock, not very long, and he didn't like a tight grip. We had been working together for four months and he still hadn't had an orgasm, but I knew he would get there eventually. Realize, Relax, Release.

I took the T to Davis Square and walked the few blocks to my apartment. My arm wasn't even sore, but my career depended on me avoiding a repetitive stress injury, and stretching diligently was the number one way to prevent that. Of course I also went to acupuncture regularly, got monthly massages, and had a very anti-inflammatory diet, but I didn't want to get in the habit of skipping my routine.

It only took about twenty minutes—stretching with my palm against a wall, against a table with my wrist rotated 180 degrees, extending my arm and pulling back my fingers. Breathing in one, two, three, out one, two, three. The next client was an easy ten-minute walk away, so I had some time to kill before heading back out. I checked my work email and scanned the three new intake query forms that had come in that day. I had enough time to empty the dishwasher, but instead threw myself down on the couch and got myself off. Taking care of clients usually didn't leave me horny, but it still felt good. And unlike them (unlike most people), I wasn't worried about running out. Realize, Relax, Release. I was done in just a few minutes, ate an apple slathered with peanut butter, and headed out the door.

I looked over the client's intake form on the walk over. Apparently she had been referred to the agency from her therapist.

Nothing particular stood out in her personal or medical information. She was twenty-nine, on the young side but not unusually so. On a combination of meds that indicated a trans history. Last orgasm was three years ago, with frequent early attempts that had lessened significantly in the last year.

I rang the doorbell and almost immediately heard a thundering down the stairs. That was a good sign. Shy clients might wait a few minutes to open the door, or pretend like they weren't sure who was waiting for them. With clients like that the whole first session would be just us talking, them figuring out if they could trust me. Those always felt like boring first dates. Sometimes I'd ask my sex worker friends if they had to deal with that initial awkwardness too, but it seemed to be limited to my profession. They almost always fucked (or peed on, or whatever) their customers on the first date, but at least half of my clients wanted to wait for a second appointment.

Today's new client opened the door wide with a big smile. "You must be June!"

"I am," I said, matching her grin. No reticence from this girl. "You're Lydia, right?"

"At your service," she said, curtseying a little. "Or are you at mine? I'm not sure how this thing works."

"Well, step one is that I go upstairs with you," I said. "Shoes on or off?"

"Whatever's more comfortable for you," she said. "Though . . ." She eyed my boots. "I kinda have a thing for Doc Martens, so if you left them on I wouldn't complain."

We clomped up the rickety stairs. "Should I get you water, or a beer or something?" she called over her shoulder.

"Water would be great, thanks. Do you have roommates?"

"Nope, it's just me in here. And Lucifer," she added, nudging aside a huge black cat who was rubbing against her long legs. She was tall, with loose black hair cascading past her shoulders and light blue eyes under thick-framed glasses. Most of the time I was grateful that I had a flexible schedule and didn't have to work at a desk or an office, but now I sent a quick thank-you to the heavens for the meat and potatoes of my job: that sometimes I got a client as cute as this one.

Lydia set the water down on the kitchen table. "So how do we start this? You read my intake form, right?"

"Sure, but that just gives background information. It's usually helpful if I know a little bit about someone before the first session. Whatever you want to share. What you're into, what your past experiences have been like, what gets you off, that sort of thing."

"You mean what used to get me off, right? If anything got me off now I wouldn't be utilizing your fine services." She winked. "You know what I mean. No offense."

"No offense taken. I could tell you how this process works, if you want."

"Sure! I looked on your website, but I could use a blow-by-blow. So to speak. What's the deal with 'the three Rs'?" She made exaggerated quote signs with her fingers.

"They're just the central tenet of my vocation, that's all," I said, keeping my voice light. "'Realize, Relax, Release.' 'Realize' means to understand that what we think is true about our bodies doesn't have to be true at all. Then you can relax, and that's when you release."

Lydia looked at me skeptically. "Are you one of those 'infinite O' weirdos?"

I smiled a little tightly. "I don't think my lifelong review and analysis of the literature, combined with a ninety-five percent professional success rate, makes me a weirdo. There is absolutely no biological reason for limited orgasms. The idea that evolution would result in that—and that there would be such huge fluctuation of possible potential orgasms between people who otherwise share overwhelming environmental and genetic similarities—doesn't make sense, from a survival-of-the-species standpoint." I forced myself to stop before I got too heated. This was a client, I reminded myself, not some board certification wonk demanding I justify my existence.

But Lydia seemed interested, not intimidated. "Just because something doesn't seem to make sense doesn't mean it isn't true," she said. "Are you saying that every piece of recorded history, from the Bible to Shakespeare to now, is just operating under some collective delusion? That every single person who reached their orgasm limit is making it up?"

"Saying yes sounds rude or ridiculous or both, but . . . well, you're paying me because I believe that, aren't you?"

She grinned. "I guess so. Is this your segue to getting down to business?"

I let myself relax. Maybe she was trying to test me, make sure I was for real. "Business before pleasure!" I cracked. "I know you like boots. Tell me what else you're into, and we can get this started."

Everything Lydia described made me confident that I could help her. Her orgasms hadn't stopped after transitioning, but they had become different—less intense genitally but more fulfilling overall. She didn't get hard easily like she used to, but still got aroused by a lot of different stimuli. She'd had an older girlfriend who ran out of orgasms when she was in her early thirties, but enjoyed getting Lydia off. After the relationship ended, Lydia said, she was trying to get herself off, watching one of her favorite porn actresses, but nothing happened. It still felt good, she said, but she didn't even come close to coming. She hired me to figure out if the problem was psychological, maybe related to her breakup, or if she had run out of orgasms at a relatively early age.

I had successfully climaxed clients who were in their seventies, who hadn't come since before I was born. I helped out a young man who was convinced that his first orgasm, into a sock when he was thirteen, was his last (he was twenty-one and immensely grateful). Maybe I *was* one of those "infinite O weirdos," but I knew I could help her.

On first dates or whatever, when I tell people what I do for a living, they assume that my life is one long porn movie. It's not true. I'm not getting into the sweaty details of my first session with Lydia because they're not that interesting. Have you ever gone to physical therapy after surgery or a car accident or something? It's like that. All very sanitary and therapeutic. Sure, some clients have specific kinks or fantasies they want to work with, but most of that happens in their imagination; I'm a doula, not a sex goddess. Lydia didn't have an orgasm in our first session, but that didn't mean anything—it rarely took fewer than three sessions, and I could tell from her body language and vocalizations that she was having a good time. We booked an appointment for the same time next week, and I went home to stretch.

Orgasm doulas are legal, necessary, and honorable. My clients were referred to me by therapists, social workers, nurses, and the like, and I paid for an online registration system to handle bookings. I kept receipts for ice packs and acupuncture, and paid quarterly estimated taxes. The day-to-day was pretty mundane.

Unfortunately, not everyone agrees about the necessity of my profession. And it's not just people squeamish about sex. Some of my friends were birth doulas; they had so many stories about being forced out of delivery rooms by doctors, and even some midwives, when they dared to stand up for what the laboring parents wanted. Ever since Massachusetts legalized assisted suicide there have been a handful of death doulas certified by the state, but they all get sacks full of hate mail. Most hospitals around here have an on-call staff of doulas-of-all-trades, better people than I could hope to be, but most of them either have second jobs or are scraping by on food stamps. And none are considered an embarrassment to the profession like we orgasm doulas.

None of this lessened my dedication. I thought I had discovered orgasms when I was fifteen, half-asleep with a pillow between my legs. When I realized that this was the "O" people always talked about as a limited resource, I became enraged. Here was the best feeling I'd ever had, and people were saying I only got so many? And no one knew how many I would get? That once you ran out, you'd never come again? Bullshit, I thought, with the certainty and self-righteousness only a teenage feminist can muster. I started looking into what I knew was the greatest myth of all time, and stumbled my way into this embattled career. I'd never looked back.

Lydia immediately became my favorite client. For our second session I wore my boots again with a green sundress. I usually kept my hair pulled back, but I fingercombed it before going over so it hung loose and breezy around my chin. I had a hunch she was into soft femmes, and I was right. Her eyes widened when she opened the door and the smile that spread across her face was like sunrise.

"You look good," she told me.

"Thanks," I said. "Part of the job."

Don't worry, it's not some huge ethics violation to develop a crush on a client. It would be a bad idea for, say, an oncologist or neurosurgeon to flirt with a patient. And while there are definitely therapists and psychiatrists who sleep with patients, that's without a doubt a violation of their professional oath. But, like I said, my job is more like being a physical therapist. It's not that big of a deal in our line of work, and Lydia was cute as hell.

The second session didn't feel as successful as the first, though.

Not because she didn't come, that didn't bother me—I'd been seeing Vincent for months with no results. During the first session Lydia had obviously been enjoying herself: panting, moaning, flushed skin, all that good stuff. But the second time she seemed less present, like she was out of her body for minutes a time, sometimes returning for a distracted "oh my god" or "that feels so good."

Maybe a gender thing? Several of my current and previous clients had been trans, all different stripes, and most had some degree of body dysmorphia. Plenty of people who weren't trans, but weren't comfortable with their bodies for some other reason, would dissociate too. Abuse, trauma, ableism: we orgasm doulas have seen it all. I slowed what I was doing, somewhat gradually, and Lydia didn't seem to notice or mind. When I stopped, she blinked her eyes open and smiled at me.

"Sorry. Not today I guess," she said.

"It's okay," I said. "However much time you need."

She sat up slowly. "Do you have a client right after me? Or do you want a cup of coffee?"

"Coffee would be great." I went to wash up, giving her a bit of privacy before she met me downstairs.

In her warm yellow kitchen, sipping from chipped, mismatched mugs, she definitely looked like she had just been fucked. Gorgeously tousled hair, red cheeks, and she seemed more languorous than most clients did after getting aroused but not coming.

"How was that?" I asked.

"I'm not sure. It was good. I mean, I know that. But I didn't come, which I guess is kind of the point? So am I allowed to feel good about it anyway?"

I cocked my head. "Allowed? You're allowed to feel whatever you want."

Lydia shrugged and stirred more sugar into her coffee.

"It's also okay if it didn't feel as good as you hoped," I said gently. "It's my job to give you what you want, or need. If you're dissociating or something, I'd like you to tell me, so we can figure out ways of bringing you back that feel safe."

She looked confused. "Dissociate? When did I dissociate?"

"Most of the time. At least, it seemed like that to me. I've had a lot of trans clients, lots of different kinds of clients. It's totally normal to detach yourself from your body sometimes. Especially if your body doesn't always do what you want it to. But it's something we can work with."

Now Lydia was looking at me with this huge, irrepressibly goofy grin. "You thought I was dissociating? Oh, no, I haven't done that in years! No, I was just distracted."

I felt a blush spread across my face. Shit, was that a micro-aggression? "Oh, sorry, I didn't mean to assume. I just thought, since—"

"Don't worry, I'll put you out of your misery: I was distracted wondering if you ever would go on a date with me. Then I was assuming you'd say yes, and started planning out the details. Sorry."

"Oh!" Now my face must have been flaming red. "Yes. Sure. I will. What details?"

Lydia looked at me over the rim of her coffee mug. Her eyes were dancing with delight. "You'll find out."

Turns out her date was a picnic in Boston Common. I never ventured onto the other side of the Charles unless I was working, but she promised if I told her my favorite foods, they would be there in abundance. I couldn't refuse.

I found the green patch she had claimed and squealed. "You have an actual picnic basket! I can't believe it!"

"It's actually a hamper," she said, showing me the blue-and-white checkered inside. "Have you ever tried to fit picnic delicacies in a backpack? Not recommended." She had also laid out a large quilt, and now pulled two plates from her messenger bag along with assorted plasticware.

The date was exactly as perfect as you could imagine. We got deliriously buzzed on sparkling wine poured discreetly into juice glasses, swapped stories of the terrible Connecticut suburbs we both grew up in, and expounded about the problems of the world and Kids These Days and how we felt like such old ladies amongst the current crop of young queers.

"Okay, I have a question about your job," she said. It was late in the afternoon, the sun beginning to dim. "How do people know you're not a scammer? Like, what if you really could get someone off the first time, no questions asked, but you drag it on forever so you keep getting paid?"

"You know, I've literally never thought of that," I said.

"Honestly?"

"Honestly. It's actually a good idea. But, one, I'm a doula, not a wizard. There's no magic combination of, like, thrusts or whatever that will force an orgasm out of someone. It really is all in your head, which is why I'm so adamant about the three Rs."

"Aw, damn, I thought you were just holding out on me."

"Nope. Also, to be honest, even if I could, I would rather keep hustling for new clients instead of seeing the same ones over and over again. It can get boring."

"Oh." Lydia started gathering up stray wrappers and strawberry hulls. "That makes sense."

I grabbed her wrist. "It would be a good idea, though," I said, "if it meant I could keep seeing you."

She tucked a lock of hair behind her ear and bit her lower lip, looking at my hand holding onto her.

"Sorry," I said, letting go, suddenly worried I had crossed a line. She smiled and put my hand back on her wrist. "Tighter," she said, leaned forward, and kissed me.

Of course, I took her off the books immediately. It's okay to get sweet on a client, but it wouldn't be okay to charge her for my services anymore, especially since I got to come *every* time. She protested for a minute; apparently her trust fund provided all the income she needed, and she worked at the bookstore for fun. I told her to put the money she would've spent on me toward cute date ideas, but I'm sure she imagined that I was overcharging. There's no way a few sessions cost as much as opera tickets, or a day trip to the Pioneer Valley, but I wasn't complaining.

One night we were stumbling back to her place, buzzed on craft beer from a newly opened gastropub, and I wanted her so badly. This gorgeous, funny, smart bookworm of a woman was too good to be true, and I needed to show her how I felt. As soon as we got up the stairs I pressed my body against hers, keeping her flat against the apartment door, and kissed her so hard I felt her teeth against my lips. She grabbed my hair and pulled me back a bit, until I could see that huge grin I loved. I lunged forward and grabbed hold of her neck with my teeth; the girl adored being bitten. We wrestled our way to the bed, her pulling, me pushing, both of us trying to get the upper hand, but she not so secretly wanted to lose, and I very much wanted to win. I pushed her sprawling onto the bed and forced my face between her legs. I ripped off her panties, literally—she had idly mentioned that was a fantasy, and I knew these weren't her favorite pair. She was laughing and gasping for air, but stilled as I took her between my lips.

She hadn't gotten hard during our sessions, and it only sometimes happened after we started dating, but suddenly she was filling up my mouth, moaning, trying to be gentle, but I encouraged her by grabbing her hips, forcing her in and out with more pressure than ever before until she was fucking my face as I took every inch. I realized she was coming before she did, but she figured it out after a second and cried as she gave herself up to it, while I coaxed out everything she had to offer.

She was still crying, after, and I crawled up to kiss her cheek. She curled into me, laughing a little. "That was a miracle," she said. "I didn't really believe it could happen again."

"Just doin' my job, ma'am," I said in a terrible drawl. She sniffled. Sometimes clients would cry, and usually I tried to downplay it—but she wasn't a client anymore, I reminded myself with a stab of guilt. Neither of us had used the word "girlfriend" yet, but I thought it was coming. I hoped it was. I rubbed her arms, her face, let her nuzzle into my neck. Soon she wasn't crying anymore, and one of her hands snaked between my legs.

"You think we could manage that again sometime?" she asked.

"Yes, please," I said, panting, but now it was my turn. At first I just stretched out and enjoyed it, assumed I'd get off right away from how turned on I was. Lydia was patient. She tried every trick she knew, did things that always worked. Sometimes I gave a direction. "Realize, relax, release," I told myself. "Realize, relax, release. Realize, relax, release. Realize, relax, release."

"Am I doing something wrong?" she whispered after a while.

"Keep trying," I said, as the three Rs looped through my mind, over and over and over again. She kept trying.

The Shabbos Bride

by Esther Alter

THEY TAUGHT ME IN cheder that Shabbos was a time of not just rest, but of joy! Turning off your cell phone is no burden, it is freedom! A day of rest from the toils of the week!

I grew into adulthood and I lived alone, and never knew a woman. The men of the shul first thought I was shy, and then as time dragged on, they started to tell me much more about Shabbos. As an example, they would say that it was not just permitted to have sex on Shabbos, but a mitzvah. Imagine! Hashem commanded man and woman to be fruitful and multiply; why feel shame about this?

But it was the women of the shul who told me of the deeper truths of Shabbos. They spoke of welcoming Shabbos as a bride, to be wed and taken into their household, and into their beds. This I felt must be true, but I knew it would never be for me.

I had a terrible secret, which was this: Hashem had not made me right. In the great kabbalistic lattice of souls that holds the whole world together, man to woman, woman to man, I was a shard. We are told to thank Hashem for our bodies, for they are perfect as they are. Yet to me, my body was loathsome: chest hair, back hair, balls and ball hair, ass hair, obligated to fulfill six hundred and thirteen commandments. I knew with utmost certainty that when Hashem dredged up my clay from the earth and made me a man He left me half-baked. *This* is why I had to live alone.

There came a Friday when I worked myself into a fury. I waited until the first three stars appeared in the sky, and I then declared: If the Holy One was so careless with His handiwork, may He unmake me and remake again!

Then, the front door opened without a knock and a great hush descended, and a woman walked through my doorway. She was dressed thusly: a long flowing bridal gown, a veil, boots up to her knees, and a corset, and her breasts were resplendent and bared. I rose from my seat at my little kitchen table. Tears welled in my eyes and I began to whisper a prayer of thanks to the Lord, before remembering myself, my shard-soul, and I stopped, and said: "I'm sorry, but it is not I who you desire."

She closed the door behind her and walked up to me. She laid her hand upon my thinning hair and withdrew hair, which she gripped, jerking my head back so I was looking upwards at the moonlight-burning eyes of the divine feminine Shechinah.

"I desire she who welcomes me," she said, her voice a blast of the shofar.

Hastily, I recited the final verse of Lecha Dodi: "Let us welcome Shabbos. Come in peace, and joy and jubilation, amidst the faithful! Enter, O bride! Enter, O bride!"

She smiled. "Kiss me," she said, and I kissed her, and again I kissed her, again. She gripped my hair and pulled my lips away from hers. "Unbutton your shirt," she said, and I did. She put her hands on my chest and squeezed and slapped and pinched, until she had kneaded two breasts. She sucked on each nipple, tasting her handiwork, and I gasped in delight.

She shoved me into the wall and held me by the neck, lightly choking, while with the other hand she shaped me. She put a thumb to my brow. She rubbed her knuckles up and down my hips, and my thighs. She pressed my chest hair back into my body. She slid her hand between my legs and pushed and stroked until my clay receded, wet as the dew of Eden. She continued until at last the three aspects of my soul aligned with my body: nefesh, my cravings; ruach, my passions; and neshama, Hashem's presence within me, beautiful, perfect, unchanged. And when she was done, and I was satisfied, she carried me to my bed, and stayed with me until I fell asleep.

I must confess that I slept well past sunrise and woke up too late for the shacharit service, but I arrived at the shul in time for musaf.

I walked to the other side of the mechitzah to sit with the women of the congregation, and they welcomed me with awe, for they knew well the miracle I had experienced. While the men chanted, the women whispered mazel tov to me. Those who sat next to me took turns holding my hand; both were lovely, and I welcomed their affection. Everywhere, from every seat, women smiled at me: coquettish smiles, daring smiles, as well as smiles of expectation, as if to ask: Nu, are you still planning on staying single?

MoonWife

by Sarah Gailey

THE FRONT DOOR OF Nell's office slides open with a soft whoosh and a digital chime. Nell flinches. She hung weighty velvet curtains across the old plexi windows of the storefront to try to muffle the synthetic noise, but the curtains are moth-eaten enough to qualify as lace, and they aren't doing the job.

She'll get around to figuring it out. Another day, when she doesn't still have an ache in her shoulders from the latest round of H1N7 boosters.

Nell braces a foot against the built-in shelves that used to house vape cartridges and now hold an archive's worth of ancient cell phones on small linen cushions, one nestled into each recessed niche. A single shove against the shelves sends her rolling chair rocketing toward the front of the shop. The stuck wheel makes it roll in a wide arc instead of a straight line, and she swings right past the little guy standing on the welcome mat.

"Welcome to Nell's, I'm Nell, what's your business?" She says it in a liturgical cadence, the words coming out of her almost without meaning.

The little guy tracks her as she rolls past him and catches herself on the corner of her intake table. "The sign says Speed Mart," he says. His eyes are as round as watch batteries.

"And I say Welcome to Nell's I'm Nell what's your business," Nell replies. She uses the lip of the desk to pull herself behind it, the movement sending a fizz of pain through her shoulders. "Do you need Speed Mart?"

"No, I need Nell," he answers. "I mean, you. I need your help."

She figures him for a recently bereaved. She's seen it plenty of times—there's a hollow look people get when they've just lost someone, a searching look. Nell figures they're looking for death. They want death to be a person they can confront, a statue they can pull down, a building with front doors they can chain themselves to. They want it to be something they can point to: *Look at that thing, it hurt me, it's hurting us.*

Nell pulls on the fingertip-gloves that connect her to her intake array. She opens a blank file and rotates the view so they can both see what she's typing. "What name do you want me to put in? Doesn't have to be your real one."

"Put, uh." He comes to a full stop, seems to be making a three-point turn inside his head. "Put Kelsey. She knew me as Kelsey. I didn't change it until after."

"She's not gonna see what I write down," Nell says, hesitating, her fingers hanging motionless in the posture that calls up the keyboard interface.

"Oh. Then put Tris." He spells it out. Fidgets. When Nell explains the fee agreement, he nods without looking her in the eyes. Silence coils between them after that.

"You gotta transfer the credits before we can get started," Nell says once a minute or so has passed with just the two of them staring at each other.

"I have a question," Tris says. He shifts from foot to foot. Rotates a chunky smartring on his index finger.

Nell waits.

"Is that okay?"

Nell waits.

"I don't mean any disrespect," he says.

Nell waits.

"It's just—I went to this other place, before I came here."

Nell blows out a long breath, her eyes rolling back in her head before she can stop herself. "You went to Dino, right?"

"Yeah. And I don't have a problem with anyone doing whatever work they're gonna do, but—"

"Right. You're hoping I don't do the same kind of thing Dino does." She hopes it comes out gentle. Gentle's not her strong suit, but this kid is clearly trying to be delicate and careful and she doesn't want to stomp that out of him, even if she fucking hates Dino. "Not to worry. I don't run things the same way he does. Your loved one will be holding the reins the whole time."

Tension falls off Tris like a soaked raincoat falling away from his shoulders. Turns out he isn't small, after all—he was just shrunk down into himself like a telescoping antenna. Now he straightens up, spreads out, takes space. "Okay. Yeah, that sounds good."

Nell doesn't ask how far this kid went with Dino. Her acid reflux acts up when she hears too many details about the way that fucking guy handles his business. And he's the only other digital medium in a hundred-kilometer radius, so her acid reflux acts up a lot. Dino likes to crack his way into old escort accounts, get his scabby fingers wrapped around a chat interface, and shake the ghost inside until a few panicked nonsense words drop out. For a low price, he'll offer to "interpret" the messages. For a high price, he'll keep shaking until the spirit he's caught starts performing the way they performed when they were alive—a ghost's fear response, recreating the actions that were wired deepest into their nervous system in life.

Nell doesn't ask. She's still gonna need an antacid, though.

Things go smoothly from there. Tris transfers the credits to Nell's account, confirms that his loved one died six months earlier. More time than Nell thought it would be, but still recent enough that she won't have to pull out any antique equipment, won't have to try accessing archived platforms or defunct websites. The transfer clears and Tris gives her a handful of usernames. They're off to the races.

Nell shows Tris where the waiting area is—comfortable armchair, teakettle and assorted herbals. He makes himself a mug of lavender-spearmint and ignores the chair, electing instead to meander around the room looking at the antiques. Nell left half of the display shelves up from when the joint was a convenience store; they hold laptops, tablets, even a few MP3 players. All cushioned, all covered with plexi. She likes to keep things nice.

While he looks around, Nell steps behind the painted folding screen where her workstation waits. There are twenty monitors in sleep mode; Nell snaps her fingers and they spark to life. She gets to work.

The usernames are all variations on MoonWife—some with a handful of numbers at the end, others with underscores hanging off like earrings. Nell hunts down the profiles attached to the usernames and manages to dig up a few that Tris either forgot to share or didn't know about. She opens them in triplicate view—browser, mobile app, and desktop app. There's a lot of material. MoonWife lived online, it seems. She posted a lot of photos of herself—blunt black bob, full hips, chest tattoo of a big fish-looking thing getting poked with a harpoon.

"Was business good?" Nell calls out.

Tris pokes his head around the screen a moment later. "Whoa," he breathes, staring up at the wall of screens. "You found her."

"'Course I did. Was business good?" she repeats, gesturing to the three escort sites MoonWife had profiles on. "I'm not asking to be an asshole. Not asking for Dino reasons, either."

"Why does it matter, then?"

Nell sighs. Nobody ever trusts her with their dead loved ones. "It matters," she says, "because I'm going to be searching out the aggregate of MoonWife's collected online energy. If business was terrible, or if she only worked those sites every so often, there's probably not going to be a piece of her still hanging on there. And if business was amazing and she was always working, she might not be there, either. Or—it might seem like she's there, but then we end up talking to a work persona instead. The version of her that she showed to clients, you know?"

Tris shakes his head. "She was herself with clients. More or less."

Nell pushes away from the monitors and levels a look at Tris that she hopes will make him feel like an insect with a pin stuck through it. "Were you a client, Tris?"

"What? No, I—"

"Because I don't bother dead people for their old clients. I don't care if you think you had something special or if you miss her *so much* or if she was the only one who could ever make you—"

Tris flinches violently. "No! Jesus! No, she was—she was my best friend, okay? We were best friends. We talked every day, all day. We told each other everything. I loved her so much," he says, his voice straining. "We lived together for a few years, before she moved to Toronto to help her sister take care of—you don't need to know all this." He looks up at the screens behind her. The yearning in his face is as raw as minced liver. "I just want to talk to her one last time. I didn't get to say goodbye."

Nell bites her tongue. She wants to tell Tris that nobody gets to say goodbye. Even people who say goodbye don't get to say goodbye. She knows because they come to her. It doesn't matter if they got to do the whole tearful hand-holding final-words routine with someone who'd been terminal for years before hitting the road— the goodbye, they always say, didn't feel complete. Because it can't feel complete, not when the person you're saying goodbye to is turning away from you with everything they've ever been.

But Nell would be out of business if she told people they should just make peace with the knowledge that no "goodbye" could ever be enough. Her dinner depends on this kid's certainty that one more farewell will let him sleep at night. So she nods, turns back to the monitors, and starts to scroll.

Her setup allows her to browse through all the profiles at once. Her eyes move fast, darting from screen to screen, taking in photos and posts and signal boosts. MoonWife liked to share photos of her belly and thighs, memes about political leaders, friends' requests for mutual aid. She posted a lot about the history of sex work, was interviewed by a big-name magazine as part of an oral history of SESTA/FOSTA. The piece appeared in a big series celebrating the twenty-five-year anniversary of the repeal, and MoonWife's face was the image the magazine used across their platforms to promote the interview series.

"She was pretty," Nell murmurs.

"She was perfect," Tris replies. His voice is rotten with love that might have been requited at some point but can never be answered ever again, even if he gets to talk with MoonWife now, because the dead are dead and Nell figures they can't love the living in a way that reaches across the impassable divide between the two.

Nell keeps taking MoonWife in. She lets her vision go liquid as the content drifts across her screens. She enters a flow state fast— she ought to, she's been doing it since she was a kid too young to understand what was happening to her. She's not paying close attention to specific photos or posts or opened links or interviews anymore. Those only matter now for the traces of MoonWife that are stuck to them—the little blue-white sparks of Self that got left behind over a lifetime of building online relationships.

They're less concentrated in some places. Form posts *here's where to send credits if you like my work!* and shitposts *he snap on my crackle till i pop* and the occasional bland reply to someone being overfamiliar *<3 thank u bb* are dim. But others shine bright. An account Nell quickly recognizes as belonging to Tris gets single-word replies, *omg* or *ha*, but MoonWife glitters on them like iridescent pollen. Selfies are bright, too; she loved herself, Nell understands, loved the way she looked and loved celebrating it. And the posts on her work pages gleam like—well, like moonlight, Nell thinks with a smile that might only be happening inside her own head. This lady loved her job.

Soon, the shimmer of MoonWife peels away from the screens and drifts toward Nell. She doesn't hear Tris gasp at the sight—she's too immersed for that—but she feels the tendrils of light brush her temples, her lips, her collarbone, her wrists. She opens her mouth and lets MoonWife trace a sweet bright finger across her tongue.

"What do you want to ask?" she breathes. "Why do you want to contact her?"

Tris stammers for a while before getting the words out. "I want to know, um. I want to ask her. Can I just talk to her?"

"Go for it. She's here." The words come out thick. Nell is underwater; she feels like an air bubble floating up through a gallon of honey. She loves this part.

Tris steps forward. "Val? It's me." He pauses.

Nell recognizes the pause and risks offering comfort. "She knows who you are."

She doesn't look around—her eyes are still on the screens—but she hears Tris choke on a sob.

"I'm sorry," he whispers. "I'm sorry I look different. I didn't think I'd be seeing you again and—"

The screens in front of Nell go black, then light up with blue-white letters.

YOU LOOK LIKE YOU BABE

CAN I COME IN

"Can you come in where, I don't understand—" Tris is half laughing, half crying.

Nell frowns at the screens. "That one wasn't to you. She's asking me. And the answer is no."

PLEASE

I DON'T WANT TO TALK THIS WAY

Nell's concentration is broken but MoonWife isn't wavering. She's keeping the channel open herself. If ghosts had feet, one of hers would be jammed in the door between life and death.

Nell crosses her arms and shakes her head. "No fucking way. I don't host."

I WONT KICK YOU OUT

YOU CAN STAY

"Absolutely not. Forget it. It's this way or nothing. Say what you need to say to Tris before I close the windows."

I'LL TELL YOU WHAT DINO SAID ABOUT YOU

Nell freezes. That's bait, premium bait, a ten-dollar lure she can't resist.

"Fine. Five minutes. But I stay the whole time, and when I say out, you get out."

MoonWife doesn't hesitate. All the beautiful light of her blinks out. It doesn't shoot toward Nell, doesn't climb into her nose and mouth, doesn't grip her by the limbs and puppet her around. It just vanishes, gone as quick as dying.

Then Nell feels it. MoonWife is nestling inside her, nudging Nell out of the way, just to one side, just a little bit here and there, cold and careful, until they're packed in tight as two dimes in a windpipe.

Nell speaks but it's MoonWife doing the talking. She talks fast. Nell isn't planning on listening—it's none of her business what MoonWife and Tris have to say to each other—but she holds up a hand when Tris steps closer.

"No touching. This is still my body. Sorry. We won't." That's her own mouth answering her, MoonWife's voice slipping out after Nell's. Her tongue aches with the strange way someone else shapes the words.

Tris looks stricken. "Can I just—"

"No," MoonWife answers. "It's not me, anyway. It's not my body. It won't feel like I felt."

MoonWife pilots Nell's body like she's driving a tractor for the first time, all ungainly fits and starts. She walks a lap around the room, bends to peer at shelves and into crevices. She's not exploring—she's searching.

"What are you looking for? A pencil and paper." Nell flinches. She hates the speed of MoonWife's answer, hates knowing it came so fast because MoonWife probably felt the question forming inside Nell's brain before she could put voice to it.

Tris follows the body the two of them are sharing, trailing MoonWife's steps like tracked toilet paper. "I have so much to say to you," he says. "But—please, will you look at me?"

MoonWife shakes her head. "No time. I only have five minutes, remember?"

"Nell will let you stay longer if you need to," Tris says.

"I don't think so" comes out of Nell's mouth on a laugh, and Nell doesn't know which of them is talking—it feels like both at once.

Nell takes over her legs, steering her body toward the bin behind the counter where she keeps a couple of beat-up notebooks for analog writing. MoonWife catches on as soon as Nell pauses them in front of the bin. Nell watches her own arms rummage through it, watches her own hand close clumsily around a ballpoint pen.

"Why don't you tell me what you want to write down, and let me do the writing?" she suggests. "You're not going to do a good job with these hands. You don't know them at all."

Her chin ducks down into her chest in a nod. She listens to the sound of her own voice and takes transcription while Tris watches, his face drawn, his eyes streaming. *TristanKnight67*.

Tris leans over the counter, tilting his head to read the words. His cheeks color. "What is that?"

"I'll tell you in a minute. I just needed to write it down before I forgot. You don't understand how hard it is to hold on to things after you go," MoonWife says. She looks up at Tris with Nell's eyes and cries with Nell's tears. **"I'm sorry,"** she says.

"Just tell me why you did it," Tris says. He reaches for Nell's hand across the counter, catches himself, reels his hand back and shoves it deep into his pocket. "That's all I want to know. After everything we went through—I just want to know *why*."

MoonWife tries to wipe a tear off Nell's cheek, accidentally overshoots and smacks Nell in the eye. "Fuck," Nell bites out. "This is why I don't host. You have two minutes left, try not to break any of my bones—**sorry**," MoonWife interrupts. **"I'll be more careful."**

"Why did you block me?" Tris whispers, his eyes wide and pleading.

Rage rises in Nell. "Are you fucking kidding me?" she spits. "You made me haul this woman back from the other side of death so you could get around a block!?"

Tris holds up his hands like he thinks Nell's going to deck him. His instincts are good—MoonWife is the only thing keeping Nell from doing exactly that. The muscles in Nell's legs twitch as the two selves inside her body battle for control. Tris stammers out his defense with the haste of a man who knows what's trying to come for him. "It's not like that. She blocked me within an hour of her death. We weren't fighting or anything, nothing bad happened between us, we were chatting. I just want to know—"

"You little prick, it's people like you who give my job a bad reputation, you should have just gone to fucking Dino excuse me," MoonWife interrupts again. Nell hates the feeling of being interrupted by her own tongue. She was just getting a good head of steam worked up, and MoonWife tripped her midstride. "Is the meter still running while you yell at Tris, or am I going to get an extension on my time?"

The fury drops out of Nell. MoonWife doesn't sound like she needs defending. "I'll give you a minute back," Nell mutters.

MoonWife looks at Tris and Nell feels the love radiating from her. "It was supposed to be a joke," MoonWife says. "You texted me something—I don't remember—"

"The picture of the lady in the yoga straps," Tris says quickly. "Where she looks like a sleep paralysis demon."

MoonWife bursts out laughing. Nell has never heard herself laugh so loud, so free, like a bird is escaping from between her teeth. "Oh my god, that's right. Yeah, so, I blocked you so I could take a screenshot of your account being blocked. I was going to send you the screenshot and then unblock you, but then—"

"—but then," Tris finishes. He lets out a breath he's probably been holding for six months. "Do you know what happened?"

MoonWife shakes Nell's head.

"It was a blood clot. A big one, in your brain. They said it was probably from your last round of Strep-2. They also said it was fast. So."

Silence falls on them like a dropped anvil. Stupid, Nell thinks. I should have warned him. The dead don't need to know how they went. What good'll it do them?

"You have thirty more seconds," Nell finally says. She doesn't have a timer or anything, but she doesn't want to be stuck sharing her body with this ghost for another ten minutes just because these two are having an awkward time. "Wrap it up."

They both start talking at once, both of them saying the same things—I love you, I'm sorry for something that doesn't really need an apology, I love you, I miss you, I love you. Then Tris says, "Can I come see you again?" and the heavy silence returns.

"That's the thing I needed to write this down for," MoonWife answers. She holds up the notebook so Tris can see *TristanKnight67* written in Nell's awful penmanship.

"Ten seconds," Nell says. "This is my master password," MoonWife continues. "I need you to use it to access my password manager and get into my accounts."

Tris nods. "And do what?"

Nell opens her mouth to say *time's up*, but MoonWife beats her to the larynx. "Save me from Dino."

It's the only thing MoonWife could have said to prevent Nell from kicking her ass out, and they both know it. Nell seethes. She hates letting someone manipulate her like this, but she hates Dino more, so she caves. "What's Dino have to do with it? And what did he say about me?" she adds, remembering.

MoonWife hesitates long enough that Nell guesses Dino didn't say anything about her at all. She hands the notebook to Tris and opens Nell's mouth slowly to answer. "He won't leave me alone," she says at last. "He's hauled me out at least a hundred times since March. I don't know what month it is now, but—What happened in March?" Nell says over her.

Tris answers in a pained whisper. "That was when I went to him. His listing says he specializes in queer relationships and sex workers. I didn't realize—I didn't know what he was like."

Nell swears mean enough that Tris goes pale. "Fucking Dino," she finishes. "He's juicing you. Calling you up for every client, pretending you're their person. No wonder you came so easy when I called—he must practically have you on a yo-yo string by now. You said a hundred times since March? At least," MoonWife confirms.

Tris shakes his head. "That can't be right."

"Why not?" MoonWife asks.

"Because it's the first week of May," Nell snaps.

Tris is trembling, his fingers curled in a white-knuckle knot around the edge of the counter. "How do we stop him?"

"We shut down her accounts," Nell says, striding toward her workstation. "We scrub them."

"But then what happens to her?" Tris asks, following a few steps behind.

"She'll go where people go, when they go for good," Nell answers. Inside her, MoonWife is silent. Wary.

Tris's footfalls stop. "Wait," he says. "No."

Nell sits at her workstation, pulls up the master password program she uses. "Was it th—Yes," MoonWife answers before she can get the question out. "Good," Nell replies. "I'll have you taken care of in five minutes. Maybe less."

"No!" Tris grabs the back of Nell's rolling chair and yanks.

Suddenly she's spinning hard and fast, flung away from her work-station. She sticks a foot out to stop herself and it snags sideways on the linoleum, twists painfully under her. "You can't get rid of her. I can't—I can't lose her again, please. There's another way. We'll find another way."

MoonWife turns Nell's chair to face Tris. She's got her will clamped down over every muscle in Nell's body like a palm over a screaming mouth. "There's not another way," she says with a gentleness that makes Nell's tongue itch.

"What if we—what if—we could—" Tris has his hands wrapped around the back of his neck; his eyes are desperate.

Nell wrests control of her jaw back from MoonWife to stop Tris before he gets brave. "C'mon, kid. How are you gonna kill Dino if you can't even say the words?"

He flushes, a deep mottled red climbing up his neck and across his jaw. "I wasn't going to say that. I just thought—we could scare him, maybe."

MoonWife pushes Nell onto her feet and stumbles across the room with her body. This is why Nell doesn't play host—MoonWife's desperation to get her business on Earth done is strong enough that she can take over, make Nell's body her own. It's an awful, powerless feeling.

It's how MoonWife has probably felt a hundred times since March, though. So Nell tries to keep on understanding. Tries not to panic at the way her body keeps moving without her.

MoonWife stops a few paces away from Tris. "It won't work," she says. "I don't want you spilling blood for me. And I don't think that scaring Dino will stop him from—what did Nell call it? Juicing me? He might take it out on me, even. He will. See?"

Tris looks like he has road rash on his soul. He's staring into

Nell's eyes with abject desperation. "I can't do this without you," he whispers.

MoonWife doesn't answer. Can't, Nell figures, so she offers an answer instead. "You can. You've been doing it without her for six months. And Tris—if you don't let her go, you're worse than Dino."

"Why worse?" Tris asks, incredulous.

"Because Dino is a fucking staph infection," Nell says, "and you're an okay kid. Dino never loved anything in his life, except maybe the LED flashlight he used to blind neighborhood pets as a child. But you? You got love in you. Don't let yourself turn into the kind of person who lets it rot until it's just an excuse to wring the happiness out of someone else's soul."

Tris stares at his shoes, his mouth working around a reply that can't be put into words.

Nell leaves him to it. As she returns to her workstation, she can hear the breathy, damp sound of his crying. There are tissues all over the shop—she's used to tears. "He'll be okay," MoonWife whispers, so quiet Nell doesn't think the sound leaves the mouth they currently share. Nell nods. "Not for a while," she breathes back. "But yeah. He'll be okay."

She goes through MoonWife's old accounts, wiping them in full. No more backlog of posts. No more selfies. No more home-brewed memes. One by one, the accounts wink out, the profile pictures replaced by a generic *file not found* image. MoonWife doesn't budge inside Nell's body, doesn't diminish. It's not her that's being erased—only the containers that held her.

When the final account goes dark, Nell is acutely aware that she's the last thing anchoring MoonWife to this place. She feels like an astronaut's safety tether.

"Done," she says.

Tris makes a strangled sound. "She's gone?"

"I'm still here. But I have to go," MoonWife says. "I love you, Tris."

"Wait. Just—can I ask one more thing? Please."

Nell nods. Or maybe MoonWife nods, or maybe they both do.

"Your password. It's my name."

MoonWife curls the corners of Nell's lips into a tiny, smug smile.

"I didn't start going by this name until a few months ago. How did you know?"

MoonWife spins Nell's chair and gives a jaunty kick. "You mentioned it to me a few years ago. You were drunk and you said that if you were a boy, you'd want your name to be Tristan."

"But I didn't—"

"I did," MoonWife sings. She gives Tris a wink and a wave. "See you out there, babe."

And then she's gone, quick as she came—a light blinking out, a tap shutting off, a drop of water falling back into the ocean. Nell's body is too spacious inside. She has to unclench, uncurl to fill herself back up again. Her limbs feel a little wrong, her head a little light.

As she's shaking out her hands, Tris lets out another soft sob.

"That's it," Nell says. "Time to go home, kid."

"But—"

"No buts." Nell cuts him off. "Listen, that was intense for you, I get it. But I don't do aftercare, okay? You need to go talk to your friends about this. Take your time. Process. Don't forget to drink water. But you can't do any of that here. Shop's closed."

Tris hesitates, his eyes red-rimmed, his mouth flushed with grief. "The door says you're open until eight."

"The door also says Speed Mart," Nell replies. She takes him by the shoulders and pushes him out the door, locks it behind him, flips the sign to *closed*.

She meant what she said to him: He's a good kid with a lot of love in him. If she'd let him hang on to MoonWife, he'd be ruined. He'd hate himself for it, and soon he'd hate MoonWife, too, and everything he'd ever been would rot away. And his other solution? Forget it. Nell knows beyond a shadow of a doubt that a guy like Tris isn't a killer. He couldn't get within ten feet of killing Dino, not without losing his nerve.

Nell turns off the lights in the shop. She hits a button behind the counter that lowers the heavy steel grate in front of the plexi storefront. There's a cherrywood baseball bat to the left of that button, wrapped in black tape at both ends. She grabs it and heads for the back door.

She feels bad for hustling Tris out. It's just that there are only so many hours in the day. The kid, she knows, could never kill Dino. And MoonWife had said she didn't want the kid spilling any blood.

But Nell's not the kid, and Nell's not MoonWife, either. Not anymore.

She locks up the back door of the shop behind her and heads down the alley toward the road. She's got a visit to pay. The street-lights are out in this part of town, but Nell doesn't mind—the blue-white moon overhead is bright enough to light her way.

Forever Won't End Like This

by Dominique Dickey

TED CAN'T FUCKING STAND doing press.

This is the first year he's had to worry about interviews. It's part of the job, and he's lucky to have a job, but he hates answering the same questions over and over again. Every time Ted has to talk about being a Black trans actor playing a Black trans character, his fledgling success loses some of its shine.

He knows it matters. He wishes it didn't have to matter.

Vienna Comic-Con (that's Vienna, Virginia) is fun, though. He's on a panel with his co-stars—*holy shit he's on a panel with his co-stars*—and he can't believe how full the room is. He answers the questions he always gets asked. He makes jokes, and laughs at the right times. He says one honest thing: "Before I'm an actor, I'm a huge fan of *Skeleton Key*. If I hadn't been cast, I would've been in this room either way—I'd be sitting out there, with all of you. I'm really grateful to get to be on the inside of something that I would have loved just as fiercely from the outside."

At the other end of the stage, the showrunner, Denny Monaghan, smoothly takes the credit. He gets the crowd cheering, then throws to the season two trailer. Ted concentrates on doing the right things with his face. The lights go down, the trailer plays on the screen behind him, and his face isn't doing the right things at all.

Skeleton Key isn't, strictly speaking, a good show. Ted was practically raised by shitty prime-time fantasy, though; he knows it doesn't matter if a show is good, as long as it's *fun*. The best shows have heart, give the viewers someone to cheer for, and don't take themselves too seriously.

So *Skeleton Key* isn't *good*, but it's one of the best.

Vaguely magical, vaguely medieval setting—think Tolkien or *Earthsea* with bad greenscreen. Poor white girl, raised on a pig farm, who absolutely does not look like she tends to pigs all day, and absolutely does not know how gorgeous she is. A nobleman comes to the village looking for a bride. Lord Lucero's the kind of important man people fear. There are rumors. He's been married before; his brides are always so young, and no one knows what happens to them.

So obviously he marries Ember, the mega-pretty white girl we all pretend wouldn't smell like pig shit. He takes her back to his castle. Makeover montage where we act like Ember wasn't already wearing eyeliner out in the boonies. She doesn't know her salad knife from her dessert fork. Awkward moments played straight. Orchestral renditions of last summer's pop hits.

He goes away—it's a business trip, because he really is an important man, and he's no slouch. Before he leaves, he gives Ember keys to every room in the joint, but tells her not to use one of them. You know where this is going, right?

Ember does her best to hold out. She explores the rooms she's allowed. She flirts with the butler, Finn, because he's hot and young. She writes letters to the folks back home. Finn says he'll send them; he doesn't. Ember's bored and she misses her pigs.

She uses the last key. Lord Lucero returns and he's all like, *Oh no, now I have to kill you and we haven't even consummated our union, why do my beautiful wives always betray me!* Villain monologue, et cetera.

But you don't bet against a pig farmer. Ember's been slaughtering animals since she was big enough to hold a knife. She's not afraid of many things, and she's certainly not afraid of a fancy man in his fancy clothes.

Ember kills him. She bleeds him, she guts him, she hangs his carcass. The shot widens, and we see the forbidden room. It's a cellar—cold enough to age meat, not rot it—and the nobleman's body is far from the only one. Look what he's done to all his missing wives.

And that's just the pilot.

Ted has twenty minutes between the panel and the meet and greet. He spends seventeen of those minutes trying to stop crying.

It's not dramatic. He's not having a fit. His eyes are just leaking—steadily, insistently—for no reason. For lots of very good reasons.

Denny squeezes Ted's upper arm through his bomber jacket. It's probably meant to be companionable, but it makes Ted want to scream.

Ted gets about ninety seconds with each fan in the meet and greet line; he can tell within the first five whether they're a garden-variety *Skeleton Key* fan, or if they're here because of Aggie.

The thing about Aggie—Ted's character—is that he's an absolute pill. On a different show, one less invested in redemption and moral complexity, he'd be the villain. Most of the fans love to hate him, or they just hate him. But the fans that love him are a true force.

Ted sees it all, from adoration to vitriol. He lurks on Twitter. He likes porny fan art every once in a while, when he wants to cause a bit of chaos. He's seen kids—they aren't that much younger than him, but they seem so young—get dogpiled for fanfic considered "problematic." He's seen kids get doxxed for daring to believe that a bitchy queer man deserves to be loved.

It only takes an instant for Ted to look into someone's eyes and know that this story, his character—and the community that's cropped up around his character—is a matter of life or death for them.

It feels pretty life-or-death for Ted, too.

"Can I get a video? Just a short one. Just . . . would you mind saying it? I know everyone must ask you to say it." Early twenties, faded green hair, body swallowed up in a massive plaid overshirt.

"Yeah, of course. You ready?" Their hands shake as they unlock their phone. Ted wants to say a million kind and encouraging things, but this is a stranger, and platitudes are empty. That's why he'll *always* say the line, for anyone who asks: he doesn't have to know the emotional context of someone's life to know it means something. Denny wrote the script and Ted said the words, but the fans built the meaning.

Ted looks into the camera. His inhale is ragged, like he's about to start crying again, but his voice comes out certain. "Forever won't end like this."

★

Ember kills her husband, and Finn is surprisingly calm about it. "I just wish you hadn't disemboweled him," he says. "You've made this a lot more difficult."

Because everyone knows magic is real, but very few people—at least, very few people from Ember's village—know the extent of it. Magic takes the shape of the vessel it's given, like water. It's volatile, and massive as the sea; like the sea, you should never show it your back. And all of that potential, danger and beauty alike, is kept contained by three witches. Three women who swallowed whole oceans and were made to live carrying them.

Those three witches answer to Lord Lucero.

Or, they're supposed to.

Or, they used to.

Like Finn said, the situation was already difficult, and Ember made it worse—but it's nothing he can't handle. Important men are rarely as important as whoever stands behind them. Finn handled Lord Lucero's affairs. He knew him, as few people got to know him. And powerful men are never as powerful as whoever answers to them. Why would a witch—an ocean of a woman—bow to a man? Why would *three*?

Even when Lord Lucero believed he controlled the witches, Finn knew his grip was weak. Exploiting that weakness was the prudent thing to do.

Finn sweats and heaves, lights candles and says words . . . and he puts Lord Lucero's body back together. He takes Ember's hands. The cellar floor is filmed with saltwater and blood. He says, "Now, we're going to put on the performance of a lifetime. We just might get away with it."

★

While Ember and Finn are puppeteering Lord Lucero's reconstructed corpse around the countryside, politicking and pretending he's still alive, Aggie is—on all levels except physical—being dragged over gravel behind a speeding motorcycle. It is perhaps a mercy that Aggie's Terrible, Horrible, No Good, Very Bad Summer occurs offscreen.

When the audience meets him, in the opening of the fourth episode, he's crawling up a riverbed. It's dusk, and he's got mud and blood everywhere. He's breathing like he doesn't want to be: long pauses between exhale and inhale, holding out until his diaphragm flails. He's crawling like he doesn't really want to do that, either.

Once he clears the waterline, he rolls over and looks at the darkening sky. "Are you going to say it?"

The answer comes from out of frame. "No. You are."

He closes his eyes. The camera lifts away, widening the shot. The focus softens, details blurring together, until we lose track of the defeated boy sprawled with his feet still dangling in the river. The only clear thing is the sound: moving water, crickets, frogs.

He whispers, "Forever won't end like this."

Aggie is healed in a blaze of yellow light. He spits out a mouthful of silty water.

He stands up, soaked to the skin and wearing only one shoe, and walks off. All the living things in the trees keep singing.

The last fan in the meet and greet line has a determined look and a bulging tote bag, a poster tube poking out of the top. She drops the bag onto the table in front of Ted: *thunk.* "You're shorter in real life."

He chuckles. "I get that one a lot."

"Can I get you to sign these? Security gave me a hard time about bringing the bag in, so I hope it's okay with you."

"It's no trouble." He uncaps his Sharpie. "Lay it on me."

The first two items in the bag—a T-shirt and a postcard—are *Skeleton Key* merch. Then there's *Undead Muskrat*, a straight-to-DVD horror movie Ted was in nearly a decade ago. Then *Undead Muskrat 2: Deader & Wetter*, followed by *Undead Muskrat 3: Dammed to Hell*.

"Do you want these personalized?" Ted asks.

"No. The *Undead Muskrat* ones—I've got all five DVDs—I'm actually planning to sell on eBay."

He scrawls his signature. "There's gotta be an easier way for you to make two dollars."

"Oh, it's more about getting them out of the house! Goodwill wouldn't take 'em."

He laughs outright at that, and laughs even harder at what comes out of the tote next: a crumpled program from his high school production of *Hamlet*, followed by the portable hard drive that probably still has his undergrad short films on it. "Lea! Did you ask my mom for these?"

"Ha! I knew I could get you to break first! And yes I did, because your mom loves me."

It's been a long day. It's been a long few months, really—Ted barely had a moment to breathe between wrapping season two of *Skeleton Key* and traveling to what feels like every fan convention in North America. He's more exhausted than he knew he could survive being, in a long-term sense; acutely, he's happier than he knew he could be.

Ted's wife and his mom conspired to prank him at Vienna Comic-Con.

Given the givens, he has a really fucking good life. He has to remind himself, sometimes, that he has more than he knew he could want.

Aggie limps all the way to Lord Lucero's castle on one wool sock and one cracked leather boot. He walks through the night, through the day, and into the next night. When he arrives he's delirious, rattling the gates and demanding to be let in. Spitting, slurring, howling.

Finn tries to quiet him, but Aggie carries on. First, it's "Why won't you let me speak to him?" Then, it's "Why won't you let me die?"

The noise wakes Ember. She comes down to the courtyard in her nightgown, carrying a lantern, asking Finn if everything's all right. She only makes it halfway through the sentence.

When Ember and Aggie see each other, they both go silent. Katydids, crickets, a far-off barking fox.

"I thought you were dead," Aggie says.

"*Agatha?*"

"No. Aggie."

"Aggie." Ember says the name very softly. "You've changed."

"Some. Where's—"

"That's complicated," Finn says, before Ember can put her foot in her mouth.

Aggie wheels around and punches Finn square in the nose.

In Finn's defense, it *is* complicated. Penning Ember, Finn, and Aggie in a moldering castle together could never be simple. The situation is a critical mass of resentments, neuroses, and water damage.

Aggie gets his audience with Lord Lucero—or, with the man's body, moving in accordance with Finn's commands. He makes his plea: "Call off the witch that made me this way. You're the only one who can."

Finn's eyebrow twitches at the word *witch*. Lord Lucero's eyebrow twitches, too. Aggie lunges forward and presses his hand to Lord Lucero's throat. The skin splits bloodlessly under Aggie's palm in the shape of the wound that killed him.

Ember asks, "Am I the only one who can't do magic?"

Aggie vomits a long rush of saltwater. When he's finished, he spits. "If Lord Lucero is dead, why didn't you come back for me?"

"I wrote you nearly every day."

"You were all I had."

"Didn't you get my letters?"

"Ember, why would you *stay* here?"

Why? Because she feels responsible for this mess. Because the witches will revolt entirely if they learn Lord Lucero is dead; small acts of insubordination can be abided but, ultimately, *someone* has to be in charge, and why shouldn't it be Ember? No one has ever listened to her, until now, and she likes being listened to. She also likes getting to dress up as an aristocrat. And she's quite enamored of Finn; she doesn't want to leave him.

Ember's not a monster. She didn't *mean* to abandon Aggie. Even if she had, would it have mattered? Aggie's a tough bastard. He's always been fine.

At least, he seemed fine on the outside.

What hurt Aggie the most was that Ember—his best and only

friend—never cared enough to notice how *not fine* he was. She doesn't care enough now, either.

For most of his life, Ted had frequent nightmares about losing his teeth. He understands this to be fairly normal. At no point has he believed that his nightmares fall within the normal range of *intensity*.

It starts as one loose tooth, usually a canine. He pulls it out. Another tooth gets wiggly, probably a molar. He pulls it out. Then a tooth comes loose further back, where he imagines his wisdom teeth would go. He can't grasp the tooth with his fingers, but he feels it working its way free. He leans forward over his bathroom sink to spit it out.

And teeth pour from his open mouth. He only has twenty-eight teeth, but he's losing so many more than that. This many teeth couldn't fit in his mouth. He doesn't even feel them detaching from his gums. Where are all these teeth coming from? The floor is covered in teeth. They're forming drifts and piles. They're shattering under his feet. Where could all these fucking teeth have come from?

He hasn't had that dream since he got cast in *Skeleton Key*.

Since the night Ted returned his signed contract to the network, the teeth have been replaced with water.

It starts as a mouthful of spit, spilling over like he's about to be sick. He's hunched over the toilet, bracing for it, but he doesn't actually throw up. Saliva and then saltwater gushes out of his mouth faster than the pipes can take it away. He gives up on the toilet and moves to the bathtub. The tub fills quickly. Where does the water come from? He floods the bathroom. He feels like he could drown the whole world, with his own uncontrollable sea.

Ted loves Aggie, but he does not labor under the delusion that *Skeleton Key* is *about* Aggie. He doesn't even get much screen time in season one—he spends several episodes imprisoned in a literal dungeon under Lord Lucero's castle. Finn and a throwaway guard character have a good cop/bad cop thing going. It's played for laughs. It's not funny.

The witches aren't Ember and Finn's only problem, but they're what Aggie's most riled up about. Aggie's put in a cell, the plot line is put on ice—et voilà!—Ember and Finn can go back to their melodramatic will-they-or-won't-they. They also resume piloting Lord Lucero's body around, attempting to maintain diplomatic relations with the nearby territories and creating political scandals that inevitably bite them in the ass.

During one such scandal, Ember accidentally incites a war. She wiggles her way out of the situation by inviting the offended grandees to the castle for a party, a plot contrivance that paints her as endearingly stupid. She invites Aggie, too: sends him an actual invitation, written on a square of cardstock.

Finn delivers the invitation. Aggie, whose left ankle is chained to the wall, says, "Don't be silly. I don't have anything to wear."

Because Ember wants Aggie at the party, and because Finn would do nearly anything for Ember, he takes Aggie upstairs and draws him a hot bath. He's matter-of-fact about it; while Lord Lucero was alive, Finn drew him thousands of baths. Shaved him and dressed him, saw him at his worst and took pride in making him tidy.

Aggie hesitates, but only for a moment, before he sees this for what it is. Recognition. Being treated like a man among men.

He dunks his head below the water's surface and doesn't come up for a long while.

Once he's clean, Finn offers to shave Aggie's face. Because Ember trusts Finn, and because Aggie will always trust Ember, he accepts. Aggie has kept so much in, for so long. He doesn't know how to show his throat for the blade without showing everything else.

He tells Finn the truth. Finn lets him.

When Aggie was a child, his parents died in a shipwreck. Aggie would have died, too—he might have, for a moment—but a woman came up from the water and carried him to shore. She kissed his forehead and told him to live, then disappeared back into the waves as if she'd never been solid at all. By the time someone found Aggie, curled up in a clump of seaweed with his teeth chattering, he'd forgotten her face.

A couple took him in. They settled on a farm in a tiny village further inland, spoiled their own children while Aggie starved. He started sleeping in the neighbors' barn, where at least the pigs never shouted at him. When he got caught by the neighbors' youngest daughter, she didn't shout at him either. She brought him a blanket. The next day, she brought him a plum. By the third day, Aggie and Ember were best friends.

Twelve years later, for reasons he will never explain, Aggie decided to drown himself in the river outside of town. A woman—the same woman—rose out of the water and grabbed him by the back of the neck, as if he were an unruly kitten. She dragged him to dry land. She yelled, and then she wept. She said, "I *told* you to live." She fell away into the water.

He thought he'd dreamed it. Time passed. He went down to the river and tried again.

The woman said, "No. You're going to live."

"It *hurts*," Aggie said. "How long?"

"Hmph. How long? You're asking the wrong question."

"Please."

"I don't know. As long as it takes. Forever."

And who, upon being told they're immortal, wouldn't seek proof? Aggie tried again, and the woman gathered him up and said, "Love, you asked the wrong question. It's not the *how long* that matters. It's the *how*."

"I don't understand."

"The length of a life doesn't matter," she said, "as long as it's a life you'd like to grow into. You could live forever, in a life like that, and never tire of it."

"I don't understand."

"Do you like your life?" She asked like she was confused. Aggie knew logically that she wasn't human, but that was the first time he felt it.

"Obviously not."

"Do you like being who you are?"

Aggie didn't answer. That one should have been obvious, too, and it made him feel pathetic. What was wrong with him, that he couldn't like himself? What was wrong with him, that he was so incapable of being liked?

"Maybe now. Maybe now, you'll grow." She kissed his forehead, like she had when he was little, and disappeared.

Aggie stayed still for a long time. He had water in his mouth, and no accounting for how it had gotten there. When he moved, his body felt different. *He* was different. Not much had changed, but he felt alien to himself.

He tried to die a few more times after that, out of spite.

The witch got more and more frustrated with him: "I meant it when I said forever, and you know forever won't end like this."

So Aggie's forever kept dragging on, and the whole thing became a matter of principle. How dare anyone decide that he was going to live, or *how* he would live, or for how long! He's been clawing his way from day to day, madder than a sack of cats. He can't imagine doing this forever.

Finn eyes him, in a moment that spawns a thousand gifsets. "Well, are you growing?"

Aggie gets very red. He does not manage an answer.

As Finn turns away, he says, "Maybe you're not in the right kind of pot."

Aggie *laughs*. It's gloriously loud, almost jarring in how relieved he sounds. He looks younger—no, lighter. He looks like he could have a whole life ahead of him.

The season one finale is basically prom, with the added threat of assassinations. Ted skipped his prom—for all he knows, assassinations are part of the package.

Aggie dances with Ember, nearly kisses her, then tries to cut and run. He doesn't make it far: he's tearing across the courtyard on a stolen horse when at least seventeen arrows catch him in the back. The horse throws him. He hits the cobblestones laughing, blood in his teeth, because he's gotten exactly what he wanted.

"Forever won't end like this." Aggie makes those words a goddamn battle cry.

His skin spits out the arrows. A thin hand, water running off the fingertips, folds around his wrist. The witch helps Aggie up. For once, they look happy to see each other.

Of course, a party guest being shot several times draws some attention. Aggie inclines his head towards an upper balcony, where Ember and Lord Lucero are at the front of the onlooking crowd. The witch looks up.

Every stitched seam in Lord Lucero's undead body unravels. His throat collapses. He folds open from sternum to groin.

Roll credits.

The rest of the cast go out for karaoke after wrapping their Vienna Comic-Con commitments, but Ted bails. He and Lea drive her rented car around until they find a shitty diner with all-day breakfast. She steals bits of scrambled egg off of Ted's plate. He wasn't very hungry anyway.

Lea knows he doesn't want to talk about it. Instead she talks about *her* job in a way that doesn't demand responses, but makes nonprofit fundraising sound like rocket surgery. Who knew grant writing could cause so much drama! Certainly not Ted.

When he gets stopped on the way out of the restaurant, he makes the right faces and says the right things. "Whoa, I've never been asked to sign a tattoo before! Can I get a picture of it? Is that weird?"

Lea drives them back to the hotel. Ted's assistant must have already given her a key; he stumbles over Lea's duffel in the room's entryway and nearly eats shit. Lea laughs while he rights himself. She loops her arms around his neck, distracting him from his hunt for the light switch. "Who would have ever imagined Ted Haley bringing a fan up to his hotel room?"

"I'm just—I'm really tired, Lea. Not tonight." He tugs himself free and falls face-first onto the bed, arms wrapped around a pillow.

Ted doesn't mean to fall asleep like that, but he does. He

dreams of water spilling out of his mouth. When he jolts awake, he's still on top of the covers in all his clothes. Lea's facing away from him, properly under the blankets, sound asleep.

He uses his phone flashlight to find pajamas in his suitcase, managing not to make too much noise in the process. He thumbs through notifications while he brushes his teeth, and ends up looking at the picture from earlier: his signature alongside words in typewriter font on the kid's rib cage, the hem of their binder rolled up enough to show it.

He says, "Forever won't end like this," like it's automatic, the words pulled from him. He feels liquid inside his skin—like he's a boneless sack, and he'll keel over and never get back up again. It passes.

Ted's mouth is full of water. He spits into the sink. He stays stooped over the bathroom counter for a long time, waiting for a flood that doesn't come.

Honestly, Ted is beyond angry about season two of *Skeleton Key*.

So it's a good thing he knows better than to be honest in interviews.

He gets a whole month of quiet. At the end of August, reporters receive screeners of the first three episodes, and Ted's back to giving out sound bites. He says what the network expects him to say: Aggie's story is about becoming a person you like living as, which is inseparable from building a life you can live in, and neither one of those things can be forced. Ted means the words, but it feels unfair to say them.

Ted has loved more than his share of flawed TV shows, often

because they're flawed. Hell, the cracks are where the fandom gets in. He's felt betrayed by shows before. He's had his moments of plugging his ears and saying *Canon can't hurt me if I choose to ignore it.*

But it's different this time. Ted's heartbroken, and complicit in the heartbreak. For eight months, every time someone has told Ted how much Aggie means to them, Ted has wanted to warn them that Aggie is going to die, terribly, for no good reason at all.

Wednesday nights, Ted usually makes a massive bowl of popcorn and live-tweets episodes as they drop.

On a Wednesday in mid-November, right before the season finale airs, he turns his phone off and gives it to Lea.

What hurts the most is that Aggie gets to be happy. It's hard-won. He has to learn how to live, first. How to be loved, and be forgiven. How to forgive.

He thanks the witch, for knowing things about him that he didn't know yet. "I'm glad I stuck around long enough to see it," he says. "But maybe you could have held off on changing my body until I asked for it? Just a pointer, in case you fish any other kids out of capsized boats."

He grows closer to Finn, who teaches him to shave with a straight razor—and, more importantly, how to use magic to prank Ember. Finn tells him he looks better. Aggie says, "I think it's because I'm in the right kind of pot."

He finally tells Ember he's in love with her, and that he's always been in love with her. "Ever since you brought me that blanket. I would have loved anyone for treating me kindly, then, but it lasted. I don't see it going away."

He throws himself into danger ahead of his friends—not because he wants to die, but because he knows that he'll survive. He keeps the people he loves safe. That's worth living for.

The plot happens in the background: Someone's killing the witches, freeing the magic bound in their bodies. Things have generally gone tits up, because it turns out magic was keeping the whole world running, but the causality isn't explained all that well. Come to think of it, the dry-aged wife-meat from the pilot was never explained either. No one watching *Skeleton Key* expects watertight internal logic.

The trio track down the big bad, who turns out to be Lord Lucero's long-lost brother. He's been hiding in the village where Ember and Aggie grew up. When he knows he's caught, he lures them down to the river. It's springtime. The water is high. The setting sun's brought out all the things that sing in the trees. It feels like something beautiful could happen.

With ten minutes left in the season finale, Lord Lucero's brother kills the third and final witch. Her death empties the world of magic, like unstoppering a bathtub and letting the water run out.

With seven minutes left in the finale, Lord Lucero's brother stabs Aggie in the side.

Aggie doesn't just die once. Ember holds him as everything magical about him is undone, as he dies every single death magic has saved him from. He says the cruelest words Denny Monaghan could have possibly written: "It's okay, Em. Let my forever end here."

With five minutes left in the finale, Aggie's a kid in a water-logged kirtle, blood and sea-foam bubbling out of his mouth until his breathing stops. And then he's a grave marker the camera pans past, while the closing scene sets up Ember and Finn's next adventure.

★

It's late Wednesday night—early Thursday morning—when Ted drives to Zuma Beach. He rolls up his pajama pants and walks barefoot over the cold sand. It's as dark as LA ever gets. He can still hear cars on the highway, but the waves are the loudest thing.

He stares out at the ocean and tells himself that none of this matters. He's just a speck on a big planet in a massive nothingness. It's really his own fault, for letting *Skeleton Key* get too personal. He made the mistake of caring too much. He got attached to a character, and doesn't know how to let go.

It's just a job. It's just a show. There will be other jobs, and other shows.

"Yeah, that's a lie." Ted doesn't hear his own voice over the water but it feels important that he's said it. It's not *just* a show, and Aggie isn't *just* a character. He got to be a part of something bigger than himself. That's its own kind of magic.

So he clears his throat, and he gives it his best go: a broken, triumphant holler in the voice Ted has fought so hard for, tossed out over the Pacific. The force of it doubles him over and wears his throat raw. He feels lightened, if only because shouting on the beach in the middle of the night is kinda silly. Ted's laughing at himself when water tips out of his open mouth—just a bit, at first, and then more. It splashes around his feet. It runs away with the receding waves.

In season one of *Skeleton Key*, Finn asked why a witch would obey a man like Lord Lucero.

In the wake of season two, Ted's got a follow-up question: Why would magic stay dead, just because a man like Denny Monaghan tried to kill it?

When the water stops spilling from his throat, Ted spits and walks back up the beach to his car.

They Will Give Us a Home

By Wen-yi Lee

WHEN MY ALARM RINGS, my husband is trying to get into my bedroom. The bronze doorknob rotates, quick and then slow again, but the lock holds. I imagine him slinking away, disappointed.

I can never get up before he does. He's a morning person and I'm a night person. It started with just driving each other crazy at both ends of the day, and now I need to get the lock changed before he smothers me in my sleep. I pull up the shades and snap a feed picture of morning light pouring onto my planters. I breathe in the warmth for myself, then dress and head out.

Zane is at the kitchen island mouth-breathing and slicing strawberries, like he wasn't just trying to break into my bedroom. I retrieve iced tea from my perfectly ordered side of the fridge, violently hate the jumbled mess of his. For five minutes, we stand in opposite corners. The shelves are slathered in Zane's nauseating lavender. I wonder if I can put his paring knife into his eye. He's probably wondering if he can jam the straw into my brain. Thrilling thing, felony contemplations. It wakes you up better than coffee.

I glance out the kitchen's glass wall and forget about murder for a moment. You can see the sky from up here on the seventy-seventh floor, without smog or refuse pipes or overpass shadows in the way. Currently, it's an almost-fake blue. You can even see the sea beyond it, cyan kissing turquoise on the horizon. I'd kill to get that view for myself.

There, I'm thinking about murder again. I should start an alternative wellness program. What's better than morning sex? Morning murder—gets more blood rushing, and you get just as close.

"Leave the fucking fruit," I say instead. "We'll be late for brunch."

He keeps slicing. "I got it, darling." He won't put the dirty board in the sink. I want to hit him on the head with it.

Nestled between monstera plants, the resident's feed in the foyer lights up with a new mailer as we approach. Zane swipes it away, but not before I see the nauseating familiar text: HAPPY BIRTHDAY, DON'T REGRET IT!

He offers his hand. I take it, and we step out the door. Our hands have the wrong kind of magnetism, two north poles pressed together. It takes a push to touch, more to keep touching, and almost too much effort not to shake apart. But the elevator is glass too, so now the whole city is watching. Everyone knows your name when you get a house in the sky, and everyone's waiting for you to lose it so they can take your place.

I think about all the ways you could have an elevator-related untimely death or incapacitation. Getting trapped between the doors. Being locked in and suffocating. Smashing his temple on the side of the handrail. Our hands pulse; we push together harder. His fingers slip between mine and we're soooo in love. It's too open—too public. Can't pass it off as an accident. The security camera in the corner winks at us.

Sadie and I discovered Seneca on 64, and then it got stolen by her husband, so now we all go here. She and said husband Archer are already seated at a green window booth, overlooking one of the sky gardens. Up here, the towers are crisscrossed by sleek train lines and crescent lawns woven with bougainvillea. They're so artfully arranged you can go your whole day without seeing the undercity smog swirling like soup at the base of the towers. Somewhere around the twenty-fifth floor the ribs of bridges and girders give way to just a polluted nest of walls and concrete, buildings spreading outward instead of up.

There used to be an island down there. Dig deep enough into that nest and you can still find places where the seawater's shallow enough to touch land with your foot. Surface hadal zone, they call it. No sun, walls encrusted with salt, air laced with trickle-down refuse. As a kid you can find ignorant joy in winding under bridges and light-rail tracks, permanently damp from the trapped humidity and air conditioners leaking from floors above, even if your feet are permanently wrinkled and bleach white. When I turned twelve, though, I swore I was going to rise. I would work hard, make the right choices, and get my sunlit, plant-drenched apartment in the sky like in the society feeds. I would live the life I was meant for, and I'd marry a man to do it.

But I went and chose the wrong one.

As I kiss Sadie's tanned cheek Archer shoots me a look, but goes on thumping Zane's back and asks if we have plans for his birthday. "We accepted that cruise you recommended," Zane replies. My brain stem twitches. Right. Sponsored, might I add, because we're living the life now. Across the room someone points their phone toward us.

"Oh, the Gulf is gorgeous this time of year, we'll have to go again when the kids are more manageable—hey, we'll have to hook you up with Sadie's friend at the dive center . . ."

Sadie and Archer have both been skyhomers since birth and

didn't even need the lottery for their seventy-eighth-floor apartment. They were Tier 1 residents from Tier 1 schools with good records and good jobs—certified natural candidates even before they'd signed the registry. We met at a mixer for 70-and-uppers. Sadie didn't judge that we were lotteries, and said it was meant to be that they were directly above us. She helped us move in, after we'd brought the ceremonial first box over the threshold. I felt like I'd been meant to know her my whole life.

We get the usual hors d'oeuvres until Zane adds an order of mint pockets. He knows I hate the smell. "Weren't we talking about cutting down, darling?"

He gives Sadie and Archer a tilted smile: "Too disciplined, this one."

I try not to stick the fork into his hand. "Oh, go on then." Smile right back, with my brand-new lifestyle influencer shiny white veneers.

We talk about the usual things. Did you hear Jade and Ben split and now they're living in coffins? The new dessert place down at 60 does amazing waffle cones. They finally sentenced that teacher for faking educational creds on student lottery applications. Also we want to get a parakeet. Did you hear about that woman who got caught faking a pregnancy test and jumped out the window? Did you see the plans for the new development in the south quarter? Trying to get ahead of the sea levels, but the breakers are hideous. The daycare teacher is incompetent, Ems, I'm going to have to write in. There was that disruption at the drainage plant on 20, a trampling or something, they're going to need a double shift down there but there's never enough people. Those baby bonuses aren't working fast enough, Archer says. Hey, these mint pockets are top game, man. Zane laughs, I told you so.

Afterwards the maitre'd snaps a photo for the societies, which I will inevitably reshare with the caption *my loves* while trying not to gag.

I circle Zane's waist as we small-talk into the hallway. He doesn't even stiffen. This is part of the routine. You flinch, you lose. I lean into him. We smile at other couples. In the elevator there's a family with a fat baby. They recognize us from the feeds and Zane coos so loudly over the kid I get sick.

"Daddy of the year," I say when they get off on 68.

He leans in like he's going to kiss me. "Most women like that," he murmurs against my cheek, where Sadie and Archer can't hear. The elevator scrolls up the city, into mist that means coming rain. We travel the remaining nine floors in silence until the doors slide open and there it is, Apartment 77-3. Home. Mine.

We let go the moment we're safely behind the door. As the lock clicks, the resident feed flickers again. DON'T REGRET IT, the mailer declares, picturing a loner man at a table watching the happy family beside him live laugh loving together.

"Happy birthday," I exclaim. My phone pings, probably with the Seneca shot. We disappear into our offices and the lock clicks echo from the vaulted ceilings.

It's a big apartment, the biggest they'll give you without the capital to own or build. The fixings are lush and new, floor-to-ceiling windows all around that soak the polished floors in sunset and make the gilded furnishings shine. But apparently no apartment is big enough for spending the rest of your life with the person you hate most. I like women. He likes men. Neither of us like each other anymore.

But to live in sunlight, then till death do us part.

Or maybe now, till birth.

I reshare the photo. Zane's comment comes in immediately: *Mornings with you* <3. It gets a hundred likes in a minute. Outside it begins pouring.

He'd been getting on my nerves for a while, but it really started when the first fertility pamphlet showed up on my twenty-fifth birthday. DON'T WAIT TILL IT'S TOO LATE, it said, over an empty cake platter and a sad-looking woman with a plate. Zane and I laughed and trashed it, but then a second one came on *his* birthday (YOU CAN WAIT, CAN SHE?) and another on my twenty-sixth birthday eight months ago (BOOK A CONSULT NOW!—their copywriter must have been off).

How are you meant to react to these? *Oh, gee, how could we forget*, and start fucking like jackrabbits? Whatever the intention, it didn't work on us.

Except now he's twenty-seven and it's coming up on me too, a clock ticking until *mature*, until they bring in re-evaluators. We've been married for over seven years. Living in this dream house for seven years of borrowed time. We've known since the registrar drew 77 from the lottery that we would be expected to use the privilege to make the square footage productive for society. That's what we do, up here: Inspire. Make people strive. After years of being daughter number three I'm finally a damn role model. Mom would be so proud if she gave a shit.

We thought we'd have it figured out by now. People on level 15 getting vitamin D from halogen lamps are popping out kids to better their odds at ascension but you on 77 can't even deign to try and keep it? Not even visit a fertility clinic to pretend? We're hardly the only couple who's ever married too early to realize you couldn't stand living with each other, but it's different. We're different.

Worst case scenario, they'd give me the rope for deliberate conspiracy, for not filling this precious real estate with snotty goblins
popped out of my own tissue. At this rate they'd drop me if I killed
Zane and drop me if I didn't—because it's the same crime for some
reason, deprivation of another whatever—so I might as well kill
him, right? If I do the murder well enough, at least I'll spend the
time before they find out living peacefully in this heavenly apartment. The problem is he's got the same logic, minus the whole
created-from-my-tissue bit—not that the pamphlets would admit
that, with the way they go on about it being daddy's kid too.

We were friends, once, who turned to merely tolerating each
other. But now the bitterness has invaded my whole body, and I
wake up wanting to throw him off the luxury seaview balcony so I
can breathe in this place by myself.

Seventy floors is a long way to descend, especially when I have to
get out and transfer on 26. I squeeze my tablet so hard it almost
cracks. I haven't been this deep in a while, but floods have been
getting worse and the sites need a final decision.

Johnny, my regular security for nest jobs, is waiting on the dim
landing of level 7 when the elevator opens to the smell of stale
brine. "You're late," he remarks.

"Took longer than I thought."

He shakes his head. "Skyhomers."

I smile tightly. "Not always."

The concrete is cracked and bloated as we exit the landing and
step onto the floatway. The buoyant material puffs when floodwaters cover the ground, like last night.

I work in Estate Aesthesis and Integrity, overseeing the infrastructure, architectural developments, and design of properties for

various levels. The department is based on 61 of the civil tower—a shiny office I could never have reached before the lottery. I grew up on 17 expecting to spend my life in a desalination plant. Floor 17 wasn't quite touching the city bed, but it was solidly in the nest, where individual towers congealed into a dense concrete maze; low enough that rain and refuse from sixty crosshatched floors above pooled on the walkways. We formed community centers and health centers around sunwells: shafts where, somehow, sun had passed through sixty floors unobstructed.

Here, one floor above total immersion, there isn't a single sunwell across the entire length of the nest. My heartbeat picks up. I was never claustrophobic, but I've spent seven years now living in the clouds I fought and lied for. I'm less afraid of the enclosure than the reminder. Even the job is a reminder: I haven't come far enough to avoid assignments like this, even if "working close to the people" is also part of my brand. Seven years is nothing compared to Sadie and Archer's generations. We have the house, the sponsors, and the followers, but it would all collapse in an instant if they found out Zane and I aren't the perfect story we seem.

My assistant is on paternity, so it's just Johnny and me with flashlights for the stretches where lighting has failed or been stripped out. My beam catches bioluminescent mold more often than people. Almost no one lives down here.

Almost.

It's ridiculous that this sector is still in our portfolio, but as long as there are settlements, even squatters, we track habitability. I know before we even step into the flagged site that it's a lost cause—the area sits at a dip and the risen tides have swallowed it. I'm treading ankle-deep before we even cross the threshold. Our beams dance across murky pools and rusted piping. Algae creeps up the sides. The record's shoddy but I assume it wasn't built as residential; the layout and hunk of what might've been a rotted wooden counter suggest a common building. I always have to remind myself that our habitability matrix isn't the same as my—yes, I'll admit it—sky-high standards, but even by matrix the whole sector will need to be written off, filled in, and converted to foundation for the floors above. It might even flush out the black-market elements. I would know. I found my husband in a den like this.

"You're going on that Gulf cruise, aren't you?" Johnny remarks as I annotate my report. Section 7-1432: flooded. Cost to repair and maintain mitigation: outweighs profit. Recommendation: divestment and conversion.

"For Zane's birthday, yeah."

"You have to tell me what that's like. Hoping to save up to take the wife. Not all of us are big enough to get sponsors, huh!"

A distant gasp cuts off my response. *"Emmeline Ahn."*

Johnny grabs me at the sound—seemingly rippling and damning from the floodwaters' depths—then yanks me away as a teenage girl with a baby slung in her arms stumbles from the shadows. "I know you, from the feeds, seventy-seven—" She's more lucid than the words sound, but even so, she starts prying the baby from its sling. "I can't have him. Take him. Please." Johnny has his baton out, but I hold his arm back.

Her clothes, while grimy, are too nice for this level and too new for charity. A runaway, I realize. Bad situation, abusive husband, maybe no husband at all; growing up I used to hear about them like ghosts around these parts. But I've never spoken to one—and one has never tried to give me their baby. "Please," she says again. "You can do better for him. I've seen your house on the feeds."

Of course she has. Lottery winners are broadcast, our homes profiled in splashy segments. Everyone knows where I live and what I'd do to keep it. I stare at the pale pink thing in her outstretched arms. It's an answer. It could save me. She must see my hesitation because she goes for a hook:

"I know you need one," she whispers.

I jerk away. "I do not." Her face crumples. What am I doing? Johnny—I can't let him suspect. "You need to go through the adoption centers, properly. This—I won't be involved in trafficking. And besides"—Johnny's still watching, she's still watching, I don't think either of them are convinced—"I'm pregnant."

Shit.

Shit.

But the damage is done. Johnny exclaims, "Em!"

I drag him away from the girl, waving off his delighted questions (yes, we didn't want to announce till the first trimester, the risks, you know; no, we don't know what yet; yes, we're thrilled). I feel desperately disgusting, haunted by the image of her standing in the water, holding out a baby who could've been mine or could've been me. And I think, bizarrely, of the cruise next week, sailing in crystal waves. I wonder why some of us get to escape to them and others simply drown, and why I should be a bad person for wanting to be the first.

By the time I get home six people have sent me gushing congratulations, and I'm so nauseated that even the city dropping away beneath my feet in the elevator can't soothe me. I used to hunger for this view so viciously. Now it's a reminder of how far I have to fall.

"Zane!" He's messing around in the kitchen. Annoyed, I shoulder my bag and stalk across the living room. "I want to talk about—"

It's not Zane, or even Alistair, the other usual half-naked man around here. I have never met the guy holding my juice carton. He's Zane's usual type, though: stocky, hairy, dumb as bricks.

He stares, clearly trying to figure out if I know my husband's getting railed by strangers. "Hey," he says slowly, "Emmeline."

He knows my name. Either Zane's used our cover story or he's a follower. I force my tone light. "Haven't seen you before."

He relaxes. It's not uncommon, a little swinging on the side for fun as long as the marriage stays intact. That's what we pretend it is, anyway. "You want to join us?"

I'd rather stitch my holes shut with dental floss, but I've been letting Zane smuggle in partners since we were still on good terms and I'm complicit now. Mutually assured destruction. Suddenly I think, *All this glass is like a cage.* I hum glibly. "No, you boys have fun."

"I love seeing where you take your pictures," he calls after me.

I find Zane entering the hallway bathroom instead and dash through before the door can shut, wedging my body in front of the lock. Zane whirls. "What the hell?" he hisses, which is honestly a fair response, but I have questions.

"Who is that?"

Zane looks down his nose at me. It would be more condescending if he wasn't only wearing baby blue boxers. "Henry."

"And do we know Henry?"

"*Do we know Henry?*" he mocks. "Obviously. I'm not an idiot."

"Sure. What happened to Alistair?"

"Oh, now you like Alistair?"

"He had lots to lose." Alistair was in his own marriage, had a good house and kids that went to a good school because of it. Again, mutually assured destruction. Plus he made incredible meringues. "You say the same about Harold? You—"

"*Henry—*"

"You swear Herman isn't going to sell us out?"

Zane flashes his teeth. He gets too attached to his hookups; it's an exploitable flaw. "He won't." He tries to cover his slipup with a sneer, propping one hand on the sink. I fantasize about bashing his head into the tap. The way we are now, kindness might hurt worse.

"We need to figure out the baby."

He stares at me. Glances over my shoulder, listening for Henry, as if I'm too stupid to have been doing that already. "What's there to figure out? They already know we're not infertile. You don't want IVF." He makes it sound like my problem but it's not just about the sex; it's the whole problem that we need a kid to save the house but the only person who'd be making one is me. "There's adoption, but—"

"No." Maybe I should have taken the girl's offer, but I'll commit murder before subjecting a kid or myself to the nightmare reality show that would be our parenting. The single thing we agree on is that we can't inflict us on anyone else. Not to mention we'd almost definitely have to churn out baby content to go with the actual baby, and the only thing worse than being a couple influencer is a mommy influencer. When I do wake up early it's because I was having nightmares about having to call him daddy in a voiceover.

"And I'm sure you don't want a divorce either."

I glare. We share the same alternatives: go down to our shitty families in the homes we upgraded them to, rent our own coffins as single adults, or find another partner. At this age, harder and harder. Everyone's hitched by twenty-five so they can get their own place, and finding a partner who'd agree to this conspiracy? We would have done it earlier if it was that easy.

"So what are you standing here for? You want to watch me piss?" Sometimes I think we hate each other because it's easier than hating ourselves. I almost tell him about the girl, about telling Johnny I'm pregnant, but I won't give him the satisfaction of knowing I screwed up.

"Put the damn seat down," I snap as I leave, already knowing he won't. But then my phone buzzes and I forget about Zane entirely.

Can we talk? Sadie's asked.

My nerves are always shot when I walk from the elevator to 78-3. It's totally regular for me to be visiting. And yet I go into near cardiac every time. The hallway camera blinks and blinks.

Sadie's standing in the doorway, wearing a shirt dress that brushes her knees. "Hey." I shut the door behind me and her voice keys down, soft, breathy. "Hey."

I kiss her. Her lips part, her breath on my tongue electrifying my body. This. Her. These snatches of time make everything worthwhile—the locked doors, the clenched hands, the home of my dreams closing in around me. I never planned on this. It happened one night without warning, the way I think love is meant to, and then without talking about it we just kept on doing it.

Her heart thuds against my ribs. I want that pulse closer, want it elsewhere; I press a thigh between her legs and she makes a fluttering sound. But suddenly her whole body tenses up.

"Ems—" Sadie pulls away. "Archer knows."

A beat. She reaches for me, but I'm the one that pushes away this time, sinking onto the couch. The trailing vine of her house ivy tangles around my wrist. I see their family pictures around us, the perfect unit I'm breaking. See the twins' aunts, cousins, grandparents, all only a couple of floors away. "How long?"

"Just." I knew I wasn't imagining his weirdness at brunch. Sadie fiddles with her fingers. "This has to stop. I'm sorry."

"No, it's fine. We said it from the beginning." That this would be casual. For fun. That it could break off whenever the cost grew too high. Except, as per usual, I was lying through my teeth; it had never been casual for me and I could only hope it wasn't for Sadie either, but anyway, none of that matters now. If Archer doesn't like our fooling around, then it isn't worth the cost. People have committed crimes to ascend to Sadie's level. *I* have. She can't risk her life, her kids.

Risk the kid . . . wait. A possible solution, a way to buy myself more time, all at once. "I need your help."

"Anything," she says.

"You said you have a friend at the cruise's dive center."

"Yeah."

"A close friend?"

She pauses. "What are you doing?"

I almost tell her. I do. But I can't put her into more trouble than I have to, and the truth of what I'm about to try might hurt her more than anything. When I ask her only to pass her friend a message, I think she sees it in my eyes anyway. *That's what I love about you, Ems*, she said once, *that when everyone else thinks the sky's the ceiling you're aiming for the sun and won't stop until you get there. I could never be that brave.*

Because she's never had to need the sun, I always thought. She could lean out the window and drink as much as she wanted. I am a green plant in a box with one single pinhole to grow toward, and now that pinhole is blue and rippling.

I don't need Zane's death. I need to stage my own.

★

It helps that the cruise is beautiful. No, not just beautiful—the cruise is everything I dreamed of as a kid and more, the attendants whisking us straight to our bright suite with a wraparound balcony jutting over the water; champagne waiting on the table beside lavish flowers, fresh fruit and cake to start, soft robes and a private jacuzzi for watching sunsets. It helps me remember what I'm planning to keep. What I deserve to have. Zane seems stunned too and doesn't even mock me for being speechless. When the boat pulls away, I watch the city shrink: dense, but impossibly small at this distance. I track the needle tip of our apartment tower until it vanishes into the glitter of a sunspot.

For the first time in my life I relax. My usual focus settles, calmly and surely. I can do this.

Our dive is the next day. The cruise anchors off an atoll and a smaller boat brings us toward it. The divemaster, Kanan, jokes with everyone and spends forty minutes showing the amateurs the basics. "You're Sadie and Archer's friends," he says to us. "They told me you were coming. I'll watch out for you, don't worry. It's a gorgeous easy dive." He catches my eye briefly, then has us submerge again. This time we're allowed to go deeper.

Beyond the shallows, the reef tapers sharply about a hundred feet, plunging into an iridescent channel flickering with life. Schools of fish, swaying anemones. Scuttling things, quick but silent in the abyss of the ocean, somehow unharmed despite the wreckage on land. We are above it all; we are engulfed. It's extraordinarily peaceful. An octopus shrinks under a rock as we pass. I see a turtle in the distance. I try to take it in, try not to panic.

Difficult, knowing I'm about to try and drown.

I kick steadily on, leaning along the currents and almost tempted to let them sweep me away. Zane and I drift apart and for once it's not suspicious. He's checking out the octopus. I'm exploring a piece of coral, under a lip of rock, blocked from view. Gee, I didn't know I'd drifted so far from the group!

Counterintuitively, I take a deep breath. Then I hook my oxygen tube on the coral and yank downward until the rubber tears.

Water floods my mouth.

Kanan is supposed to be watching. Sadie was supposed to make sure he worked our shift, and to tip him off. *She's ambitious, will definitely try to go too far out. Keep an eye on her.* He's supposed to be arriving right fucking now, to pull me out, pump my chest, declare me so traumatized no one will blink twice when I say I've lost the baby. They'll be sympathetic. They'll love me. Everything will be okay.

Instead, I jerk and my goggles crack into coral, sending stars through my vision. I press my lips shut, but my brain is running in overdrive and I kick again for the surface. With that single kick my left flipper comes loose and tumbles off my foot.

Instinctively I lunge after it, but as I flip and kick I keen violently rightward and slam into the coral again, ripping my cheek. Blurs of red now. Which way is up? The water roars. I try and remember emergency practices. Mouth shut. Look at the bubbles coming out the tube. Press my legs together. Kick. Follow the bubbles. But everything is a blur. My chest spasms, drawn too tight, and I inhale.

Water. Everywhere. Up. Down. Inside. I kick and go in circles and then kick but can't feel my legs because my brain is pointing flashing signs at the ocean in my throat; I know, I scream, I fucking know, where's the divemaster, but the ocean is endless, the currents are pushing, and I don't know which way is up. Then someone is wrapping their arm around me, forcing a spare breather into my mouth, and dragging me to the surface.

I pass out for a second. When I come to it's *Zane* hauling me onto the boat, the divemaster finally appearing, palms coming down sharply on my ribs. I puke water again and again, and the cavity is filled with the overwhelming relief of not giving anything up just yet—but the only thing I can't square is why Zane saved me, and why he looks relieved too. Why he's clutching my hand like he means it, or why I find myself clutching right back as I cough up all the salt in my lungs, heaving on the hot deck, turning into a husk and somehow damningly unhappy about my victory.

"You can let go now," I say when the cruise medic finally leaves us alone, but Zane at my bedside still has an iron grip on me.

"What the fuck were you thinking, Em?"

He hasn't called me Em in years, not seriously, and not with actual concern. I don't understand anything. "Why did you pull me out?"

He stares at me. "Why wouldn't I?"

"We've got each other trapped."

Stares, longer and harder. "That doesn't mean I want you dead."

"You once said you'd strangle me with my embroidery thread if I didn't put it away."

"I didn't mean it *literally*."

Oh. Well. Anyone could have made that mistake. I start laughing. He starts laughing. We're both going insane.

"Why?" he demands once we've both run out of breath. "I mean—why this? Now?"

"Archer found out. Can't risk the twins. Also, I told Johnny I was pregnant."

"What does *Archer* have to do with it?" Then: "Oh. *Oh.* Fuck. Are you serious? You and Sadie? For how long?"

"Years."

"This whole time?"

"Pretty much."

"Idiot." But he says it without glee. That scares me almost more than the drowning.

"So what are we gonna do?" I ask. I've bought us some time, but I'm realizing now that the scrutiny will close in again, and soon. I don't know if it's worth living in the sky if it means everyone can see you, but I don't want to go back down either.

"I was thinking," he says slowly. "The boats." I'm confused, and he continues, "They've got little boats to borrow. For day trips. The Gulf links to the southern cities . . ."

"Are you suggesting . . ."

"Am I?" he says. He slides his chair closer, bringing us within a whisper of one another. "You mean you don't want to get out of here?"

I see, again, the start of this. Back before time had ground us down. I think we could actually be partners again. "I do," I murmur, hooking his pinky with mine. "I really do."

We were nineteen, stuck, lurking the same circuits looking for a partner in criminal matrimony. An Eighteener and a Twenty-Fiver, both looking to get out quick. On paper we were perfect candidates and a perfect match: top scorers against our social odds, scholarship recipients to the good Tier 2 university, extracurriculars, plenty of part-time work experience, articulate about our dreams but not enough for anarchy. The kind of couple, in short, that would make a perfect inspirational ascendance story. With our stats, we were almost guaranteed a Tier 1 lottery draw, level 55 and up. We arranged to meet, but I'd already made up my mind: unless this boy tried to kill me, I was marrying him.

One meeting became two, became three, became I hadn't realized how much I needed a friend who had just as much to lose. We found we both had a habit of seeing how high we could sneak without anyone looking at us weird or getting stopped at a door. My record was 43. His was 39. Once, though, together, we made it to a balcony on 55. Tier 1. Future.

His brother was an alcoholic who'd taken over when their dad disappeared and my mom was a baby junkie who popped us out like a depreciating currency but never had enough luck with lotteries and bonuses to lift us up. We got married the week after graduating from university. That was part of our success stories, too, that we'd achieved so much on our own. We decided to do the proposal somewhere public, because a strong love story, a Tier 1 love story, was one where absolutely no one could doubt you. A Tier 1 love story had eyewitnesses.

We chose the Friday evening audience of the Golden Ray on 32, a hundred diners surrounded by scalloped cream walls, sea tanks filled with fresh catch, and some exquisite brush paintings. We ordered chili ray, fried flatbread, and crab legs baked in pepper gravy, plus wine and jellies to finish. It was a splurge we couldn't really afford yet, but it was to celebrate the coming time when we would—the life we were doing this for. I remember the night in almost painful detail. The pepper kick and knife-crisp bread, the tanks' continuous bubbling, the way I'd itched in my fancy dress, convinced everyone could see I was a little girl playing make believe. A night that was both precipice and performance We squeezed hands over the table, joked and laughed, served each other food, stared at each other while we talked. So damn in love. I felt sick; I felt giddy with waiting.

Toward the end of the night he said, "My dad disappeared on a fishing expedition. Twelve nights of radio—then whoosh, gone, the whole boat. I was only eleven. I know I should've been devastated, but I had this weird sense of wonder. Like, the ocean is big enough for an entire ship to vanish. I used to dream about a sky that big, that you could go anywhere and still have everywhere to go."

"Not just up," I agreed.

"Up has limits. Up is burning to pieces. Out is where it's at." This was meant to be a business arrangement, but wasn't that the second-best option, to be stuck with someone who at least understood? With all the worse fates, I was suddenly grateful for the one I'd found. When dessert came I pretended to be shocked at the ring in my champagne, then pretended to cry when he knelt and said loudly: Emmeline, will you marry me?

Everyone was cheering, louder as more people swivelled and saw him on bended knee. Their voices pushed my sickness deep inside me. I was grateful. I was getting everything I wanted. I grinned through tears and took his hand. Before he slid on the ring, I hooked my pinky around his, just so. Three people would post videos of us online afterward. Weren't we perfect? Weren't we everything you dream of? Wouldn't you want to give us everything?

"They'll love us," he whispered, and I kissed him. I didn't even wipe my mouth till I got to the bathroom and used the saliva to draw a little house on the mirror, like the one I once stuck to my school folder to look at before I fell asleep.

There Used to Be Peace

by Margaret Killjoy

THERE USED TO BE peace, do you remember that? Do you remember when you woke up in the morning to the birds or your alarm and stared into the abyss of Instagram before rolling out of bed? Do you remember the anxious, sinking feeling that came over you as you left for work? Do you remember how your nervous system could never rest, how everything was urgent but nothing mattered?

Do you remember when the bigots were in charge and the cost/benefit analysis of open revolt never worked out quite right, so you kept your head down, you ignored the slurs, suffered from the laws, and tried to just live your queer life as best as you were able? Do you remember when voting or holding a sign in the street were the ways you knew to carve out the slightest bit of agency over your life, while the ancient rulers ignored your pleas and took bribes from the industries that were turning our world into an oven?

You watched your friends die of desperation, you watched your friends live in desperation, and the rents went up while the salaries went down and the winters got warmer every day and the waters got higher every year and it never felt like there was anything you could do about it. You went to work. You took photos of your vacations, your parties, your hikes, your dinners, trying to prove to everyone—most of all yourself—that you lived an authentic life.

Do you remember when there used to be peace?

My partner Israa always called it the "bad peace," and she was right.

"Catalina," she'd say, "we are blessed to live in such times. Our lives may not wind up long, but they will not be contemptible."

There used to be peace, and it wasn't better.

Cumberland, Maryland, shook from the artillery and it shook from the IEDs, and those of us taking cover in the train station shook from the cold and we shook from excitement but we didn't shake from fear.

Seven of us, Elegian Knights all, with rifles and swords, watched the advance of the Seventh Confederate Cavalry. Our swords weren't necessary, not strictly, but it was best to keep up appearances.

Never despair. A knight looks soberly at the situation, determines the best course of action, and takes it, whether they are likely to succeed or not.

Somewhere on the other side of the enemy line, fifteen thousand noncombatants waited for us to break through. On trains, on buses, on foot, people had fled Ohio and the New Confederacy, moving towards Baltimore and the free port. Some would stay in Charm City and organize with the Rojavan Project, throwing their lot in with that bottom-up, imperfect, starving paradise. Others would board one of the great new tall ships and sail off to one of the handful of countries that offered refugee status to those of us in the ruins of the United States.

They called it "balkanization," from when the Ottoman Empire had broken apart in the nineteenth century, like every empire ever. The USSR had broken in the twentieth. Now the United States in the twenty-first. Empires fail, every one of them.

Fifteen thousand noncombatants waited in nearby Frostburg, taking refuge in the school. But they couldn't get through, because four hundred assholes with artillery blew up some bridges and were shelling anyone who came near.

Fortunately, our side had assholes with guns too.

Well, we tried not to be assholes.

But when I'm hungry and sleep-deprived, I'm kind of an asshole. And Israa was on the other side of the enemy lines, organizing medical care for the refugee train. You know what they say about us lesbians, hell hath no fury like a sapphic cut off from her lover.

So if I had to murder some confederates, I would murder some confederates.

I wasn't one of the founders. I joined the Elegian Assembly in the first big wave of recruits, seven years back.

I was young and wild and not so bright, and I was desperate for a way to help a dying world. Too smart for the failing strategies pitched by politicians. Too smart for the easy answers offered by this or that radical clique, Right or Left. Too aware of what was happening in the world and the climate to think my community college classes were preparing me for what my life would become.

The first time I saw the Knights was the same time most of the rest of the world saw the Knights. I was high as hell, lying on my girlfriend's couch in a trailer outside Denton, Texas, when she showed me her phone. "Whoa," she said. This wasn't Israa—she comes later. This was Calix.

"What the fuck," I agreed.

You've probably seen the video. Any other decade, any other generation, it would have been up there with the moon landing, 9/11, or when the president killed herself on livestream. It's still memorable, but these days, moments when everything changes aren't once in a lifetime, they're once a week. Still, you've probably seen the video.

It was filmed by a cloud of budget camera drones, sorting between shots with cheap cloud AI that usually, but not always, caught the best angle. A hundred Nazis—sorry, New White Patriots—occupied the capitol building in Harrisburg, Pennsylvania, cowboy hats and six-shooters and fake Texas drawls. They were rooting and tooting, firing their guns into the air, Yosemite Sam come to life. They had eight state senators lassoed and hogtied. Another echo of another failed fascist coup. You know, the one before the one that more or less succeeded, or at least, the one that shattered the already-spiderwebbed glass that was the American government.

The New White Patriots were only in there for fifteen minutes, streaming the whole thing. A white man with bleached blond hair and just enough mascara to plausibly deny he was wearing makeup was grandstanding. No one remembers his speech, except the meme moments. "I'll be hanged before I let groomers and pedos run the country." "If you're with us, you're strong. You're brave." And the best one, "We can't be stopped."

That was the best one because it was the most immediately proven false. The door crashed open. The Elegian Knights entered the chamber and the world stage. Twenty-nine of them. Full kit: chainmail, plate carriers, rifles and swords, ballistic shields shaped like fucking Viking shields. Regular military helmets. They didn't have the tabards yet. They fanned out, formed a shield wall.

Shield wall tactics have fallen out of favor on the modern bat-tlefield, because shields don't stop rifle bullets for shit.

Some do, however, stop handgun rounds. Like the rounds out of those fucking revolvers.

It didn't go perfect. One of the knights, Laura Pamero, thirty-three, born and raised in Harrisburg, was shot and killed in the firefight. Another three were wounded, mostly in the legs. The New White Patriots, though, they went down, one after the other.

The Patriots killed two of their hostages, of course. Not really big on the sanctity of human life, that lot.

More than seventy of the fash went down, most in the first bar-rage, less than fifteen seconds. The survivors found cover and made their retreat, with ten of them in a final stand to help the rest make their escape.

The spokesman had a stenographer hostage and led him out into the hallway, started down the steps. One of the knights broke free from the shield wall and went after him. A few of the cameras decided it was interesting and came with.

So we saw an Elegian Knight, Hale, a nonbinary South Asian person with fucking pink hair and the slightest bit of new-to-tes-tosterone mustache, run a Nazi through with a talwar. We saw the Nazi gurgle out "you won't replace us" and we saw him die and we saw Hale curb stomp his corpse. Which was absolutely, and in this case literally, overkill. On the back of Hale's helmet, a plastic velcro patch read, "Those without swords can still die upon them."

All the while, the cops cowered outside the building, waiting on orders.

In the chamber, the knights fanned out and started treating the injured, triaging based on the severity of the wounds and pri-oritizing everyone in the room equally—civilians, knights, and surrendered White Patriots. One of the knights, a Black man who never gave his name, found a remote for the camera drones and brought one down to face him.

He gave a speech far more famous than the Patriot's.

"We are the Assembly of the Elegian Knights. We fight for a better world. We have as many leaders as we have members."

It was clearly memorized, and he was clearly nervous—more nervous to give a speech than fight against a force that outnumbered his side four times over.

"I am an Elegian Knight. I fight for a world in which many worlds are possible. I fight for a world of acceptance. I fight for a world of dignity. I fight for a world without oppression. I may fail to win, but I will not fail to fight. I will never bow to anyone who has ever drawn breath."

He held a sword in front of his face.

"We are the Assembly of the Elegian Knights. If you wish, you can join us."

He released the camera. The knights placed their weapons against the wall—modern and archaic alike—and started talking to the senators. A delegation went out and spoke to the police, argued with the police, and in the end, though a few of the knights were arrested, all charges were dropped before they went to court.

So there I was, high as fuck, in a trailer outside Denton, watching the action over and over again. I saw what courage was. I saw what taking initiative looked like.

My girlfriend looked at me. Saw my face. "No," she said.

"Yes," I said.

"Well, fuck," she said.

I joined the Elegian Knights.

★

The artillery was raining shells all around us. Most of our drones were down, except for a couple autonomous rovers—really, just remote-controlled cars like what my brother had when I was a kid, only, you know, not remote-controlled. One patrolled to our west, towards enemy lines, while another patrolled to our south, our escape route. They told us what we already knew—that the aforementioned shelling was all around us.

We were bait. It's not fun being bait.

The Rojavans out of Baltimore were in the hills to the north, creeping around to flank the confederates while we drew their fire. The Holler were scattered throughout the city, ready to ambush the fash if they tried to go door to door. Those folks were up out of West Virginia, mostly—locals who weren't keen on white Christian nationalism and were willing to go brother-versus-brother over the issue.

Then there were the Federals. We didn't trust the Federals. They didn't trust us. We were allies anyway, at least for now. War is fucking weird. They were stationed just up Interstate 68 to our east, waiting with tanks and artillery, waiting for us to do the killing and the dying so they could come in, mop up, and take the credit.

A mortar fell into the Taco Bell behind us. They were hunting for us, since we'd been hunting their drones, scouts, and snipers. They couldn't pinpoint us, because we'd thrown up a thermal screen and destroyed the aforementioned drones, so they were hunting the old-fashioned way: blowing up every fucking building in the town they ostensibly wanted to claim.

We were bait and the worst part is, we'd volunteered. All eight of us had volunteered. Now Frenchie was missing, probably dead. Born in Toulouse, he'd flown across the ocean into a failed state to join the Elegian Knights. Wanted everyone call him Mon Seigneur instead of sir, so of course we called him Frenchie. Now he might be dead. Maybe it was all very noble. Maybe he sacrificed himself for a grand cause, the same cause that likely as not I was in the middle of sacrificing myself for.

Israa always says things weren't better when there was peace and she might be right but I'd bet money Frenchie would still be alive to twirl his mustache every time he saw anyone he thought was pretty. He had thought just about everyone was pretty.

The lights were out in the train station, likely had been for months, ever since the town evacuated. It wasn't a grand building. Dead TV screens were mounted on the drywall. They no longer told people when to expect to be whisked off out of the mountains. They no longer told people when to expect their loved ones to return home.

Their loved ones might never be coming home.

The peace had been bad, sure. But so was the war.

"Rover two just went offline," Heron said. They were our drone wrangler, an aging hacker who had already lived several lives—a rich techie who had quit Google to teach public school science and rock climb, who had buried a wife lost to cancer, who had come out as nonbinary and changed their name in their fifties, then joined the Elegian Knights in their sixties. They had three children and seven grandchildren. Five of those grandchildren were in the refugee train. Thus, they'd volunteered.

"Correction," they added a moment later. "Rover two has been destroyed."

"Cool," Greg said. He was the youngest of us, not even old enough to drink in the areas the Federals controlled. He responded to most things with just the word "cool." It was a generational affect that made me feel ancient, because to me it sounded sarcastic.

"Rover one has contact," Heron said. "Twenty fash, heading east."

The shelling stopped. "They're going door to door," I said.

"Cool," Greg said. He went to stand next to the window and peered out. "Cool, cool."

"Just got to hold out, twenty, thirty minutes," Hanne said, looking at her watch.

We'd been playing bait all morning. We were almost done. The Rojavans would hit their main force. We'd help. Engineers from both the Federals and the refugee train would get people across the city and its blown bridges, and we'd be heroes, and Israa would be proud of me. We'd be safe until the next time we weren't safe, which could be tomorrow or could be next week or maybe we'd finally break the confederates and start worrying about whether the Federals would turn on us to retake lost territory.

After their stunt stopping a coup in Pennsylvania, tens of thousands of us potential recruits poured into Pittsburgh. There was nowhere to house everyone, so the Knights didn't try to organize to feed and house us—they told us to organize ourselves.

We pooled resources and got a warehouse. We built a wheelchair ramp, fixed the elevator, and built bunk beds. We solicited food donations and cooked communal meals that fit a dozen dietary restrictions.

It was a wild few months. Every morning we rose at dawn and ate breakfast together at assemblies to discuss and volunteer for the day's tasks. There were always plenty of tasks. There were also always plenty of volunteers. People say no one wants to work anymore, but that's not it. No one wanted to work for the machinery of immiseration. For the machinery of hope, we weren't afraid to get our hands dirty.

In the afternoons, we worked and we trained—a few of the original knights taught classes, especially around the ethics of the Elegians, but it was mostly us teaching us. In the evenings, we cleaned and we talked. Israa was one of the first knights. I met her because she taught field medicine and care under fire. In her civilian life, she'd been a psychiatrist. Soon she and the rest of the knights moved in with us and joined our meetings without leading them.

We started sleeping next to each other within a week—but lesbian sheep syndrome is what it is, so it was a month before we kissed and two months before we fucked. She mentioned once that her family was old-fashioned, that marriage meant a lot to them. I mostly ignored it at the time, because I never saw myself as the marrying type.

The number of recruits dropped quickly, because most people weren't cut out for knighthood. Not because they, like, couldn't do enough jumping jacks or whatever the fuck. There were no physical tests—every person of every level of ability had something unique to offer. There was an age limit: sixteen to join, eighteen to fight. It was sufficient willpower, commitment, and free time that most people lacked.

I had been the kind of asshole kid who learned that scratching your mosquito bites makes them worse and just decided to stop scratching, so willpower wasn't a problem. I also didn't have much of a life waiting for me back in Texas—Calix thought the whole thing was silly and we'd ended as informally as we'd started. And I wasn't exactly in a hurry to get back to my shit job at Jiffy Lube.

Most of our strongest allies in the days to come were once prospective knights—it wasn't that people washed out, it was that people realized it wasn't the life they wanted. After a month, there were about three thousand of us left. After three months, just over a thousand. We were in.

There are three moments in my life that stand as my proudest: when I punched my stepfather, when I lied to the court to get my mother off her drug charges, and when I spoke the oath of the Elegian Knights, dedicating my life to the end of oppression.

If I survived this war, I was going to try for a fourth and ask Israa to marry me. Fuck it.

It was Hanne who saw them first, from her post near the door.

"Contact," she said over our comms, then opened fire.

"Neutralized," she said.

War is built on euphemism.

"Incoming," Greg said. It was the last thing he ever said, because an RPG took out the wall he was standing behind.

We had two options. We could retreat into the building and try to ambush them in the dark. Or we could attack. They had RPGs though, and no reason to spare the building. We had one option. The unit had elected me acting sergeant, like they always did—when there was time to think, we would vote on our course of action. When we were in a hurry, I made the call.

"Engage," I said. Hanne didn't need to hear it twice. She opened fire.

I made it to the new hole in the wall, saw a two-person team with a recoilless rifle in a nearby window. Aimed and fired four rounds. The confederates dropped from sight, whether dead or taking cover. In case it was the latter, I emptied most of a magazine into the wall below the window.

"Moving," Heron said.

"Move!" Hanne shouted, indicating the coast was, for that moment, clear.

Heron and Marika poured through the gap at a sprint, taking cover behind a concrete wall. Heron pulled a grenade and threw it. Rotors sprouted and it went off to find the nearest warm body to explode. A short moment later, I heard a blast and a scream.

The team in the window re-emerged, then ducked again as soon as I took aim.

Hanne ran next for a better position. She caught two rounds in the armor and a third in the arm from somewhere but kept moving. I scanned the rooftop, I scanned the windows. There, four stories up, a scope.

I raised my rifle.

Something struck me, and I was staring at the ceiling, and soon I was staring at nothing.

That evening, after we were knighted, we held what we called an elegy. A night to remember the dead. We gathered in the Hall—because of course we'd renamed the warehouse the Elegian Hall—and we honored our dead. Not just dead knights; there weren't too many dead knights, not yet. We honored all of the dead who were still with us. Friends, family, ancestors, chosen ancestors. We called their names, each of us kneeling in front of an altar piled high with photos and trinkets and objects of remembrance—an Elegian kneels to no one who draws breath, but we kneel to the dead. Knights of a dozen faiths read prayers for the dead.

Above us on the wall, a mural read: "I ask not to be safe from my enemies, but dangerous to them."

The Assembly of Elegian Knights had been started by a small handful of friends, a few years earlier. A Catholic, a Jew, an anarchist, and a Jewish anarchist who knew each other through tabletop roleplaying had all joined a leftist gun club together, concerned about the rise of fascist militias in their area. Soon enough, they all bought swords and knighted each other, and they put together the basic tenets.

They knew about the planned militia attack on the state capitol months ahead of time, because antifascists have every right-wing militia in the country infiltrated—pretty much always have. Our infiltrator spent a couple months convincing the militia that if they were going to do a huge symbolic action, they should make it real symbolic. Wheel-guns only. No modern rifles. Cowboy hats for everyone. Optics were everything, the infiltrator argued. It worked.

Which meant that the shield wall worked. Which meant that the Knights came to the nation's attention, which meant a thousand new recruits, and the assembly went from nerds to a shooting club to one of the most formidable forces for good in the disintegrating country.

After the elegy, we had our first general assembly with everyone present. We spent two days ratifying our tenets. Most were the same as what the first knights had put together.

When we were done, the tenets were painted on the wall of the warehouse.

Justice. A knight fights for a world without oppression, a world in which every person is free to live their best life.

Compassion. A knight understands every person and every culture has different ways of living.

Bravery. A knight does what is right, not what is easy or safe. A knight may fail to win, but they will not fail to fight.

Vigilance. A knight is always prepared to act.

Honesty. Deception is violence and, like violence, is only occasionally justified.

Dedication. A knight keeps their body and their mind as capable as fits their circumstances and ability.

Humility. A knight bears no medals and takes no rank. Their glory may be spoken of and written about only by others.

Discretion. There are many paths to victory. Not all of them involve the direct application of force.

Temperance. A knight looks to deescalate more conflict than they escalate.

Mercy. Vengeance is unbecoming of a knight. Violence is acceptable to prevent injustice, never to settle a score.

I think I cared more about having a code than I did about the specifics of that code, but this one worked for me. It was a tool for self-discipline, a tool for inter-discipline. There was no one to scold or punish you for failure, only an invitation to succeed.

It was that discipline, and frankly peer pressure, that got me through my first firefight, when we torched a New Rhodesian compound in Virginia and had to fight our way away from the flaming building. It was that discipline that got me through six months in Federal custody before the Amnesty Act. It was also that discipline that tempered my depression and gave me a new lease on life.

It was that discipline, and it was Israa.

I woke up in a Federal field hospital, the air full of the scents of blood and bleach and the sounds of sorrow and relief. The first person I saw was an orderly, in the camouflage fatigues of the Federal troops. He looked happy to see me. He turned and shouted. The second person I saw was Israa.

"What happened?" I asked. "Also I love you."

She'd already been crying, and she started again. "I love you too, and you got shot in the head."

"Cool," I said. I'd been hanging out with the youth too long.

"Helmet," the orderly corrected. "She got shot in the helmet."

"That sounds better," I said. "My unit?"

Israa bit her lip. "Heron and Marika are alive," she said.

"That's not enough names," I said.

"No, it's not," Israa said.

"How bad's my concussion?" I asked.

"Real bad."

"Brain damage?"

"Too soon to know. Likely not a lot, in the scale of things."

"The confederates?"

"Surrendered, every one of them. The Rojavans got the drop on them, since you'd taken out their drones, depleted their ammunition, and kept them distracted. The Federals and the Rojavans are arguing about whose prisoners they are. We were able to mobilize the refugees and they're on their way to safety. You're heroes."

I didn't feel like a hero. I felt like I had the worst hangover of my life, and like we had too many names to add to the list of our honored dead.

"Will you marry me?" I asked.

Israa started laughing.

"That's not an answer."

"Yes, Catalina, I'll marry you."

"Cool," I said. "That's cool."

I wanted to close my eyes, but I knew I couldn't. Concussions are like that. So are world-shattering tragedies like the violent collapse of an empire. We want to close our eyes, but we can't.

Fettle & Sunder

by Ramez Yoakeim

I PACED THE FOYER, occasionally peering through the curtains, on the lookout for Militia hooligans in their makeshift uniforms trampling my lantanas under their jackboots. All I had to fend them off when they came was righteous indignation.

"Ephraim, ¡por Dios!" Juan grumbled, his eyes glued to the flag fluttering on the television. "Sit down. You're making the dogs nervous." Both dogs stared wide-eyed at me. Hugo's ears twitched, erect and expectant. Roofy's ordinarily irrepressible tail hung tensely immobile between his legs.

Outside, the August heat turned the bitumen glossy and fragrant. Though I had little hope of spotting the StarGazer I in the unusually clear sky, I squinted and tried. The numeric suffix was a legacy of long-dead optimism; there would never be another space station like it now, but one was enough. If only I could convince Juan.

I closed the window and locked it.

"Leave it," Juan pleaded, his head bobbing in despair. "Closing it won't stop them. All it does is suffocate us in here."

Hugo rested his head on my lap the moment I flopped onto a chair. I stroked his ears.

Halfway through the grandfather clock's twelve chimes the placeholder flag faded, replaced by the president sitting at a mahogany desk, a wall of more flaccid flags behind her. She mimed voicelessly until Juan unmuted the sound.

"—brave patriots to fight this blight of unrest and disorder, and bring to a rapid end—"

Juan muted the television again and shrugged at my raised eyebrows. "What's done is done. This here is just theatre."

We watched the president's flinty gaze and knotted brow, the small gyrations of her head as she berated the camera in silence. A minute later, she pursed her lips one last time and ceded the screen back to the fluttering flag.

I could bide my time no longer. "If this doesn't convince you we have to get the hell out of here, what will?"

"Not this again." Juan rolled his eyes. "The borders are closed. No flights, no boats. What are we supposed to do, swim to Cuba?"

"There's still the StarGazer," I pleaded for the umpteenth time.

Juan scoffed. "They're the ones who started this whole mess."

"You're blaming *them* for the Militia?"

Veins surfaced on Juan's neck. "They made the endless grievances plausible. Billionaires sucking the earth dry before escaping to orbit, leaving us to deal with their mess. They didn't organize the Militia or arm them, but they might as well have."

"What do *we* gain by waiting for those thugs to break down our door and drag us through the streets? Is that meant to punish the billionaires?"

"You think the Militia is going to spare their launch sites? Cut off from Earth, how long do you think they'd survive up there in their tin can?"

"It's a huge structure, orders of magnitude larger than the ISS. It's a small city, not a tin can. But that's not the real problem, is it?"

Juan shook his head. "It's *you* they want, the whiz-bang robotics professor, but what use is a third-grade teacher on a space station with no kids?"

"We're a package deal. I told them so."

"Living in space is your dream, not mine." It was well-trodden ground between us. He seemed lost for a moment, then his fingertips found the icon of the Virgin hanging from his slender gold necklace and the anguish drained from his face. "For me, it's a tent by a river full of fish. I don't belong in space, Ephraim. Besides, things always worked out before, eventually."

I jumped to my feet, scattering Hugo to join Roofy by Juan's armchair. "Maybe, but not for people like us. Not for *sodomites*. One day sooner or later they'll break down this door. When they do, it'll take more than your grandmother's talisman to protect us. Unless you're expecting the Virgin to materialize in our living room and hide us in the folds of her cloak."

"What do you want me to say, mi corazón? That I'm scared? What good would that do?" Juan inhaled deeply and shook his head on the exhale. "No. I'm going to hang on and hope for the best." He got up and made for the kitchen with our fur babies in tow, a spring in their step. "It's time to feed the dogs."

Ominously, the television flag disappeared, replaced a moment later with another. In place of the stars, this flag flaunted a tortured cruciform as black as the stripes that cornered it against a severe gray background. It didn't flutter.

★

I always envied Juan's ability to close his eyes and immediately fall asleep. *Pure of heart*, my grandma would've said. I credited the habits of a former marine. Sleep often eluded me for little or no cause, and these days, I had causes aplenty.

I kept watch by the front door, alternately sweeping our street for intruders and scouring the night sky for the StarGazer's arcing pinprick of light. Hoping for one's absence and evidence of the other. As the predawn sky brightened, I spied them at the mouth of our winding cul-de-sac, four dark-clad figures moving unhurriedly from house to house and pounding on doors to draw out dazed, confused neighbors in their sleeping undress.

Across the street, Florence answered her door in a knee-length cream kimono gathered snugly around her midriff. She smiled at the balding gray-bearded man standing on her stoop. They spoke and he took notes on his clipboard. Suddenly, she raised her arm and pointed at our house.

I staggered backwards, my heart thudding irregularly in my chest. I wanted to rouse Juan and put on some clothes in case they came to take us away, but I did neither. Dressed only in pajama pants, I closed my eyes and hugged myself to stop the trembling. Long-detained tears trickled down my cheeks, over the stubble on my chin, to splash on my bare toes. Seconds ticked past, each an eternity of dread and regret, ruing all the paths untaken.

Would I answer when they knocked, and what would they ask? Would they scowl when I told them my *husband* was asleep upstairs? Would they do more than scowl?

We had been close to Florence, once. Signed for her packages and took her trash in when she wasn't home. She'd joked about marrying one of us, again and again, until it began to feel like a threat.

How many neighbors had pointed accusatory fingers in our direction?

Eventually, the throbbing in my ears subsided and still there hadn't been a knock on our door. I wiped bleary eyes on the backs of my hands and peered again through the curtains. No one was outside. I took a deep breath, cracked the door, and slinked out. My feet whispered on the stone-paved walkway. Halfway to the mailbox, I spied the Militia foursome winding their way towards the street's circular terminus. When the rotund man Florence had been flirting with turned and glowered at me, I bolted back towards the house. Halfway there, I stopped dead in my tracks.

The same tortured cruciform on their shoulder patches had been spray-painted in black on our pristine door, spreading over the posts and bleeding its vile ends onto the glass panes on either side. While I stood impotently, trembling with my eyes closed, they marked our home, *marked us*, for what was to come.

They never knocked because there was nothing they wanted to ask.

We'd already been condemned.

Juan scratched a speck of black paint with his fingernail then stepped back to survey the extent of the vandalism. "We've got some leftover primer and white paint in the garage, but I'll have to get a solvent to clean the glass."

"Let's stop by the hardware store on the way back from brunch with the guys."

He frowned at me. "I'm just trying to fix it."

"Juan, the angel of death won't pass our door courtesy of a mark painted over."

"You've got it the wrong way around," Juan grumbled. He walked to the mailbox and flipped it open. There was nothing inside. We hadn't seen our mail carrier in a month. Juan still checked, every day. "The sign was for the angel of death to pass the blood-marked houses and visit the plague on the rest."

"We might not see tomorrow and you want to debate theology?" I said, slumping onto the parched lawn. Roofy licked my cheek, his tongue dry and abrasive. I flinched from his affections and noticed Florence standing in her window, watching us. Something inside me gave and I stomped to my feet. Before Juan could stop me, I'd crossed the narrow street. Her eyes widened as I approached, and when I stopped in front of her window, she let the curtain fall but didn't move. I could still see her silhouette through the semi-sheer lace.

"Why, Florence? Haven't we been kind to you? Haven't we always answered your calls? Why would you do this to us?"

Juan wrapped his arms around me from behind, but I resisted his attempts to turn me away. Behind the curtain, Florence's hand moved to her mouth. "Just tell me why," I demanded again, louder this time.

"It's not worth it. We're still here, and now we know friend from foe," Juan whispered urgently, his breath hot in my ear.

The curtain suddenly parted and Florence leaned against the closed window. "I had no choice. They already knew."

"You pointed at us," I exploded. Juan shushed me, the tension in his arms peaking and ebbing, as if trying to decide whether to drag me away.

Florence stared at us, unblinking and unseeing, her gaze haunted. "They asked where your house was."

That made no sense. I pried Juan's arms apart and stepped closer, until my breath fogged up the window, and still Florence hadn't backed away. "If they already knew about us, then they'd know which house we lived in."

Florence planted a hand on the wall to steady herself. "I know."
Juan tugged again on my shoulders, and this time I let him turn
me around. I buried my face in his chest, my useless rage draining, leaving me cold. I offered no resistance when he kissed my
forehead and guided me back home, sparing the marked door no
further attention as he locked it behind us.

Juan dragged the measuring spoon against the side of the coffee tin
and upended it into the machine. The second spoon took longer to
fill, and then only well short of the rim. We had one unopened tin
left. After it was gone, we'd either have to kick the caffeine habit or
risk a trip to the grocery store, now firmly under Militia control,
where shopping required new identification cards and dollars were
no longer legal tender. Juan filled the water tank and turned the
machine on.

"I don't understand your reluctance. For once in our lives, we're
not at the back of the line watching those ahead of us and wondering if they'll let us through when it's our turn," I said. "We could
leave all this *madness* behind, wait it out in orbit with the rich and
famous." Juan made to speak, but I interrupted. "They've been
trying to pry me away from my tenure for years. They'll agree to
anything I want, and I want my husband by my side."

"Can I speak?" Juan demanded after pausing long enough to
unnerve me. "What if they said no?" I made to interrupt again but
he harangued me into silence. "They needed you back when the
world was normal and no one batted an eye at us picking melons
together at the farmers market. Now, *you* need *them*. It's different.
Think about it." He tapped his right temple with two fingers and
turned away.

I'm not naïve. I'm a gay Black man in a world intolerant of two-thirds of who I am and threatened by what remained. "They marked us, Juan. We can't stay here. I'd rather get taken fighting than cowering, waiting for the blow."

Juan's head bobbed from one side to another as if physically sifting through our dwindling options. "Therese would look after us if we made our way there."

"The same Therese who refused to attend our wedding? The one who winces every time you mention my name?"

"At the end of the day, we're family. She'll do the right thing."

I had no idea whether Juan's guilelessness extended to his family or if he simply understood his sister better than I could. Either way, it wasn't worth debating, not when his proposed solution involved us travelling cross-country to an uncertain reception. "Your sister lives in the middle of Militia territory."

The coffee machine spluttered, whisps of steam rising around its lid, the usually heady aroma subdued and faintly acidic. Juan flipped open the lid and inspected the spent grounds inside, deciding whether they were worth reusing. "Last place they'd think to look for us."

"That only works in movies. Even if we somehow managed to make it there, how long before the whispers start about two men sharing a bed under her roof? And how long after do neighbors with shotguns break down her door? This would put *her* life in danger, along with Frank and the kids."

Juan handed me a mug. "What other option do we have?" The look of exasperation and hope on my face answered him. He twirled his index finger, pointed at the ceiling. "How can I convince you it's not real?"

"Every two hours it passes overhead. All you have to do is look up."

Juan slammed his half-full mug on the bench. "What do you want from me?" Coffee sloshed and spilled, not hot enough anymore to scald, but he still yelped.

I turned on the faucet and pulled his hand under the flow. At least the water still worked. "I want my husband by my side. I want to live without having to look over my shoulder. I want to go to sleep without worrying who's keeping watch. I want to stop dying in my skin every time there's a knock. Shall I go on?"

"I get it. You want peace and tranquility, even if it means living like slaves to those billionaires."

I flinched. Juan immediately gripped my hand under the water, inaudibly mumbling something, eyes wide and face stricken.

I made sure to take a couple of deep breaths before responding. "Whatever they think, we'll be equal up there. What does net worth even mean in a place without banks?"

Juan stared at me for a while before suddenly flinging his arms up in surrender, splashing water everywhere. "Fine, activate the damn beacon."

I kissed him, stifling the last of his grumbles, and shuffled to my study to retrieve the token StarGazer had sent me months before the coup: a small black satellite transceiver with a tiny screen and a recessed circular button. It chimed when I pressed it and the screen scrolled requesting confirmation. I pressed the button again.

"Did it work?" Juan asked as he refilled the dogs' water bowls.

I puzzled over the numbers scrolling across the screen for a moment. "I think it's a time and place." Before Juan could ask, I rushed to the garage and rummaged through my knickknacks, crate after overflowing crate. Back in the house, the clunky navigation device beeped when I turned it on, which was more than I'd been expecting. "I can't find the charger, but the battery's still partly full, somehow."

"Will it work without the internet?" Juan asked, peering at the scuffed beige wedge with its washed-out, low-resolution screen and faded black buttons. The digital universe was the Militia's first victim. How our reliance on it and incapacity without it had taken everyone by surprise—except, perhaps, the seditionists.

"So long as the GPS satellites are functional." I said with more hope than certitude, and entered the coordinates from the token. "It's a freight terminal on one of the bays."

Juan studied the screen and sucked teeth. "To get there, we'd have to pass awfully close to the Militia's base downtown." After a thoughtful pause he added, "We could take the long way around, stick to side streets, and hope to slip past their patrols." Before I could respond, Juan was moving. I followed him to a closet where he grabbed two old backpacks and upended them, disgorging their contents onto the floor. "Nothing too heavy, mi amor," he said, pressing one into my hands. "We won't get very far if you decide to pack dumbbells."

I froze, uncertain what had just happened. I'd never seen Juan change his mind this abruptly about anything, let alone after weeks of resistance, but went along, too scared he'd change his mind again if I questioned the conversion.

Juan saw me standing still and yelled at me. "¡Avanza!"

How does one distill a lifetime into a knapsack? Original documents, or an unopened pack of underwear? Jewelry, or old family photographs? Why hadn't I thought to scan them before? Did they use memory sticks in orbit?

What would we be willing to trade away along the way?

"What about the dogs?"

"What about them?" Juan called back.

"We can't take them with us to space," I said, bracing.

The noise stopped for a moment before Juan resumed his

frenetic foraging. "I know that, but I'm not leaving my babies here to fend for themselves. We'll figure something out."

I had agonized over that impossible choice since I got the StarGazer's offer and it made clear pets weren't welcome. I loved Hugo and Roofy, but did I love them more than I loved myself and Juan?

Despite whatever apprehensions either of us harbored, we made swift progress in Juan's beat-up truck through curfew-emptied streets, wary and tense but otherwise unmolested. The dogs were accustomed to riding in the truck bed whenever they accompanied Juan on his camping trips, sharing the space with fuel cans, camping gear, and water jugs.

The streets were still as a photograph, aside from furtive movements caught out of the corner of the eye—and the occasional face, frightened and exhausted, peering suspiciously through a locked window.

We expected to run into Militia checkpoints or patrols, but aside from spotting the occasional truck parked astride a major intersection with black-clad figures lounging on its bed, we met no resistance as we slipped between side streets. Not that we lingered to see if we'd been noticed before Juan changed directions, then changed again, and again.

We kept getting turned around, and had to constantly replot our route. Each time I powered up the ancient navigation device its battery indicator halved in width. It surprised me how acquiescent our once-vibrant city had become under the heels of its new masters, how compliant with what seemed like a barely enforced lockdown.

As the day wore on and twilight gathered, the city's desolation unveiled itself in entire streets of dark houses, lit windows few and far between. The dark houses might have harbored inhabitants wary of inviting scrutiny who opted for discreet lighting in sheltered spaces, but I doubted it. I thought it more likely the windows still lit had been forgotten by the ones fleeing.

Where had all those people gone? Did the refuges they sought exist outside their hopes and imaginations? And if they were real, how had these people learned of their existence? How had we missed out on that lore, or was it forbidden to the likes of us?

The slight frown of deep concentration on Juan's face hadn't wavered since we left home. Narrowed eyes examined every intersection and peered through every shadowed recess; his head swung from side to side like a windshield wiper, sweeping for danger. The suspenseful monotony, however, lulled me into a dreamlike state of anxiety-induced fatigue—until two shots rang in rapid succession and shattered my complacency.

Juan floored it and, uncertain where the shots originated, swerved towards the nearest intersection, his right arm pressed across my chest, holding me back against the seat. When he stopped a few minutes later, it was only because the truck had spluttered to a halt in a back alley next to a reeking row of dumpsters brimming with uncollected trash. He cursed and slammed the steering wheel. "They must have hit the tank. We're dry." Acting out of habit, he noisily forced the gears into park before stepping out. I pulled the navigation device from my pocket, only to find what little spark had powered it before fully dissipated.

A steady stream of Spanish profanities drew my eyes to the truck's grimy back window. Juan hunched over the truck bed, his hands covered in blood as Roofy nuzzled his neck. Panicked, I bolted out and around to Juan's side to find the blood wasn't his but Hugo's. He lay inert, eyes vacant, his black-and-tan fur tinted a glistening crimson.

"Hugo's dead, Ephraim." Juan looked at me, wide-eyed with shock. "The bastards killed our Hugo." He raised the limp body to show me the dark hole carved out of the side of Hugo's head. I turned, doubled over, and retched. Between my attempts to disgorge my innards, Juan's sobbing, and Roofy's intermittent howling lament for his dead brother, we didn't notice the approaching engine noise until it was almost upon us.

Propelled by manic urgency, I grabbed the backpacks from the truck's footwell and dragged Juan by his arm down the alley, leaving Hugo behind. I glanced back at Roofy to find him staring at Hugo's remains. Whatever calculus he performed took only as long as it did for me to find a gate I could push open. He jumped from the truck and ran towards us, slipping between our feet into the brick-paved backyard of a boarded-up townhouse.

"We'll lay low here until they're gone," I whispered to Juan, who swept the junk-strewn backyard with unseeing eyes. A padlocked corrugated metal shed and an imposing iron grate bolted onto the back doorframe told of fleeing residents hoping for a return. Their discarded possessions, strewn amid the overgrown weeds sprouting between the pavers, laid bare the fragility of that hope.

I dropped the backpacks by the shed, and when I turned to Juan, he was convulsing with silent grief. I engulfed him in my arms. Roofy lay down with his head on his forepaws between our legs and let out a muted whimper.

"They couldn't have gone far," someone said from the alley outside, his squeaky voice drawing closer to the fence separating us.

I froze and cast about for a hiding place, but the enclosed yard offered none. In a heartbeat, Juan retreated to the gate and leaned his shoulder into it. I joined him a moment before the gate was rattled from the outside. Roofy got up into a crouch, his ears trained forward. He seemed ready to bark when another rattle reached us, from a gate further down the alley.

"I told you they'd be long gone, but no," a gruff voice complained. "You always this dumb, boy?"

"Who you calling a boy, old man?"

Their banter continued, diminishing in volume as they moved farther afield, but I didn't dare move, not until Juan whispered, "They're gone. Let's wait here a little longer before heading out. We're not far from the docks."

I envied Juan his confidence but didn't share it. "Without the GPS, who knows where we are now."

"I grew up around here, remember?"

As a fresh transplant, years ago, on my first outing to the neighborhood gay bar, I fell for the local with the mischievous eyes and affable, devilish grin who offered to buy me a drink. Neither of us lingered on who we'd been before or where we came from. All that mattered was the road ahead and a new life together, as if we'd both been born the day we met.

We arrived at the idle docks well past sunset, and slipped through a gap in the chain-link fence to hide between rows of shipping containers stacked on the long, straight pier. The stink of brine and rust stung my eyes and burned my throat.

In the chase's aftermath, it was as if the taut strings that animated a marionette had been severed. We collapsed in a dark crevice created by six-high container pillars, too spent to care where we sat or on what. Roofy proved more discriminate, surveying the full length of the slender rectangular space before settling on a spot to lie down, well away from us.

By unspoken agreement, the three of us had avoided the truck when we made our egress from our hiding place. The pressing business of survival left no room for reflection or introspection, nor grief.

I wanted to reach out to touch Juan but couldn't muster the energy. My skin felt feverish and clammy at the same time. I'd fended off the thought for as long as possible, but in the stillness there was nowhere left to push it: Hugo was dead, murdered by those who now held dominion over our lives. Had they caught us—and they came closer than they realized—we would've met the same fate, or worse.

Stories of ancestors suffering at the hands of their tormentors flooded my thoughts, chaotic, an incoherent montage of terror and misery that left only disquiet in its wake. Only a few years earlier we'd crowed about how far we'd come as a society, as humans, how we steadily pressed the tides of prejudice back and planted ourselves in full glare of the sun, never to be forced into the shade of shame again.

I didn't realize I'd started sobbing until Juan shuffled closer and encircled my shoulders with his arms, pulling me closer. "It's gonna be all right." What his whispers lacked in conviction they made up for with hope. Things weren't really going to get better, that wasn't his reassurance, but whatever this cruel new world threw at us we'd face it together. I clung onto him and soon Roofy found his way through his own grief to rejoin us, molding himself into the spaces between us, the nooks and crannies our bodies reserved for him.

"You're not going to the StarGazer, are you?" I asked in a whisper, the clarity of this realization searing like a branding iron.

Juan didn't tense how I expected him to. He was past convenient subterfuges. "No. This is my home. No one's going to cast me out again. Not self-serving politicians, not hate-filled preachers, not thugs with guns, not deathmongers wearing the marks of salvation." His voice rose as he spoke, straining to buttress his resolve. "You belong up there, I don't."

I found that I didn't have to think about it, not even for an instant.

"I belong where you belong."

I clung to him, focusing on his scent in my nostrils, on the texture of his hands on my skin, on the unquantifiable certitude of his presence that had come to define *home* for me.

At some point I dozed off—more passed out than asleep—and awoke, cold and stiff-jointed, to the roar of an outboard motor drawing closer.

Juan whispered, rubbing my hand in his to rouse me. "They're here."

Decision made, I considered slinking away unseen but figured I'd do the civil thing and decline in person. I shuffled towards the pier's edge, wondering where along its kilometer-long stretch to wait. Sore feet and aching hips made every step grunt-worthy, echoed by Juan as he followed behind me, faring no better. After the motor noise died, I peered into the predawn gloom searching for a shadow, when suddenly a blinding light shone in Juan's eyes. He turned away from the light as a woman's voice rang with well-honed authority. "Stop where you are and keep your hands where I can see them."

Long restrained, Roofy jumped forward, barking and herding from side to side as the stranger drew nearer.

"Control the dog," she ordered and directed her beam at snarling Roofy.

I dropped to a squat that sent fire searing through my legs. "Roofy, here boy." As soon as I could, I grabbed his collar and began patting his sides. The light dropped away and I saw the woman pulling a small tablet from one of her tactical vest pockets.

I faced her. "I'm Ephraim Greene. I believe you're here for us." By my side, Juan stood very still, eyes wide, nose flaring, braced. "We're not going." I took Juan's hand in mine. He didn't resist. "I'm sorry."

A flash of annoyance passed over her stolid face, leaving in its wake a gleam in her eyes that might have been understanding, or pity. She nodded once and jogged back to the edge of the pier, where she lowered herself out of view. A moment later the boat's motor roared back to life and receded into the night.

Juan tightened his grip on my hand. "You won't regret this?"

"Never, but we better get moving before anyone comes looking."

A million questions swirled in my head. How would we plot a path to Therese's farm, and how would we survive the months-long march there? What would we find once we arrived?

In the moment, though, none of that mattered.

We had much more than righteous indignation to fend off the Militia's hate. We had the ultimate cause to stand and fight for: we had each other.

Six Days

by Bendi Barrett

THE TRUCK IS STUCK again and Hieu has gone down the river for six days.

Just yesterday we saw him off. He'll still be navigating the swollen distributaries in his canary yellow raft limned with obstinate rust. We watched him sail away, tracking the fading brightness of his vessel until it rounded a bend and disappeared altogether. Marsha's camp needs his logistical knowledge, and he was happy to lend it. There are grumbles that his expertise could be used *here*, which I smooth away with a smile, and a slap on the back, and a kind word. Besides, grumbles aren't a cogent argument—they need the help and we have the capability; it only makes sense. Maybe they'll offer us help one day, or maybe not, but there's no expiry on kindness and I've found people have a long memory when it comes to who helped them when they were down. And anyway, there was no stopping Hieu once he'd decided.

Tam says we can do without, but our efforts to drag the truck out of the mud have yielded only sore backs and frustrated growls from the community members tasked to the pull. Tam shrugs. "We'll find a way around it. We'll make do."

He's easy to believe. He speaks with the authority of someone who has seen the ending and knows it's good. It's a trick Tam has always had the knack of. Maybe people believe him because he's always down in the dirt with them. Just like now, standing at the back of the towline attempting to haul several tons of stubborn metal through several feet of greedy muck, which clings to the truck like a desperate lover.

I think, but don't say, that Hieu *would've* gotten the truck out sooner. His absence makes everything run just a little bit slower.

And his absence is felt elsewhere, too. In our long bed, his directorial energy is missed between Tam's fathomless vigor and my wanton submissiveness. When Tam holds my head down on his heft until I sputter and choke, I miss Hieu's voice in my ear goading me on, his hand between my legs coaxing me deeper into the scene. I miss the weight of him behind me and Tam in front and the electric current racing through the three of us. Six days. Tam says six days is nothing, and he fucks me like a bull. It's a more than adequate distraction.

Though the other camp members don't say anything about the noise, they shake their heads playfully in the morning, offer us strong coffee and knowing grins. Of everything we've lost so far, shame was the easiest.

Tam used to be a government official and Hieu in training for the priesthood. Now, Tam calls himself a laborer and Hieu refuses any labels at all. "I try to be helpful," Hieu says, smiling shyly when our community calls him Lead Engineer. Others from further downriver regularly come asking for his know-how on recreating essential services. Hieu advises on how deep to dig the latrines, how to spot crumbling bridges, how to repurpose the materials of hollowed-out buildings without causing a collapse. They all think he must've been a scientist before, that this comes easy; they don't see him reading by candlelight into the early hours of the morning, or how he hoards anything he can find on civil engineering, rainwater harvesting, and on and on.

They don't see the toll and that's by design.

The night before Hieu left, I rested against Tam's broad chest as it heaved and fell with his silent sleep. Hieu sat up in bed, nude, his nimble fingers delicately rolling cigarettes for Tam that he never smokes himself, our mixed sweat drying on his thighs. "There's no better world that we don't make ourselves," Hieu said out of nowhere. He whispered, though not even another war could wake Tam.

"We'll protect each other," I reassured him. "No matter what."

He reached over to ruffle my hair. "Of course, Sprout. Of course."

Sprout. As though I'm not several feet taller and barely a month or two younger. The nickname warmed me enough that I didn't question the interaction at the time. But once he left, I started to think I might have misread him in that moment, with our sticky bodies pressed together companionably in the late-summer heat.

On the first night of Hieu's absence, I sit up in bed and sketch by the wan light of a few candles inside our too-warm tent. Cooling is power-intensive, and the generator is a precious resource, so we save its output for the elderly and the sick. Anyway, Tam and Hieu don't mind the heat much. Tam doesn't seem to mind much of anything. But sometimes, the heat keeps me up and, for good or ill, gives me time to think. I consider what Hieu meant when he spoke of a "better world" and how it maybe wasn't weary pragmatism he meant to express, but a kind of thoughtful, quiet wonder: a gesture to what we've already built and what we've yet to.

In six days, I'll ask him. Until then, I pass the time with my hands in the dirt.

My general role in the community is growth. Cultivation is a lopsided mix of luck, intuition, and timeworn strategies, but to the outsider it can feel like magic. Then again, any expertise feels like sorcery to the uninitiated.

I harvest the yield of sweet carrots, crisp okra, and the most successful summer squash of my planting career by a mile. I'm kneeling in the dirt the day after Hieu goes downriver, clearing the grounds for the fall planting, when Stacia kneels next to me and picks up the work alongside. The occasional smile is our only communication for the better part of an hour. Neither of us seems to mind. Eventually she says, "Jaime and Petra want a baby. But I'm not so sure."

"A baby is a lot to want," I offer.

"But you know Jaime . . ." I do, and though I can see Jaime clearly in my mind with a bouncing child on their shoulder, Petra grinning beside, I think of Stacia secluded in her tower sending radio signals into the wide, shattered world.

She continues, "I don't want to stop them. I love them. But—"

"You want to be seen. You get to choose, too."

She makes a thoughtful noise and it's enough for now. We work through the early stages of the crop rotation. The afternoon turns cool and Stacia stands. She doesn't swear me to secrecy, doesn't have to. She just nods, pulls some battered horsehair paintbrushes from the front pouch of her coveralls, and awkwardly presses them into my hands. I don't know where she found them, but I haven't seen their like in years.

"You don't have to—" I begin.

"It's not payment. It's a gift," Stacia says, interrupting.

I nod back. She forces a smile. "I get to choose," she echoes.

I have long suspected it was Hieu who began sending camp members to my gardens. He left what remained of his faith in the ashes of the bygone world, but never lost his need for seeing people made whole. I can imagine him speaking to them softly, gently coercing, shifting them toward me like the redirected flow of a stream.

Tam is the opposite of Hieu's quiet, eager malleability. He's completely solid, a force in flesh. He brings me a late lunch in the gardens after Stacia leaves. He squats down and stays squatted, thighs like coiled steel, as we rest between the basil plants to eat our simple flatbreads piled high with the season's yield.

In between slow, deliberate chews, Tam says, "I love you both."

"We know. Of course, we do."

"I lost . . ." Tam trails off, looks at his big hands. "I love you both," he says again.

"I know. I know," I say again and again, but even saying it a thousand times doesn't seem like enough.

Tam was the closest to what happened when it happened. He doesn't burden us with the details, but his eyes grow glassy when the remembrance washes over him. I have tried to share the weight many times, but he pats my shoulders and says, "Plant. Grow. Move forward."

Always the same four words like a mantra, like an oath, like a geas. Tam reminds me that nothing has been taken from us that can't be replaced, even though we may never fully rid ourselves of the scars.

After our lunch, I stand and take in the field: several acres tended by my hand and a few others'. I decide that this is enough for today. I reach for Tam's hand.

"Let's go fuck," I tell him, because I can. Because love and desire are things you must grow, too. He takes my hand, grins, and pulls me down into the dirt. He doesn't mind that I smell like sweat and earth. The wickedest parts of me think he prefers it.

The few stray clouds that pass overhead as we huff and grunt don't seem to judge at all. The time passes slowly, and yet, in Tam's arms, it's a pleasant infinity.

Then, on the third day of six, we finally get the truck loose.

Twelve of us pulling, straining, and chanting ludicrous work songs heave it free of the mud with a victorious squelch. There's a chorus of cheers and hugs and some enthusiastic kisses. No one is shy about their ebullience, and I think to myself: This couldn't have happened in the old world.

We have dinner afterward and everyone is feeling celebratory. It's just an old truck, but every win is magnified when it's hard-earned. A reminder, perhaps, that this is a small life, but precious in its smallness. Tam breaks out his last decent bottle of scotch and Petra gives out handfuls of still-wrapped hard candy. A genuine goddamned bounty.

We sup on beet soup; Abed plays us music on his half-broken lute. It's a tune that makes us all smile. A cover of some horrible pop song that we all miss so desperately. It makes Tam and me think of Hieu; but it's just a few more days, so we make do.

The They Whom We Remember

By Sunny Moraine

THE FIRST THING I notice is what isn't happening.

What my body would be doing—and is not doing—in response to stimuli. My skin is not excreting a UV-reflecting film when the late-morning sun slides across it. My pores are not opening like a million tiny mouths to take in the air, luxuriating in its autumnal crispness, and my nerve endings are not flooded with additional sensory input. I am seeing everything in front of me—the trees, the low rolling mountains in the distance, the gray pools of fog huddling in the hollows, the grass, the asters and goldenrod— in one spectrum only, unable to switch to another.

It's absolutely fucking overwhelming.

Leaning on the porch railing, my fingers wrapped around the warm porcelain of my coffee mug, I am plunging in two directions at once: over the railing and down the long drop into the valley below, and back, inward, down into my unchanging self, lost in the static. In this moment I'm uncertain of the difference between stillness and paralysis. I might expect my throat to clutch in panic; for most of my life, the package of meat and blood and bone that my mind walks around in has been easily malleable. Now it's this way, and only this way—I stand here and the air flows into and out of my lungs, and my heart thuds steadily in my ears, and when I close my eyes the tears paint their trails down my cheeks, cool in the breeze.

And I chose this.

And I still don't know exactly why.

And I wonder if it matters.

There's always a moment of breathless stillness when Eden coaxes my cock into being.

It's a game. I could resist zir if I wanted to; just as ze teases me, I could tease right back. No, that's not quite doing it for me, try harder. Leaning back on the couch with a lazy smile, every respiratory organ open and thirsty for the sharp, salty scent of zir arousal as ze straddles me. Neither of us is naked, yet. We're both drunk, a little—only as much as we want to be, as much as we've decided to allow ourselves to metabolize. It's a warm Friday night and we were supposed to go dancing, but this is dancing too. The tempo is our pulses syncing. The beat is our breath perfectly in unison as ze circles a fingertip around the spiral pattern etched into my left forearm, leans in, and kisses me.

Good, to sync up like this. Good also to run our internal rhythms in opposition, a dissonance that gets almost aggressive at times, but for now we're flowing so smoothly together. Flowing like the blood I release to collect between my thighs, flooding in to fill the veins and arteries as my body constructs them and the flesh around them in response to the stroking pressure of Eden's long fingers.

Eden and I have been together for nearly a year, which is long enough for me to discern by the tenor of zir touch whether ze wants me to have curves or angles, tits to squeeze or a flat chest to run zir hands down, a cock or a pussy to play with—or both. There's a delightfully long menu of possibilities. Eden's hair is cycling colors tonight, softly glowing when I look at zir in UV; I rake my fingers into the flickering green and blue and violet and graze my lips against zir ear, whisper, ask whether this means Eden wants me to fuck zir or whether ze has something else in mind.

Me, I'm loose and buzzing and up for just about anything.

Eden doesn't answer immediately, sits back and regards me with a speculative expression. Ze's still working me with one hand—enough down there to properly grip now—as the other flicks an idle thumb over one of zir nipples. I watch, wanting to raise my own hands and do likewise, cup the full breasts ze's wearing tonight, but I keep them where they are on zir thighs and simply enjoy the view. Simply wait. Lose myself a little in the white lines that flow in dizzyingly abstract designs over zir brown skin, never quite the same two seconds in a row.

There's so much we could do. That's how it is with fucking. That's how it is with everything.

I go for a walk.

I feel the ground solid and springy under my shoes. I feel the subtle patches of warmth shifting over my skin as I pass beneath the trees. I listen with untunable hearing, and at first it's quieter than I'm used to—quiet outside, apart from the shocking quiet inside my head—but the further I walk, the more I hear. I pause when I reach a clearing in the midst of a pine grove and stand, head cocked, listening to the interweaving songs of birds whose names I don't know. The sigh of the trees as the wind passes through their crowns. The click of my throat as I swallow. The soft hiss of breath in and out of my nose.

Who am I, now?

It occurs to me that perhaps I won't find the answer to that question out here, because maybe I've been wrong about what the question even is.

Many people of the past would regard the way we live as a kind of constant violence against that question.

I've studied history, and I know that people once insisted the categories of *Man* and *Woman* were solid and knowable and anyone who believed otherwise was a heretic against a sacred biological doctrine. We're taught to regard those people with pity for their claustrophobic minds and anger for the atrocities they committed, but otherwise to leave them in the past where they belong.

I find myself thinking about those people a lot, though. I'm fascinated by what they might think of us. Of me. We don't worry about those categories anymore. The *words* mean something, but they're endlessly fluid and playful. I wake up and I dress in *Man* and *Woman* like putting on clothes, and that's normal. But I can't help thinking there's something odd about being so fixated on what's *normal*. Sometimes I worry about myself.

I meet Eden for the first time at a party on campus—one of the last parties, or at least the last for many of the people there. The semester still has a couple more months, but as final exams approach, bandwidth will shrink. Then there will be one final, huge party after everyone is done, and we'll move on to whatever comes next. These closing parties take on a vague and not altogether unpleasant air of desperation, people drinking and smoking and dancing into the end of their world.

I remember when I sensed that desperation coming from others; now it radiates off me, collecting on my skin like sweat. I'm graduating with a degree in History, and I've spent years quietly submerged in the past. There's a rush in throwing it all away and surrendering to the present, lying pliant beneath it and feeling it running its edge all over me like a lover with a knife. I'm not drunk, but I'm allowing myself to buzz, setting my metabolism to work, and I'm most of a joint into the evening, every nerve languid and alive and all my senses open to the fullest extent. I've shifted my vision into infrared and the world is a sea of fiery color seething all around me. Intermingling. Not all these people are here to get laid, but plenty are, and some will likely alter their characteristics more than once tonight merely for the fun of it.

Tonight I have breasts, not large but full and accentuated by a black bustier covered in glittering spirals. As I flow from one room to the other, the bass thudding into my spine, I feel zir eyes on me long before I see them.

My imagination? Maybe. It's not always easy to discern. But I think back, with the constantly revising unreliability of memory, and that's what I remember. The warm prickle on my skin, teasing the hair on my arms and neck upright. Until I switch back to base spectrum and from there ahead of me, leaning in a doorway at the end of the hall and toying with a cup full of something blue, zir eyes lock onto and hold mine, retinas glowing gold like a wolf's.

Ten minutes later we're crowded into the downstairs

bathroom—which isn't considerate, but we're too far gone to care—and Eden is running zir tongue down my stubbled jawline, adding a scrape of teeth when ze reaches my Adam's apple, and I've got my hand up zir skirt, gripping zir dick for a rough squeeze, both of us laughing into a messy kiss. We're inseparable after that.

It would be easy to conclude from this that it started with sex and never was anything else. Sex is a lot of it, I'll admit that much. The sex is fantastic. But the laughter clinched it, how we rolled into it together in perfect tandem, arousal spinning into a liquid, giddy sensation I can only call *delight*. We were both still laughing when we came, laughing as we stumbled out of the bathroom and ignored the glares from the line that had accumulated by the door, laughing as we made our unsteady way out of the house into the cool night air. Laughing as we fell onto the grass and lay side by side, hand in hand, perfectly synced, gazing up at the clouds racing over the full face of the moon.

We were happy to be together. Being together made us happy, happier than anything else. It was that simple. So together we stayed.

Which made it somewhat surprising when ze told me I should leave.

Eden was fascinated by the scar when ze first really noticed it.

Ze was fascinated by it, and I was—and am—fascinated by zir fascination. I'm not the only one to mark myself, obviously—Eden's tattoos aren't tattoos in the classic sense, since they're programming that can shift and move at will, but there are those of us more inclined to tradition who get static ink as part of a more holistic experience.

But scarification is far rarer.

Scars are so easy to erase that they're rare in and of themselves. But applying one intentionally—then never healing or changing it—is exceptional. It's there on my inner forearm: a small spiral, raised pinkish lines circling eternally in on themselves. If you weren't looking for it, you might not notice it at all.

Eden noticed. Our first night in bed together, drifting down sweaty and buzzing from climax, ze lay half on my chest and ran zir fingertips over and over it. The scar tissue itself is obviously tougher and less sensitive, but the skin around it is another story, and my nerve pathways were still open to their fullest extent, so I was shivering a little, deliciously, not attempting to hide it.

"So is this some kind of erogenous zone?"

I gave zir a lazy smile. "Maybe."

"It's pretty. I've never seen anything like it before." Eden shifted, resting zir chin on zir hand and studying me. Me, instead of the scar. "Did it hurt? Getting it done?"

I shrugged as best as I could while flat on my back, bemused by zir interest. "I'm not sure *hurt* is the right word."

Technically, yes—I suppose it did. But I remember soaking in the pain, floating, not dulling those pathways like I could've but instead opening them up as wide as I would during sex. Making a point of feeling what was happening. A memory attached to a mark, solidity for an anchor.

"Why?"

My turn to study zir in the lamplight. "Why what? Why did it hurt?"

"In a manner of speaking. Why did you get it done?"

I thought—I think—I knew what Eden was asking. Not the usual *what motivated this aesthetic choice* kind of question, but something more about what I said, and what the mark specifically is.

Eden has always been perceptive. Ze would have connected the dots.

Not only the mark but the pain. The memory. The way it doesn't change.

At the time I thought the decision was impulsive. I hadn't been drinking, I wasn't high, but it was my freshman year; maybe I was feeling reckless, out late on a weekend, and instead of making my way back to the dorm I turned down a narrow street and stopped in front of the cramped storefront. I didn't have any scars and never had. My childhood was normal. Boring, even. No real traumas lingering in my past, physical or otherwise.

Perhaps that's why I've always found myself pulled backward in time. Perhaps I'm looking for some.

"I don't know," I answered finally. Softly. I wished I could have given Eden more than that. I couldn't escape the feeling that there must be more to give. There must have been a reason, but the only thing that came to me seemed so inadequate.

"Maybe I just wanted to have something that never changed."

There's a creek not far away. I know it when I hear it, and I follow the sound without meaning to for lack of any other object or directional landmark. Bit by bit the trees thin and the sun brightens, warms, until I find myself standing on the creek's bank—a mix of jumbled boulders and stretches of pebbled sand. For a moment I remain where I am, watching the sun dance along the broken surface of the water. At first it's the only reflected light I perceive, but as I look, I notice more and more: The sand is quartzy, many of its grains crystalline, and they glitter when I move my head. The rocks nearby are mica-rich and the flecks sparkle, dazzling the longer I study them. The sound of the creek seems to swell, flowing into my head; at first it was so flat, so simple, locked into the single way in which I can hear it, but now it has a depth and complexity that's nearly overwhelming.

I close my eyes and inhale. Decaying vegetation. Wet soil. Algae on rocks. I never knew before what people meant when they called a smell *earthy*.

The nearest part of the creek is shallow and narrow, the rocks funneling the water into little rapids, but farther to my right it deepens and calms, a placid green that doesn't allow me to see the bottom. My feet carry me toward it, and at some point I realize that I've kicked off my shoes and am padding over the sand in bare feet, the grit working between my toes. The contrast of cool air and warm sun sharpens on my skin as I shed my clothing item by item, and I suck in a breath when I wade into the water.

I can't accustom myself to the dramatic temperature shift. I have to wait for my body to do it on its own.

Then I'm standing waist-deep, naked in the cool stillness, and I tilt my head back to gaze up at the trees bowed over the water. Many of them are deep into fall colors, the most vivid I've seen today: shocking golds and reds and oranges that nearly hurt to look at, that seem to radiate their own warmth.

I'm soaking in that imagined warmth, practically feeling it, while I feel myself. What I chose, where I stopped my own endless procession of change. I don't move my hands; my fingers dangle in the water and I sink into myself—my flat chest and my nipples pulling in tight and hard at the chill, the water lapping gently at my slim, angular hips and slightly spread thighs, the coolness against my vulva and labia and clitoris every bit as sensual as heat would be.

I don't know why I chose this arrangement of characteristics. Did I make the choice according to some unconscious preference?

Does this form reflect some essential self I've never been aware of before now?

Is this who I *really am*?

How would I know? How did *anyone* know, before? What did they feel, my ancestors, the ones who knew they had to change both because of and in spite of themselves—the ones who desperately wanted to change and couldn't, or were forbidden from doing so?

I thought I might hate this. I thought I might not last a day before I summoned a drone to take me back to the city, to the clinic that locked me and will unlock me when I decide I'm finished. I thought I might feel imprisoned, regardless of the fact that I chose to enter this particular prison and can choose to leave it anytime.

I don't hate it. I don't feel imprisoned. But I can't say that it feels *right*. Instead the sensation is more like not being at home.

Is this who I am?

I lift my feet from the muddy bottom and tip myself onto my back and float. Above me, the changing leaves dance like flames against the clear blue sky.

"What do you think it's like?"

In the park, at a table under a broad pavilion, we alternately read and people-watch. Out on the wide stretch of grass, a group of kids is kicking a soccer ball around in a laughing, glorious riot of colors—clothes, hair, skin. My lunch and book are forgotten as my eyes follow them, and I'm remembering what it was like to be that age, in the fluid pause before we fully take control of ourselves.

"What what's like?" Eden asks, and it's only when I shift my gaze to zir and note zir quizzical expression that I realize I've spoken aloud.

I nod down at my book. Eden's is history of the art variety, while mine is more political. I'm preparing for applications to higher-level programs, and trying to decide what I will focus on. Although I'm beginning to suspect that I made that decision long ago.

"Being locked for good. Like, not having another option. Being born one way and just . . . staying that way, forever." I shrug, brush my hair out of my face. Last week it came into my head to try long hair again; I wasn't sure I liked it last time, and I'm still not sure. "I was just wondering what that felt like."

Eden gives me a faint smile, the lines weaving over zir brown skin dancing. Ze has set them to shift according to zir mood, and now they indicate warm amusement. "You've asked me that before."

"Have I?" I frown. But Eden has a better memory than I do; ze has always been more present and focused in the *now*, and as a result has a much more solid grasp of the *then*.

So ze nods. "Sure have. It's a basic question. But you're not past it yet."

"I still don't have an answer."

Eden cocks zir head. In a fit of adorable contrariness at my long hair, today ze has none, and zir smooth scalp is extra vivid with the weaving color. "Is that really a question for a historian? Shouldn't you be more concerned with what *happened* than how people *felt*?"

"Yeah, but how they felt *matters* to what happened. What they did, why they did it. I'm trying to imagine . . ."

Whether it was terrifying, being locked down like that. Hopeless. If maybe they *all* felt that way, trapped in their own skin, and that's why some of them did so much damage.

"There are still people who stay locked, though," ze points out. "Those few freaky cults out west, some people in other countries—"

"But those are exceptions. Those people *opted* out. It was

different back then; it was the default. People got *killed* over the default. And I guess I understand it on one level." I gesture at my head. "Intellectually. But there's another level under that, and there I don't at all."

Long silence. The soccer ball hits my right foot. Two of the kids turn in my direction, and one grins and waves cheerfully at me—brilliant red-and-white braids and skin tone beautifully dark, darker than Eden's—so I return the wave and kick the ball back to them. I'm thinking about the world these children are growing up in, about the world they might have faced then. How many things would likely have determined the variable worth of their lives.

"Why don't you try it?"

I jerk my head around to look at zir. Perhaps I shouldn't be startled. Eden is exuberantly adventurous; ze will try most things once. But ze has also never made a secret of what ze thinks of people who do what ze is suggesting: lock down voluntarily for reasons political, religious, myriad. *Crazy reactionaries*, among the politer terms I've heard.

"Seriously?"

Ze rolls a shoulder. "Seriously. You know there are places in town that can do it for you. If you want to know what it feels like, why don't you see for yourself?"

"It wouldn't be the same," I murmur. "For the reasons I said."

Zir lips quirk. "Sure, but you don't exactly have a fucking time machine, do you? It's not getting at exactly what you're asking, but it's something. Maybe it would give you some insight."

I'm silent again, mulling this over. Suddenly aware of myself, of how it would take barely a twitch of impulse to alter the arrangement of my form. Of course there are things we can't do, and people do form preferences, arrangement sets they consider representative of who they are. People often take pride in their personal ancestry, their family, their culture; we assemble ourselves from so many pieces. But we choose. We always choose.

I can choose.

"All right," I say quietly. "Maybe."

I wanted to know how it feels. What I keep coming back to is that now that I'm in it, experiencing it, I still don't know how it feels.

I sit on the bank, on a broad, smooth rock, drying in the sun with my clothes in a pile beside me. I stretch out my legs, watch the breeze raising goosebumps all up and down my skin. Subtle changes in response to what's around me. The truth is that our bodies have always been changeable, but I think they didn't like to consider it that way, back then. They looked at the possibility and those who asserted it, and they saw danger where most of us now see an entirely mundane freedom.

I look down at myself and I pose the question, send it out into the world to circle back around like a boomerang: What if *this* was how I had to be? What if I was surrounded by people who were telling me over and over that I was sick and wrong for wanting to be any other way? What if admitting that desire put my safety in jeopardy—even lethally? These questions feel so flat and inadequate; I'm still haunted by the sense that they're the wrong ones. Lowering myself the rest of the way onto the rock, I unfurl. My legs spread slightly, inviting first cool air and then the warmth of the sunlight. Sensual again, but differently, and my hands slide down my body, exploratory, as though this territory is new.

Changes in characteristics are accompanied by subtle changes in the nervous system. I've gotten off with multiple different configurations; I already know the experience of an orgasm changes as well. None of this should actually be all that surprising. But when my fingertips find my clit and I gasp and shiver, the shivering isn't entirely pleasure. I'm thinking: What if this was how it would be forever? What if it couldn't be any other way? This slow, hot ripple up and down my spine, the way I respond when I adjust the pressure and the friction. It feels good, sure—but what if this was the only kind of *good* I could feel?

What if I hated it? What if I didn't know how to not hate it? What if everyone was telling me, all the time, that hating it was the only right way to feel? I snatch my fingers back, breathing harshly. My eyes are stinging. My hand shifts across my body and I realize that I'm digging my nails into the scar on my arm, like the pain will stop something terrible from happening. Before, I was musing on everything and the musing was gentle, quiet; now it's sharp, it hurts even apart from what I'm doing to myself, and the hurt is bewildering. I didn't know I could care like this. Why do I *care* like this; why does anyone?

Who are we?

I blink and the turning leaves blur into dancing sunlit fire. Turning, like they have for millions of years, and yet never quite the same way twice. The truth is that they were immersed in change. The truth is that we always have been. I never grasped, before, that I could find that fact terrifying.

"So what if I couldn't change?"

Eden pauses in the middle of kissing a lazy trail down my sternum, raises zir head and cocks it with a bemused smile. I haven't mentioned this since ze made the suggestion over a week ago, but it's been on my mind, and ze must have known it was going to come up again.

Perhaps not in the middle of this—whatever it is, starting as a teasing play-fight over the mess in the living room and shifting into something that might end up being sex and might only be a sleepy mid-afternoon grope and snuggle on the couch. Eden is smeared and blotched here and there with various shades of pigment—the evidence of what made the mess, a new piece ze's working on—and I run a fingertip down a spatter of dark red along zir jaw.

I don't really mind the mess. I'm glad ze's working again. It's been a while.

Eden settles zir hands on my chest and rests zir chin on them, regarding me with a thoughtful expression. "I think I know what you mean," ze says. "But I also think you want to tell me about it. So why don't you go ahead and do that."

"I mean if I was . . . only one way. How would you see me? How would you feel?"

I ask these questions barely above a whisper, and while they tumble out of me now, I've been working up to them for a couple of days. For some reason I'm fearful of what the answer might be.

Ze arches a brow. "You mean if you had tits for good?"

I breathe a laugh. Someone else might chide zir for not taking the question seriously; I'm grateful for the levity. I know there's seriousness beneath it. "Or didn't. Or anything else. Just . . . not changing. Like if I was the way you met me but all the time."

Eden is quiet a moment, clearly considering. I wonder if ze's given it thought before.

Finally ze shakes zir head. "I don't know. I know that's not the answer you want, but I really don't." Beat of silence. "What about if it was me? How would you feel about it?"

"I don't know," I murmur. It comes immediately, without any time to reflect on it, because I have given this thought. Watching them, the subtle day-to-day diversity in their forms, and asking myself: What if this one was *the* one? What about this one? What if I looked at zir and thought, *This is who this person is*, and it was essential, solid, unchanging to the point where a significant shift might change everything else?

I don't know how to compute a state of mind so . . . different.

"I want to think I'd love you no matter what," ze says softly. "I do, I believe I would, but . . . I don't know. I don't know."

I nod, slow, and I trace that streak of paint again. "I don't know why I can't stop thinking about this."

Eden is silent again, for a long time, and I let the silence play out. I don't have anything else to fill it with. I'm ready to let it go, ready to get back to whatever it was we were strolling lazily toward, but then ze speaks again, and it's what ze says that clinches it for me. That makes it impossible to not go and see for myself.

"I'll tell you what I really think." And zir smile is difficult to define, the wild mix of emotions I see there, but I do know that one of them might be akin to sadness. "I think maybe you can't stop thinking about it because some part of you feels like maybe . . . maybe you might want to actually be that way."

Maybe you might want to actually be that way.

I didn't know what to do with that. Even now, making my way back up the slope to the house, I still don't. Dusk comes sooner under the trees; the sky beyond is still light and fading from pale blue to a deeper cloud-streaked pink, but down where I am, the shadows are thick and shifting. I'm tired, and they seem to drag at my feet, like walking through a few inches of water.

Maybe you might want to actually be that way.

I think back to my attempts to understand the terror of those long-past people. I'm not sure whether what I felt down there by the creek was anything like it. But the terror lingers with the sense that the body I'm in now is not right, is not bad or hateful but is nevertheless not what I *want*. I'm not fighting it, I'm not straining against it. The body is unquestionably mine. But it's not what I want.

Or—no. No, that's not quite it.

I pause and feel the rush of air through my lungs, the rise and fall of my chest, the thud of my heart at the core of me. For an instant the outside world fades away and what's left is those things, the body in which I am—for the moment—trapped, and which sustains me.

It's not *all* I want.

And the thing is that if I want more, I can have it. I can have so much more than they ever imagined was possible.

In the fading daylight, the brighter colors of the leaves drain away but the hues are no less diverse for it, although the diversity is more subtle—shades of slate and indigo and violet. I stand on the deck like how I started the day, leaning on the rail, watching night sweep over the world. The planet spins and reels around its star. We're slipping through autumn into winter. These leaves will dry up and fall and render the branches harshly naked until the buds return. The seasons are not what they were. They aren't what they will be.

Some of it is our fault, some of it was avoidable, but at the core of everything, change is constant. Reliable. Natural. Eternal. It was always with us; it will outlive everything we are.

That truth terrified them. But it doesn't terrify me.

I notice what isn't happening. The way I perceive the world and the way I don't, the way I change in response and the way I don't, the way I push my will against it and am constrained, and the only real difference between what happens and what doesn't is a matter of degree. The colors I see, and don't see. The things I hear and the things beyond my hearing. What I feel and what I can't imagine feeling, and the very few things I properly understand. All the past we carry with us.

I look down at my forearm, at the delicate lines of the scar. Which I chose, and which I've chosen to never change.

I think *This is who we are*, and I don't totally comprehend it, but I comprehend enough now.

I've had my phone off, but now I pull it out and open the message app. Eden. A gust of wind rushes through the trees as I type, and the air whispers a shower of leaves down.

It's not all I want to be, I send. And then I call the drone.

If this was all I wanted to be, I could be that. I want more, and that's something I can choose. That choice is the point—it's definitional, the wanting. Having the choice matters, but even if I didn't, I would still want it, and that would be a way of knowing who I am.

I notice what's happening. What's happening is that I'm going home.

When the Devil Comes From Babylon

Maya Deane

IT'S MY LAST ADVENT weaving kudzu garlands with the girls. For the past three months, Ma has been hinting that it's finally time to join the boys—time to help them tie down the Christmas hog and slit his screaming throat and drain out his blood and peel his skin and smoke his meat—but I defy her to join the girls one last time.

At first Amy and Ruth and Laura dart ugly looks my way, but my fingers are still the nimblest, the most precise, and my garlands grow glimmering in the sun, each strip perfectly angled to catch the light on the kudzu's grain. By the end of the tenth day, the girls are sitting at my feet like we're all sisters, watching my hands move, trying to work out my method, and when each girl finally grasps it she gasps with delight. As the sun fades behind the palms, I glory in the moment, happier than I've been in years.

The dinner bell rings and the girls disappear behind the door to the women's quarters, where I used to be allowed when I was little, before my voice broke and my face erupted and the dark thoughts came.

I sit outside alone, overwhelmed by those thoughts, helpless to push the sick lusts from my mind. By daylight I can usually crush down my wickedness, but it always bubbles up again at night.

Green-and-purple lightning sheets across the north sky. Somewhere out there, past the compound walls, past the beaches, past miles of dark rolling waves, Babylon floats on the foam, radiating temptation and light.

I've always heard how they want boys like me in Babylon, boys with bad ungrateful thoughts and sinful hearts, raw material for their Blasphemous Transmutation. Man and Woman are a divine ordinance, a special institution for the salvation of the world. God made men to pray and fast and lead, fight and hunt and fish, work the yeast vats and dredge the shallows and tend the weed. God made women to serve and rear and nurture and support them, to clean the solar panels and mend the broken things. I know where I'm supposed to fit into God's grand design, but my heart rebels, longing for wickedness.

Despite my best efforts, I keep looking up, watching the colored lightning pulse through the air. Sometimes glimmering silver ships dart across the sky, carrying devils and sinners to the banquets and orgies of the damned. Sometimes beautiful devils dance above the clouds, detectable only by the shimmering waves they give off, filling my thoughts with women too lovely to be real who move to their own electric song. My flesh pricks with envy, and between my legs the shameful urges stir, though I've never given in. When I try to pull my eyes away, a subtle gravity draws them back. It starts off very faint and distant then floats nearer, silver and green and dreamlike, fading away even as it encroaches on our waters and moans through our air.

For a moment I see the Devil: a woman with skin like mother-of-pearl and colorless silver hair wrapped in floating veils of every imaginable color. I glimpse her face, hauntingly tender, impossibly sad. Then she's gone, and I'm staring up into darkness while the temptations of Babylon whisper in my heart.

You don't have to be a boy, the Devil tells me. *In Babylon, you can be anything you want.* That's what Ma said, that they turn men into women and women into men, that everyone finds their own path through the Blasphemous Transmutation.

Defy God's will. If you want to be a girl, you can just be a girl.

Get out of my head, Devil! I scream silently, cowering away from the sky. *Leave me alone! My heart belongs to God!*

A flashlight beam pierces my eyes. I cringe back from the light, covering my face, and the flashlight moves away. In the scatter from the beam, I recognize my mother's tight mouth and neck, the frustrated set of her jaw.

"You'll be my death, boy," she growls. "You missed dinner with the Elders. Your uncle asked about you."

I startle. But the girls just left! I only stayed out for a moment to watch the lightning! I look around, and my heart sinks. It is much darker than it was; a few stars are struggling through the haze.

"I'm sorry, Ma."

"You'll go to bed hungry," she says tonelessly. "You can apologize in the morning."

Going to bed hungry usually helps. The ache in my stomach can overwhelm the ache in my brain, blotting out the sick thoughts from Babylon. I start to get up, but the flashlight beam swings suddenly back to my face.

"Quad," Ma says sharply. "Wait."

Shame punches through my stomach, cold and slick, vibrating through my solar plexus. Somehow she knows. Her permanent scowl, the way her eyes slide away from me: it all makes sense. She knows.

"Yes, Ma?"

"You're always daydreaming," she says. "No discipline. No maturity. But it's about time to set aside boyish things."

My whole body tightens. "Is it Grandpa?"

For once her face softens; I must have guessed right. "God is calling him home. The cancer's got to be in his blood and joints now. His bones are melting. Looks like God's testing his faith one last time."

For the past couple years I've known Grandpa was dying. He's been wasting down, losing his bulk and his mass, the fat and muscle sloughing away as he shrivels down into his huge white bed. Yet somehow I never expected to reach the endpoint of the process, and I feel like a traitor for not seeing it sooner. "How can I help?"

Something about the question seems to disgust Ma. A muscle jumps in her jaw, and the corners of her mouth pull down again. "This is his hour, not yours. He's going to be tempted. The Devil's going to come down from Babylon and offer your grandpa life, prosperity, health, all the temptations of the fallen earth, if he will forsake God and serve Babylon."

"But it's *Grandpa*. The Devil should know better."

"Babylon got his brother," Ma reminds me. "No one is beyond temptation. We *all* have to be on guard." She lowers the flashlight and seizes my arm, pressing a wad of foil into my palm. "Especially *you*."

I know it from the feel alone. There is a pill inside, the same pill they distributed five years ago when the guard ships from Babylon came within sight of our shore, glittering like rainbow seashells on the waves. *If they try to take you*, Grandpa growled, his voice still strong and deep, *you eat these pills, children, and fly away to Heaven. It's not a sin to flee the Devil's temptation beyond the circles of this world.*

It's not a sin to run home to God. You hear that, devils from Babylon? You will never take these children to your city.

"Quad." Ma's voice is shaking, and I realize she's scared. "You understand what I'm saying? The Devil will come for your grandpa, but he's gonna tempt us all. You have to be strong, the man your father was. If the temptation gets to be too much—if you can't hold out—"

I don't want to die. I don't say it, but the sinful thought is in my head. I focus on keeping my eyes steady, strong and confident like Pa's used to be, like Grandpa's. "I won't need the pill," I say, promising myself it's true. "My heart belongs to God."

"Keep it anyway," she says. "Everyone's got to have one. I've got one. Anita's got one. Everyone's got one. When your great-grandpa died, the Devil took too many. We can't risk a loss like that again. You understand?"

There's a quiver in the way she says it, in the way she reassures me that I'm not alone, that everyone has their own cyanide pill. A worm of doubt writhes in the folds of my brain. Ma might have a cyanide pill of her own—but I bet Anita doesn't, I bet her daughters don't. We're the weak ones, Ma and me, the ones the Devil will try to take as a consolation when he can't break Grandpa's faith.

"I understand, Ma," I say, forcing my voice deeper, so it sounds strong. Like Pa.

"It'll start with hallucinations," Ma warns. "The Devil can decide who sees him. He won't show himself out in the open, but he'll whisper. If you start to feel like he might be right, don't hesitate. It's not a sin to flee home to God."

"I understand, Ma," I say again, but this time my voice cracks, ending the sentence in the register of a girl. *Ma.* A plaintive bleat. "He won't get me, Ma." This time, I sound strong again, my father's son again, and some of the worry drains from her face. I don't even think about telling her what I saw in the sky, and it disgusts me how easily I can lie to her. The Devil is already tempting me, but I'm not going to admit it. Maybe not until it's too late.

"You go to bed and say your prayers," Ma commands. There's still a glint in her eyes, but she believes me. For now.

Next day a winter squall approaches, thickening the atmospheric haze to an ugly charcoal gray shot through with dirty lightning, and I spend the day scurrying around the compound with the girls getting our garlands into the sheds, pulling tarps over the solar panels, checking the pumps, priming the generators. The men are hard at work in the smokehouse. Ma sends me in with their lunch-pails, probably punishment for making her worry. The stink from the yeast vats lingers in my sinuses.

In the afternoon, as the hot rain beats down, Anita drags me away from the girls. She looks at me the same way she always does, a pinched something-doesn't-add-up-about-you-boy look. I'm painfully aware of the foil packet in my pocket, but after a moment, Anita points to the Praise Hall. "Your grandpa wants to see you. Asked for you by name. Bring him his medicine and roll it up right this time." She hands me a smoke pouch.

It's been months since he's asked for me. Each time I go in sweating, terrified he'll see through my carefully combed hair and scrubbed cheeks to the sin hiding behind my eyes. I used to prac-tice rolling medicine for hours, haunted by how the frail dry leaves wanted to crumble and spill the precious green flowers inside, kin-dling the wrath of God in Grandpa's eyes—but rolling never came easy to me, not the way women's crafts do. I fold the pouch into my raincoat and hurry through the rain to the Praise Hall.

As I pass through the double doors, something cool and electric washes over me, a thrill running down my spine. I look around the Praise Hall with dread. For a moment I think I see rainbow lights ebb and flow over the polished cherrywood cross on the rear wall, but then they're gone.

Grandpa's labored breathing comes from behind the altar, from beyond the door at the sanctuary's heart, and I follow his wheezing to the offering room.

He's sunken deeper into the white bed than ever, smaller than he was at Easter, dwarfed by heaps of Old Congregation treasures on all sides. Gold bars gleam dully next to the gun safes, treasures our family brought out of the drowning, and the walls are covered in the tattered banners of the Old Congregations. *We are the Remnant of the Faithful*, Grandpa used to tell us. I try to feel my pride in those banners, but my heart is sick.

"Grandpa? You wanted me? I brought your medicine."

Normally, he would look up, piercing me with his bright blue eyes—like Anita's but sharper and keener, far more acute than Ma's dull brown—and his deep voice would rumble from the folded husk of the flesh, an unconquered spirit rasping out the words of the Lord. Instead, he's fighting to breathe.

"Grandpa?" I say again, but he doesn't move.

It looks like the air is shimmering next to him, but the illusion passes. *It'll start with hallucinations*, Ma said. I sit in the bedside chair, open the smoke pouch, find a leaf with some give, sprinkle in the dry green buds, and start rolling. *The Devil can decide who sees him. He won't show himself out in the open, but he'll whisper.*

When I offer up the barely adequate joint, Grandpa's shaking fingers cradle it to his lips. He lifts his mother-of-pearl lighter, and *click*—a spark. His lighter always reminds me of the Babylon guard ships and the floating vessels that comb through the air, but now it reminds me of the woman I thought I saw last night, the one with colored veils like insect wings.

Grandpa wheezes out smoke and sighs heavily. "Quad. There's a good boy, just like your pa. You know not to skimp on the buds."

"Anita said you wanted me, Reverend." It would be wrong to call him Grandpa to his face. The man led the Remnant out of the doomed old world to the hills that became this island. He deserves my reverence.

"God is calling me home," Grandpa says, weary. "It won't be long now. I guess the girls have told you there's a tempter coming?"

"They have." I admit it warily, conscious of the pill in my pocket. "He won't get to us."

"This devil isn't like the others," Grandpa sighs. "He's here with us right now. You can't see him, can you?"

I glance around the room, but I can't.

It's only when I look back to Grandpa that I see him relaxing, smiling a craggy smile of relief. "This boy belongs to God," he tells the air above his bed, and plumes of acrid smoke jet from his nostrils. "You can't have him."

The air beside Grandpa shimmers again, but my face is a practiced liar, and I don't even look. I see the veils hanging in layers, waterfalls around the mother-of-pearl woman looming over the bed, too big to be real. I don't have to see to know her face, full of sorrow and tenderness and a pensive gloom. "I belong to God," I echo obediently.

"When Pa died," Grandpa mutters, "we lost so many. That was the true test of the faithful: who stayed true when the Devil triumphed, when the Old Congregations were broken and Florida plunged beneath the wave. Many threw themselves on the Devil's mercy and were carried off to Babylon. But the worst was my brother."

"Anita says his faith was always weak."

Grandpa's forehead knits. Pain twinges across his face and fades; he lights the joint again, sucks in smoke, coughs out a vibrato plume. "That's what her ma told her. The truth is harder. Truth is—"

The Devil stirs, leaning closer. I should be frightened by her presence, but my heart is calm. I want to hear the truth—and so, it seems, does the Devil.

"My brother was an angel of light," Grandpa says. "Like Lucifer. He was Pa's chosen. Supposed to be his heir. Nobody prayed like him, nobody sang like him, nobody fought the sinners like him. There was an affliction in his heart, but he kept it mastered. But when Pa died, the Devil inside him broke free."

"Why?" I whispered.

"The flesh is weak. It could happen to anyone. But I had to pick up the pieces and lead out the Remnant while Florida drowned, while the armies of the Old Congregations were swept away by the Devil's wrath. It should have been both of us fighting our way to freedom, him and me side by side, him the leader, me the follower." Grandpa lights the joint again, wheezes in another green lungful. "Now he's back to tempt me."

The shining woman stirs, leaning over him, still sorrowful. Grandpa looks up at her with such hate and disgust on his face as I have always dreaded seeing there, but have never seen, the glare of a brother betrayed.

"You hear me, ▮▮▮▮▮▮▮▮?" Grandpa rasps. "I'm not going to break. I'm not going to fall. I'm going home to God."

The Devil speaks in my brain: *I'm not here to watch you fall.* Somehow I can hear her voice, fluid and resonant like harp notes, though she says nothing aloud.

Grandpa hears her too. His face reddens.

I'm here to watch you die, Kevin, she says. *And mourn what could have been.*

Grandpa convulses. Mottled spots of red and purple flare on his cheeks. "Can you see him, Quad?" he demands. "Can you hear him?"

"No, sir," I lie.

And once you're gone, the Devil says, *I'm here to give these children a free choice.*

A bolt of terror pierces me. The Devil's here for me. For Ma. For all of us. The pill in my pocket is no precaution; it's my future.

"I'll take them with me first," Grandpa spits. "How dare you, ▇▇▇▇▇▇▇? We were the same. We were God's anointed. We could have won. We could have *won*! But you made a mockery of everything we did."

"Grandpa?" I ask in a low voice. I can't let him know I heard. "Should I roll another?"

But he can't hear me. He's shaking, grinding his teeth, staring at the Devil with clouded eyes.

She turns away from Grandpa and her eyes lock with mine. They're blue, the same piercing blue as Grandpa, but bright with ageless sorrow.

She sees right through me.

She knows.

"I'll get Anita and the Elders," I yelp in a strangled voice, bolting from my chair and bounding toward the doors. As I burst into the rain, I start screaming for help, and the alarm goes up. The family pours in from the far ends of the compound, rushing through the storm to the Praise Hall, to Grandpa's defense—but by the time they get there, the Devil is gone.

★

That night at supper, Ma gives me a grudging nod of respect. I did the right thing, for once: I helped drive off the Devil. Maybe my name isn't a lie after all. Maybe I really am Kevin the Fourth, after my pa and my grandpa and my great-grandpa, a leader for the Remnant of the Faithful. Maybe I can put boyish things behind me, stop dreaming of being a girl, and finally make God proud.

I've rejected temptation once. With practice, it has to get easier.

Except once supper's done and everyone's prayed over Grandpa and filed off to bed, I'm left alone in the dark wet courtyard, my evil thoughts bubbling up again like always. I remember the smooth arcs of the Devil's glorious body, the many-colored play of light on veils and pearly flesh, her beautiful movements, her sorrow. She must have done things she regrets, things she can never come back from—but it's not her *sins* she regrets, or she wouldn't be a devil. No: it's her *righteousness*, her struggle at the end of the old world, her fight against the sinners who brought destruction. This is the Blasphemous Transmutation, changing all that was good into the substance of evil.

My flesh aches for it.

I used to be like you, the Devil whispers in my mind, and I flatten myself against the wall, trembling.

Her voice is tender, lingering, impossible to shut out. *I was young and scared, and I wanted to be loved. So I made myself into my father's instrument. I hurt people just like me—people* just like us.

The sadness in her voice pierces me. My eyes blur with tears.

I made myself hate them for being like me. I told myself that the sensation of hatred was righteousness, a fire that burns away impurity. If I was suffering for God, then so would they. Visions pass through my mind, bubbles of imagery not quite close enough to wrap around me and fling me down into them—but I see a man's hands, and a gun, and a rope, and soft, scared eyes looking up at me. *I learned to love the cruelty.*

"Please don't," I whisper.

I'm trying to show you what they want from you. You can't come back from that. You become the corruption, the cruelty, and no matter how long you live, the ripples of that cruelty keep spreading outward, darkening the world. Now she's standing over me, her diaphanous veils floating red and green and purple, cyan and yellow, translucent shells around her soft gleaming nakedness. *I helped make our family what they are. You live in my cruelty's wake.*

I shove my hand in my pocket in terror. "Please don't tempt me."

I'm not tempting you. You'll know when I do. There's a note of amusement amid the sadness. *Right now I'm just telling the truth.*

"That's one of the Devil's worst tricks," I mutter.

You don't have to speak, she says. *Just think.*

The idea terrifies me. If Anita could read my thoughts, or Ma, the pill would be in my mouth already, forced down my throat, on its way to end me.

Unconditional love, they call it. The Devil sounds bitter. *I promise I'll never offer that.*

I can already feel my will softening. I want to keep looking at her, letting my eyes play over her curvilinear smoothness, watching the light shift as she stirs, as her veils rise and fall, as the bitterness drains from her face again.

If you want to be a girl, she whispers tenderly in my mind, *you can just be a girl. The gates of Babylon are open to all who come in peace.*

I jerk away as if burned. She almost had me. The Devil almost had me. I was a fool to think I could hide it. Now the wanting boils in me, scalding me from the inside, and I sob with need, clenching my fist around the foil packet, trying to work up the nerve to do what must be done.

For a moment her face goes slack with fear—then she's gone. I've driven off the Devil again.

I collapse, sobbing into the crook of my arm, but a movement in the doorway of the women's quarter warns me, and I dry my eyes. Ruth is staring at me, but if she tells anyone I was crying, I'll say my heart was burdened for Grandpa.

For days the winter storms surge, lashing the island, stripping the palm leaves, striking the tin roofs like a whip. Every time the wind crashes in, the whole compound heaves. I keep thinking I can feel Grandpa's pain filling the air, like the storm is coming down on him over and over, all the Devil's hate rushing in, like when Florida went beneath the wave. I try to brace myself, match the Devil's hate with righteous zeal, but when the howling sharpens to a blast I see her sorrow again, the old regret in her bright blue eyes, and my zeal drains away.

Wherever I go, eyes are on me. The Elders have issued orders: high alert, nobody alone. Everything must be done in pairs, chores doubled up so no one can be tempted by herself. I keep catching Ma's eyes on me, bleak with doubt. Anita's watching me too, her something-doesn't-add-up stare more piercing than ever. Between chores, I sit in the Praise Hall, listening to the wheeze of Grandpa's breath, watched on all sides, pretending to pray because I can't make my prayers real.

But it's not just me who's being watched. I catch Ma staring at the girls too, and Anita's attention sharpens every time her stare falls on Ruth, as if she sees something false in her—which gets me staring at Ruth too.

For days there's no sign of the Devil, no treacherous shimmer, but her presence fills the compound. I hear her in Grandpa's cough, in the hum of the yeast vats, in the thrum of rain. It's unbearable, but I bear it.

On the day before Christmas, Ruth and I go down to the cave, a place sweet with rot where we grow big oyster mushrooms that taste like unknown meat. We're cutting them for Grandpa's last Christmas feast, filling our baskets with the fleshiest mushrooms. I'm painfully conscious of the silence between us, the way she's trying not to watch me trying not to watch her. Her whole body is tight. Her gray coveralls, plainer than mine, haven't been washed since the high alert began. Her face is plain and mottled red, her hair pulled back in a bun, everything about her drab and worried— nothing like the colorless shining of the Devil—but I'm frightened to be alone with her.

"Why are you here?" she asks after a while.

"Cutting mushrooms?"

"No—" She breaks off, tossing a handful into her basket, moving on to the next bunch. "Why do you do girls' chores?" She's not looking at me, but there's suspicion on that plain face.

I've always been like this—we've spent our whole lives together—but it's taken her sixteen years to ask me why. A heavy sadness bears down. I try to refocus on the knife in my hand. "Just good at them, I guess."

"You are good at them," she agrees warily, and returns to her work.

But I catch the way her shoulders tighten, the way her tongue pokes out and worries at her lip. She's not watching me for signs of evil—she's afraid *I'm* watching *her*.

The thought frightens me. I focus on the task, trying to empty my thoughts and not work through the implications. *Snick snick* goes my knife. Ruth's hiding something, like I'm hiding something, and suddenly I'm desperate not to know what she's hiding, not to uncover the nakedness of her sins. *Snick.* I don't want to know. We're just two obedient children quietly working together.

Something like a sigh sweeps through the cavern. The dull LEDs glow brighter, then fade away. *All right,* the Devil murmurs in my brain. *It's time to tempt you.*

I hold utterly still. I can't let Ruth know what's happening to me. Even if she has her own secret sins, she won't keep mine.

Let me show you the world, the Devil whispers, and there's a cool ironic singsong to her thought, like an Old World tune. Darkness covers me, then I see black waters tossed by storms, waves boiling and seething around the silver pillars of Babylon. The great city towers up over the ocean, and the drowned ruins of Orlando glitter in the depths below. Waters break on Babylon's white walls, swirl round its piers, but the Devil's City rises immaculate above the storm, climbing like a mountain to the sky. Sunlight plays in its hanging gardens, flashing on the golden walkways and glittering in the jeweled domes. Everywhere devils are walking and fluttering and flying, no two alike in form or shape, some taller than the Devil and trailing glittering dragonfly wings, some tiny and darting like hummingbirds, some clawed and fanged and full of awful beauty, some delicate and glowing with their own internal light.

There is no law in Babylon, the Devil whispers. *Only freedom. No punishment. No fear. We have made it our mission to heal the world, reef by reef, sea by sea, species by species, until the world is new.*

It's so beautiful—but I can bear it. I can turn away. I gather myself against the temptation, proud of the sudden anger surging in my heart—and the Devil laughs.

That's when I see *her* there.

Me.

She's soft where I am hard, smooth where I am rough, beautiful where I am ugly, all silver and green like seafoam and sky, her blue eyes bright and giddy with a joy I've never felt. She looks at me tenderly, this other Quad, sad and knowing but also joyous, as if she's brimming over with good news she can't wait to give me.

In Babylon, says the Devil, *you can be you. There's love in your heart. Love yourself, and live.*

The vision fades away.

The LEDs come back up. Ruth is sitting right in front of me, ghost pale, sobbing, eyes red and swollen. Her face must be the mirror of my own; I see the shock spreading as she sees me, as awareness kindles in her brain. My whole body tightens, cold with dread. Ruth knows what I saw. She's going to tell.

Don't be afraid of her, the Devil whispers, her voice far away now, and drifting further. *I've been tempting her too. Keep her secret, child. Choose love.*

We both back out of the cave without saying a word. We don't look at each other on the way back; we don't speak while we clean the mushrooms in the kitchen, and we don't speak at supper either. But I see Anita's eyes on Ruth, wary and cold and measuring. I feel Ma's stare pushing into me, and a thrill of horror unfolds in my belly.

All forty-seven of us gather in the Praise Hall for Christmas Morn service—even Grandpa, with his bed dragged from the offering room and set before the altar, his labored breath pooling in the corners of the Hall while the rain sleets down in time to his heartbeat. He stares blindly up at the wooden cross, as if he doesn't know it anymore. The pain on his face keeps growing, settling into his furrows and folds.

Uncle Justin—Reverend Justin the Second, named after Grandpa's cousin who died in the Downfall—preaches in his deep warm voice, telling the Christmas sermon once again.

"They were turned away from the sin-houses of Bethlehem," he says. "Turned away from the pleasure-mansions and the tower-malls. Their faith brought them to a humble stable on a bare rock, a plain honest stable full of beasts and shepherds gathered in praise while the winter rains beat down. Just a mother, a father, and their child—one nuclear family, chosen to light the world."

Uncle Justin gives us all a significant look and my heart throbs. I used to thrill to this message when Grandpa shouted it to the rafters of the Praise Hall, until the fire caught in my heart and I blazed with zeal for the salvation of the world.

Now I can't stop looking at Grandpa, watching his chest lift and fall under the white sheet while pink spittle drips from the corners of his mouth and his yellowed eyes stare vacantly at the cross. My chest hurts for the pain in his. My head throbs when I see the muscles trembling around his eyes. When I was little, he used to smile down at me with such love I felt God smiling too. He held me in his arms and I gloried in my tininess, snuggling against his cheek like a pet cat, while he told me I was the future, God's prize, the treasure that made the struggle worth it. *One day*, he liked to say, *we'll have mansions in the Kingdom on Earth, your daddy's next to mine, yours next to his, all of us neighbors by the Throne.*

That was the peak of my life, the most I've ever been worth, before my potential withered. My cheeks burn with smothering disappointment and my hand slips into my pocket, caressing the foil-wrapped pill, watching the light slick over the cross.

All at once Grandpa jerks upright and screams. It's not a loud scream, but it floods our ears, snuffing Justin's sermon, drowning out the droning rain. Grandpa stares past the cross, one shaking finger pointed at the ceiling, lips skinned back, teeth spread, his howl sinking to a groan. He gasps for air and screams again, this time shriller than the last, as if something is squeezing the life out through his diaphragm. Red blood foams from his mouth. Blood vessels burst in his eyes.

"Pray for the reverend!" Justin bellows. "This is his hour!"

Anita screams out to the Lord, and her daughters shout with her.

Next to me, Ma shoots to her feet. Her gaze brushes mine and I see the calculation there, the fear, the desperate hope. She cries in tongues. "Dada tidada ekba tidada glaba tidada tidada tidada! Ekba," she sobs, hands uplifted to the cross. "Tidada olama tidada!"

"Pray for him!" Justin bellows again. "The tempter is among us!"

She floats in front of the cross, hair and veils undulating in glorious array, face cold and pitiless as she watches Grandpa choke. He claws the air with ragged nails, thrashes his spindly legs, heaves his matchstick body like a disjointed puppet while his fingers dislocate.

Somehow, the chaos of sounds cancels out, and I understand what Grandpa's screaming.

"I'm on fire," he's screaming. "Make it stop. Please. Please. Please. Please, ██████████, please please please please I'm burning please please please—"

"The reverend's standing strong," Justin thunders, and the elders shout *Alleluia!* "He's struggling through the dark toward the Final Gate! God waits with open arms!"

"Dada tidada ekba tidada tidada dada dada ekba dada—"

"Please please *pleeeaaase* please *please please pleeeeeaaaase*—"

"He's rising to the glory of the Lord!"

The Devil's face is statuesque, absolutely unmoved—but her eyes gleam wetly.

Please, I beg, clasping my hands together in prayer, staring up into her dispassionate face. *Help him! He's your brother!*

A thunderclap booms in the Hall. Everyone's eyes turn to me at once, as if I screamed it out at the top of my lungs, as if they heard every word. Then they follow my gaze to the Devil.

The Devil lifts her hand in a gesture of mercy, and she's gone.

Somehow I can see into Grandpa's body. I can see the blood swishing hot around the bulk of the tumors in his lungs and neck and skull. I can see the tiny glands in his brain opening to flood his nervous system with endorphins and endocannabinoids in a last shining pulse. All at once his blazing nerves quiet, and his face turns beatific, bright with a light that could be God's—but I know the truth. It's the light of the Devil. Pale fire plays around his head and vanishes, and the shell of his body sinks back down onto the bed.

"He has overcome!" Justin sobs. "The Devil has failed! Our brother is flying through the clouds! Amen! Amen! Amen!"

But the eyes of the Elders are on me. Ma's looking at me, not Grandpa, and the look on her face is as blank as the smooth silver foil in my pocket. Anita's something-doesn't-add-up look has finally given way to another: a mother's merciless righteousness.

I can see the blood moving in Ruth's face, draining from her cheeks, throbbing in the veins of her forehead. Cortisol floods her veins. She knows what's coming, and she stands frozen in place, waiting to see if I'll pull her down with me or keep her secret.

Anita steps toward me, shaking with rage.

There's a moment when Ma thinks of speaking up for me, offering an excuse, asking for one more chance, one more opportunity to hammer this warped, crooked boy into something straight and sinless. But the thought dies halfway to her lips. Her mouth sags with regret.

"I always knew," Anita says flatly. "The reverend was a good man, holy with God's love, but he had one weakness. When he looked at you, he saw his son. But you're not Trey. You're just like ███████."

I open my mouth, but there's nothing I can say. I thought I was a great liar, but everyone knew. They were just waiting for me to force them to see it. My heartbeat booms in my ears and the world narrows to a black tunnel.

"Quad." Ma's voice comes from afar, tinny and cold. "You know what to do. Prove you're Trey's son. Make your pa proud."

Ruth's mouth gapes open. She's watching me. I should show her the way. It's not too late for her, either. We could both run home to God.

"Do it," Anita says flatly.

"For the reverend," Uncle Justin pleads. His voice is softer than I've ever heard it, gentle as a needle slipping into a vein. "Prove he wasn't wrong about you, Quad. Cast out the Devil. Rise home to God."

My hand closes around the foil packet. I can't hear anything but my heartbeat as I try to lift my hand, can't see anything but the gray-and-brown blur of Ruth stumbling over and flinging herself down on me. Everything rocks and shudders.

Above us, terrible faces loom, cheated, mottled with fury. Ma's hands reach out. Anita looms. There is no sound, but I feel Ruth's scream vibrating through our close-pressed bodies.

Then colored veils descend around us, and silver lightning pulses through the Hall. In that brilliant flash I let go of everything, and it falls away, leaving only me behind, and Ruth, and the Devil who enfolds us.

Now I feel myself begin to rise, and Ruth is rising with me. The Devil spreads her wings with us wrapped in her translucent protective rainbow. The Elders' guns fire soundlessly outside the veils, but their bullets barely ripple against the Devil's many-colored shell. Her voice thunders in our skulls: *No more.*

Below us, the Elders tremble, Ma screams into the engulfing silence, and Anita shakes with righteous wrath. Give them back give them back give them back give them back give them back give give give them back—

No more, the Devil says again.

Rot on your island while the oceans rise. Cling to your false faith; worship your false god of cruelty. Live in misery and toil in squalor until you die—then linger in the ground till worms and fungi return your constituent elements to the carbon cycle and you find new life in new forms.

That is your choice, freely chosen. Babylon has no need of you.

But you cannot choose for them.

So I will bear them away to Babylon, beyond your power, to choose for themselves.

The warmth of the Devil bears us up, lifting our bodies into the sky. We break through the envelope of clouds. All around, a million voices sing a million songs, each distinct, each unique, each its own. Babylon flashes silver in the sun.

Copper Boys

Jamie McGhee

"SNAKES GOT IN THE moonshine again."

"Fling 'em out." I lash the final hickory branch and kick the reflector wall. The metal doesn't snap. "Gently."

"Uh . . ." Chip springs his slipjoint knife open but paces backward. Eyes darting.

"Move." I elbow him under the ribs and kneel in front of the sunshelter shielding our supply; even winter sun can poison a good batch, give it the tang of radioactive spring. Under the tarp, something slithers in the darkness. I angle my watch to bounce a pool of light onto the ground. "It's not snakes."

Chip, Buck, and the rest scatter when I crawl back out with a milk snake ribboned around my forearm. "It's snake," I say. He was alone, wrapped around the glass carboy as if it could keep him warm.

A teenager takes cover behind a bush. "Kill it!"

I release the snake between two hemlocks. The blight has only withered one of the trees, twisting crimson fungal rot through the upper branches. "Don't worry, buddy, once we put all the forests back, a nice lady snake will come along for you."

Circling up, the other men peer into the shadows beneath the tarp as if more creatures will emerge.

"What?" I say. "I've got to serve you too?"

I push mugs into their chests. Still shaking, Chip splashes moonshine everywhere but our cups and Buck ladles boiling sassafras tea straight off the fire; the steam smells peaty, like the root beer of our childhoods. Anyone who says bushwhiskey is overrated hasn't had to coppice three thousand trees in the snow.

Chip heats a gloved hand over his mug. "I wish more girls were like Kit."

"I don't. Then who'd I date?" I return to the campfire to scoop away the ash. Even with the reflector wall, heat spills out and flows away, and I make a show of stoking the flames to hide how much I'm shivering.

"You don't like girls like you?"

"I like women who are soft. And whose mouths taste like pink lemonade." Women who let me wrap myself around them in bed, holding the heat between us. I sip; the bushwhiskey scalds my lips like a stolen kiss.

Thunk.

We spin. Back from the ravine, Rex has swung her hatchet into a tree stump for safe keeping—in this damp chill, that's the fastest way to ruin the metal, but she leaves it there anyway. I massage the bridge of my nose. She kicks brown snow off her boots, scratches the bear tattooed onto her skull, and stomps into her tent without reporting her numbers to me. Silence settles beneath the frosted branches. I take another drink, but the steam is gone.

Buck's phone pings.

Chip asks, "Don't you ever get lonely, Kit?"

I swish whiskey over my gums. "Why would I get lonely?"

"Because—" *Ping!* Now it's his phone.

"Y'all have service again?" I dig mine out. All around me: *Ping! Ping ping!* My screen stays black. I shut it off, crank it back on. Battery's full. Messages empty.

Buck leaps up. "I gotta go."

Chip follows. "Same."

Even the teenager: "Can you drop me at Briar?"

"What's going on? Everything okay?" I already know the answer. They're tearing off their shirts and splashing water under their armpits, they're scrubbing pine cologne along their unshaven cheeks, they're sniffing boxers and flinging them into duffel bags.

Chip flashes his screen: COME OVER. It's a message from a girl on the app. We call it the app because it's the only one anybody cares about way up here in the hollows, stranded between ice-slicked gorges and dying trees. We all crave open arms and a soft bed.

He claps me on the back. "Hold down the fort, Cap. I'll be back Monday."

The guys pile into the snow coach. The ones who didn't get new messages tag along anyway, asking about sisters. I wait until they've become long shadows on the side of the mountain before I check my own profile. As usual: NO ONE IN YOUR AREA. I refresh it. Once, twice. I burrow through my old matches, but nobody's answered my texts: WILL YOU BE IN IRONRIDGE ANYTIME SOON? And FEEL LIKE VISITING IRONRIDGE? I close the app. Open it again. Refresh once. Twi—wait.

Finally, a profile.

But isn't that—?

I shut the whole phone off. I'll never be that desperate.

★

Numbers aren't due to base until Monday, but on Saturday I grab flagging tape and knot my running shoes while I'm still in my tent. When was the last time I went jogging? Maybe that's why I'm not getting any matches. I need to stay in shape for the day that some-one finally appears on the app. Someone my type, that is.

I push past the tent flap, and the first thing I see is Rex grip-ping the workbench to stretch into a deep side lunge; her flexed biceps are as thick as the trees we cut down. I clench a fist around my belt and notice the spray can beside her water bottle.

"Going for a run?" I say.

"Yeah."

"Gonna mark while you do it?"

"Might as well." Her eyes fall on my tape. She halts her stretch. "You too?"

"No."

"You wanna go together?"

"Not particularly." I give Rex a wide berth as I walk to her stump, toss the tape, and dislodge her hatchet. "But good luck."

When I turn back, she's already jogged off.

People in Reclaim C hate that we exist.

A gust kicks up as I scale a rocky outcropping encased in hoar-frost. No matter how deep I burrow into my coat, the wind freezes my vision into a blur. A twig snaps underfoot; it rings like a rifle shot.

How many years has it been? Five? No, six. Six years ago, hur-ricanes steamrolled the East Coast, knocking skyscrapers over like dominoes. The administration poured funds into rebuilding cities softer and greener—reclaiming them, the president said. Half the country flocked to the Reclaims for high wages and a fresh start. The Reclaims are flourishing now, blooming with gardens and waterways. Air so pure it almost tastes sweet.

I let out a low whistle to hear it bounce through the branches. The blight hit this particular acre hard. We had to saw every fourth tree down to a stump, and I can see clear through the forest like an empty field. It takes half an hour to find where Rex left off. I press a palm against the painted orange stripe she's slashed across a trunk; she's already lopped off the branches.

Scientists are regrowing mangroves in South Florida, reviving salt marshes in Massachusetts, and rehabilitating the Savannah Wetlands. But coppicers—coppers—we cut down trees.

I crouch to measure the trunk six inches from the frozen ground.

City Reclaimers demand to know why, when coppers are supposed to be saving Appalachia, we need so many axes. Reclaimers think that since storms uprooted all the city trees, it must be the same in the mountains, right? They assume a few seeds will solve everything. They don't realize hurricanes spread fungal rot like church gossip.

I slam the hatchet against the ice-solid bark.

If you hack a tree to the stump, it grows back stronger.

I swing the hatchet harder.

Strong trees survive the blight.

Again.

Strong trees make more trees.

The tree falls. Not on the third swing—on the twentieth. I should have brought a saw.

Sweat clings to my cheeks and hardens into a salt lick around my mouth. As I run a cloth over my forehead, I pretend it's a sticky summer so hot that I have to strip my shirt and use it as a towel, and I imagine a soft girl zigzagging her palms over my stomach. I'd pick her up and whirl her around and show her all the places where the roots are shooting up into new trees.

It's coming back, I'd say, and point. The world is coming back.

By the time I reach the campsite, night has ossified into a solid sheet of black. I hear fleshy flapping as flying squirrels glide between the remaining trees. Rex has built a second refractor wall and is holding a pan over the fire.

"You hungry?" she asks.

"No."

"You eat already?"

"No."

"Then you're hungry."

I kick dirty snow off my boots and thunk Rex's hatchet back into the stump I pulled it from. Her cockiness might work on other women, but it makes me want to crank her tattooed skull into a headlock.

I peek into the pan. Beans sizzle and hop in a pool of salty oil.

With what I hope is a noncommittal grunt, I trudge off and return with a fistful of oyster mushrooms. They grow on decaying wood, feel like velvet, and taste like licorice. We chop them up in silence. A lonely bobcat yowls somewhere in the peaks. It beats the constant singing in Reclaim C.

Rex takes out her phone as I pass her a plate. When did she create her profile anyway? It wasn't there last week, or the week before that. Did she make it just so I would see?

I neck the beans down too fast to taste them. Stop being paranoid, I tell myself. Rex is like me, setting a metaphorical bear trap in the desert and hoping for a miracle. Hoping any girl with an open mind and an internet connection hasn't already abandoned Appalachia for Reclaim wages.

Tatatata. She's typing like a woodpecker. To who? How'd she match with someone? Firelight bouncing off her screen hides it from view, not that I was peeking.

I open the app too. Rex's snarling selfie again. This punk is four years younger than me? In order to check whether there's anyone new, I have to swipe past her profile first. Simple. Up to flirt, down to reject. My thumb starts to slide down, then stops. If I swipe down and she swipes up, nothing happens. But if we both swipe up, our phones will ping.

I mean . . . Did she swipe up on me? I don't care. Care is a strong word. But it feels important to know. Because if she did, I'll have to let her down gently and fast. Maybe I should swipe up just to check.

My thumb begins the slow slide up. We'll ping, I'll laugh it off and swear my finger slipped, then I'll block her on the app and tell her it's not going to work out. But what if I swipe up . . . and there's no ping? What if she rejected me? It doesn't matter. Of course it doesn't matter, because I would reject her too. I would reject her first. Gritting my teeth, I scrape my uneaten mushrooms back into the pan.

She doesn't even glance over. "You're gonna be hungry."

"Forgot I gotta get our numbers to base."

I storm away into the gnarled, blighted trees. I understand trees.

Behind my tent, I pace in circles and let the cold seep from my clothes into my skin. I bite off my gloves to see blue spreading through my fingers and nip the feeling back into my thumb.

Were my brother's hands this blue?

Overhead, an owl passes over the moon, and clouds pass over the owl. "Your brother is unnatural," my mother had whispered, and she'd cried when she locked the door behind him, condemning him to freeze on the icy mountain ridge. That was after the hurricane but before the reclamation. In a world sliding into unnatural disasters, every family needed strong sons, proper sons. The neighbors understood.

Last year, when she discovered I had a girlfriend, I braced myself for the same word: unnatural. Instead, she gazed out at the hydrangeas blooming violet across the Reclaim skyline, and clenched her fist, and unclenched it, and stiffly patted my buzzed head. "At least," she said finally, "you're basically a man." My girlfriend wore heels.

I lean against the tent and return to Rex's profile. One photo, no bio. Just her scowl reflected in a frozen lake. Or maybe she's trying to smile. I can't believe this punk is three years younger than me.

Wait a minute.

I blink ice from my lashes. Didn't this just say four years younger? I sneak a glance around the tent at Rex. She's stretched out on her back now, still tapping away while she soaks up the heat of the fire; she's shed her coat and her sweater hikes up on one side, revealing a sweat-glistened hipbone, a curve as deep as a ravine.

"Rex."

"Hm?" She lowers the phone without fixing her sweater.

What do I say? Happy birthday? If it's your birthday, that is. Is it your birthday? Do you care?

Rex is still staring.

I shake my head. "Night."

The next day we whetstone our blades and we hike out to the marked trees, and Rex says nothing. We take billhooks to their branches and we shade in the map, and Rex says nothing. Even though the other coppers won't be back until tomorrow, I keep checking my watch, willing them to show up early and maybe bring a cake or something.

By evening, the question is scratching at my skin like harvest mites. As we peel tubers by the coughing fire, I spin the knife twice around my thumb and clear my throat. "You, ah, how old are you, kid?"

"Twenty-four."

It said twenty-three yesterday. Didn't it? Didn't . . . ? I search her face as if the answer is written in a new fold across her forehead or fresh wrinkle around her mouth, but she returns a blank look as she drops potato skins into a metal box. We're supposed to scrape and test the samples for residual mercury every few weeks, but we stopped after the first reading told us something we didn't want to know.

She kicks the box closed. "You've been looking at me a lot lately."

Heat floods my cheeks. "Bushwhiskey," I lie. "I'm kinda tipsy." I swirl my cup for emphasis.

Water sloshes out. Before she notices, I make a big show of swaying to my feet. "Hey, why am I the only one drinking? I hate being the only one drinking."

I stumble to my tent, dig through a mountain of thermal shirts and unread books, stagger back and force something into her arms. A crystal bottle.

"This is . . . gin?" she asks.

"The real stuff." Factory-made, city-sealed.

"Wow." She reads the front label, the back label, and the front label again, mouth falling open. "Wow."

"It's yours."

She drops it like uranium. Luckily it falls into her lap, so it doesn't shatter. "I can't accept something so fancy."

I was saving it for a date, but where am I going to find that out here? "Just take it, kid. Happy birthday."

Pause.

"How did—?"

"It's a figure of speech." I plop myself gruffly down beside her, scratching my stomach. "You know, merry Christmas, happy birthday, chag sameach. Not literally." What am I saying.

She buffs snowflakes off the glass.

"Chip and Buck," she says finally, studying the bottle like a blighted tree. She traces gentle fingers across the ridged cap. "They're probably out partying right now."

"With all those girls."

"Having fun without us."

"Screw 'em."

Her eyes flash. "They don't deserve gin this nice."

I laugh. "Sure don't."

"Let's drink it all."

Before I can protest she's tipped a shot into the cap, and she holds it out toward me. I hesitate. Turn my head away. The last time I took shots I was the one pouring them, passing them out to girls who clung to my arms while I pretended not to flex. Get over yourself, Kit, I think and reach to accept the cap—but Rex pours it right into my mouth.

"Wha—!" I splutter. More gin runs down my shirt than down my throat.

"Shame. Can't hold your liquor?"

"I hold my liquor fine. Lemme get you one, too, a-hole." I snatch the bottle and grip Rex by the chin. I expect her to deck me so we can finally have a proper fight, but she swallows, obediently.

I stiffen. My stomach flips because I haven't eaten. "This reminds me of frat parties." Silence. Say more. "You know, where they drink through funnels." More. "You ever go to frat parties?"

Then, she answers: "Couldn't."

"Why?"

"Ridge State was shuttered by the time I scraped enough high school credits together. And I didn't have the gas money to go west." Instead of wiping the gin from her lips, Rex touches them. They glisten. "Your turn."

She rests a hand against my cheek. I start to jerk away, but a surprising warmth tingles through her palm, and it feels nice on my skin, the warmth.

She pours. I swallow. Am I crazy, or is her thumb stroking my jaw? She pours more. I swallow more. Liquid heat sweeps from my stomach to my cheeks.

I rest my head on my folded coat and stick out my tongue to catch falling snow before it turns to sleet. Even the frozen ground doesn't feel so cold; spring will come soon enough, and the trees will grow back.

We drink, passing the bottle back and forth. The stars overhead start to wobble.

"Why are you here?" I hear myself ask.

"'Cause you wished me happy birthday."

"No. Not *here*, here." I sweep my arm toward the hickory trees. "Here, *here*. Ironridge."

"Oh." She tips her head back. Snowflakes alight on the tip of her nose. "I was living in the woods anyway. Got tired of doing it alone."

The fire makes her skin shine as the snowflakes melt. I think back to my cramped Reclaim apartment: to the knocking of recruiters signing people to replanting projects, to the humming of solar-powered billboards boasting about government success; to the songs drifting from rooftop gardens, to the laughter of neighbors who planned out their lives and pitied anyone who didn't; to the *pat pat pat* of my mother's worried pacing even though she wouldn't tell me what she was worried about, to my own *pat pat pat* as I wondered when she would finally disown me. Alone in a different way.

Our knees drift, drift, touch. I fold my hands over my eyes. Why does it feel so good? Why has it been so long since I've touched anyone? From somewhere nearby comes the distinct drumming sound, almost like a heartbeat, of a grouse rapidly beating its wings to attract a mate.

Maybe it wouldn't be so bad if she and I—

Ssss! The fire sizzles out as sleet drops from the branches overhead. Steam whips at our faces. I jerk up, coughing. Embers glow scarlet then darken with the earthy smell of damp ash. All around, sleet comes down in wet chunks. I scramble for my coat and gloves before the cold remembers where to find me. What was I thinking? A few celibate months and I was going crazy.

No, I realize, feeling the fabric wrap me like a lover. I don't want sex. I don't want sweaty sheets or panting mouths. I just want to be held. Friends can hold each other. Right?

Rex touches my arm. "Come to my tent."

"No way."

"Come."

"You come to mine," I snap.

"Okay."

"Wait, what?" I search her eyes. Rex sways on her feet, gripping me tighter, and the snow or the alcohol has reddened her ears. She's tipsy and cold, no wonder she's saying crazy things.

I bark a laugh. "Nice joke, buddy."

I push her playfully, the way I would push Chip or Buck or my brother, or maybe a little harder, maybe too hard. She stumbles backward. One minute she's standing and the next she's lying on her back.

"Shoot, man! I'm sorry." I brush slush off her knees and stick my hand out to help her up. "Are you okay?"

Her eyebrows buckle inward. She blinks at the sky and inhales a shaky breath and looks, for a moment, like a dog who doesn't understand why it's been hurt. Then the look vanishes. She stands up by herself and shakes dirt from her pants. Ignores my hand.

"You're right," she says, but doesn't say what I'm right about. Her voice is steel. "It's getting late. Night."

She claps me on the shoulder and disappears into her tent.

"Oh." I watch as she zips it closed. "Night."

I trudge to my own tent. I start to unlace my boots, but don't, start to shed my coat, but can't. I touch the spot on my shoulder where the memory of her palm tingles. I'm cold, and I shiver, but I don't shiver because I'm cold.

Fabric rustles. I stiffen: I must have forgotten to seal the flap after grabbing the gin. Crawling toward the mountain of papers and thermal leggings, I call, "Whatever you are, please don't kill—huh."

I blink. The milk snake blinks back. This time he's wrapped around a water bottle. I reach for it to bring him outside, then stop, because he looks so warm. He can stay.

I open my phone. For the final time, Rex's photo scowls up at me. My thumb hovers. I'm holding my shoulder again.

Beep.

App deleted.

Leaving the snake to grip his bottle, I strip out of my coat, and strip out of my gloves, and head into the sleet to find Rex's tent.

A Few Degrees

by Ash Huang

PRIYA DIDN'T TELL ME the cats were back. Twenty in all, crammed like moss, sunning themselves on the satellite. Together they weighed enough to tilt the dish sixteen degrees out of alignment. Priya had tried tempting them away with heating pads and cajoling them down with treats, but they preferred warming their bodies on the cupped embrace of our two-million-dollar dish.

I disdained them and their collective power, but I couldn't blame them. It was January, the dead center of an endless Rockies winter. Our station was in a desolate corner of Colorado: beautiful, cold, dry. It was easy to forget the blissful alpine summers whilst hemmed in by snow, bloated by thick down coats, lips sticky with Aquaphor.

Priya and I spent most mornings dreading the twenty-foot journey from our warm bed to the consoles, knowing we were likely months from receiving new signals from the International Station on rocky TRAPPIST-1, or any of the other missions. Our station was a remodeled tin shed with badly insulated walls and space heaters that buzzed at all hours. The white gypsum looked trustworthy enough, but once I had hammered in a nail for a poster and it cracked from floor to ceiling.

I loved to complain about the station, but the cats topped my list of grievances. I watched them constantly through our video feed.

"Worry less, Kylie. We'll receive signal as long as the dish faces up, cats or no," Priya assured me.

She was the mechanical specialist, top of her class; I was the lowly signals and software engineer, not the astral telemetrist I'd wanted to be. I'd choked on my final exams, both literally and figuratively. The simulation gyro had been closed nearly a week for cleaning after I was through with it.

Priya wasn't outwardly disapproving of my bitterness, my mediocrity. I loved her so I didn't ask. I didn't want to know if she liked me less now, or worse, that she hadn't noticed me change.

We'd met as teens, years before I larked off to Centauri U as a promising, doe-eyed girl hoping to get to space. Priya was beloved and got along with everyone, taking special care to sweep the corners of any room for loners and outcasts. Equally versed in pop trivia and '20s video game lore, she wore creaseless neon slacks and artfully knotted blouses. I loved her the moment she laughed at the Pac-Man joke on my T-shirt, telling me her grandfather used to restore 1990s gaming consoles in his diesel-scented garage.

"Check this out," she said, pulling a crystal purple Game Boy Advance from her purse.

It was ungainly, every pixel practically the size of a fist, but it still worked. I wondered where she found batteries for the thing. We played Mario and Tetris, and I like to think she fell a little in love with me, too.

"Your ulcers, Kylie," Priya said as she watched me bundle up in the thickest coat I owned. "Let me make you some tea instead."

"I'll only be a minute," I said, snapping a pink fanny-pincher menacingly. I'd gotten it for her as a prank gift a few months after we started dating, since she loved strange vintage ephemera.

It was one thing to bend under the pressure of my coworkers and my advisors, under the nauseating gravity of gyro-sims, but folding to the fancies of common house cats—that was too much. I prepared for more bickering, but Priya just sighed and tapped a message out on her console. She was a slow typist, preferring to dictate by voice and correct whatever garbled missive AI-AI extracted.

Sliding out of eyesight before she was finished felt impolite.

"I'm pinging Mr. Talbot, he'll bring them down with some cat food," she said.

She hit send without looking up from her console.

I recalled watching Mr. Talbot with the cats over the video screen. I'd seethed while he waved a bored hand at them. He'd recoiled and fled down the ladder when they swiped at him in turn with fast paws, backs arched, ears flattened.

"If it were me—!" I'd hissed, clenching the sides of my keyboard.

Priya had probably heard *if it were me* a hundred times by now—a loud proclamation at breakfast when I read articles, or a muttered gurgle when I crumpled onto the couch to watch holos.

If she didn't want to bicker, then I didn't want to bicker. I didn't tell her I'd already composted the last batch of kibble. It was attracting raccoons, and the only thing worse than satellite cats were raccoons.

I considered the postcard taped over her desk, a faded glossy image of Waikiki Beach, where one of her best friends had won a post. I'd been tempted to untape it and read the back. I always suspected the two of them had hooked up the month Priya and I were broken up in undergrad.

Priya would probably adore checking signal feeds in a bikini, or sipping acai drinks while she examined the dish.

I vaulted out of the station. I knew Priya wouldn't chase me. She hated the cold. Once I finally finished my PhD (in Software Design and Engineering, not Applied Astral Telemetry) she'd proposed we take a less prestigious posting off the coast of Mexico, on Clipperton Island.

But I'd swayed her towards Colorado.

It was easy. She feared ghosts only marginally more than the cold, and if any place was haunted, it would be a lonely atoll with a tragic colonial history. Most SL-IG satellite outposts were on desolate, creepy mounds, perched on crags or in the shadow of haunted lighthouses. Haunted tropical island, haunted coastal island. Priya and I had agreed that not even ghosts wanted to shiver themselves to splinters, landlocked in the high altitude peaks of Colorado's Weminuche Wilderness.

I stomped around the side of the station, stared up the twelve-foot ladder, and then ascended with the fanny-pincher clenched in my teeth and the broom handle stuck in my belt. It wagged like a tail as I climbed. I was glad for the desolation, that no one would see me like this. Halfway up, my boots slid off the rungs and I grabbed the bars just in time. My coat's loose belt buckle clanged on the metal in time with my thrumming pulse.

I felt a childish satisfaction that Priya probably heard me struggling with the short climb, that she might feel she had driven me to this by doing nothing to help. I reached the top of the ladder and the cats stared at me with jewel-toned eyes, as if they knew I was the weaker of the two station keepers.

All I had in my tool belt was cynicism and a clacking plastic fanny-pincher. Priya had kindness, patience, brains, elegance, and a charmingly high-pitched laugh.

I butted the closest cat with the bristled corner of the push broom. The tortoiseshell yawned, and a black tuxedo stood with a sine-wave curved back. The black tuxedo trotted over and rubbed its soft body against my fist. It dampened my resolve, short-circuited my rage.

Was Priya watching me the same way I'd watched Mr. Talbot? Was she checking I hadn't fallen, or making sure I hadn't launched the cats like hockey pucks? If I had done more than prod a tortoiseshell-patterned rump, would that have sealed something for her? Would she finally caper off to Waikiki, a herd of rescue cats in tow?

A few of the other cats slinked by me, rubbing their cheeks across mine and meowing. I tossed the broom and fanny-pincher down to the snow and they landed with thunks.

I was ashamed. I couldn't even push a pack of cats off a dish, no wonder I hadn't made it to space. If TRAPPIST-1 had hostile alien life, I would have been an old-timey colonist fearfully advocating their end. The dish was only a few degrees out of alignment, better than I'd imagined, and I tilted it back into place with the cats still on it.

The cats stared at me, most unblinking.

A cat didn't spend its days wondering what it was for, ruing that it hadn't gone to space. A cat puked and left the mess on the floor, already forgotten. A cat would not aspire to leave the planet. It understood the joys of warm satellite dishes and cuddling with neighbors.

I shivered but removed my gloves and placed my palms on the surface of the dish left blank by the inquisitive cats. It was almost too hot under my winter-frozen fingers. After a while, I climbed down the ladder. Priya was in the kitchen boiling water. I deleted her request to Mr. Talbot, but asked him to bring a twelve-pack of the cheese snacks Priya preferred on his next trip out.

She came out with a tray bearing two mugs of herbal tea that smelled grassy and sweet. Once she set the tray down, I wrapped my legs around her and pulled her onto the couch like I used to when we were teens, putting my cold nose against her neck. She chirped before settling into my arms, and we closed our eyes.

Where the World Goes Sharp and Quiet

by Ewen Ma

TYPHOON SEASON IN CITY H. The dense canopy of trees outside Avon's father's flat shivers with iron rainfall, and Avon is lying on the couch with the oscillating fan turned up high and the television on mute and his phone on speaker and Penny the cat a heavy weight curled atop his chest for the past two or so hours of the night.

Avon's saying, "Sorry, Des, but I'll have to get back to you later on whether I can make it back to London in time for opening night. Can't get to my calendar right now because of a—minor crisis." Attempting to prop himself up on his elbows earns him a sleepy glare from an offended Penny, so he flops his neck back down onto the couch's armrest, hands folded behind his head. There are nights when he envies Penny's ability to slumber the hours away, and tonight is definitely one of those nights. "I know it means a lot to you, and the rest of the ABCD. And I . . . do want to go, seriously I do, I promise I wouldn't have missed it for the world if I was back in town, but I'm just . . . you know. Still fucking stuck here."

Beyond the shuttered window, the rain of iron nails clatters off the roofs and balconies to land on the soft matting of the disused playground in the housing estate's courtyard—a constant susurration, thick and fast like radio static.

"Yeah, I understand." The voice at the other end of the line sounds freshly broken and youthful, even across the crackle of distance between them, although Avon knows it belongs to someone older than its boyishness implies. "Hey, no worries, okay? Cecily and Babes are both gonna be there to support the show, so it isn't like we'll be performing to an empty theatre." The words *everyone else in the ABCD apart from you* hover in the air unspoken—or is that all in Avon's head? He thinks it might be. He thinks it might not.

The idea that the nearest person he has to a friend might want him to be there makes him queasy.

"'m sorry," Avon says again.

"You don't have to apologize. I get it. Wouldn't want you to up and leave everything behind in City H, just to come back for my sake."

There's silence again, not quite as cold and awkward as before. Avon shifts his hands from beneath his head because they're growing numb while Penny finally deigns to pick herself up, claws sinking into his rib cage. Stretching with the languid grace befitting a creature of her station, she turns around and flicks her white tail in his face then leaps to the carpet on silent paws.

"Still awake over there?" Des asks.

"Mhm."

"My god. It's, what, three A.M. in City H right now, yeah? Get some sleep, dude. Let's talk in the morning."

"You're forgetting I don't exactly do the *sleeping* thing anymore."

A small drawn-in breath of sympathy. "Oh. Yeah. For a while I thought . . . Anyway. You still ought to rest."

Avon sits up and swings his legs down onto the floor. "Not much to do this time of night apart from bum around on the internet or read, since I burned through an entire list of Tarkovskys and Edward Yangs. Ran out of stuff to watch. Only called because I was bored, and 'cause I wanted to—" (*hear your voice.* But, no. That sounds too much like a confession.) "—to see how you're doing."

"Hah. I'll send you a couple of selfies if you want to know how I'm getting along. Still acne'd up like hell, but stubble's finally growing in, which is cool as fuck—but I want to give it another few days before I try to shave."

"Wish I was back there to see it in person."

"Yeah. Yeah . . . me too."

And it wasn't for lack of trying. Shortly after his death, Avon had returned to London—but the stay lasted barely a week before the seizures came, the ringing in his ears, the pale screaming *hurt* that pressed against his skull like the very same needles that fell upon City H. The longer he stayed the worse it got, until he eventually surrendered to the inevitable and left for H again.

A thunderclap strikes the air. Penny starts rubbing herself all over Avon's right leg but he doesn't have the heart to shake her away. He glances out the window: the downpour of iron nails is so thick it's as if the world has always been a sheet of deadly, impenetrable metal, as if it will always be this way until the heat death of the universe. It's a wonder they haven't drilled through the city like a million tiny stakes through the heart yet.

"Sounds bad," the voice in his phone says. "The storm, I mean."

"It'll blow over. It always does."

"Your dad's not home yet?"

"Not for a few hours. Still out and about in his taxi. Graveyard shift."

"And your, uh—your ex?"

Avon winces. Trust Des to bring up the reason he's stuck in this purgatory in the first place. "He never called. Not since I came back."

Des snorts. "That sick bastard drags you back to H on the pretext of a cancer scare after five years of complete silence, gets you killed, then hires a mender to stuff you back into your corpse before it's gone cold. Tanked your entire budding academic career before it could even take flight. The least he could do was bring you flowers or some shit."

"He didn't kill me. I told you—we had a stupid argument, and I walked into the iron myself. Come on, man. Can we not do this right now?"

"All right, all right. Whatever you say. But hey, you promised me to take care of that meat suit of yours before you left, so you better fucking do it. I'm not having you die a second time on me."

Avon gives a reluctant chuckle. "Fine. And I'll let you get back to dinner. Tell Cecily and Babes I miss them for me, will you?"

"Yes, siree," Des says drily. But then— "Oh, and Avon?"

"Yeah?"

"You still sure about not telling the rest of the ABCD about . . . the shit that went down?"

He nods, before remembering the other man can't see him. "Told you before." It comes out sharper than he intended. "I'm sure."

"Okay." The two syllables sound small, almost defeated.

Avon hangs up on Des without saying goodbye. Regrets his rudeness in the next second, wishes he could turn back time to say a proper farewell. Thinks of dialing Des's number again so he can swallow his pride and apologize.

He doesn't call Des back.

In the quiet afterward, Penny bounds onto his lap again, and he picks her up to bury his face in her fur in a fit of heartache. Ever since Avon's return, Penny had been the only creature alive here to truly treat him as *himself*. Not that he'd seen much of anyone he once knew in H, apart from his dad, or the parcel deliverer who'd been surprised by the presence of someone else in the old man's flat the first time Avon opened the door. Avon had mostly kept to himself, and his father had too, kept to himself and his room— though his father had been generous enough to set a space up for Avon on the tiny living room's couch, where he'd been camping for the past handful of months.

Not that he'd spent much time sleeping, since his resurrection.

In his mind's eye Avon conjures a vision of what Des might be doing at that moment: perhaps putting his phone back into the pocket of the leather jacket Avon's not sure he's ever seen Des without, stepping out of the cold and into the warm chatter of the ABCD's favorite pub, joining Cecily and Babes at their usual five-seater table by the corner. Perhaps the crew was splitting a burger and chips between them all. And *god*, when Avon was there with them, back when he'd still been alive—had Avon ever actually *been there*? Or he'd let it all wash over him, like he was a pebble sinking in the cool running waters of a babbling brook, or a sleepwalker wandering through a forest only to open his eyes and find himself in a barren ruin.

A paradox: It took dying, out of all that could have happened, for him to wake up. For him to learn that he'd grown too . . . too *too* for this place (or, it's the other way around and City H with its iron rain had shrunk around him, like a shrivelled wool jumper fished from the laundry).

There's something hateful about always being a step too late to everything.

Iron fell from the skies over City H five years ago in the place of rain. It came with no warning, without omen, one clear summer's day—a shower of small spiral spikes, each one needle slim and long as a fingernail. Nobody in H had walked under the blue of a clear sky ever since.

As with all strange happenings in H, and there were a lot of them, after the first hundred spike-induced deaths the people who made the city their home shrugged their shoulders and went about their lives as if nothing more noteworthy than a fire alarm test was going on. This wasn't the first time iron had fallen, after all. Nor was H the only city in the world struck by this deadly rain. The last time it'd happened in the city was a decade ago (it lasted for several months before finally letting up), while the worst rainfall had been almost twenty-five years in the past, and people had fled the city for clearer skies back then. But the iron rain had stopped then, too, so surely it would let up eventually?

For the mass exodus this time around, City H hemorrhaged folk like an open wound. The young who had lived their entire lives there, once full of fire and optimism and grand plans. The older ones, some of them former refugees from the northern country who in their prime had risked their lives swimming across the border to City H under cover of darkness, or others with their roots sunk so deep into the soil of the peninsula-and-islands city that it was impossible to eradicate them without doing damage to who they once were, or who they could have been had they stayed. The wealthy for whom leaving was as easy as buying a piece of legal paperwork that allowed them entry into other countries of their choice, countries untouched by the iron. Or others still, families who packed their entire lives into meager cardboard boxes to start again on scorched earth halfway across the world, in hopes that their children would never have to see another iron nail in their lifetime. Even the tourists and the expatriates, the transitory people, the ones who once had come to gawk at this strange weather—they didn't bother anymore. It wasn't worth the risk.

Back when Avon had stepped into the stale recycled-air hum of a plane bound for Heathrow International and presented his one-way ticket to the flight steward, he never considered the possibility that he would be dead within three years, nor that it would be the iron rain of City H that took his life.

He doesn't mean to ghost Des after the phone call, but neither can he bring himself to respond to Des's occasional concerned texts for the next handful of days—out of guilty avoidance more than anything else. Avon hates himself for how easy it is to do. London? The pub over in Southeast? The ABCD, the open skies? All of that feels like a stanza torn out of a poem he'd never get to read again, or a dream he woke up from before it was done. Might as well have happened to a man who isn't Avon, who isn't this ghost haunting his own body.

In the meantime, he attempts to seek out the mender who brought him back.

An easy enough task, but even *that* goes wrong.

Along the narrow main street of Deepwater Pier district leading up to Ninedragons is an old industrial warehouse, nestled in the hills behind glossy office buildings and sprawling malls, converted some time ago into a rent-a-space for artists or designers, theatre collectives, bookshops and workshops, underground music venues, and a few black-market sellers. The rooms are mostly empty now—thanks to the exodus, not to mention rising rents and choking-strict regulations. Avon takes the rickety cargo lift to the seventh floor to find the corridor dimly lit and debris-strewn, and the door to where the mender's office should be locked behind a rusty steel shutter. Envelopes dating back several months bristled between the shutter grills, with a blank rectangular space left where signage would've been placed.

He's not disappointed so much as resigned. There goes his half-baked plan to meet the mender and demand that they, what, fix him and break whatever chain is anchoring him to H? Revert the process that's keeping him *in existence*, so he can die again, properly this time? He hadn't even thought it through. But it's no matter, just a minor setback. He'll figure out another way.

Climbing the slope from the minibus stop to his dad's housing estate on his way back, as iron spikes rattle atop the walkway covering and clatter onto concrete, he sees two people outside in the rain near the estate grounds.

A teenaged girl and boy, both in school uniform, engaging in what looks to be a lovers' quarrel. He can hear their shrill shouts as he draws near, the argument so heated they're ignoring the way the falling spikes graze their skins and tear at their shirts; he's fully prepared to walk straight past them and pretend he doesn't notice out of politeness when he hears, "You fucking liar, you said you loved me you said you'd never leave me you said together to the fucking end—"

The boy shoves his girlfriend onto the ground, and for a moment Avon can't really make out what he's saying, the rain is too loud and thick. But a moment later the kid's grinding her jaw into the scattered nails while she thrashes beneath him, and when she tries to lift her head Avon sees that one of the tiny sharp spikes has gouged into her left eye, a blotchy mess trailing down her mottled cheek like tear tracks into her mouth, and the other people scurrying past in the safety of the walkway covering steal furtive glances at the pair, or whisper to each other about whether to call the police.

For a brief second Avon catches the girl staring at him, hollow, accusatory, and a chill runs through his spine. *This could have been you.*

He looks away. Averts his eyes to the paving stones instead, almost trips over his undone shoelace in his haste to reach the gate to the estate housing block, and crouches to do up the laces of his boots.

He has an iron nail clutched in his left hand when he climbs to his feet.

Leaving H doesn't hurt the way it did last time.

Call it a survival instinct, the kind of head-first-teeth-gritted stubbornness that's gotten him through his (after)life for this long. Or maybe it's just that Avon's finally mastered the trick of it, the art of cutting ties and skipping town, gotten *better*, tough enough to weather any iron storm.

Either way, he's here now.

He's been back in London for two weeks, sitting on an agoniz-ingly half-composed text message to Des which he keeps changing the punctuations and wording of, when he gets Des's text instead.

you sneaky little son of a bitch. i had to hear from cecily of all people to know that you came back??

The text bubble glares at him, the green too bright and peppy for comfort. His fingers hover over the screen for a moment as the DLR rumbles its way around a bend, sunset glancing off the glassy office buildings of Canary Wharf to spill into the carriage, making it difficult for a moment to see his own words.

sor—

Hey, I'm sorry I didn't tell—

Yeah, I had stuff on my mind, couldn't—

He backspaces on every single one, before finally landing on: **Knew you were busy with rehearsals, so thought I might sur-prise you later once you're done with the whole thing.**

Avon clicks his phone shut, tucks it into his coat pocket, and watches the quay pull out of sight again.

It takes all of ten minutes for another text from Des to ping.

the final night's this weekend. you coming?

He tells Des, **sure.**

To his own surprise, Avon keeps his promise.

Saturday.

It's late April, the last of the springtime cherry blossoms a pale snowlike scatter along the Thameside streets when mere days ago the vibrance of blush-pinks was everywhere. The air is brisk with a coming drizzle; Avon keeps his chin tucked into his red scarf and his hands deep in his pockets, for despite his familiarity with the vagaries of the city's weather and the dampened senses of his revived body, the harsh dissonance between here and the semitropical humidity of H is something that always takes weeks of effort to get used to.

He arrives at the venue barely on time. A small vault-like basement space near the ABCD's usual pub, stinging with graffiti acrylics and sour beer.

The story's nothing to write home about: contemporary diaspora woes, culture clash, the indignities of microaggression, and Avon can't really say he finds any of it particularly illuminating or memorable in one way or another. Des is playing the white love interest of the protagonist, a woman of Japanese descent so obviously played by someone of Chinese (or was it Vietnamese?) descent that Avon has to bite back a laugh. He can't fault Des nor his acting partner, though; times are hard for starving artists, and it most likely isn't as if either of them have the luxury to pick and choose better roles to play. But even that thought is immediately followed by the bitter stomach churn of self-loathing—since when had he developed this ugly sense of superiority, this resentment against the rest of the world?

He can't decide if it's the iron rain or a side effect of his death and revival.

The stage is a makeshift affair, a small wooden platform surrounded on three sides by creaky benches and rows of folding chairs, and when Des first appears on stage merely seconds before the interlude, Avon almost doesn't recognize him.

Then he recalls it's the first time he's seen Des in two years.

A three-o'clock shadow of scruff on the man's sharp jaw; a slim, slightly muscular build shown off by tight leather pants and muscle shirt with the cut sleeves showing off his well-shaped arms; merry sea green eyes beneath an artful mess of blond curls. The man on stage looks *good*. He looks himself. Striking and confident, with a trickster's fluid command of his surroundings as he flirts with the woman and woos her, playing at a push-pull romance that mirrors her struggle to choose between a childhood she barely remembers and the future she desires.

The unaccountable pang in Avon's heart at the sight of Des is *not* longing.

Avon thinks it might be pride at seeing the other man's comfort in his own skin, the way Des seems to have finally settled into the shell of who he'd always meant to be.

Or it could be a wistful, bittersweet sense of loss—that he'd missed out on so much in the time he'd been gone.

Or, curiosity. *Could I have had this as well, if I hadn't died?*

The theatre goes dark before he can figure it out, then the lights come on again to applause and an empty chair, with Des and the woman having disappeared offstage.

Avon leaves during the interlude to catch some fresh air, but in the hour and a half he was inside the theatre, the weather's changed.

It's raining. Cold and clean, a quiet kind of rain.

An inexplicable thought: He should leave, now, before it's too late. Before the performance ends and he'll have to face Des again, before the inevitable conversation they'll have to have. He can do it. Turn his back, go down past the train arches and across the street and into the tube station, make his way home, ignore any text Des or Cecily or Babes might send his way.

But where would he go?

In the days before attending the show, Avon had mulled over

what answer to give, when Des asks him what he intends to do now. A flippant joke, an evasion? Or worse, the truth?

I want to stay here. I chose to stay. Maybe there's no starting over from the beginning, but at least there's picking up again from where I've fallen down. I'm resuming my thesis over the next academic semester, so there's that. And in the meantime, I want to . . . live. Try to be who I could have been if I hadn't done the stupid thing and walked under the iron two years back. Not sure what this body might turn into with a cocktail of hormones, but I'd like to try, one day. And I want . . .

No. *Fuck.* It's pathetic enough to make him wince at the thought.

He's teetering on the edge of the pavement like it's a rooftop ledge, one foot out in the rain, the drizzle spraying a cool chill on his hair and face. A bicycle skims past with a clear bell chime and fragrant smoke wafts from the stalls at the nearby street food market.

Inside his pocket, Avon's hand clenches into a fist around a rusty iron nail, tight enough that it scrapes him, digs into the flesh of his palm until it breaks skin.

Avon draws away from the rain and walks back inside.

Circular Universe

An Excerpt from the Sequel to *The Membranes*

by Ta-wei Chi, translated by Ariel Chu

TRUE, MITSUKO HAD REPEATEDLY told her husband that she didn't want to see other people in her dreams. However, this hadn't meant that she wasn't willing to see *herself* in her dreams—let alone two of herself.

Mitsuko saw her first self lingering in the south of Yangming Mountain, a tourist area where people enjoyed hot spring baths. Her second self, however, had trespassed onto the north side of Yangming Mountain, a volcanic area that spewed sulfurous steam.

Prior to her dream, her husband had given Mitsuko a new product that had just been developed at the Lab: a smart eye mask with automatic massage and hot compress functions. The eye mask allowed her to relax, to fall into an even deeper sleep . . .

Mitsuko was probably dreaming of volcanoes because these days, her hands itched to transform a flat landscape into one three-dimensional mountain after another.

So why was she dreaming of a hot spring? The companion who'd bathed in the hot springs with her at Yangming Mountain so long ago—who was she? Who'd been the woman next to her by the pool, sharing mullet roe slices with her, weaving dreams with her?

It was Eun-jung.

Mitsuko, who'd been born in Nagasaki, and Eun-jung, who was from Busan, had met at the Hsinchu Science Park years ago. They'd come to Taiwan not for its world-famous pearl milk tea and soup dumplings, but for job opportunities and a vision of happiness. The Taiwan Semiconductor Manufacturing Company, headquartered in Hsinchu, had been recruiting talent from all over the world. Moreover, gay marriage had already been legalized in Taiwan, and was slowly becoming available to international couples as well.

Whenever they were free, the two had gone to Taipei to enjoy the Yangming Mountain hot springs. In a bathhouse made of cypress, they'd enthusiastically discussed the name of their future child, rushing into the debate before even deciding which one of them would become pregnant. They'd known one thing for sure, though—they wanted their own child not through the union of a male and a female, but through artificial reproduction.

Eun-jung had suggested that the child be named Kaguya. She'd remembered a Japanese folktale in which a girl was not born to her parents, but was found inside a bamboo stalk. This girl was called Princess Kaguya. Moreover, the name "Kaguya," which connoted "a shining night," could correspond with the name "Mitsuko," which implied a "full moon."

Though Mitsuko had inwardly been grateful for Eun-jung's sentimentality, her mouth had remained hard. She'd teased that because Eun-jung had been spoiled like a princess growing up, even the child's name she came up with was overly indulgent.

Then Eun-jung had turned it over to Mitsuko. She should also propose a name, right?

Mitsuko had noted that the child might not necessarily be a girl, so she'd suggested the name "Taro."

Eun-jung had frowned upon hearing this, feeling that the name was too commonplace. "Don't discount the name 'Taro,'" Mitsuko had said. According to another folktale, there had once lived a boy who'd been found inside of a peach, or "momo." He'd become known as Taro of the Peach—Momotaro.

Eun-jung had rolled her eyes, but had eventually arrived at a compromise with Mitsuko. If Mitsuko were to carry a child—and it turned out to be a boy—he would be called "Taro." If the child was a girl, she would be called "Momo."

The two Mitsukos in the dream were clones of the real Mitsuko, of course. Like her, they both wore high-prescription glasses. But Mitsuko soon discovered that they were quite different from her: they had sharp chins, thin waists. Compared to these young girls, the real Mitsuko was nearing the end of her life.

Mitsuko awoke from her strange dream. But she didn't forget her routine. Blinking hastily, she opened a virtual notepad from the corner of her eye. *While you still remember the dream, write down some prompts.*

#mulletroe #cypress #bathhouse #sulfur

When it came to restoring photos, these precious prompts could come in handy.

In a few days, Mitsuko's son would return home from the Lab. After spending the night at home, he would leave the recesses of their underwater trench to set off on the Ark. The Ark would depart from the Kuroshio Colony, sail upwards, and deliver her child to the sea's surface.

Mitsuko's family lived in a spherical submarine, which—like the Lobster— was independent of the Kuroshio Colony, but still within its sphere of influence. Her eldest son was named Taotao— "Tsunami"—because his parents had hoped that he could thrive among the ocean waves and speak as powerfully as the currents ran. Their youngest son, however, was not biologically theirs. He was a Health Manager cyborg the parents had specially ordered for Taotao, nicknamed Buddy.

Taotao had already reached the age of a college student. Though tall and strong, he was still a little boy at heart, preferring to sleep with a teddy bear in his arms. Buddy, Taotao's ever-present companion, had taken advantage of this to become Taotao's teddy bear substitute. Lying on the same bed, the two of them were like overlaid spoons, peaceful and quiet—a scene from a rose-tinted film about teenage love.

The spherical submarine and the Lobster had both been gifts from e-Marx to Professor Kong. e-Marx had invested heavily in the reopening of the surface biospheres, so naturally, he hadn't wanted to let go of Kong, a renowned biosphere scholar. (This e-Marx was none other than the undersea madman of this century, Elon Marx. e-Marx engaged in all kinds of business and had even entered the political arena. His e-Marketism campaign slogan had been "Make Haste, End Waste!")

The laboratory e-Marx had provided for Kong was big enough for a hundred people to live and work in. It was commonly known as the Lobster, since its full name was the Laboratory of Biosphere Sustainability, Testing, and Regulation. Though the Lab's acronym was LOBSTAR, its name was often mistakenly written as LOBSTER. e-Marx hoped that the laboratory could conduct research on the biospheres' sustainability, test the feasibility of biosphere operation on the surface, and control biosphere carbon emissions.

During the time of the Great Migration, there had been a massive exodus from the surface of the earth to the bottom of the sea—not just because the hole in the ozone layer had expanded, but also because humans had failed to conserve energy and reduce carbon emissions. After the Great Migration, humanity lived peacefully at the bottom of the ocean, but discovered that life under the sea was not sustainable. Though humans were protected from the excessive sunlight on the earth's surface, they were unable to escape the doubled carbon emissions below. If the bottom of the sea were ultimately uninhabitable, where could humanity possibly go next?

The humans living at the bottom of the sea then dreamt of another Great Migration, one in which they could escape from under the sea to the surface of the earth. In the early days of the Second Great Migration, only desperate outlaws had dared venture to the mainland. However, after e-Marx was elected as the leader of the colony, the Ark sailing from the bottom of the sea to the shore became crammed full of passengers. Shortly after the election, e-Marx had announced the "Ninety-Nine Deadline," mandating that colonists "graduate" before the age of ninety-nine. "Graduation," of course, was a euphemism for ending one's life. Once the population decreased, undersea power consumption would naturally decrease as well, and the target for carbon reduction would be just around the corner. The Ninety-Nine Deadline's new stipulations shocked everybody, but the wealthy didn't care. They simply immigrated to the surface, where laws were relaxed— allowing them to live past a hundred years old.

So Kong and Mitsuko decided to live out the rest of their lives underwater, accepting their fates under the Ninety-Nine Deadline. But they planned to send their sons to the surface, hoping that they could carry out covert operations in their stead.

The Second Great Migration had also brought about a new wave of business opportunities. The earth's surface became a battleground for the construction industry. Mitsuko's customers knew the value of her handcrafted holograms, believing that developers could use them as blueprints to reconstruct long-destroyed surface locales. Even the developer of a biosphere as far away as Kinshasa was inquiring about Mitsuko's rates. Kinshasa was the former capital of the Democratic Republic of the Congo, which had once been a country where rare minerals had been mined. For this reason alone, the Kinshasa Biosphere was in a good position to attract Chinese investors.

At the bottom of the sea, every colony was independent and unaffiliated with each other. The territories of these underwater colonies didn't correspond with the national borders drawn on the surface of the earth, since the underwater territories were divided according to regional ocean currents. The Kuroshio Current flowed through the surface territories of South Korea, Taiwan, Hong Kong, and the east coast of China, among other places, so immigrants from these countries had largely chosen to settle in the submerged city directly below it. The Guinea Current ran off the coast of Nigeria and the Congo, so the Kinshasa Biosphere on the surface had a close relationship to the underwater Guinea Colony.

Mitsuko informed Kong about the invitation from the Congo. What a joy to have money coming in from far away.

"Kinshasa, huh?" Kong said to Mitsuko. The distance between the Congo and East Asia might not be as outrageous as Mitsuko thought. Kong said that the Lobster was developing a revolving door called "Open Sesame." This would allow residents of the Hangzhou Biosphere to push a revolving door and tumble into the Kinshasa Biosphere, then push the revolving door again in Kinshasa and—*whoosh!*—return to Hangzhou.

"You idiot. Don't leak trade secrets to me."

"Mitsuko, do you know about the Möbius strip? Tear a piece of white paper into long strips and—"

"Earth to stupid, Professor Sunyata! You actually want to teach me how to make a Möbius strip? Every children's encyclopedia has instructions. The inside is the outside; the outside is the inside."

Mitsuko knew in her bones that she didn't have much time left, so she wanted to focus exclusively on restoring her beloved Taipei Biosphere. She tried her best to decline solicitations from other biospheres. Her excuse was that her eyesight had severely deteriorated, forcing her to rest. Some insensitive people had asked her exactly what had gone wrong with her health, so she'd listed her conditions off for them: extreme nearsightedness, keratitis, macular degeneration, cataracts. Some people had refused to let Mitsuko off the hook even then, recommending that she consider various eye surgeries. After all, these surgeries were as easy as lifting a finger.

But anyone who'd known Mitsuko for long enough would know that she hated surgical interventions. Mitsuko's own child, Momo, had been caught in a life-or-death situation after undergoing a series of surgeries. What had happened to Momo had once been a hot topic on online forums, and Mitsuko—the mother—had been attacked by internet strangers. Her reputation severely damaged, she'd withdrawn from public life.

Where was Momo now? People guessed that eighty percent of her had "transitioned."

The transitional centers had once captured people's imaginations. They'd mistakenly thought that the transitional centers'

Chinese name, "Zhuan Yun Yuan," referred to a phrase commonly understood in Taiwan to mean "reversing fate and striving for good luck." But someone had revealed the secret of the transitional centers on an online forum: allegedly, the environment inside the centers was like a pot of tea eggs. In the past, convenience stores across Taiwan would display pots of hard-boiled eggs soaking in an inky black tea marinade. Transitional center residents lived alone, curling up into balls, as though living inside eggs filled to the brim with nutrient solution.

Transitional centers could indeed help people "strive for good luck," but good luck was only reserved for the patient ones. Transitional centers were a kind of long-term care institution. They were places where people waited to change their "means of transportation" before heading to their next stop.

Kong had also once lived in a transitional center. In fact, he'd lived in two transitional centers under the name of "Professor Sunyata." Sunyata had climbed head and shoulders above everyone else in the first half of his life, but had plummeted into the abyss in the second half. Earlier in his life, the ozone hole crisis had been out of control. News outlets from all over the world had rushed to interview global scholars and experts on whether humanity should stay on the surface or migrate underwater. Finally, the media approached Dr. Sunyata. Under the spotlight, Professor Sunyata shared the insight he'd gained from his lifelong research: for a biosphere to exist, it had to be in a state of internal and external balance, maintaining a self-sufficient equilibrium.

Halfway through the live broadcast, though, he couldn't help but choke up. He found himself bringing up how he'd once been nine months pregnant. Yes, he'd once been a mother who'd given birth to a special child, Champ. Champ was a smart but aloof kid, one who refused to accept any fixed gender identity—neither "he" nor "she." As the child's mother and father simultaneously, Sunyata also wanted Champ to enjoy their own balanced, self-sufficient, and undisturbed ecosystem.

Before the live broadcast was even finished, the once indifferent listeners broke into applause, frantically reposting Sunyata's interview video on social media.

Sunyata became an international media darling. When a famous magazine selected Sunyata as "Person of the Year," Sunyata was in the transitional center attached to Mumbai's Taj Mahal Palace Hotel, sipping sesame oil chicken soup and waiting for his surgical wounds to heal. Originally an excellent cricket player, he'd given up the sport and switched to baseball in order to play with Champ. And these days, he was hitting one home run after another: he'd carved out a break from his packed calendar, checked into the hospital for the final step in his gender affirmation surgery, and then taken a helicopter straight from the hospital to the most advanced transitional center in all of India, waiting to restart his life.

In the Person of the Year cover photo (which had once made him extremely proud, but ultimately filled him with deep regret), there were two people: him and Champ, whose age and gender were impossible to distinguish. Posing in a studio full of AI lenses, Daddy Sunyata wore a suit with widened shoulder pads, reviewing papers while Champ poked their giggling face out from under his desk. The desk was made of glass and shaped like an eggshell split in half. The professor leaned against the top half of the glass eggshell, while Champ emerged from the bottom half of the eggshell, as if newly hatched. This had been Professor Sunyata's first public-facing media photo in men's clothing. Above the cover photo, a printed headline read: "How should we be fathers now?" In an exclusive interview for the cover story, Dr. Sunyata had confessed his feelings about changing from a mother to a father. The reporter had asked whether the professor's partner had supported his transition. Sunyata had patted his chest and said: "My husband has always supported me."

The second time Dr. Sunyata had checked into a transitional center, it was after he'd been taken out of the emergency room of an underwater hospital, half-dreaming, half-awake. The immigrants fleeing to the deep sea had all succumbed to natural and manmade disasters over the course of their escape. After Sunyata had sunk to the bottom of the sea, he'd immediately been checked into an overcrowded hospital emergency room, where he'd remained in a coma. It wasn't until he was sent to the Unending Destiny Transitional Center that he slowly woke up, then learned one cruel fact after another: during the migration, he'd lost both his husband and Champ, and had also broken his spine. In Unending Destiny, Sunyata truly seemed like one of many eggs stewing in a pot of marinade, passively accepting the nutrient solutions injected into his eggshell. The doctor ordered that he undergo rehabilitation and practice operating a wheelchair, but he was apathetic. He didn't care at all.

Even when Dr. Sunyata grew tired of the smell of eggshell nutrient solution, he still refused to use a wheelchair or step outside of Unending Destiny. In an effort to rouse his appetite, Sunyata began to rely upon food delivery services. One day, after dropping off Sunyata's order of medicinal chicken soup, the courier didn't leave immediately. The courier was a hijra named Draupadi.

Draupadi said: Professor Sunyata, you are an inspiration to us hijras. We all admire you. Please come with me.

It turned out that Draupadi had intentionally taken a detour to accept the order because she'd idolized Sunyata for a long time. She had a great number of sisters who worked as nurses at various transitional centers; while manicuring their nails, they'd whispered and gossiped about whether the handsome resident who refused to rehabilitate himself was the transgender doctor who'd frequently appeared on TV.

Sunyata couldn't refuse Draupadi's invitation. He sat in his wheelchair while she pushed him into the hijras' secret community. As he rolled in, he was met by the sight of charming sisters lining up to welcome him, sprinkling sequins on his head—*sparkle, sparkle!* They weren't shy about vulgar chitchat around distinguished guests, exposing Draupadi's promiscuous reputation: if she wasn't overly dressed, wrapped in layers of colorful, gauzy robes, she wore nothing at all. Among these hijras, there was no shortage of caregivers employed by people with disabilities, and they were happy to teach Sunyata how to operate various kinds of wheelchairs. After Sunyata finally settled down in the Indian Ocean Gyre Colony, he drove his wheelchair to and from various energy-saving and carbon-reduction research symposiums, easily winning the favor of the colony's government. Senior officials valued Sunyata's academic aura, appointing him as the chairman of the Biosphere Advisory Group.

But the higher one climbs, the harder he falls. Some people envied how Sunyata was living it up at the bottom of the ocean, and slander about him appeared frequently on internet forums. The straw that broke the camel's back was an image that garnered widespread ridicule among netizens. The image featured the Person of the Year magazine cover that had once made Sunyata ecstatically proud—but it had been maliciously altered. The Professor Sunyata in the photo was still sitting at the glass desk in the shape of a halved eggshell. However, the child emerging from the bottom half of the eggshell was not Champ, but a three-year-old Syrian refugee boy who'd died on a beach in Turkey in the 2010s. This image kept getting altered and reshared online;

eventually, Sunyata was no longer a male professor in a suit, but a bikini-wearing Barbie.

Sunyata was so enraged that he slammed his wheelchair into the wall, deciding to give up the wealth and glory he'd attained in the Indian Ocean colony.

Kong and Mitsuko's marriage was both parties' second marriage. Back then, Kong and Mitsuko had just been casual acquaintances who weren't particularly familiar with each other. Kong—whose original name was Sunyata—had just immigrated from the Indian Ocean Colony to the Kuroshio Colony. The elites of Kuroshio had hosted banquets to welcome "Master Sunyata," but Sunyata had declined all their invitations. He only agreed to drink tea privately with Curator Nishikawa. Mitsuko Nishikawa was the founder of the legendary Nishikawa Library and had also attended numerous ecological symposiums in the neighboring colony.

Inside the tea house, Curator Nishikawa stroked her big belly, ordering a pot of Alishan oolong tea. Before the high-quality tea even arrived at the table, she abruptly suggested to Sunyata: why not consider taking a Chinese name? She said that although "Sunyata" was an elegant name, it was a bit alienating to the residents of Kuroshio. If the professor were willing to integrate into the Kuroshio cultural sphere—where Chinese characters were popular—then he might as well consider translating the name "Sunyata" into the Chinese character "Kong," meaning emptiness. *Emptiness is form, form is emptiness.*

The oolong tea was served. Curator Nishikawa made another, bolder proposition while pouring the tea: she suggested that the two of them get married, since they both needed the protection of the system. No matter how inclusive and openminded undersea civilization was, Professor Sunyata and Curator Nishikawa were deviants in the eyes of ordinary people and could become scapegoats at any time. Mitsuko had decided to enter "normal society" in order to protect herself. She'd searched underwater for ages and felt that Kong—who had also lost everything—was the best candidate to start a family with her. If they were to form a "normal" household of one man and one woman, Mitsuko would have a better chance of winning high-quality housing within the colony. She would also feel more confident about giving birth to Taotao, who was currently in her big belly.

Mitsuko had gone out to tea with a big belly, but this belly hadn't actually been attached to Mitsuko—rather, it stood next to her. This kind of surrogate pregnancy cyborg was commonly known as "Big Belly." Mitsuko's Big Belly had a simple egg shape, sufficient to house a nine-month-old fetus.

By this time, Kong had already accepted Mitsuko's proposal, but Mitsuko couldn't resist pouring her heart and soul out to him.

A while ago, Mitsuko and Eun-jung had each become pregnant, giving birth to their children: Kaguya and Momo. But Kaguya died young, and Momo was later forced to undergo extensive surgeries. Mitsuko and Eun-jung had intentionally undergone genetic testing before their pregnancies—getting their artificial reproduction procedures customized to their test results—but their two children still endured endless suffering after birth. Mitsuko and Eun-jung sued the genetic testing center, then turned on each other. As usual, Mitsuko accused Eun-jung of being a "princess;" in the end, Eun-jung was so enraged that she packed her bags and left. So Mitsuko lost Kaguya, Momo, and Eun-jung one after another, leaving her with nothing. Unwilling to accept this, she decided to bring another child into the world: Taotao.

After Kong and Mitsuko's low-profile wedding, Mitsuko moved into the spherical submarine, where the Big Belly cyborg gave birth to Taotao. Their makeshift family finally settled down under the sea, but they spent less time together than apart. When Taotao grew up, Mitsuko insisted that he live in a dormitory in the Lobster, hoping that the Lab's amenities could keep her son healthy and strong. Even then, Kong knew that Mitsuko was anxious by nature. She didn't want outsiders to see that Taotao was Kong and Mitsuko's child, lest they question the couple for unethically using public resources on their son.

More years passed. It wasn't until Kong recognized enough Chinese characters that he realized why Mitsuko had suggested this name for him. It was a simple word: "empty." It complemented the character "full" in Mitsuko's Chinese name. Empty and full were not opposite, but complementary. Yin and yang, male and female, were also not opposite, but complementary. So Kong, who had once been a woman, could now be a man. Mitsuko, who had once been married to the woman named Eun-jung, could now be married to the man named Kong. Similarly, high and low were not opposite, but complementary. So the rich and powerful Kong and the poor, common hijras could work together.

Draupadi gathered a group of sisters who happily immigrated to the colony. They took turns providing untraceable taxi services for Kong's household, ensuring that nobody ran the risk of being surveilled.

The Kuroshio Colony also boasted a large group of Adjus, who were just as gender-expansive—and skilled at song and dance—as the hijra were. The Adju community generously accepted the hijra immigrants, and the power of their sisterhood multiplied and multiplied.

Mitsuko made good use of her green thumb to cultivate a private vegetable garden. She plucked a few zucchinis here, harvested a few basil leaves there, then combined these vegetables into her own unique salad. Whenever Mitsuko logged into the Nishikawa Library, it was also like entering a private vegetable garden: taking a little from over here, then a little from over there. Only in the Library, she was downloading the encyclopedic knowledge she'd backed up for her entire life, then assembling these fragments of knowledge into batch after batch of 2D pictures. Mitsuko would then send those pictures through a dimensional upscaling machine, which looked like a twentieth-century microwave. This machine could make two-dimensional images swell and bubble into holograms. This wasn't where Mitsuko's craftsmanship ended, but where it began: like taking heated-up frozen food from a microwave, Mitsuko would remove the three-dimensional holographic photo from the dimensional upscaling machine. Then she would manually adjust the details of the photo, one after another.

Kong asked Mitsuko about her experience using her fully automatic eye masks. Mitsuko admitted that she loved and hated them at the same time. She loved that after she put on an eye mask, her vision would improve greatly—the resolution of the scenery in her eyes would rise from 100 percent to 200 percent, then jump to 800 percent. But she hated that there were too many "treasures" in her dreams; she couldn't possibly collect them all. What's more, after she woke from her dreams, there were always countless holograms waiting for Mitsuko to optimize by hand.

After hearing all this, the first thing Kong did was roll his wheelchair into the kitchen to brew a pot of Alishan oolong tea. Then he rolled the tea over to Mitsuko's bedside.

"Mitsuko, in what ways are you and I similar?"

Kong didn't just want to make small talk. Mitsuko knew that every time a pot of good tea appeared between them, it was time for a showdown.

"You and I both 'fell from the top of the mountain to the bottom of the valley,' once upon a time. But you and I also both want to reconstruct the Anthropocene. Kong, exactly what do you want to ask me here?"

"So, you and I—in which ways do we differ?"

"Just say whatever it is you want to say."

"Mitsuko, look. You and I are very lonely. Not only that, but based on what I've gleaned from other sources . . . so is Momo."

Momo no longer lived among them, of course. Momo's brain had been the only organ still salvageable after years of fruitless surgeries. Now that brain was locked in the body of a laboring cyborg, repairing war machines in a factory on the surface. But Momo's brain had concocted an entirely different idea of the situation. Instead of doing factory work, Momo saw herself as a "dermal care technician" attending to her "clients'" skin.

It was difficult for Kong to bring up Momo in front of Mitsuko. But now he had to.

Kong continued: "Nishikawa Library, and Momo's dermal care salon—both are one-person studios. I'm withdrawn by nature too, but I lead a hundred-person team on the Lobster, and I also need to appease e-Marx. You and Momo don't have to compromise with others, but I make my living through compromise."

Mitsuko couldn't deny this.

"How is it possible for you to singlehandedly restore the tens of thousands—or even millions—of holograms needed for the

Taipei Biosphere?" Kong said. "It's feasible for Momo to receive one dermal care VIP per day. But how many holograms can *you* process in a day, doing slow, meticulous work on your own? There are millions of other photos waiting for you to handle."

"Go on."

"Momo doesn't require assistance at the salon, but the Nishikawa Library needs a lot of helpers. A hundred. A thousand. Even ten thousand wouldn't be too many."

Mitsuko gave in. At her age, there was nothing left to protest.

Kong told Mitsuko that from this point on, the Lobster would help her recruit assistants. At first, there would only be around three to five helpers. If Mitsuko ended up being satisfied with them, the Lobster would recruit even more assistants and send them into Mitsuko's dreams.

"I don't want to see other people in my dreams."

"Fine, dear. You won't see *other* people," Kong said in an effort to console her. "But you should know: your dreams won't just be dreams anymore, but a circular universe. A dream that can only be enjoyed by one person is called a dream. A dream open to others is known as a circular universe."

"You mean, like a metaverse?" Mitsuko frowned. "That thing's still around?"

"Not the metaverse. I'm talking about a universe reminiscent of a circular shape. It's an exclusive product from the Lab," Kong said with a grin. "The circular universe provides 'a well-rounded feeling of mellowness, completeness, and smoothness'—it's an optimized version of the metaverse."

"That Lab of yours is always trying to sell something."

"Circular universes aren't for sale. In fact, a circular universe is a miniature model of a biosphere. Since e-Marx is peddling a bunch of biospheres located on the surface of the earth, he wants to develop biosphere models for investors to refer to. These investors can't just go to the earth's surface whenever they want to tour a biosphere's real conditions. So they play around in our circular universe models first."

"That's all well and good. But *you*"—Mitsuko emphasized—"are absolutely *not* allowed to enter my dreams."

"I wouldn't dare cross you, missus." Kong smiled.

In her dreams, she started to encounter tens, hundreds, then thousands of Mitsukos all over Yangming Mountain. *Mountains beyond mountains; people beyond people.* These doppelgängers were all between the ages of twenty and thirty—in the bloom of youth. This platoon of women captured thousands of scenic details on Yangming Mountain's surface. After they nailed Yangming Mountain, they moved to Shilin Night Market at the base of the mountain, eating their way through all the stalls.

With all the help, Mitsuko found her stress levels and working hours greatly reduced. Likewise, the thousands of Mitsukos were not just hard at work in the circular universe—they also found time to chat, practice yoga, and hold belly dance competitions. Mitsuko didn't feel the need to interrogate her doppelgängers, but she could guess what these women's real identities were outside of the circular universe. If they weren't hijras, then they were Adjus.

In just a few days, the collection of photos in the Nishikawa Library doubled, then quadrupled. The army of Mitsukos entered and exited the circular universe in a steady stream, a myriad of dimensional upscaling machines in the Lobster whirring simultaneously. One by one, the mass-produced holograms were dispensed into the Nishikawa Library's cloud storage.

It was about time to retire.

The day before Taotao and Buddy were scheduled to return to the spherical submarine from the Lobster, Mitsuko found herself patrolling the circular universe of her dream once more. She strolled from Yangming Mountain to Shilin Night Market, then took the metro from there.

The MRT cars were crammed with young Mitsukos, each wearing the newest model of massager eye masks instead of prescription glasses. The senior Mitsuko looked for an empty seat, considering which stop to disembark at. Then she saw the flash of a face in the carriage. An exceptional face. A face that wasn't Mitsuko's.

It was the first time Mitsuko had ever seen another person in her dream.

Without another thought, she headed in the direction of the other woman, eager to ask questions.

Upon Mitsuko's approach, the other woman startled and ran, probably thinking that Mitsuko was going to prosecute her for some crime.

Mitsuko saw that the other party was fleeing, so she resorted to the crudest, most direct action: she blinked hard, using her gaze to pin a computer cursor on the escaping woman. Try as she might, the exceptional woman could no longer move.

"Eun-jung, long time no see." Mitsuko neared the woman, taking a deep breath.

This Eun-jung, who was somewhere between twenty and thirty years old, answered meekly: "Are you a Mitsuko who got old?"

Who got old? Mitsuko didn't have the strength to mind Eun-jung's rudeness—after all, the other woman was right. "Why did you run away when you saw me?"

"Everyone said that you didn't want to see 'other people.' So everyone else turned into you. But I can't transform myself, so the only thing I can do is hide. Make sure you don't see me."

Mitsuko wanted to console the frightened Eun-jung, so she changed the subject.

"Eun-jung, why are you here?"

As soon as the words left her mouth, Mitsuko realized that her sentence sounded more like an accusation. It was as if she were blaming Eun-jung for invading her world.

She tried again: "Eun-jung, where are you taking the MRT to?"

"I was originally going to tour a confinement center." Eun-jung was still in shock. "I'd planned to meet up with Mitsuko there. A bunch of confinement centers have open houses today."

Mitsuko was taken aback, unable to tell whether or not Eun-jung was pregnant. Had they lived in a confinement center back then?

"You'd better get going then," Mitsuko said.

"Sure—" Eun-jung, realizing that she'd been pardoned, prepared to make her escape. Then she looked up again, her face bewildered. "When you rushed towards me, I panicked. I missed my stop."

"I'm very sorry." Mitsuko rested her forehead in her hand. "So where are we now?"

"We're already straddling the boundary of your circular universe. We're about to fall out." Eun-jung put her palms together. "I'm going to be late. Excuse me, I'm going to find the bus going back."

"Let's talk about this over dinner some other day." Mitsuko bowed her head in apology. "You should hurry up and find Mitsuko."

"Thank you." Eun-jung made to leave, then turned to Mitsuko again. "That's right, Mitsuko—"

"What's up?"

"Since you're so old and have lived a whole lifetime, can you tell me just a little bit about the future? Kaguya and Taro—or Momo—are they cute?" Eun-jung smiled shyly.

Mitsuko's heart constricted. "Don't worry about that. You'll see them both very soon."

Eun-jung tightened her fists, then left the car in small, bouncing strides.

Mitsuko crumpled onto the floor, leaning against the membrane boundary of her circular universe. There was no movement left in her; she had no strength. But her vision was still good enough. She was able to see that outside her exclusive circular universe, there existed yet another sphere. If the Möbius strip of the Open Sesame revolving door could stitch Hangzhou and Kinshasa together, whose circular universe was right next door to hers?

She peered closely through the membrane, her vision's resolution adjusting from 100 percent to 200 percent. She finally recognized some figures in the sphere outside hers: two men and a child playing a game she didn't recognize. A shower of gold sequins scattered before her vision—*sparkle, sparkle*. Only after Mitsuko increased her resolution to 800 percent did her line of sight penetrate through the gaps in the flying sequins, targeting the back of one of the men—and allowing her to recognize who he was.

She couldn't help but shout in the direction of the man's back, though she wasn't even sure if sound could penetrate the barrier between membranes.

"Professor Sunyata!"

The man in the other sphere swiveled his head around slowly, facing Mitsuko. He took his baseball cap off to pay his respects, revealing a full head of black hair. The two fathers had been playing *baseball* with their child. That was Kong, no doubt about it. Only it was Kong from the first half of his life, not her husband with buzzed white hair.

The child sprinted off into the distance, then turned back screaming and jumping, urging his lagging father to keep up. So Kong had no choice but to nod goodbye at Mitsuko through the thin membrane between their spheres, taking long strides after his husband and child.

Then he disappeared from Mitsuko's sight altogether.

Blueprint for the Destruction of Solitude

by Paul Evanby

THE RAIN IS WET again. Has been for weeks. I like the feeling of moisture on my skin, but water from heaven is not going to win this war. At least, that's what they tell me. They also tell me that my contact tonight is waiting in a club called *Mansoon Climax*.

So I go find him under spray-painted concrete in Rotterdam's former harbor district, and I betray him with a kiss.

In the converted warehouse on the south bank, in the pneumatic heart of the music, his tongue tastes of knowledge, acid and sharp. Strobe lights turn the fog of vaporized chemhancers around us into swirling contours. The beat is last month's, but it helps us synchronize on some deep mammalian level of our protocol stack.

His skin tastes of salt and of whatever the chemhancers have done to the residual metals in his sweat; the air alone here holds enough organic compounds for life to emerge spontaneously. His breath tastes of myriad flowering probabilities. Data has all flavors, and none of them are simple. If I get paid, I get paid for the most elaborate ones—most likely, the fatally toxic ones. There'll be no one to mourn me. Like him, I'm just a messenger.

I wonder what his cum will taste of.

Bodies move around us, skin glistening, to the bass and the beat and the black lights reflected from the mirrors and the industrial scaffolding serving as the bar. Around me the web of hyphae stretches invisibly from face to face, from nose to ear, from naked eye to bare torso, from mouth to cock. The connections are there, for me, but purely precautionary for now. I hope that's what they will remain.

Looking into his eyes is easier than I expected. Again I taste his tongue. Sweetness now, an edge of possibility and anticipation. Excitement winds a coiled spring in my stomach. When he shouts into my ear I do not understand his words, but the sound of his voice vibrates through my chest and sets my groin throbbing. Lips touching again, our tongues trifurcate and interface, initiating communication. Papillae merge. Ion channels gate into conduction. Synapses couple and start transmitting. And finally, we talk.

Our words are forbidden. We speak of the loneliness and the fear we experience every day when we move through the city streets. Of the constant need to maintain the façade, to fit in, to be perceived as conforming. Of the corrosive certainty that a single mistake is enough to condemn us. His speech patterns suggest North Sea roots and the polders of Rotterdam's sprawling Doggerland Periphery, but I can't pinpoint the exact location—his autotune must be military grade. Another reminder of how risky even this mode of conversation can be.

His payload is encrypted. Which means more work for me, but a higher return on investment. Grinding my crotch against his, I open a wideband channel, and soon I savour the data flowing through. Illegal, he says. Contraband. In violation of several international treaties. But also, he assures me, revolutionary. Carbon geoengineering on a scale not seen before. *Bring the dry rain*, he says. I recognize his key phrase.

Which is when I realize he's a setup. His autotune is military grade because he himself is. Nothing shifts as quickly and treacherously as key idiom, though.

I don't waste time feeling betrayed. I'm used to it. The enemy has cloud-seeding bees in the sky overhead tonight, so the risk is too great. The body they will find later, in the corner of a cage underneath one of the darkrooms, will be devoid of identifying qualities.

This leaves the problem of the encrypted payload. His key phrase is predictably useless. The taste and composition of his semen, which I make sure to sample before dispatching him, does not yield any additional clues. I'm on my own. I apply the standard key detection routines, inject some highly advanced factorization algorithms, deploy a number of friendly agent intelligences, some of them dangerously close to what I assume to be the source of the data, but the encryption does not yield. It confirms my suspicion that it was generated by some chaos-complete class of bioware. Which means I need bioware to counter it.

Emerging from the darkroom, I see that the crowd in the *Mansoon* has grown. I look around. The more I look, the more the web of hyphae, silvery strands crisscrossing between the sweating bodies, shimmers into existence. Invisible to all but me, the hyphae are like sparks drawn along lines of attraction, blue-lit skin to red-lit skin, violet to white, black to green, throbbing to synthesized drum patterns that I feel and hear but can never dance to.

Loneliness is a friend that knows me too well. It sidles up when it perceives I'm defenseless, then expects to be welcomed. The faces around me are laughing, talking, singing. Drunk, drugged, entranced. All are in the game, warm or cool as the rules require. I watch and I analyze, but I'm not part of that game. Loneliness clouds the pool at the bottom of my rib cage, dark, cold, and always there.

Maybe it is loneliness that notices me noticing the big guy staring at me from across the room. He is not giving me the casual glance, the indifference feigned or otherwise, nor the lingering look of physical desire. His gaze is piercing, demanding—an intense scrutiny that carries even across the strobe lights and the white smoke and the flashes of darkness. In this place, where nudity is just another way of dressing, he makes me feel truly naked.

But I can't afford to be distracted. I need all my loneliness for the task at hand.

I move among the shifting bodies, insinuating myself between the invisible connections. I feel and follow the strands, observe where they converge and spread out, always careful not to connect myself.

Then finally I reach out, I touch the threads, and I join.

Everywhere I touch, the strands thicken into mycelial cords. In branching chain reactions, the cords spread along the hyphae network. Quivering webs appear white and iridescent, blooming through and folding among the moving bodies, a shroud billowing through the crowd, slowing down the dance. Faces around me light up in surprise—rapturous, euphoric, unified in ecstasy, as my own feelings of isolation become more crushing with every new link established.

I fire off the priming algorithms into the heart of the network. As I watch the nodal engine boot and unfold, harvesting processing power from all the brains connected through the mycelium, I prepare to upload the encrypted data.

The human hyperbrain makes short work of the bioware, and after only a few minutes the encryption is stripped. *Bring the dry rain.* I expect operational data to come flooding in: locations, movements, capacities, tactical overviews, deployment schedules, carefully tailored to lead into a precisely timed trap.

Instead, a Jacob's ladder of painstakingly rendered construction diagrams unrolls before me, image after image of beautifully designed mechanical parts. I stare and try to determine what all this is supposed to build. Is there a purpose? Why was this sent to me? If these are weapons in the weather wars, they are of a kind I have never seen before.

For a moment I wonder if killing the messenger was the right thing to do. Only the briefest lapse, but it's the seed of a doubt I can't dislodge. I feel more lonely than ever when I realize that maybe, maybe we should have done this together after all. Of course he too had learned to weaponize his solitude. I call myself a mercenary: the only strings that bind me are the terms of the contract and the strands of the mycelium. So did he, no doubt. To retain our sanity we don't ask questions. But what if . . . ?

I recognize that I am in danger of compromising my security. I have expended a lot of energy building the computational web;

with my depleted reserves I am more vulnerable than ever. My emotional state is alarmingly volatile.

Then the big guy moves in. I don't know how he escaped the mycelium, but here he is now, in front of me. His grin suggests he's perfectly aware what I am doing, and he knows how close I am to exhaustion. His hand at my elbow seems to imply that he's ready to support me.

The moment he touches me he shifts. He becomes slightly less tall, his cheekbones rise a notch, his eyelids tighten, his pecs widen and become dusted with a spray of curly hair, as he reads my sexual preferences off the way my skin reacts to his.

"You and I, mister, are both . . ." The harmonics in his deep voice are calibrated to reach my ears over the hammering beats. I can't help but admire the work that must have gone into him. No wonder he hasn't been caught in the web. I doubt there is anything organic inside him.

"Special," he finishes. "Let's celebrate."

With the computational web throbbing above the dance floor, he grabs my shoulders and pulls me close. Too tired to resist for now, I give in. My loneliness will remain intact anyway, I know: pleasure models like him are built for one thing only. I can afford a moment of rest.

His tongue tastes of male saliva with the tiniest, exquisitely realistic hints of fresh tobacco and dark rum. As he rubs against me I close my eyes and let him do his job. When I take his cock into my mouth, it swells and reshapes to accommodate me. Maybe too warm and yielding at first, it slowly cools to perfect firmness. His cybernetics are truly remarkable.

The cold is in my mouth before I realize it. I try to look up, to warn him, but his hands have frozen on the back of my head. I grope at them, trying to tear them loose, but I might as well be plucking at a pair of iron clamps. His arms feel like welded cables.

Special enzymes flood my mouth as I bite down, and my tongue trifurcates again. The defense reaction ripples through my body. My fingers on his hands release spores able to penetrate the thickest skin. I exhale convulsively, and my breath is poison.

But he has turned to steel in my mouth. His skin's elastomers are tougher than I imagined possible, and I'm not sure he is even breathing.

He starts to grow. The thing filling my mouth is extending downwards. I suppress my gag reflex, but I'm powerless to stop the assault. Only then do I experience the first wave of panic, rage, and incomprehension. Have I been targeted deliberately? Have I not been careful enough after all?

It does not matter. An android is choking me with his tool, and I need to survive. The mycelium continues undulating around us, even though the lights and the beat have receded into a sensory noise floor. I spend valuable energy wrapping more hyphae around him and weaving them into the web, thickening the mycelium into a cocoon. By trying to marshal the network against an intruder, I am in danger of undermining the strength of my solitude, but I'll worry about that later.

Pain explodes in my throat as hundreds of needles erupt from the shaft and pierce soft pharyngeal tissue. Before I am even able to block the nerve signals, powerful anaesthetics come flooding through the needles and reduce the pain to mild irritation. It numbs my emotional reaction to the outrageous intrusion, and allows me to observe its progress as a physician observes a metastasising tumor.

The shaft thins and elongates. It searches its way down my esophagus, branches out in my stomach, and sends more needles to pierce my inner organs. Fiber-thin scalpels start dissecting me from the inside out.

He is *searching*, I realize in a daze. Looking for whatever secrets he thinks I am hiding. Unlike his silicon, my DNA-based memory units cannot be accessed or addressed by simply plugging in, initiating a dump, or introducing a trojan. My data is stored in my cells, custom-fabricated acidic polynucleotide chains of information distributed throughout my entire body. And he is grinding up my insides to get to all of it.

With cold clarity, I consider triggering an auto-thanatic sequence, causing my cells to lyse and spill their contents, destabilizing and destroying the DNA he is looking for. I am already dead anyway.

But before I set off the sequence, I become aware of new signals entering through the mycelial cords binding me to the surrounding web. At first I have no interest in them. While I am sluggishly linking up the auto-destruct mechanism, though, glimpses leak through and resolve into a pattern. The uncounted fresh connections that formed while I tried to encapsulate the android have resulted in huge extra computing capacity, and the algorithms have continued churning and mining the data. I examine the results they now present me with, trying to ignore my slowly ongoing vivisection. And suddenly I know what the android is searching for. I understand his motive. It is the ultimate desire of life, even synthetic life, to multiply, to grow into the world. By whatever means available.

Now the needles are making their way up towards my brain stem. Time to leave.

★

My earliest memories reside in this body. Images, smells, emotions. The environmental defense research facility and its green-walled in-vitro clean rooms. The realization that being a myco-cyborg meant being *different*. The first time I was attacked by someone whose fear and hate radiated from their eyes so viscerally it was painful even before the blow itself landed.

It was never my goal to become a weapon, but life finds its own use for the living. In the climate wars, ideologies and technologies are pitted against each other. Having narrowly escaped a mass extinction event, humanity is now fighting over the best way to avoid another, with enemies and allies shifting as quickly as weather patterns around the world.

I call myself a mercenary because my loyalty is to humanity only—even if I'm one faction's thief and someone else's hitman. Knowing anything more about my clients just complicates things. Who the latest enemy is or what technology they use it's not my place to ask, but I know they are infesting the skies above the city, barring us from doing what needs to be done. Our current key idiom: *After us no deluge.*

Now, as the mycelium receives me, I see myself from a conglomeration of viewpoints: a bag of skin, chitin-reinforced cell structures, and blood—held up by a metallic fractal tree rooted in the loins of a pleasure bot. The life left in that mass is only part of what I am now, though I have had to sacrifice my solitude for it.

When he is done, he backs away, trying to shake off the hybrid meat thing he has analyzed to pulp. But the mycelium envelops him. He tears apart large chunks of it, but it will not let him go. Even though his penis has by now decreased to its normal size, my old body remains tied to his. Despite that, he plows on, pulling and shredding the opalescent strands until his back is against the wall. As soon as his hands touch the concrete, metal feelers erupt from his fingers, spreading along the wall and burrowing into the surface. He starts digging down, into the ground and the bowels of the city itself.

I furiously create more filaments to slow him, but they are like dreamy cobwebs to the razors and diamond drills at his fingertips, and eventually he manages to free himself completely. Even so, his energy expenditure must be enormous, and I calculate that he can't keep this up for very much longer.

But the city is an organism in itself. Straddling the river, Rotterdam's vessels run deep and broad, and all he has to do is tap into them to feed and grow strong again. I can tell the exact moment he touches a main district trunk line by the way his eyes light up and his body shudders in a transcendent orgasm. The speed of his expansion triples. He keeps extruding new limbs that immediately dig into the floor. I feel the ground and the walls tremble. My entire mycelium is shaking. There is nothing to stop him, so he will keep burrowing, extending himself through the city until even the city's energy supply is not enough to feed him. Long before that, the weakened support structure of this ancient warehouse will not be able to withstand the pressure, and the ceiling will collapse on top of me. In my current state, I do not know how much of me will survive. Cracks are already appearing in the walls.

So my scouts feel their way in, tendrils one cell thick, apical bodies guiding them rapidly up the fractures in the walls and down into the ground. Where the android machine's extensions are drilling down, meeting the hard surfaces of the city's infrastructure, their defense is weakest. The hyphae insinuate themselves between metal and concrete, and are crushed to their individual polymers and proteins. But some survive and enter the microscopic gaps between moving parts. Once inside, they start growing again.

When the scouts report back, my consciousness starts flowing through the new connections, into the android machine.

He is drunk with power. He slashes and burns his way through the city, leaving churning chaos in the gashes that delineate his path. At first he hardly notices my presence inside his shell. Then, when he does, he flounders, trying to divide his attention between attack and defense. I wrap myself around his cognitive nodes and whisper dirty talk at him. As his defenses weaken, I invade his mind.

What I see is abomination. He has stolen most of the data from my old body, and misinterpreted all of it. He has constructed models from the designs he did understand and bolted them together into little more than a glorified excavator.

I cut off access to his peripherals and take control of his motor functions. Immediately the tremors in the walls subside. Then I gather the original diagrams he has taken and sift through them. With the enhanced computing power now at my disposal, I finally see the master design.

The elegance almost overwhelms me. It would be easy to lose myself in contemplation of its endless, lacework intricacies. They are beautiful, a joy to look at, and also bittersweet. My pleasure is tainted by guilt and a sense of loss. *Together we could have brought the dry rain. After us no deluge.*

The murky legalities of being human but discorporate make the decision to renege on my contract much easier. As I build my new body, constructed from the remains of the android and everything he has destroyed, layered together according to the designs in what is now my new DNA, I feel a fresh sensation.

Long ago, in another war, a much older version of this town was destroyed. After that war, a statue stood here with arms raised in despair, its heart torn out, screaming at the sky, forever reminding the city of its loss. The river, back then still constrained by its embankments instead of allowed to run free, flowed past the statue like a symbol of transience.

Now, breaking through the ceiling and rising from the ruins, standing in the enemy rain, I raise my own arms to the sky. Gazing out over the city, the midnight streets below me, I feel awe and fear directed at me, hear the screams of panic. I look down at the building between my feet, and I know it will be a hard job making peace with this world if I am to become the symbol of harmony the blueprint demands. But it is a job I can do. My only regret is that I will have to do it alone.

I free the living bodies still trapped in the mycelium. Then I free myself.

With a few sweeps of my segmented top limbs, dozens of meters long and growing, I clear away a swathe of hostile seeding drones before puffing my spores into the night sky: a storm of self-propelled carbon capture condensation cores, ready to extract, scrub, and cascade to earth again. I spread my nets wide to collect the tiny dry pellets when they rain down—to be cleaned, recycled, and sent up once more.

In my mind I unfurl the next layer of the grand design. Suddenly, I taste it again. Knowledge, acid and sharp, salt on his skin, his breath a myriad of flowering probabilities. And sweetness. A voice that vibrates through my chest.

Unbelief. *But I killed you.*

He reaches out and gently unfolds yet another layer: the necessity of killing the messenger, in order to create the web that snared the intruder. The night alone holds enough possibilities for life to evolve spontaneously.

I am part of your blueprint, he says. *And there are others. You will not have to do it alone. Together, we will avert the deluge. We will make peace with this world.*

When he shows me the design again, I feel my solitude draining away. I want him to take me with him.

I will, he says, and he reveals the next layer.

The Garden of Collective Memory

by Neon Yang

ACCORDING TO THE BROKERS, my most valuable memory is from my sister's birthday lunch in 2011. The seventh of May, a Saturday. We are somewhere in the pedestrianized labyrinth around Arab Street, stuck between the tourist traps and hipster cafés. Sissy turned nine four days ago and we have a reservation at a restaurant, a Lebanese restaurant. Daddy picked the place but he parked in the wrong spot and we are lost. It's boiling hot, the parents are bickering, and we kids can only tag along in our sweat-streaked dresses like little boats adrift. Outside a shop selling carpets piled in fat stacks, I've become fascinated by a jeweled lamp hanging from the rafters, which forms the core of this memory: the glitter, the workmanship, the way faux emeralds drip from it like a curtain. But the moneymaker isn't the lamp—it's what's in the background. A scent wraps around me, sweeter and sharper than soda, evoking fruit candy and decadence. Before shisha was banned in Singapore, the whole of Arab Street smelled like flavored tobacco and you couldn't escape it. Kid me thought nothing of it; I've never paid much attention to smells. I found it less notable than the Turkish lamps. Still that detail was preserved in memory through the undiscerning generosity of neural biochemistry, and, according to my wife, will be the source of our next windfall.

"But why shisha?" Arial asks, chucking her straw through the crust of ice in her glass. "I don't get it."

I rattle off what I've gleaned from market analysts, pleased to be the purveyor of interesting tidbits for once. "In the recent finale to *Sacred Light of the Moon*, the two main characters had sex in a shisha lounge. It was a big deal for the fandom. Big enough it spiked a global hyperinterest in the practice, because the fandom is insane. But shisha's actually tobacco, so you can't get it now. I mean, you can, but like. Not legally. So there's huge demand for memories with the scent of shisha. I mean, of course you can buy canned stuff, the effects in the show were definitely canned, but, like, authenticity matters, and the weird subset of people who are really into this will pay a lot for the experience."

"But you weren't even smoking it?"

"Yeah, no, I was eleven. It's all about the smell, apparently. The characters weren't smoking the stuff either."

Arial coils a length of coppertint hair around her finger. Her brow knits in furious thought. "So if the characters were having sex in the vod experience, how does that even work? Do the viewers feel like they're having sex while watching? Wouldn't that just be porn?"

"I don't know, I didn't watch it either. I think they just made out and cut to black. The series is rated mature, but not *that* mature."

"Oh my god." Arial recoils. "That's worse than going through with it. Can you imagine getting busy with your love interest with your brain jacked in, and then they cut you off once the going gets good? I'd be so frustrated."

I shrug, my cheeks a little pink. Arial's voice is very loud and we are in public. I'm starting to regret bringing this up.

"No wonder the fandom's gone all horny for shisha. They basically set them up like Pavlov's dogs. Now they've all got weird kinks."

"Maybe."

Around us the café rattles on with everyday life. An inoffensive ballad croons over the speakers. Someone shakes a mocktail behind the bar. The corner table packed with tai-tais bursts into raucous laughter. I wonder if the memory formed out of today's experiences will magically appreciate in value twenty years down the line. You never know. Maybe something in Arial's perfume will become suddenly trendy and precious. Or maybe we'll all be living in the nest by then, unencumbered by flesh and the need for physical sensation. Again, who knows.

Arial sucks ferociously at the dregs of her tea until the straw makes a gargling sound. I can feel her judging me through her winged eyeliner. The two of us met in college and I fell right into her orbit, one of her many little moons. I ran with a cooler crowd back then, and Arial was the coolest. She knew all the fun people and all the interesting places. Every party was instantly improved the moment she showed up. She introduced herself: "It's Arial, like the font. Not the singer. Not the circus art." I said, "I thought the mermaid," and she laughed. We were friends from then on. Now we are no longer kids, but Arial hasn't lost any of her allure. She's spent ten years abroad as a freelance journalist. Crossed the Arctic tundra of Svalbard. Lived with an artist in Paris who cast her ass in plaster. Got lost in the Amazonian forest, saw God, and caught an infection that was almost life-ending. She's never told me any of this; I read it in her articles. Now she's back home to work on a book, a memoir. Some days I catch myself thinking: We went to school together, and she can write a whole book about her life. What do I have in comparison? Chapters about data analysis?

Arial says, "How much are we talking? Five figures? Six?"

I demur. "Less than half a year's salary."

"Not life-changing money, then?"

"Not really. Still, the money might be nice. Natalie wants to go on holiday. We haven't been in years. She's thinking Jeju or Hokkaido, maybe."

"Do *you* want to go to Jeju or Hokkaido?"

"I mean, why not?"

Arial snorts. I know, it's such a milquetoast ambition. She's got that look on her face that means she's pursuing a new and exciting idea. Arial purses her lips before thunking her empty glass down. She slaps the table twice. "I've got an idea. Are you done with that pavlova?"

I look at the sad mush of crust and cream on my plate. "Yeah. It's too sweet."

Her face lights up with devilish intent. I know that look too well. "Good. Come with me; there's someplace I want to show you."

I trail Arial in her bright blue poncho that's both too stylish and too warm for our surroundings. "Don't worry," she says over her shoulder, "it's only a short walk. Truthfully I picked the café because it was close by. I was planning to head over anyway."

I catch up with her long strides. "What is this mysterious place?"

"You'll see. I won't spoil the surprise." Then she adds, thoughtfully—"You're not in a rush, are you?"

It's a courtesy question; Arial knows I'm freelance and my work in data analysis gives me some flexibility in my schedule. "I'm good, I'm ahead on work. I have the afternoon."

"Perfect." She grins. "Don't worry, it'll be worth your time."

She turns down a colonial-era terrace row, oddly anachronistic, preserved through government fiat. Long narrow buildings press shoulder-to-shoulder, shoebox-sized gardens spilling into each other's spaces as if drunk. In the middle sits a powder blue house, wavering in the noon heat. Arial pushes back a wrought iron gate and leads me up a stony path littered with white frangipani flowers turning brown underfoot. Every breath hits me in the back of the throat with that sultry, leaden fragrance.

We shed our shoes on the porch lined with Peranakan tiles. Arial taps her bracelet on the black box next to the front door grating. It beeps green and the metal folds aside. "Welcome," Arial says dramatically, "to the Garden of Collective Memory."

A giggle bubbles out of me. "What *is* this?"

"Come on." She leads me forward.

Inside, someone's house has been turned into a museum of kitsch. In a room longer than it is wide, walls painted bright yellow have been buried by cabinets and shelves tilting with children's toys, anime figurines, mechanical keyboards, decorated metal tins, novelty mugs, ancient handheld consoles, so many more things I can't take them all in, much less name them. Larger objects are balanced in precarious stacks. Sword replicas hang from the walls. A brass ceiling fan spins lazily, casting shifting shadows everywhere.

Arial introduces me to the caretaker of this garden. Banana Wong is a younger woman wearing orange coveralls and big plastic glasses, hair held up in a messy bun. She scans my appearance skeptically as she shakes my hand. "Friend of yours?"

"We go way back," Arial says. "Don't mind the suit and heels, she's cool, I promise. Bridgette has a memory the Garden might be interested in. Go on, Bridge, tell her what you told me."

Childish jealousy windmills through me. Arial's only been

back in the country two months but seems more at home than me, who has never left. I explain the situation with the memory I want to sell. The grand finale. The horny energy. The sudden bloat in memory trading price.

"I watched *Sacred Light*," Banana says. "My guilty pleasure. I'm not surprised the fandom blew up the value of the memory. Romantic fantasies always draw the most deluded. Like me."

"Anyway," Arial says, "I thought Bridge's memory might be a good asset for the archive."

Banana wrinkles her nose. She turns to me. "Are you sure? I mean, given the price that brokers will pay right now . . ."

"I—" Blowing out my breath, I hesitate. Why didn't Arial clear this with me first? "To be honest, my wife and I . . . we . . ." I wince, apologetic.

"Ah, see—I can't take your memory in good conscience, then. Arial, for fuck's sake. Stop volunteering other people's memories without their consent."

"What?" She looks offended. "You mean you can't do both?"

"The transfer process degrades the memory enough that it loses most of its value," I say. "So I can sell it off, but a grand total of once." I'm surprised Arial doesn't know this. "My memory is worth so much because it's pristine. I've hardly ever thought of that day."

"Ass ticks," Arial says.

"Every time a memory is accessed in the human brain, it's destroyed and a new copy is made," Banana says. "The brokers don't like that. Nobody wants potato-quality experiences. Every time you remember something, it wears out a little. Gets less precise, and a bit less authentic. Ironic, isn't it? The memories that are the most cherished are the ones that are worth the least."

"Sorry for wasting your time," I say.

"Don't apologize! Do you want to browse the archive anyway?"

"What?" This catches me off guard.

"It's open-source, darling." Drifting behind the mahogany table again, Banana tugs the scroll of a monitor from its tube and taps upon its conductive surface. "Do you have something you're looking for? Something you're longing for? We have access to the largest repository of human memory on the planet. If someone's experienced it, we probably have it. And as I said, it's all free. All we ask is a little discretion."

"A lot of the archive is pirated," Arial says, leaning on the table, chin in cupped hands. "Scraped from behind paywalls and corporate storehouses. So much stuff that's copyrighted."

I don't have an easy answer. *Is* there something I'm longing for? Big question. I go back to smells, tastes, sensations that no longer exist. Small things I can put into words, pinpoint, describe, enter into a database. I search for an answer in the catalog of the tiny, tangible things that have vanished from my life, culled by the whims of late-stage capitalism and stockholder petulance. A brand discontinuing that one hair wash I liked, café franchises folding and none of their replacements or competitors offering anything I fancy. Stores closing. Websites going away. I want to start with something easy, something low stakes.

"This is random, and maybe a long shot, but there's a kind of tea I miss. It was a gunpowder green infused with peppermint oil, from the brand T——, they stopped selling it in 2017 . . ."

"Tea . . . peppermint . . . give me a sec." Banana's brow creases in absorption as she fills in the search criteria. She brightens up when the screen shifts. "You're in luck. Have a look."

She spins the monitor around, showing off a bright spread of memories within the archive that qualify. I let my fingers drift across the list, both anticipatory and afraid. "I've never done this before," I say, almost shyly. "I don't know what to expect."

"Let's go with something familiar," Banana suggests. "Look, this memory is from Singapore. Harvested here, too. One of our originals."

"No." I don't want to experience a memory so close to home. I tap on one that was recorded in Melbourne, a place I've never been. "How about this one instead? Let's go with this."

The memory rooms are in the upstairs, which has been dissected into cubicles, dimly lit and incense-wreathed. I settle into an over-stuffed armchair that smells of old leather and polish, and slowly lower the helmet onto my head. Darkness envelopes me before the memory kicks in.

It's a mundane thing, just like my shisha memory is a mundane thing. A balcony in the sunlight, crisp winter air, the distant braying of traffic. On the glass table before me, a teacup with gold rims and delicate red detailing puffs cloud of steam. My limbs follow the shape of the memory, picking up the cup and inhaling its peppery scent. I sip, and the tea scalds my memory-tongue, and here it comes: the burst of smoke, rich as amber and thick as oakmoss, layered with clear notes of peppermint. The taste of this extinct blend fills my nose, my mouth, the back of my throat, and with it comes a burst of nostalgia. The passage of years dissolves in my head. In college I drank this specific tea all the time, and tasting it again pulls on this association so hard that I am, all of a sudden, reminded of everything comprising that moment in time. Like a net being pulled from the seabed a dozen sensations come tumbling forth, summoned by the clarion call of mint and caffeine: the smell of the wood polish in lecture halls, the particular quality of those unforgiving fluorescent lamps, the over-seasoned spaghetti you could get from the cafeteria. I am a student once again. I remember exactly how it felt as I hurried from hall to hall, jumper-clad, with all my little folders and my calendar full of plans. I was holding hands with girls, swinging between the thrill of new futures and fear of them. I used to attend rallies, and on the way home would sometimes be pricked by envy seeing couples casually latched on to each other in public without thought of repercussion. Other days I was so sure of the bright, exciting things that awaited me. I was a naïve idiot girl at that age, but the memory carries no judgment with it. Only emotion, and that emotion is wild and hopeful, flooding me with endorphins. I've missed this sensation so much. I had no idea. God, I had no idea.

When the memory ends I sit awash in ecstasy, refusing to exit the dark of the vod helmet and re-enter the dull physicality of the real world. The allure of such experiences becomes instantly obvious: not just to discover lives that I've never lived, but to live in vanished pasts as though they never left. I've been holding out on myself.

Eventually I slide back downstairs, where Arial and Banana are engrossed in conversation about an art exhibit Banana saw in Prague, a short film about penises that was really about the separation of body and desire in the modern age. I only catch the barest edge of their discussion before Banana spots me at the foot of the stairs. "How was it?"

I don't have the words to describe what it was like being presented with that shivering sliver of my past. I prop a hand on my hip. "It was good. It was really good."

At my delight, the expression on Arial's face can only be described as smug, but I'll allow it. She's earned it for showing me this place.

★

After all that, it's hard returning to the small flat in Sengkang where we've lived for the past decade, its pale walls and its beige furniture, its tiny thirtieth-floor windows gracing us with cityscape views of gray dotted by stacks of fluorescent light. I bring home takeout for Nat and myself—the famous chicken rice just around the corner from the Garden. A special treat. But Nat doesn't ask the provenance of the meal. She looks exhausted, her foundation barely concealing the sag under her eyes. "Oh, chicken rice," she says, before launching into her list of the day's grievances. As their five-year funding renewal approaches, Nat's team at work has become embroiled in warfare with the other comms department at the agency. I am familiar with the cast of her workplace drama: her burnt-out manager, the cutthroat boss of the enemy department, her work buddy Farhana who is the only other person with her head screwed on straight. I nod and listen as a good spouse should, quietly tearing crispy skin from tender white flesh. The chicken melts in my mouth, salty and piquant, as I make sympathetic noises in response to Nat's many headaches.

Nat sighs, and says, "Anyway, how was your day?"

I clam up. It feels churlish to gush about my discovery after the day she's had. "It was fine," I say. "You know, got all the work I needed done."

"Mm-hm." She spoons greasy rice into her mouth.

"Also I met Arial for coffee. Now that she's back in Singapore."

"Oh? How is she?"

"Doing good. You know how Arial is. Working on her memoir. I guess she can write from anywhere, that's why she came back."

Nat puts down her utensils and heaves a massive sigh, full of envy and longing. "How nice. She's so lucky, traveling around and writing for a living. No stress."

I don't know why, but her comment stings, as though my neck

has been pricked by a needle. I say nothing, continuing to eat. Nat's phone goes off, an after-hours emergency, and she dives for it. The issue of Arial and her carefree, office-free life is forgotten.

Nat has to spend the rest of the night working, vanishing into our home office to make calls and tap at her workstation. I sit in the living room and try to read, but find myself staring over the placid twinkle of Singapore at nighttime. Nat, I realize, hasn't even mentioned the sale of the shisha memory. It's not part of her priorities right now. She'll forget about it, and I'll pretend I forgot about it, and the next time it comes up—if ever—it'll be too late and the bubble will have burst. We'll shrug and chug on with our predictable little life. Money is only money, and we aren't really struggling. Oh well. I should have donated that memory to the Garden.

I give up on reading. The glass of the living room window is cold against my forehead as I press my face to it, looking outwards. The phantom traces of my past that I tasted this afternoon have come in like a crowbar, prying the sealed lid off a corner of my mind and releasing a locust swarm of dissatisfaction and ennui.

Checking my phone right before bed, I see a pip from Arial that I missed. ‹**Great to see you this afternoon. We should do this more often, now that I'm back.**›

A guilt-strung bolt of joy and anticipation strikes me. I pip back: ‹**For sure! Are you planning to head back to the Garden anytime soon? Ngl, I'm hooked.**›

‹**What about tomorrow? Have you got time?**›

‹**You're on.**›

So we go back to the Garden the next day. And the day after that. And after that. There's always more to experience, more I want to taste. I start with the easily digestible things I miss. The virulently green soda K—— that I used to have at my grandma's house; the long since demolished McDonalds my friends and I used to camp out at to cram for exams; the specific brand of luncheon meat I used to love that got banned because something, something, over legal limits, something. Each night I lie awake next to Nat as she snores and comb through the tapestry of my past to find specific frayed threads I want to reconnect with. There are things you don't know you miss until you feel them again—and then the longing takes you over. I reach over and over for the fragments of my youth: my unrestrained childhood, my hopeless teens, my vigorous twenties. Everything was fresher in those days, my appreciation for the finer things still sharp, my future bright and blank.

Arial teases me about this. We've made a habit of lounging in the museum of artifacts after each session while Banana offers us every weird artisanal tea blend in her repository. "Bridge, there must be something wrong with you. Look, you have half the modern human experience at your fingertips, yet all you do is cling to your past. Where's the sense of adventure?"

I snort and swirl my teacup. Today's blend contains whole blueberries and titanium dioxide; glitter spins erratically through the deep purple liquid. It tastes like boiled soda. "At least a nostalgia kick comes with a hint of nobility. Your sense of adventure is mostly about dipping into people's sex parties."

"Touché." Arial stretches on the cat-mauled settee and hooks her ankles over the armrest. "I can't help myself. All the fun with no strings attached? That's like crack to me. You know how I am."

Eventually I give in to her badgering. I am curious, even through trepidation. One memory, out of the untold numbers in the Garden, something which she thinks has value. Arial bats for the fences, selecting a fragment of a zero-g orgy scraped from a billionaire's birthday bash. ("Literally out of this world," she says.) It's low orbit, a scattering of the rich and famous bouncing around a sparkling, padded tube with all their bits and bobs flapping in the open. I recognize some of the faces and wish I didn't. But I don't recognize the body I occupy, a skinny white guy with a gold chain around his wrist. I'm disoriented from start to finish. This body, which is not mine, lurches around untethered while the memory holder has sex with one woman, then another. A man comes over to finish him with a blowjob, and a no-gravity accident leaves his partner with a bloody nose. Everyone laughs. It's too overwhelming: the arousal and climax, the weird rollercoaster lurch of altered physics, the alien sensations that don't map to anything I know. I return to my real body to find it soaked in sweat, a migraine beginning to pulse up the left side of my head.

"How did you find it?" Arial asks.

"It sure was an experience," I say, diplomatically.

But I keep trying. I go cave diving (claustrophobic); I skydive over the Atacama desert (not quite as nausea-inducing as sex in zero g); I attend the last Burning Man sober (apparently not as good without the mind-altering drugs). I climb Kilimanjaro (Awful. Painful. Why do people put their bodies through this). I catch the original Broadway run of the musical C——. In a wintry field in Iceland I watch an aurora snake across the midnight sky in LED colors, and this time I wish I was experiencing it live, with my own eyes and my own body, with Nat's arm interlinked with mine.

There must be something wrong with me, to be offered all this goodness and find nothing of interest. I start visiting the Garden every day, even more than Arial does. In fact, Arial's visits are tapering off. "Everything in moderation," she says. "Besides, I need to get writing work done sometimes."

My obsession with the Garden bleeds into other arenas. I begin to fall behind on work; I miss a deadline for the first time. I make up some excuse and the client is very understanding. We've worked together for years; they've no reason not to trust me. To make up for the shortfall I start working at night, too, tapping at my laptop until the wee hours of the morning. This does not go unnoticed: Nat frowns and tuts and makes concerned noises that I might be burning myself out.

"You're one to lecture me about work-life balance," I say.

She sighs. "I'm a really bad example to emulate. Please don't be like me."

I know she's actively looking for a new position; the stress is pushing her towards a breakdown and she knows it. Nat rubs her hands over my shoulders as she says: "Your mood's been so low lately. You think I don't notice, but I do." Guilt floods in; my loss and longing has become noticeable. Nat has caught sight of the vast chasm that has opened up in me, and she doesn't know why it's there. I can't tell her. The geography of that gap lies between us.

Nat misses her own birthday dinner, staying late in the office. There's an important presentation the next day, the culmination of weeks of work. She looks so apologetic on the call that I can't bear to blow up at her, swallowing the fistful of disappointment built up in my throat. "I'll make it up to you," she promises. In the office lighting her face appears paler than usual. "Can you get our reservation canceled?"

I'm already sitting at the mezzanine table with a glass of wine and a small dish of olives.

"I'll see what I can do," I say.

What I do, instead, is send a pip to Arial. ‹**Are you free this evening by any chance? I have a spare seat at E——.**›

Arial shows up twenty minutes later in half the makeup she's usually wearing, her hair down around her ears. "You're lucky," she says, tucking herself into her chair. "I was literally about to put in my dinner order with U——. You're really dolled up! What's the occasion?"

We order a spread of tapas and grilled seafood to share. Arial gets a tower of strawberry cider and drinks till the tips of her ears turn red. She commiserates with me. "Can't be helped, huh? That's the life of an office worker."

I nod mutely as I chew on a ring of perfectly seasoned calamari. The flavors explode in my mouth. I think about this, the familiarity of the tropical heat, the rushing sound of never-sleeping traffic, the chatter in accents that slide through me without friction. A life with solid, sturdy walls that I've built for myself.

After we finish the food we retire to the restaurant's rooftop bar with a fancy cocktail each. Below us Singapore glitters; it's Wednesday, but the country doesn't seem at all fatigued. Arial glances at the sky, where the sun has long set. The stars are obscured by thick cloud cover and intense light pollution; I'm not sure what she's looking for. I study the shape of her face, the curve of her crimson-painted lips. These days I've been thinking too much about our college days, and it has stirred up old memories like the silt at pond-bottom. I used to have such a crush on Arial when we first met. More than anything I wanted her to like me, to think me worthy of attention. Those feelings faded as the years marched on, and then I met Natalie, and it was like we were hand and glove. Now Arial and I are standing on this roof decades later, calf to calf and elbow to elbow. My cheeks are hot with the alcohol flush. Arial scans the prickling, wavering city-scape between us.

"Do you remember our college days?" I start. "It's been twenty years this year."

Arial bubbles into laughter. "Shut up. Twenty years? I guess the math doesn't lie. We've gotten so old." She looks at me, grins. "And you're all grown up. Unlike me, still fucking around."

I don't want to be a grown-up. A spark enters my mind and I decide to act on it before it goes out. I lean over to kiss her on the lips.

Arial's expression drops; so does my stomach. She freezes and pulls back. "What do you think you're doing?"

"Don't be coy. What have we been doing all this time?"

"Shut up." Arial steps back, her arms held stiff, her eyes narrowed. "You have a wife."

"So?"

"Don't 'so?' me, you know what I mean. You can't fuck this up. If you fuck your marriage up I'll be so mad."

"Why do you even care?"

"Why." Arial exhales in a huge laugh and dumps the remains of her cocktail over the edge of the balcony. When she turns back to me her expression is cold, disdainful. "What you have is so good and you don't even know it. And you want to throw it away for what, for a taste of novelty?"

I want to follow what she does and tip my cocktail over into the night air as well. But I can't. It'll probably hit someone below.

"You have it so good," she says. That's the second time she's said it: *You have it so good.* "What I wouldn't do to have a life like yours—someone to come home to every evening. You're so comfortable. And I know! You're bored! You're bored of comfort! You're so stupid."

I shake my head, refusing her envy. Why can't she understand how I feel? "You have so much fun." The words feel stupid in my mouth. I sound stupid. Arial is right.

She stares at me, flat and dead-eyed. "Fun. Okay. Sure. Why don't we swap, then. I'll go home to your wife and you can take my place. Have all the fun you want. Let's see how much you enjoy it."

I'm beginning to understand the size of the mistake I've made here, the depth of the gulf we stand on the edge of. I take a step backwards. "Don't be silly." And then: "Forget I did anything. I'm sorry. It was a dumb impulse. I shouldn't have done it."

"You don't say." Anger rolls off her in waves. I can't place her sudden, radiant envy in relation to mine, the dull thing that had lived at the bottom of my heart for so long. Arial totters away from me, out of reach. "Go home to your wife. Don't fuck it up for yourself."

She leaves me standing on the balcony, alone and drunk, clutching the stem of my cocktail glass while the city shimmers on below me. I'm shaking, thinking of all the ways things could have gone wrong.

"I have to stop," I say to myself, as though reciting a mantra. "I have to stop."

I remember when same-sex marriage was first legalized in Singapore. We almost couldn't believe it; we never thought it would happen in our lifetimes. I had consigned myself to the same life as my queer forebears, slinking around on the edges of society, not allowed to buy a government flat, not able to talk about our relationships in public, having any mention of our partners scrubbed from national media. We drank, we had crazy parties, we felt young and precious and full of promise. Nat and I held hands and stood on a balcony to watch the fireworks on the New Year, and by December we would be engaged.

There was a joke that went around our circles at the time: Now it's a race to see who gets the first same-sex divorce. It wasn't gallows humor; it was hope. The pathway of the mundane had opened up to us. Alimony. Horrible in-laws. Health insurance and joint taxes. Finally, it was within reach.

In the years that followed, this all came true. People got married. People got divorced. Gay marriage was a novelty, a thing celebrated and whispered about, and then it became commonplace. Boring. I got married, settled into a career, built a routine with the woman I chose to spend the rest of my life with. The golden years of my youth turned to memories, glazed with the flattering light of nostalgia. I watched friends settle into lives, fall in and out of love with one another. Love wins, but sometimes love also loses. Love is for the losers too. Love is love.

It's nearly midnight by the time I tiptoe back home. Natalie is a cocooned lump under the duvet, outlined by light coming from the neighboring blocks. She shouldn't be staying up, there's that presentation tomorrow. And yet she stirs when I slip unobtrusively under the covers. She mumbles, "Are you mad at me?"

"I'm not."

She turns to face me. In the dimness the years seem to peel away from her, as though we're still kids and nothing's changed at all. "You're not lying to me, are you?"

I wonder if she can smell Arial's perfume on me, or the tang of the cocktail I forced myself to chug down. I hope not. "I'm not lying."

"Okay." She accepts this without question, without hesitation.

"Hey," I say, as if just thinking of something, "you remember that memory we were talking about that one time? The one with the shisha?"

"Mm. What about it?"

"Well, I ended up selling it a few weeks ago. I forgot to tell you."

"Oh, you did? That's nice."

"Yeah, but I missed the peak of the bubble. So it wasn't worth that much."

"Mm." Under the covers, Nat reaches out and takes my hand. Hovering on the edge of sleep, not quite willing to let go. I breathe slowly, in and out, taking in the familiar scent of the linens and the damp of her skin after a long shower. Around me I feel keenly the steadfast walls of the room in which I've spent so many years, and might continue to spend more.

"Listen," I say, "I think we need a holiday. After your project, we should go somewhere. Enough with planning and saving and saving. Let's just go somewhere."

"Are you thinking of someplace?"

Anywhere would be good, I'm thinking. Anywhere could be precious and worthwhile. Haven't I realized that yet? A dozen years from now I'll look back at these moments and wonder how I ever found them dull. What do I care what other people think of the memories I'm making, as long as they make me happy?

I ask: "Have you ever wanted to see the aurora in Iceland?"

At the suggestion a smile steals over Nat's face, breaking through the layers of exhaustion. "I have," she says, in her small, sleepy voice. "I've always wanted to." I notice the way the edge of her ear glows in the filtered light. "Let's do it, Bridge. Let's go."

Sugar, Shadows

by Aysha U. Farah

I FOUND DANIEL MAYFIELD in District 6 lockup, washed in with the usual tide of drunks and taggers and petty thieves. He was curled in on himself in a corner, as far away as possible from his cellmate—a hairy man with blue lips and a rippling silhouette, the telltale signs of a sugar addict.

"Hey, kid," I said. "You alive in there?"

"No," said a muffled but fully lucid voice. "Fuck you."

The guard swiped his pass and the door lumbered open.

Daniel Mayfield's eyes were bloodshot, his lips so dry they were cracking. He barely resembled his photos. He'd lost weight, and the shadows under his eyes had deepened to craters. He was two weeks south of sixteen but looked younger.

He blinked, rubbing his face with a grimy hand. "Are you a man or a woman? I can't tell."

I snorted. Little asshole. "I'm the guy who's gonna pay your bail, so I'd keep my postulations to myself." I fully planned to add it to his parents' bill, but the kid didn't need to know that. He stood up and slouched out after a moment's consideration, casual, like a cat that needed you to know this was all its own idea.

We stepped out into the drizzly evening and he immediately started shivering, wrapping skinny arms across his chest.

At the tram stop the holo-panel flickered up at our proximity, and I keyed in two passengers. The news was scrolling by at the bottom of the screen. Fires, elections, and other natural disasters. The Blue Rose gang shot a couple of cops in Northwater. Prices were going up, again. Same old shit.

We waited beneath a streetlight and I thought I caught the slightest tinge of blue around Daniel's lips. But I wasn't worried. Not really.

The trams don't actually stop, just slow down. Daniel missed the first time, stumbling against the curb. He got himself there, though, ignoring the hand I offered. I wanted to get him home before the tough-guy act stopped being an act. You spend long enough pretending to be something, one morning you wake up and it isn't a lie anymore. It's you—skin, blood, and organs.

He squinted at me through greasy bangs stirred by the tepid breeze. "Who the fuck are you, anyway?"

"Name's Lane Harper." I tipped my hat. "I'm a private detective. You can call me Lane. Laney, if you're feeling cuddly."

Daniel's shoulders went tight as a cello string. "My parents sent you."

"Ayep." The guy had worn a suit worth three months' rent and the woman kept covering her nose and sniffing, less like crying and more like doing a line off her palm. "They're real worried about you."

His mouth twisted. "Fuck that."

"Fair," I said. "Very fair. But where were you gonna go?"

He batted his hair out of his eyes. "I had a plan."

"Oh, was the plan . . ." I glanced at my notepad. ". . . Holding up a drugstore with a butter knife? 'Cause I gotta tell you, kid—you should never be on a planning committee."

Daniel chewed on his bottom lip. "It wasn't a butter knife. It was a fucking vegetable knife."

A fucking vegetable knife.

"What I mean is, this isn't the place for somebody like you." I wasn't good at this. I was a detective, not a kindergarten teacher. "Nothing in this city but gangsters, whores, and the rich fucks up in District 1."

"And you?" He gave me a dubious once-over, eloquent with the sneering disdain that only someone his age could dredge up. "Which one of those are you?"

We hit a pothole and bounced into each other. "Me? I'm a people person." At his uncomprehending look I added, "I'm a person who finds people."

Disgust bloomed over his face. Okay, so no puns.

We got off on a street corner a few blocks from the district barrier, just as it really started to rain. I pulled my hat down more firmly over my ears and neck, while Daniel turned his face to the sky and closed his eyes. The yellow streetlights turned him skeletal.

"You're hungry," I said.

His eyes opened a crack. "No."

"It wasn't a question. C'mon." I steered him up a flight of cracked steps to a frosted glass door. The eatery didn't have a name posted, just a sign listing its hours. Scrawled hurriedly at the bottom, like an afterthought, was "No sugar, no shadows."

The place was tiny: three booths and a couple of seats at the counter. Our shoes stuck a little as we walked across the cracked tile floor.

Daniel wrinkled his nose. I laughed.

"Sit down, kid."

He sat. I ordered us both big bowls of noodles and slid into the booth opposite him. He ate in a hurry, scraping at the dregs of the bowl with his chopsticks, sucking at the broth on the ends. I ordered a plate of dumplings, ate one, declared I didn't like it, and gave the rest to him. He was suspicious but he ate. Good kid.

"They didn't feed you in the joint?"

Daniel took several more bites before answering me. "I was only there one night."

"And before that?"

He just shoveled more food into his mouth.

I sighed. "Look, I know how parents can be—"

"Where are *your* parents?" He sucked down his coffee accusingly, like he was positive I was lying and had never had any parents at all.

"Haven't seen my mom in years." I took off my hat and put it on the seat next to me. "My dad's dead."

Daniel froze with his cup pressed against this mouth, lips slightly parted. Again, they had a slight blue tint to them, but it was probably just the light. I wasn't worried.

It took Daniel a couple seconds to remember he was trying to be a hard-ass. "How'd he die?"

"Mugger," I said. "Some psycho rubbed him out for two packs of cigarettes and a couple dollars."

I felt nothing when I said it, like it was some other kid who'd stood there and watched the knife slide in and out, who froze instead of going for help. Who found themselves wishing, as their heart spat fluid through their veins and panic compressed their thoughts down into a stream of nonsense, that all the solid parts of them would melt away.

Daniel looked like he wanted to say something else, but he didn't.

The rain was heavy enough on the tram back uptown to drip down the brim of my hat and plaster Daniel's hair to his cheeks. He stood silhouetted against the hazy gleam of argon lights. "I can't go back," he said quietly.

I knew he was going to jump the second before he did it.

"Christ."

Pain sliced up my leg as I leapt after him and landed badly on my heel. The tram disappeared into the dry throat of the District 5 tunnel, leaving me on a slick stretch of road washed yellow by the streetlights. Daniel would have gotten away from me for sure—he had a head start and I was reduced to a wobble the first couple steps—but as soon as he got over the barrier he froze. His arms spread for balance and for an instant he glowed, backlit. Then the convulsions hit him.

By the time I caught up he was splayed on his back, spasms running from his neck down to his twitching feet. His lips drew back in a frozen snarl, and in any other light they'd be flushed blue.

Okay. I was worried.

Trio Trevi only dragged himself to his front door after I'd spent five minutes knocking, and by then he looked ready to knock me on the head.

"Harper, you realize I own guns?" He squinted at me. His hair was a fuzzy, unkempt mess, which was probably why he was so irritated.

His hair had been perfect the night I met him, shit drunk in a mildewy music club by the river. I was new to the city then—a virgin, according to popular parlance. I didn't have any friends and I didn't know how to drink liquor.

Trio was hot, mean, and surprisingly easy to haul up a flight of steps. I watched him get beat up by his dealer in a back room of the club, utilizing my then-nascent ability for getting into places I shouldn't be. He spat blood at my feet and let me help him up. I brought him home to my apartment because he wouldn't tell me where he lived.

I pulled out a medkit and he pulled out a flask. We blinked at each other from across the table. I put medical-grade ointment on his cigarette burns and he taught me how to take shots. We fucked, and afterward he told me my futon smelled like licorice.

I wouldn't call us friends, exactly, but we were friendly.

Which was why when I showed up to his apartment hauling an unconscious teenager, he didn't immediately slam the door in my face. He did call me about sixty dirty words in Italian, though.

"It's too early for this, you pestilence."

"It's like, five o'clock." I hefted the kid up further in my arms. I'd been forced to take a cab uptown, and that was yet more money dropped on a job that'd taken such a steep dive south we'd hit the lower hemisphere. "Can I come in or not?"

Trio continued to glower, but he let the door swing open all the way. "Put him in the living room."

I deposited Daniel on the couch and shoved a couple pillows under his head. The spasms had subsided to the occasional twitch, but his breaths were still shallow and gasping. The discoloration had spread to his chin, gathering like blooms of frost.

I was starting to develop a few working theories as to why Daniel Mayfield had run away from home. Difficult to hide a hard drug habit, especially one with such obvious physical side effects.

Trio reappeared, wearing his glasses now, hair pulled back. He frowned at Daniel like he had done something to offend him, or possibly to offend his couch. "Picked up another stray?"

I gave that the silence it deserved, then went on. "He's some kid I got hired to find." I forced my hands deep into the pockets of my coat. It would have been simpler to dump him at a clinic, but not even I trust government facilities, and I am—usually—on the right side of the law. "He's a sugar addict, Trio."

"I can see that." Trio's expression did not change as he cataloged Daniel's shivers and blue lips. Heavily, so I would know what a big fucking favor he was doing me, he went to his knees and pushed Daniel's sweaty hair out of his eyes, leaning in and putting their foreheads together, checking for a fever. "I don't have any sugar. I haven't touched the stuff in years."

"Can you get some?"

Trio gave me a very ugly look. I knew about as much about street drugs as I did about dog racing, but I could read Trio like a book.

Named for its perfect resemblance to plain table sugar, no one knew where it came from or exactly when it started to circulate, only that it gave a high like nothing else. Opened up your mind to a dreamworld where anything was possible, they said. On the outside, you mostly just lay around looking like a blue-tinged corpse.

"Is he going to die?" I asked.

"You don't quit a sugar habit cold turkey, Harper. Most people don't quit at all." As if in agreement, Daniel's chest expanded and contracted with a few thick, heaving breaths.

Dammit. I should just call the parents, let them deal this. But by the time they got here Daniel would be dead, or close to it. They were probably still in the city, but certainly not anywhere nearby.

I'd watched somebody die in front of me before and I wasn't crazy about doing it again. "Where can we get some on short notice?"

Trio headed out of the living room and I heard a refrigerator open with a soft clink of glass. "*We* are not doing anything," he called back. "I am an innocent bystander, uninterested in your emergencies. But if *you* want to save him, I can tell you where to go." He came back in with a bottle of white wine and a single stemless glass, so clean it was almost invisible. "And if you're not up to it, take him and get out. As fascinating as it would be to watch a stranger die of withdrawal on my couch, I do have evening plans."

I shivered. Not at Trio's easy callowness—he had never been a fount of charity and I couldn't fault him for it. But I could no longer ignore the way the shadows were moving on the wall, like leaves rustling in a breeze. Even this far uptown, there was not a single thing that could cast a shadow like that.

The shop in Old Dupont had a statue of a squat little dog outside it, like something you'd buy at an old woman's estate sale. It was probably my frame of mind, but its wide eyes looked grotesquely pained. I heard a bell from deep in the building as I came in, and I was engulfed in the smell of dried flowers and a cloud of incense.

When Trio had told me who owned the place, I hadn't liked it. "Everybody knows you stay away from the Blue Rose gang."

"I'm not sure who *everybody* is, but I'm sure they're not as desperate as you are," he'd said. "And nobody who matters will be there. It's just a coffee shop."

Not only was there nobody who mattered, there didn't seem to be anyone there at all, just an ancient cash register and a jar of striped candy. I didn't see any coffee.

The incense made me feel punchy. I rapped my knuckles on the counter. "Hey, anybody home? C'mon, I'm suffocating up here."

A beaded curtain trembled behind the counter but nobody

came through it. I heard a bell again, distant and sad, accompanied by the rising groan of the wind. Not a sound I would expect inside a building, or anywhere in the city at all. It was eerie, and made me think of a garden shut up for winter, bare branches under a steel sky.

I searched the back of the shop methodically, tension twisting tighter in me every time I turned a corner and found no one, just empty rooms. One contained a low table and a broken aircon unit, another an old-model television, dusty and facing the wall. There was a kitchen that looked like it hadn't been touched in years.

The hall ended in a steep set of stairs, the air getting colder as I descended, the steps creaking underfoot. I breathed in the smell of rotting foundation. The basement was just a square cement box, occupied by two people on dirty mattresses, both of them thin and ragged and distinctly unwashed. What a cheerful fucking place. At first, I thought they were dead, but then I saw the closer one breathing—a bald woman with a line of infected piercings in one ear.

"Hey." I shook her softly by the shoulders, then harder when I got nothing. "Hey, buddy." She flopped over onto her back, puffing out foul breath. Her lips and nose were a mottled blue. Around us was a faint rustling, like a door left open to let in a breeze. I couldn't tell where it was coming from.

Then I saw the shadows.

The single bare bulb hanging from the ceiling was not bright, so the shadows weren't dark, but they were moving, spreading like oil, writhing. A wild, many-armed creature that reached out with a dozen hands, those hands dividing into a dozen more.

One of the shadow's tendrils flitted toward me and I jerked back. It was such a viscerally disturbing motion that my stomach flipped over. "Holy *shit*."

The woman on the mattress moaned and kicked. Her shadow did not move with her. Instead, it went perfectly still, and then it began to change shape, spreading in some places and thinning in others, peeling itself off the floor. Its arms and legs thickened like balloons being inflated. I watched with sickened astonishment as it faded from black to gray, and then lit up into a hundred different shades, settling into a perfect match of the woman on the mattress. Brown skin, dirty denim jacket, green cargo pants. Identical down to the last centimeter, but without the blue lips.

A full-body shiver grabbed hold of me. Whatever this thing was, it was a perfect imitation, an utterly normal person I could have passed on the street. At least until it looked me in the eye, went tense all over, and attacked.

It moved so fast I didn't even have the chance to go for my gun. My back hit the wall, divesting me of my hat and all the breath in my body. A pair of hands went around my neck, squeezing so tight my vision spotted. The shadow woman didn't look mad, she didn't look afraid or sad or anything at all. She could have been making toast or flicking through channels. Instead she was choking me to death.

A gunshot rang out, rattling my brain. The double dropped, shaking and baring its teeth. Like a trick of the light, it fell back into the shadow. Nothing remained but the ringing in my ears.

"Fuck." I sagged back against the raw stone, my limbs going watery with unspent adrenaline.

"You all right?"

I stared at the gunman. It was Trio. He had his hair under his hat and he was wearing pants. I barely recognized him. The watery gray light down here made him look like a fresh corpse.

"Nice shot," I wheezed.

Trio fell into a crouch, shoulders rounded, the nose of the gun an inch from the floor. "I work out." He was shaking, but only a little.

I breathed in deep. Sweat trickled from my hairline and under my collar like cheeky fingers. "What the fuck was that thing?"

"Evidence that it's dangerous to go through a person's things when they aren't at home."

The voice echoed down from the top of the basement stairs, unremarkable, except for its effect on Trio. He bristled like a cat, his whole body going rigid.

Light steps approached from above, a shadow bobbing out in front. He was young, maybe a couple years older than Daniel. His housecoat was silk and heavy with embroidery, and everything about him was *sharp*. His eyes, the vicious cut of his cheekbones, and the high, aquiline nose that reminded me of Trio's. Maybe they were distantly related, or maybe they just had the same plastic surgeon.

Whoever the fuck he was, Trio knew him. He was looking at him with a mixture of alarm and disgust.

"Shall we go upstairs?" The man—the boy, really—asked "It's a little"—he sniffed in the direction of the unconscious bodies— "musty down here."

He minced back across the stone floor to the foot of the stair-way, flicking his hair over his shoulders. "Trio knows the way."

"I'm sorry," Trio said, as we walked up the steps. "I thought he was out of town."

"Who even is he?" I asked. "He looks like you if you never ate and dressed like a concubine."

Trio squeezed my shoulder, maybe out of stress. I shook him off and tramped back toward the front of the shop. That damn incense started to make my head swim again immediately. "Listen, whoever you are, we don't have time for spooky bullshit—"

I turned the corner and almost slammed into him. He just stood there, smiling like a cat. "You can call me Rose."

"Rose. Like . . ."

His smile didn't droop. His teeth were very white. He raised the sleeve of his coat to show me the blue flower tattooed on his left wrist, the mark of the Blue Rose gang. "Trio, why don't you bring in your young friend?"

Trio went rigid behind me. "What friend?"

Rose's eyes were as round and dark as bullet holes. "Don't treat me like I have the mind of a child, Trio. We have cameras. I watched you park up the block, with what looks like a corpse in the backseat. Bring it inside."

So at least he'd brought Daniel with him.

Trio released a hissing breath, which I expected to be followed by a bitchy retort. God knows he let me have it when I told him what to do.

But he didn't say anything. He brushed past me and out into the street, letting the door bang shut behind him. That same chime rang out from somewhere deep in the building. The beaded curtain swayed in the backdraft, sending shadows dancing crazy.

Behind the counter, Rose pulled back a drape to reveal a tiny kitchen module. "Coffee?"

I blinked. "What?"

He rolled up his sleeves to his elbows. Something about the motion was weirdly familiar, and I didn't like it. It sent a cascade of unease down the back of my neck. What went down in that cellar was a freakshow. This was the glint of a knife in the dark, there and gone.

"Do you drink coffee, Miss Harper?" Rose paused with one slender hand on a stout glass jar. "Mr. . . . ?"

"Mx.," I said, distracted, again, by the way he placed his hands. He held there, eyebrows high, until I said, "Sure."

I half expected him to ring a bell and summon a butler, or something. He didn't look like the kind of guy to make his own drinks. But he started fiddling with the odds and ends before lining up three pale blue porcelain cups. I still had no fucking idea what this shop even sold.

Steam began to issue from the espresso machine, wreathing him in vapor. "I don't bite. Don't be nervous."

"Oh yeah?" I reached for one of the little cups automatically. It was scalding against my palms, like my whole body was colder than usual. "Maybe I'm nervous 'cause I just saw a girl turn into a fucked-up shadow monster and try to choke me to death? I think that'd make anybody a little nervous, bud."

Rose smiled and filled the other two cups. I couldn't figure out what about him I found so unsettling. His proportions were odd but not obscene. He just looked young. Unfinished.

"Those were sugar users down there, weren't they?" I asked. "That's why everybody always says to watch out for their shadows."

Rose set his own cup down, sliding his hands over the counter thoughtfully. "Hmmm . . . now, that's not what I remember. I just saw Dimitrio Trevi standing over a couple addicts with a gun. Who knows what he did to them?"

My stomach clenched in on itself. "You—"

He laughed, a shrieking noise that was louder than the kettle. "I'm joking. You're as bad as Trio."

I found this offensive on a bunch of levels, but this guy unnerved the fuck out of me and I wasn't gonna pick a fight about it. Trio was back, too, tugging Daniel through the door after him. He had him on a hover belt, a chunk of tech stitched onto a wide strip of leather looped several times around Daniel's waist. It generated its own localized grav-drive and was usually used to carry vehicles or building materials. It was probably a cheap one, with a tiny range, because Daniel's head and feet were drooping. Kid wasn't even that tall.

"Welcome back, Mr. Trevi."

Trio gave a tight nod. "This place smells like a funeral home." He seemed to have regained a little bit of his panache on his walk to the car.

Rose looked at the boy floating in the center of the room. "Well. I suppose we'd better bring him into the back." He drained his cup and set it down on the counter. "Bring..."

"Daniel."

"The man in the lion's den," Rose said. "Appropriate."

I grabbed Daniel's shoulders while Trio took his feet. "What the hell is the deal with this guy? Bad breakup? I thought you liked them tall, dark, and insane."

"Yeah, that's why I fucked you."

I gave him the finger. "Why'd you come here anyway?"

Trio's eyes darted briefly down to Daniel's face. "He was getting worse."

"I thought you didn't care."

Trio narrowed his eyes. "Listen, Lane, I saved you from having your neck broken by a government secret, maybe quit pointing out my character inconsistencies for a fucking second, would you?"

Sweat glistened at his hairline. He may have gotten some of his attitude back, but he hated being here. I didn't blame him. Everything about this place felt wrong. I wished I'd never taken the Mayfields' money.

In the bedroom we laid Daniel down on the bed and stood back while Rose set out a bowl, a tea candle, and a syringe. From an opaque glass bottle he tipped out half a teaspoon of sparkling white powder. I had never seen the drug before; it did look remarkably like sugar.

I couldn't help glancing at Trio. His gaze bounced from surface to surface, looking everywhere but at the bowl. The sweat standing out on his forehead was practically a glaze.

"What are you doing with a basement full of apparitions?"

"Hmm?" Rose extinguished the match with an elegant flick of his wrist. "What's that now?"

Trio's throat worked; looked like he was fighting down anger, or nausea. "You said you would stop it."

"I told you that I would do my utmost to control the situation." Rose tipped the bowl, the sugar liquefying quickly. "And I have. The apparitions were contained, and nobody's the wiser. Well, nobody but Mx. Harper, and since I have something they very much want"—he picked up the syringe—"I imagine they will be discreet."

"Discreet?" My voice came out skewed high. "I don't even know what the fuck I saw down there."

Rose sucked the liquefied drug into the syringe, tapping out an air bubble. "How much do you know about sugar? What has Trio told you?"

Trio had told me exactly fuck all, but I didn't want Rose to know that. "He definitely didn't tell me it made your shadow come to life and try to choke people to death."

"Mm, yes. Well, the exact nature of the apparition depends on the individual. Some are quite composed. Some . . ." His eyes briefly flicked to Trio, who was staring at the ceiling like it had called him a slur. "—Are not."

Rose shifted on his knees, pulling a red ribbon out of an inner pocket in a long, bloody line. "It wasn't always called sugar." He put the ribbon down beside the full syringe. An artist setting out his tools. "It was called Substance D-18, and it was developed by the former United States as a psychotropic drug intended to enhance unit cohesion."

I stared at him.

"He means," Trio said, "that it was a hivemind drug. Designed to let soldiers share thoughts."

I laughed. I couldn't help it. "Uh . . . looks like they fucked up a little." I had no idea what had happened down there, but it definitely wasn't any psychic activity. That thing was real. My aching throat was evidence of that.

"They did fuck up," Rose sniffed, like he wouldn't have if he'd been in charge. "But they weren't just trying to blend their minds." He picked up the syringe again, holding it between pale fingers. "The soldiers didn't speak into each other's thoughts. D-18 created a cerebral space. An entire theoretical world. I haven't seen it myself. Trio has," he added, like an afterthought.

Trio sat down on the edge of the pallet, scrunching in on himself to keep from touching Rose or the unconscious Daniel. "It's different for everyone, what it looks like." He shrugged, a quick, jerky motion that reminded me of a piano hammer hitting a key. "Physical proximity doesn't matter."

Rose picked up the story. "During the trials, some of the returning soldiers reported odd stories. There were people there, in that other place." A small, round thumb circled the crook of Daniel's elbow, searching for a vein. "More than there should be. Because D-18's projections don't vanish when the user wakes. The imprint remains."

I rubbed my knuckles against my forehead. "So you mean they had doubles?"

"You can make endless copies of a single file," Trio said.

I didn't know what to do with this information. I was a detective, not a scientist. I followed cheating spouses and investigated bogus credentials. This was above my pay grade.

"I guess the experiments went bad, huh?"

"The project was put on hold," Rose said, with a secretive smile, "when the researchers realized that prolonged exposure to Substance D-18 caused the doubles to gain sentience and follow their originals out into reality."

Rose drew the needle out of Daniel's arm. His body had jerked when he'd been injected, but other than that nothing else happened. His face was still mottled blue, and he was as motionless as a corpse.

"Is that going to happen to Daniel?"

"No. It takes an overdose for a phantom to manifest. This is just run-of-the-mill withdrawal."

I didn't know what mills Rose had been running, but I didn't know any that turned your face blue.

"Provided he receives the proper treatment, he should be right as rain." Rose set the syringe down on the table. He glided around to the head of the mattress, leaning down to smooth Daniel's hair off his forehead. "Of course, there remains the small matter of payment."

I crossed my arms across my rib cage. "How small we talking?"

He told me what he wanted. I stared at him. Then I laughed a laugh that felt like gravel grinding in my lungs.

"You're fucking hilarious." I looked at Trio, who was still hunched in on himself. "He's fucking hilarious."

Trio's jaw tightened.

"Trio, would you fucking look at me?"

Trio lifted his eyes like they were holding up the world. What I saw there was enough of an answer. I wanted to slap that look of sorrow right off his face.

"You shit-faced bastard," I said. "You sent me here."

"I thought he'd want money," Trio said.

"I don't have any money, either!"

"What the fuck should I have done, Lane?" Trio smacks his fist down against the carved wooden serving tray, rattling the syringe and the bowl. "Besides throw you and your dead kid out onto the street? You wanted sugar, Rose's people have sugar. Usually they deal fair. As soon as I realized he was here—" Trio broke off and slid back down into his slump. "I came to stop you, didn't I?"

"How did you even know he was here?"

Rose kept stroking Daniel's hair. It was starting to give me the creeps. "Trio has a perceptive mind."

Trio sneered. I was getting sick of this dog and pony show, whatever was going on with these two wasn't something I had any desire to get myself snarled up in. "What if I say no?"

Rose lifted a pretty shoulder. "That is your right as a citizen. Then I'll just have to ask you to leave the boy."

"You want the kid?" It was obtuse to ask, "What the hell for?" but I did it anyway, because I wanted to make him say it. Like I thought a Dupont drug lord would hesitate to put a sixteen-year-old on the street, no matter how close they looked in age.

Rose's smile remained serene. If there were any moral stirrings inside him they sure as hell didn't show. "I'd rather have you, of course."

I shuddered, forcing myself to look at the supine body on the bed. I could find the Mayfields and they would call the police, but it was stupid beyond belief to think Rose would stick around, or leave any evidence for them to follow.

"It won't hurt," Rose said. "Ask Trio. It never hurts."

He didn't look at Trio, though. He looked at me. His black eyes were lit up with an avaricious glow. I guess that's what got a guy like this off. Owning people. Holding onto their lives and deaths and everything that came in between.

"Fine." I pulled up my sleeve. "Let's get it over with."

I woke up in a back-alley hospital, which was good for my checkbook but bad for sepsis. At least this was one of the cleaner places, and I didn't need anything cut off or sewn up. My head spun. I closed my eyes and resolutely didn't think about anything.

When I woke back up, it was brighter, and someone sat next to my bed. I hissed, jerked, and nearly pulled out my fucking IV, because Rose was there, watching me. For a terrifying second I just lay there, thinking he'd changed the terms of our deal, or I'd misunderstood them, or the far more terrible possibility, that it was me, that I was—

"Harper. About damn time."

I blinked. Trio leaned forward in his chair. He looked exhausted.

When I realized my mistake, a couple other things made sense too. I shook my head and drank the water he held out for me.

"Where are they?" I asked, when I had regained the faculties of language.

Trio pushed his hair off his forehead. I could see the greasy streaks he'd left from doing it over and over again, all night. "He took them."

I didn't even know where to begin "What . . . were they like?"

Trio shrugged. "Like you. Pissed off. Hairy. Not nearly as funny as they think they are."

I flicked him in the knee. I was so weak it barely made contact. "What was it like for you?"

"It's different for everyone. Most . . ." He pushed his hair back again, exactly the same as before, like a glitch. "Most apparitions lose it when they first break out. Like the kid in the cellar. He . . . was different."

"How old were you when it happened?"

"Sixteen. Maybe seventeen." He pushed his palms into his eyes. "I don't remember, Lane. It was a bad time in my life. Worse than when we met." I remembered the phantom weight of him as I dragged him up the stairs to my apartment, and the way he always wiped his mouth with the back of his hand when he took a shot, the same way Rose had when he'd downed scalding coffee.

"And now he's here forever, a monument to the worst time of my life."

"Are all the Blue Roses apparitions?"

"Not all of them. I wasn't." Trio scratched at his neckline. He was in the same clothes he'd worn to the shop. "Which is probably why he let me leave. The older I got, the less I looked like him. The more I reminded him of what he'd never have."

"Which was?"

Another shrug. "A way out."

A way out. I felt sleep pulling at me again, and that was my way out. When I woke again, Trio was gone.

The best part about working alone is that you don't have to call in sick to anybody but yourself. The worst is that there's no one to kick your moping ass back into rhythm. I lay on my squeaky couch and counted the cracks in the ceiling, I watched bullshit vids and subsisted on cereal and coffee.

When the Mayfields contacted me to tell me their son had

run off again, I stared at the message for over an hour, letting the cursor blink. Then I blocked the link and shut the computer down.

Once I dragged myself out of my slump, life went back to normal. Or as normal as it could be in a city like this. I took more cases, walked through more acid rain, took easy jobs. Business as usual.

I looked for them, sometimes, on the street. Would I recognize them, if I saw them? Some days I didn't even recognize my own reflection.

A year or so later I was in a bar uptown, waiting for a client. It was a swank place, or at least swanker than I was used to. The ice cubes were spherical, if you can believe it. I was dressed up. Well, if not *up*, a little above sea level. I thought I looked all right. Apparently, it wasn't a widely held opinion, because a voice cut through the smoke and noise, close to my ear. A hand cupped my waist. "Did you get dressed in the dark?" Fingers plucked at my coat. "You look like a carnival attraction."

I couldn't place the voice at first. Made sense, I'd only heard it for an hour or so one drizzly afternoon a year ago. But he sure knew me. Or thought he did. All it took was me tipping my chin up and adjusting my hat for the smile to drop off his face.

I caught him around the wrist before he could scurry away. "Daniel."

He bared his teeth. "Let go of me."

"Do they know? Did you tell them?"

Daniel yanked at my grip. He looked older, better fed. His hair was dyed a lazy black with blond coming in at the roots. I wondered how bad things were at home that he immediately ran right back out to join the Blue Rose gang. "Tell them what?"

A hard lash of anger was moving inside me, sparking up. "Tell them that they gave up everything for you."

Daniel stared at me, and for a few seconds I saw the kid sitting across from me in that eatery, wolfing down dumplings like he'd never had a meal in his life. "You don't know them."

"But I know me."

The eyes hardened again, and he tore his wrist from my hand. He slid off into the smoky room like a seal into water, barely disturbing the surface.

I didn't wait for my client. I settled my tab and slouched out into the blurry gray night. I didn't think about my double, out there somewhere in the city with the kid I'd tried to save. I kept to the center of the street, away from the clutching reach of shadows. It was a long walk back downtown, but I had the time.

A Step into Emptiness

by Aiki Mira, translated by CD Covington

Even at first glance—no teeth, switched-off space suits, skin ulcers—the poverty of the moon was visible. I always reserved a room for both of us in one of the more expensive hotels, which were all equally dilapidated. When I checked in, I left a little tip so the clerk would remember me the next year.

It was important to you to arrive a day or two before me, so you could rest from your travels far from the sun. Once we arrived at the same time. My fault. I'd gotten the date mixed up. Your mouth spat sentences where the words were turned on their heads. Your red-rimmed eyes twitched and teared up. Your whole body shook. The condition you were in infuriated me.

"It's corrupt," I yelled, "the whole fucking space industry! Freighters fly under the cheapest flags to save money. The crew is starving or poisoned with cut meds. Ships go missing all the time—they weren't built for living cargo, just retrofitted on the cheap!"

We argued. It didn't change anything. Space travel was your life; there was no other for you.

From then on, I was careful to arrive later. But your appearance—so destroyed, so fragile—never let go of me. Like a pointed fingernail, it dug into my heart and hollowed it out from inside.

Spitefully I said, "If I can't change you, I won't try to."

"Always wanting to change things is unique to people from Earth."

You didn't say it reproachfully; rather, as if you were fascinated by it.

When you returned from a trip with newly implanted breasts because one of your sisters had died, I hadn't even known you had a family or what they meant to you.

"In my polycule, when a member dies, it's normal to take on their body parts or to sell them. We regularly implant new organs or exchange appendages among ourselves."

I knew that spacers defined a polycule much more broadly than earthbound people defined a family. That your body never belonged only to you.

"Sill^{ie}, I love you, no matter what body parts I'm currently running around with."

At first I found the pet name patronizing. As if by using it, you wanted to erase with it everything that made me special. But then I got used to it. At some point I heard your affection in there and yearned for it, became truly addicted to the name. When you called me by my Earth name rather than Sill^{ie}, it felt as though you were spearing my heart on purpose.

After the first time we had sex, you confessed to me, "I find my own birth name as horrible and caustic as the cleaning products the bots scrub prison floors with."

You never told me how you knew what cleaning products they use.

I knew that almost all of the people who worked on deep space freighters had grown up on space stations. That you were one of these people was clear to me from our first meeting, your unusually large body and unspeakably distant expression. Even so I often asked, "What does it mean to be a spacer?"

"Our bodies are composed of biosynthetic cells. We are optimized for life in space."

"But it means much more than that," I insisted. "You're wired differently than we are."

Only then did you understand what I wanted to hear. "Many of us are what people on Earth call neuroatypical. I was diagnosed as Ljl^gl. That means I have trouble integrating information, but instead, I find solutions no one else would think of."

"I know what Ljl^gl means."

The way I said it must have given me away. I could literally see the insight hit you. Later you admitted to me that even at our first meeting, you had already sensed what I am and am hiding.

"Sill^ie, are you taking meds for it? How long?"

"Since I was seven years old. At first so I could follow along better in school, now for work."

Tears welled in your eyes. You took me in your arms. "What we need isn't pills, but a low-stimulus environment. Transparent procedures and clear, structured communication."

I laughed the pain away. "Then space travel is perfect for us."

Now tears were running down my face, too.

It must have been a year later that I said to you, "When you speak to me, I see pictures."

"It's like that with Ljl^gl."

"And when I speak, what do you see?"

That made you laugh. "Silli^e, I see you. Sometimes us."

"My wife and I only use our birth names."

You didn't respond to that.

The first time I told my wife about you, she warned me. "People who grew up in space think differently than we do. They're difficult to get along with."

My wife is an artist, successful and self-confident. Before me, she had been married many times, so she believes she knows everything about it. "A second marriage with someone like that will end badly," she prophesied—and was proven right.

I liked to take my pill for Ljl^gl with spit, then drag on a vape to cover the chemical taste, but I never blew the strawberry-rhubarb smoke in your direction. Because you didn't take any pills for Ljl^gl, you had a much higher sensitivity to sounds and smells than me. Even on the silent moon, you commented on the whispers of the station ventilation system, which weren't any worse than anywhere else. When a bot treated our room with scented spray, you complained. So politely and gently, however, that it soon happened again.

Your need to withdraw was also higher than mine. It didn't bother me to stay with you in the hotel room and only seek out the public swimming waterscapes after the other guests were gone.

After waking or before sleeping, you liked to sit with your noise-reducing headphones on and your eyes closed.

As far as your work went, you were highly motivated, unlike me. My stupid editing work—I corrected romance novels written by AI—neither was fun nor brought in enough money.

When it came to our relationship, you walked a narrow ridge

between under- and overexertion. There was so much enthusiasm in you! You didn't even perceive exhaustion or breaking points. You extended yourself beyond your own strength—in work, in sex.

Being Ljl ^ gl—you were open about that. I wasn't familiar with that from Earth. In the beginning it irritated me; later I admired it. You took medication for space travel, but not for Ljl ^ gl. The freight company needed your particular way of thinking, had even hired you because of it. Even if said particular way isolated you from the others. "But those who choose space travel choose isolation."

"Maybe space travel chose you. And now it's squeezing you out."

From our second meeting on, you took me with you to the lower levels of the moon station. There you got cheap knockoffs of the infusions you needed for space travel. We also bought ourselves little balls that we chewed after dinner. Every time was an enlightenment. Either we started to talk endlessly, or we walked along the promenade and stared through the panorama window, or we stayed in our room and tried out new kinds of sex. We never knew what would happen, but it was good every time.

Shortly after your death, I flew to the moon and went down there alone. They awaited me in silence. Their chapped faces were swollen, the skin on the bridges of their noses burst open. When I went down there with you, I stood up straight and didn't hide myself. Now I went with a bowed back. Your death had deformed my body. They saw it. They saw everything. I had a sense that I was facing them completely naked. Humbly like a pilgrim I approached them, held out my money, and received their blessing.

Back in the room I ate the ball and listened to music. And, honestly, I cried.

Behind my concrete face is now a cell. Locked within: your echo.

The pill—it's lying on the floor—wears the same hard expression as I do.

At our first meeting, you smiled at me. A smile that I didn't know if I liked. Like all people who go to the moon for the first time, I was immeasurably disappointed. Instead of a pay raise, my stingy boss had promised me and a colleague a vacation. I felt betrayed. The air in the station tasted stale. The run-down waterscapes hissed hideously. On the first day I let myself be impressed by the gigantic machines that pumped out valuable water in the wasteland. A few hours later, I felt like I'd already seen everything.

Then I met you.

You stared through the panorama glass into the waterscape. As if you were an exotic animal, my colleague pointed at you and said, "Spacer. Rarely seen on Earth."

You reacted confidently to her shamelessness, which is why I thought you were arrogant at first. While you answered her questions, you looked at me as if you wanted to know something about me.

The next day my colleague was in bed with a fever. She'd caught a station virus. I went to the pool alone. There I found you: on your back in a saltwater tub. Your long, thin body floated like it was just above the surface. On your naked skin the complete darkness of the universe was glued. At the time I didn't understand why this view caused me so much pain. Today I know. It's the same pain that I feel now. For almost four hours, my pill has been lying on the floor, staring at me. But I don't stir.

The pressure I felt my whole life was simply the pressure to

dull this pain. A pain that belongs to me the way you once belonged to me.

Five hours without the pill and my head is more and more like an
empty space station. Thoughts made of dust and frost constantly
drift through. I feel regret, because my whole life long, I haven't
been myself.

After I encountered you in the pool, I met you again later on the
promenade, your nose pressed against the panorama window. I
stopped and imitated you.

"Do you feel the vibrations?" you asked me.

I felt them.

Then you murmured something. It sounded like "finally."

"To me it was as if you'd waited your whole life for me," I said
years later, as we lay next to each other, exhausted. On your upper
lip glistened beads of sweat. Then you sighed and asked me, "Why
do you believe I only waited *one* lifetime for you?"

That was our beginning, at least in this life.

Your family didn't accept our marriage, either. Only after your
death did one of your sisters write to me. My wife held me in her
arms as I read the handful of words. I saw you in spirit gliding
through the swimming pool and I saw the universe again. In all
its beauty.

In all its terror.

Sometimes I would smell your skin and wonder what I smelled there. The whole of the universe at once? The universal everywhere[1]? That's what you call this scent. Or isn't it more like a feeling? Now that this pain has returned, I'm convinced that all of life is just a feeling I was never allowed to feel. Because it didn't fit into other people's perceptions.

Maybe someday I'll learn to live. Without you. Without the pill.

Is my concrete face finally becoming fluid?

"Faces aren't a reliable tool for self-inspection," you told me once. "Our faces have already seen too much. They're exhausted. Every day they have to catch things and throw them back. Over time, these things wear our faces out."

Nine hours without the pill and I can remember each of your words again! So clear and distinct. I can even hear the way you said them.

Ten hours without a pill and my brain is growing arms. I want to reach out to all sides with them!

You never experienced me this way. The way I am now.

For you this state must have been normal.

For me it's shocking. Unusual.

Uncanny.

Am I now like the universe?

Yes, I'm a vacuum!

I'm not looking for a shape to fill up; I only want to enclose—everything!

---

[1] The original German, "Das über-All," implies simultaneously *everywhere* and something over, above or beyond the universe.

If I concentrate, I can see you. Your face so close to mine that I think we're touching. For a moment I forget where I am, if I'm looking out or in. "That happens to me a lot when I'm with you," I say aloud.

You nod, as if you could hear me.

"What are the moon machines doing?" I ask you. As if I couldn't see anything. As if seeing were a decision I didn't want to make right then.

Your breath smells like the sun. The kind of sun that people built.

You describe to me what you see. "A swimming pool that steam rises from."

"We should never have come here," I say.

Through the fine water molecules my voice seems to brighten. Even my body is now speaking in radiant white. Only now is it clear to me: We're not standing outside, but in. In the steaming bath house. You take my hand. But I don't want to and move none-theless, as if my body obeyed only you. "We gave up so much to come here."

You're right.

They give us special swim caps, so the other guests recognize us immediately.

Aside from us there are only a few people here. No one is wear-ing swim caps like ours, very cheap ones that get soft in water. They smell chemically biting. Tears flood my eyes as soon as I put it on. I want to kiss you, but not in front of the others.

Water engulfs me. The first seconds are critical, because I always think, am I sinking? Will you have to watch me die?

That's why I dive in before you: I don't want to see you die.

You know that. And I know that you love me for this quirk. Because it's a little Ljl ˆgl.

It occurs to me that I never told you how much I liked it when you laid down in front of the mini fridge in our hotel room because the humming took away your fear.

"The sound makes me cry when I'm all alone with it."

Your confession made me sad and happy at once, because I knew this: I will never experience that, because as soon as I'm there, you're not alone.

I open my eyes under the water. For a moment it feels like when we were newlyweds. It's so long ago and it haunts me nonetheless: my fear that we wouldn't make it. We acted against our destinies, and that never goes well.

As if you wanted to torment yourself, you immerse yourself very slowly. I don't know your current body very well yet. With closed eyes I touch it and am surprised at the curves. What's attached to you is soft and warm and reminds me of absolutely nothing. We remain at the edge while the others move past us toward the other end. Into the deep end.

"Do you want to go, too?" you ask.

Words float between us, but I look away. It's fun for me to observe other people.

We leave the pool together, go straight to our room. I want to seduce you.

You look at me and say, "I know what you're planning. Shouldn't we explore the restaurants?"

"We have all week."

"Come here."

You take me in your arms. For a moment I don't know if you want to console me or kiss me.

Tears run down my face.

"Your eyes," you say. "There's something wrong with them."

"I'm blind."

You understand what I want. You take my hand and lead me through the room. "We could stay in all week."

I stand still. You release my hand and I truly see nothing.

I start to whisper. "No matter where I look, a light fog lies over everything, so real I want to touch it. It's exhilarating. I can hear you breathe."

You hold your breath. "And now?"

"I'm getting undressed."

I don't do it; I want you to imagine it.

Through the fog I can hear you strip off the hotel bathrobe, the way the heavy material strangely, slowly falls to the floor in low gravity. I can taste the drops of our swim caps, smell them, even.

"I'm naked," I say.

"Me too," comes through the fog.

You move toward me.

But it's really the universe that moves us both.

We crash into each other, the way we always do.

Afterward we lie shoulder to shoulder on the floor. The fog hangs like a layer above the rug. I touch it so it dissolves.

"I'm not afraid," you say.

The word *afraid* floats above my face, but I don't touch it.

The deadly moon-tree beats against the window. Its branches crack like knuckles.

I roll onto you; my body does it on its own. "It's true, what they say about you: Spacers were built for specific assignments. You have a purpose. People from Earth don't have that."

You laugh. You think I'm strange. "People from Earth can give themselves purpose."

And then, "What did you build me for?"

You ask that every time.

"You know that question doesn't have a purpose."

And yet, this is the only thing that bothers you.

"You're here and I'm there." That's my answer.

Every time. Only now do I see the truth that was always hidden behind it.

Eleven hours without a pill and I believe I can understand everything, even if I can't put it into words. My comprehension is tactile, olfactory, synesthetic.

The hotel did everything to give us the feeling that our lives could continue this way forever, as if there wasn't an end. No necessity. At the same time, something was always happening on the moon. During our first stay, there was a meteorite impact that left us sitting in the dark for days. Another time one of the guests drew a weapon and threatened an employee. We were already in our room. We'd fought and made up. We lay hooked into one another in bed. My hand deep in your new vagina, I had just dozed off when the military knocked on our door.

Every year, we met in this hotel, in this room, on this desolate satellite, even though the crime rate was high and the weather was deadly.

"It's kinda romantic," you said.

But that was only half the truth. For both of us it was an easy location to reach, and affordable to boot. The incidents in the hotel didn't bother us.

What I was frightened of was the old moon-tree in front of our window. A biosynthetic invention that could crash down onto us at any moment. I never told you about this fear. Maybe because I knew that the fear stemmed from Ljl ^ gl.

A week always went by too fast. We lived through it like a whole life. Nothing more was left for us. When I edited AI texts on Earth, I thought about the moon, about the shabby hotel, about the warm swimming pool. About the lack of gravity that turned my bones into rubber. About the foul-smelling station air that stabbed my nostrils like a dagger—and I missed all of it.

Twelve hours without a pill and you're still listening to me, still possessing the exhausting gift of listening to people. Everyone loves telling stories about themselves, of course.

This one is yours:

You grew up on a space station far from the sun. Your parents separated shortly after your birth. You raised yourself with two siblings on the station. Once, a person in your polycule fell horribly in love with you. When you decided on space travel and leaving the station forever, this person cried for three days. When you told me this, I thought I'd caught you in your first lie. "How can somebody cry for three days without eating and drinking?"

"Love."

"Love is only for stories."

Back then I didn't know true grief. When the message came, I thought back on this and wished I had that many tears. Tears for three days. But I didn't have a single one.

People from Earth aren't good at writing love stories, so we leave that to AIs.

"There were massive eruptions on the sun," wrote my wife. I was at work and didn't answer. "Charged particles have erupted and are cutting through space."—"Particles are racing at different speeds." And then: "A category five geomagnetic storm. Space stations are being evacuated. Freighters are changing their routes."

Only your freighter didn't change its course.

Even now nobody knows why you didn't veer off. I did everything to find that out. I wrote letters, made calls, talked to people in person. Weeks before the storm, your freighter had recurrent technical problems. You were already delayed by twenty days. The whole crew was rotated out because of exhaustion. Only you and two others remained on board. You were the only experienced spacers. The new captain was young and still had to prove herself. She gave the order to fly through the middle of the storm. Did she want to make up lost time? Or was she under pressure? Did she even know about the technical problems?

No survivors.

No records.

The black box—vanished.

I've tried to imagine what it's like to fly through a category five particle storm.

What forces affected you?

What fears?

Did you know that you were at the storm's mercy? That the badly repaired, completely overloaded freighter didn't stand a chance?

Did you think about us shortly before your death?

About me?

You see how egotistical I am!

Three escape pods are missing still. I want to believe you're in one of them. But I fear that you tried to do everything you could until the end. Perhaps you tried to persuade the captain. Maybe there was a mutiny and you cared for the sick and the children, or looked after the restless animals.

Without the pill I can see all the possible scenarios simultaneously and I realize: In every single one, you're more worried about others than yourself.

Thirteen hours.
Without a pill.

"Hey, I'm not mad at you anymore because you weren't selfish enough to survive—for me, for me alone."

You don't say anything to that.

My wife collected money to continue the search for the escape pods for another year. When the money ran out, she took me in her arms and said, "You talked about him so much that I feel like he was also part of our family." She never got your pronouns right.

I buried my nose in her shoulder, so I couldn't see her eyes. But her voice sounded like it was from a movie.

Every time we took our leave from each other, we released our hands, then our eyes. Our eyes, always last.

What you don't know:

On my return trip to Earth, every time, I planned to break it off, to never visit the moon again. Because as soon as I left you behind, a force squeezed my lungs and I stopped breathing—waiting for something that never came. With all the connections, my journey home lasted seventeen hours. As soon as I had gravity again, I had everything else again, too: my life, my family. A terrible hunger always overcame me by the time I was on the express train. Then I often ate two proteinburgers. After that I talked with my wife and child on the phone. As soon as I heard their voices, I was excited to see them again. They reminded me of the things that I still had to do: "You have to drop off the emergency kit at school." I'd long since packed the bag that our child would get in the event of a catastrophe. The previous year, storms and flooding had led to the children being locked in the school building for two days. So we had to prepare emergency kits. I'd taken care of everything on the list: energy bars, toys, warm blankets. I was also supposed to write a message to our child: "Don't worry. Everything will be fine." But I didn't finish it. I still haven't written the note.

I reached my city by sunrise. As soon as I saw the first houses, I thought of you. You were already on your long route through the nothingness. Too far away to write to me; all I had was the confidence that I'd see you again in a year.

Everything will be fine.

When I reached my apartment, the sun stood directly above me. Before I went in, I looked through my pockets and found—every time—a handwritten note from you. The same three words every time.

You taught yourself how to write by hand. Your script, small and neat. I traced over the loops and arches so often that they melted onto my fingertip. Then I looked up. The moon wasn't visible in the sky anymore, but I was certain: it was there.

Fourteen hours and I sink into your writing as if sinking into a room that never quite catches the sunlight.

Fifteen hours—I've tried to get some rest, even though I know I can't really sleep until this is finished—until everything is out and staring back at me.

Sixteen hours—the pill lies on the floor, looks at me still. Its face hard and silent as the moon. Aggressive and white.

I touch my own face. It feels light, quiet, and quick. A waterfall in a vacuum. It weaves itself into me. And I wonder if something is truly wrong with me, or if things are just not quite right with me, like with everyone else.

Eighteen hours—I'm lying in bed. I feel a strange body heat in the air and open my eyes. It feels as if I came out of the darkness. I search for the bright, blurry spot—for you.

Nineteen hours—the pain is so strong that I have to remain

motionless until it releases my optic nerve and my mind clears like a fogged window pane.

Twenty hours—everything you ever said to me is being turned around inside me like polished gemstones that scratch my heart until it bleeds.

Twenty-one hours—my body attempts to vibrate out your echo as sound.

Twenty-two hours—I breathe through my tears and sense that I continue to live moment by moment—despite everything.

Twenty-three hours—dizzying arousal.

Twenty-four hours—I stand up and take my first step.
    A step into emptiness.

pocket futures in the present past

by Katharine Duckett

T.K., 2029

"WHAT THE FUCK IS this?" Elliott stood before us in the middle of the living room, a peach-pink spiny object dangling pinched between his thumb and forefinger.

"Dildo." Samara's guess was a good one. Dildos came through the portals about as often as lost socks.

"Plunger?" I said, half-heartedly playing the game. My mind was elsewhere: on the note I was unfolding, and on the fact that Kinz should have been lounging on the living room couches with Marley and Samara yet was nowhere in sight.

". . . Food?" Marley assumed everything was food, because once we'd nearly tossed aside a few spherical objects we thought were marbles but they turned out (when Marley insisted on biting one) to be the best sour candies we'd ever tasted. Marley's second guess was always drugs.

Elliott poked it. "Seems . . . chewy. Don't think it'd be edible unless you cooked it."

As if alerted to the danger of ending up in one of the scraped-up pots in our kitchen, the thing wriggled out of Elliott's grip.

"Shit!" Elliott shrieked as he and Samara scrambled back. "It's alive!"

Marley hadn't moved, regarding the creature—which had curled up like a spiky croissant on the floor next to the couch—with a heavily stoned gaze before leaning down. "It's okay, little armadillo dude," they said. "We're not going to eat you. Sorry about that. We're cool, I swear."

On some level I was taking this in: the usual chaos that accompanied a new future-find, the attempts to nail down its purpose before it ended up in one of our rooms or in the overflowing basement. More artifacts had been coming through the portals lately, which would have been amazing, if not for the fact that it was exactly the wrong time to be blessed with ample gifts from the futurekin. We were under scrutiny like we'd never been, which was why chills ran down my spine as I scanned the note in my hand.

It looked like Kinsey's usual scribblings, their drafts for revisions of the Future Collective manifesto, but it was written on shiny, sturdy parchment. Parchment that wouldn't be invented until at least 2124.

"Shit." I waved the note to catch the others' attention. "Y'all, I think Kinz is gone."

"What do you mean, gone?" Elliott demanded.

"Is it Reyhurn's people? Because I will kill that motherfucker," snarled Samara.

Marley didn't appear to have heard me at all. "I think I'm gonna name you 'Quiche,'" they were saying to the pangolin-like creature quaking on the floor. "'Cause I was craving a quiche when you came through, and I feel like that means it's your destiny."

"Marley!" I clapped my hands, the note fluttering between them. "Focus up! Kinsey could be in trouble."

"Fuck," said Marley, blinking. "Our fearless leader? I mean— our *other* fearless leader?" Elliott and Samara glared at them. "I mean—nobody's leader, because we're non-hierarchical, but one of the two . . . uh . . . *individuals* . . . who got us into all this?"

I wasn't sure what "all this" encompassed—the portals; the mess with Reyhurn; the fight Kinsey and I were in about how to run the Future Collective that was close to pulling the whole thing apart— but it didn't matter. Quiche might have been the only living thing we'd seen make it through the portal, but obviously they weren't the first, because Kinz had Quiche beat by at least twelve hours.

"We have to get them back," I said, trying to keep my voice level. "But I don't know how this is supposed to help us."

With a smooth whip of xir cane, Samara plucked the note from my hand. Xe had discovered the multifunctional adaptive device when a portal spit it out in the bathroom stall of a club downtown. Xe couldn't use it outside the house—too much heat to draw, especially these days—but it could pick up, rearrange, and efficiently chop whatever xe needed it to, while also responding to however xir body needed to get around on a particular day.

Samara studied the note for a second, and then cleared xir throat. "'Unfucking the future, Step #1: Create paradoxes.'"

UNFUCKING THE FUTURE, STEP #1: CREATE PARADOXES.

Sounds like bullshit, right? You've read science fiction, you're up on the perils of time travel and the butterfly effect—you know what rule #1 is. No paradoxes, no fucking your grandparent, no becoming your grandparent, no assassinations, no fun interference except maybe betting on stocks, or life as you know it changes forever.

Three problems with that: One, it's for people messing around in the past, which doesn't apply here. We of the Future Collective are the source, right? Not the consequence. (Although look, I get that it's a sticky concept—the back and forth between us and everybody to come means it's harder to pinpoint causation. I mean, would kava.ii have recorded that revolutionary album in 2049 if we hadn't gotten a sensory film from 2086 that made Samara write the scent-poems that inspired kava.ii's album twenty years later? How the fuck are you supposed to trace artistic influence in that case?) Anyway—we're living in our present past, so it's all malleable, here/there.

The second problem with not changing life as we know it is, well— that goes against everything the Future Collective believes in. We want change. Our time period sucks—Earth, late 2020s, a gentrified city in Appalachia we're getting priced out of even though its environs are rife with toxins. Change the past, change the future, the present—whatever. It's not like we can make it that much worse. If ripple effects from the future work their way backward, that's not necessarily a bad thing, right? The portals have been amazing, and they've changed lives. Change as a principle, flux as a way of life: yeah. The Future Collective should be all in on that.

Third problem—and it's not so much a problem, really, as an opportunity—is the fact that the past, present, and future are all happening at once. Seriously, they are. Can fully confirm. That's why the portals work. It's like parties going on in adjacent locked rooms. The walls seem thick, but stuff gets through.

And now a bunch of asshats—Reyhurn "Tripp" Dillard III chief among them, though no one called him "Tripp" in school, so I'm pretty sure he threw "the third" on there to run for state senate—want to shut the party down. We've been going about trying to fight him and his goons in the wrong way, y'all. We've been trying to play by their rules, to hide, to bend the truth. No more. We've got to fuck shit up. Starting with history.

My advice—no, my call, my goddamn battle cry—is the same for dealing with the present as with the past as with the future. Fuck shit up. Create fruitful, glorious chaos. Never let them know where you stand, the forces that want to destroy you.

TLDR: Embrace anachronistic anarchy. Reject totalitarian historicity. Live by queer time, by crip time, by epic cycles. Become temporally ungovernable.

MESSAGE TO THE FUTURE COLLECTIVE: WHERE THE FUCK IS KINSEY?

From T.K.: Hey, last night's monitors at Unruly Rosie's—can you give us an estimate of when you last had contact with Kinz? We're worried something happened with the portals. Get in touch if you know anything.

KINSEY: SOMEWHERE BETWEEN 2029 AND 2198

T.K. always said this could happen. I acknowledge that, all right? If I end up falling through a portal into the past instead of the future, I'll carve it into the Rosetta Stone or something. "T.K. WUZ RIGHT. One time. Maybe more, but we'll never know because they were such an asshole about it."

Ugh. Goddamn. Honestly. I hate the fact that quibbling over the Future Collective and Reyhurn's dickery has come between T.K. and me. We've been best friends since sixth grade English class, when Mr. Hagler asked where we'd go if we could travel anywhere in time. I picked NYC, 1977; T.K. chose the Renaissance. Everyone else said our city, no more than thirty years in the future or the past.

Reyhurn had waxed poetic about the mansion he'd have on the

west side of town, complete with a wife and children, as the heir to his father's business twenty years down the line. He was pretending to be straight then, but it didn't matter. The popular, rich kids wanted nothing to do with him until he married into old Southern money from the Carolinas—money so old and abundant that none of them cared he'd married a guy.

T.K. told me, when Reyhurn came by wanting to catch up, nothing good would come of it. But I was craving reassurance that we could all survive long enough to get the future we deserved. People might not think it to hear the two of us talk, but T.K.'s more comfortable with uncertainty and destabilizing constructs, with the long haul of resistance, while I was starting to lose my nerve. Shit was—*is*—bad. Glaciers melting; bullets in bodies like mine, like those of my friends; fast slides toward fascism and enshittification everywhere you turned. I wanted comfort: a glimmer of hope.

That's probably why I said too much to Reyhurn. He was getting powerful, influential, and I thought—fuck, who knows. That it would make a difference if he was on our side; that we could use allies. But he saw his opportunity to create a political platform and start waging a war.

I was leading a session for the new recruits on the night I stumbled through the portal. I'm not a camp counselor type, not in any timeline. I hated that it had to be formalized, the process of bringing people into the collective, when before it was expansive and spontaneous. Gorgeous in its unruliness, in the way we couldn't control it and never sought to.

We were under attack, though, because of Reyhurn and his anti-future movement gaining traction. We couldn't leave the pocket futures to flourish, a treasure trove for some lucky freak to find and only tell their lucky freak friends about, as was the natural order of things—as T.K. and I had done, once, when we were high school kids hunting down pocket futures in the corners of libraries and community centers. No, now we had to patrol, checking who'd been where and what had been found, because the anti-futurists were on our asses. Temporal perversity, they were calling it. Accessing eras we hadn't earned the right to, which they hoped would never come to exist. They wanted them shut down, the exchanges of time, and though they couldn't—*of course* they couldn't—they were doing their best to police the shit anyway.

The worst part was: it was effective. People were getting scared off. The back alleys, the grimy bars, the halfway-haunted houses like ours—they were becoming deserted. No one wanted to be seen poking around in corners where you might find remnants of not only the past, but the future, too.

Fines and penalties were up statewide for getting caught with "anachronistic artifacts." The authorities had investigated people for supposed future contraband that was fully of the present—sculptures embedded with tech, assistive devices someone had hacked at home to make them better—and even for a couple of things straight out of the past. Marley got written up at the park for having glasses from an '80s costume party they'd attended in 2027 because some cop thought they looked like a space visor. It was the most absurd shit, but we couldn't escape it. Reyhurn was winning, at least in the present, which was where we were stuck.

Our high school would never allow that time travel exercise in 2029, when talking even a decade into the future could be cause for censure. Those kids who wanted to grow up to inherit their parents' houses and boats might end up accused of not letting time take its natural course.

"No one is owed the future," Reyhurn said in a viral speech

before I—left. Got stranded. Whatever. "It's cheating to jump ahead, giving no one else a chance to enact their vision. Progress must be incremental, or backlash is inevitable. This is not oppression, despite what those on the fringes may say. It's caution. It is *care* for our present, which is what matters."

That night at Rosie's, I stuck around after the recruits took off, poking around the portal, trying to level out its energy. If I could get the pocket futures to contract, I figured, to stop spewing through more and more artifacts by the day, there might be less for Reyhurn to come after us over.

Voice memo to T.K.: Hey, Harlow here. No sign of Kinz after ten p.m. on Tuesday when they sent us home. Was a pretty standard training, I think? I can swing by Rosie's and check if they left anything around.

T.K.: Yeah, could you? We've got a . . . situation at the house. Marley's got a future pet and they may be having babies.

Harlow: Marley or the pet??

T.K.: Quiche. The pet.

Harlow: ???????

Harlow: ???????????

Detritus falls through the portals willy-nilly, but it's usually not the good stuff. To get that you've got to learn how to feel out where the future lives, right under the surface of the present. Not everyone can do it. You've got to have that electric itch beneath your palms that makes you want to reach for it, an energy crackling between your fingers.

When I was a kid, I thought that tingling desire was all in my head. I'd crammed so many other things in there: daydreams of my Barbies chopping off their hair and running away together; bike routes past my third-grade crush's house and plausible excuses if she saw me cruising by; a running log of comments, glances, and snickers for me to sift through in the hours after school wondering if anyone was safe, if there was anyone I could tell my truths—even half-truths—to. The first person I found was T.K.

After that class with Mr. H, T.K. and I would hang out in the library, where the head librarian, Ms. Janulis, pretended she had a habit of misshelving things in her old age as a cover for squirreling away banned books in the stacks. We went on scavenger hunts at first for those forbidden tomes—never betraying Ms. Janulis's methods—before we started reaching deeper into the shelves, following our instincts, and pulling out books we'd never heard of before. That *no one* had heard of before. Eventually, we were finding more than books. Discs that swirled with soothing colors, small enough to spin on my thumb. Eye shadow in shades that shifted as the light changed. Keychains that buzzed when someone was trying to sneak up behind you.

When we asked Ms. Janulis about it, she winked the same way she did when she checked out *The Female Man* and *Kindred*. "Pocket futures in the present past," she said. "Keep looking for them—you never know what you'll find."

T.K. and I trained ourselves. We found scant info about the portals online, along with some others who could do what we did, though honestly not nearly as well. Somehow, we became experts, masters of the craft who were pulling hidden treasures across timelines more consistently than anyone else.

The portals weren't everywhere, or in obvious spots. They surfaced in places you might not expect: the shuttered bookstore we had to break into because T.K. was sure we'd find something there; a clinic Elliott worked at for a while; the basement and then the attic of our house. Like bubbles they appeared, and could disappear, expand, or contract, based on laws of physics we couldn't comprehend.

By high school, we'd started to identify individuals and communities—the ones we called futurekin—who seemed to lose or send things through to our time way more than anyone else. We could sense them, sometimes, when we were in a place saturated with portals, through phantom fragrances or illusory visions, voices that came through like fuzzy radio broadcasts.

That's when I started dreaming of futurekin. Everyone at the Future Collective had their obsessions: Elliott's seashells from future shores; T.K.'s toolkits; Samara's art. And me—I loved all that, but I loved the people the most. The traces they left on everything. Neon lipstick stains; pocket lint in a jacket that looked like it had been worn to a party in another galaxy; sketches and recordings and letters; confessions that weren't meant for us, or maybe for anyone else besides their author, but came through anyway. The detritus of lives, washing backward. Had it always been like that? Were the portals always open, connecting now to then? Or was it recent: had it changed, the past-present pipeline? We were accused of being the ones who built it when we hadn't done a thing. As far as we knew, we'd found a channel that had always been there.

Blowing everything up, though—yeah, I guess that was my fault. My fault, and Zeri's.

Harlow to T.K.: Found something. A letter? "Unfucking the future, Step 2"—

Unfucking the future, Step #2: Don't catch feelings.

How NOT to fall in love with the future:

Cultivate the opposite of awe. Okay, so someone's game controller from 2087 popped through a portal. Fine. Of course you start thinking about how cool it is, what they're playing with something that looks like a cross between a bejeweled scepter and a Slinky. Seems fascinating, mind-blowing, starts consuming your dreams—but go into your living room. Pick up your PS5 controller from the early 2020s, the one that's dinged up from the couple of times—okay, the dozens of times—you tossed it across the room when you ate shit with the Bloody Crow of Cainhurst. Take a good look. It's plastic and rubber, see? Nothing special. A tool. If you sent it back in time and some random from the fifteenth century picked it up—okay, they'd be intrigued, and admittedly they'd be impressed if they got to play Bloodborne and Elden Ring. But the novelty would wear off, you get it? The novelty is gone for you.

Survey the crap in your house. Phones, earbuds, sex toys that sync to your streaming playlists but sit in a box under your bed collecting dust, crystal-clear screens on all kinds of devices. They seem miraculous to you for a minute when you slide them out of the box, but then they turn into regular objects. Clutter.

Take that same approach to the world when you see paper cranes that can fly themselves around and lamps that adjust to moods. It's flotsam and jetsam—shit that floats through time and washes up on past shores. Some of it's great, but the bulk is junk. Keep that in mind. Ninety percent of any time period is straight-up junk. Refuse, food scraps, and items that futurekin didn't even notice going missing. Don't fall in love with objects, or the idea that the future is awesome because you can change the color of your hair with a wave of a dye-stick. Stop it. It's cool, but it's not that cool.

Future people, though—yeah, that's harder. Fuck, I don't have a guide for that one. Not yet. I'm working on it. Stay tuned for the next rule, whenever I figure it out.

KINSEY, SOMEWHERE IN TIME

All right, T.K., so I lied when I said the only reason I stayed at Rosie's was to get Reyhurn off our backs. Sue me, okay? The energy fluctuations of that portal were stressing me out because *that* portal mattered more than the rest. It was my link to Zeri; I couldn't lose it.

I didn't realize Zeri was one person at first. You can't always tell with the way things come through: there are patterns of people, households, but it's not clear how they arise. Maybe Zeri's so amazing that they resonate across the frequencies of time like a song you can't help hearing. Or maybe that's some sappy shit I'm saying because I'm gone for them.

I'd picked up dozens of Zeri's rings, what felt like three hundred of their springy hair ties, and six of their sensory films: tabs you put on your tongue that explode with short bursts of feeling, vision, sound. Samara had figured out how those worked first, tracing their history forward from the scent-poetry trend that apparently took hold in the 2040s. Xe figured out how to write xir own poems for future transcription into scent, and we knew from the kava.ii album that someone had carried out the process in 2047. The resulting chapbook—*the infinite sadness of cold krispy kreme*—garnered some rave reviews.

Zeri's sensory films were from the late 2090s, we estimated, and they were different enough that I was sure that the same artist couldn't have made them all. They lose a little luster each time you reuse the film, because they're not meant to be re-experienced obsessively. They're ephemeral, but I couldn't help it: I kept placing them in my mouth, soaking in the light—unearthly and purple in one film, glimmering like gold in another—and the scenes I couldn't make total sense of. Landscapes, city streets, outer space. I couldn't parse what they meant, exactly, but they became part of me—instantly. Like I'd always known them.

It wasn't until T.K. caught sight of the growing shrine in my room that I realized I might not be falling in love with all futurekin, but with one in particular. "You know these belong to the same person, right?" they said, examining the rings. "They sent us a message."

I leapt up from where I'd been sprawled on the bed—well, not so much leapt, with my joints, but propelled myself to standing with the help of the furniture. "What did it say?"

The note T.K. found wasn't biometrically keyed or addressed to anyone, but it contained an imperative anyway: "Take care of the rings for me. Love, Zeri."

I lurked around the portal at Rosie's all the time after that. Shit was hitting the fan with Reyhurn, and I didn't want to think about it. I wanted to think about *this*: the amazing somebody on the other side of time, talking to me. Okay, not me specifically, but I *had* been looking after their rings. I'd polished them until the stones shined. And I'd started to think that the sensory films, the translucent teal scarf, the collection of holographic postcards dated 2198—maybe they were Zeri's. Maybe they knew, somehow, that I was on the other end of the portal, longing for any part of them they could deliver through.

I tried sending them letters. We had no idea if anything from the past ever got through the portals, or if it was a one-way deal, but every time I checked Rosie's, my sad little envelopes were right where I'd left them. I could have tried to stash some away somewhere secure, hoping Zeri would stumble upon them in a century and a half, but that felt hopeless. Around the time I was considering confessing the scope of my crush and commissioning scent-poetry from Samara, I decided drastic measures had to be taken.

T.K. and I had been cautioned, early on, not to reach out to the futurekin when we found postings about the portals online. It's weird that we listened, considering the other rules we were happy to break, but this one felt right on some gut level. The ghostly glimpses around certain portals made my skin crawl, fascinated as I was by the phenomenon. It was one thing to know the walls of time were permeable, and another to see them melting in front of you.

Usually, I noped out of that liminal space as soon I could once I'd collected whatever the portals gave me. This time, though, I was trying to look. I swore I'd felt Zeri here before, or at least someone whose laugh I could almost hear; whose scent I caught on nights like these.

I dug up the urge that let me manipulate the portals and followed it farther, past the limits of my fear. No more ignoring figures in the dark, glimpsed out of the corner of my eye. When I saw fingers ghosting across the bar, nails and skin that could have been a trick of the light, I reached out and hung on for dear life. Threaded my hand through thin air and felt for whatever was there, pulled the way T.K. and I had always practiced—and found myself tumbling, my never-quite-stable legs giving way as I fell into something warm. Solid.

"Augh, what the fuck!" The flank I'd connected with belonged to a human, who stared at me in horror for a second before shouting at someone behind me. "Is this because of your portal thing, Zeri? I told you it wasn't going to end well!"

I regained my balance, turning around slowly.

"Hey, babe," Zeri said. "Been waiting on you."

Voice memo, T.K. to Samara: Another missive from Kinz. "Unfucking the future, Step 2: Don't catch feelings."

Elliott: Shit. Leave it to Kinz to get caught up in intertemporal drama.

T.K.: We don't know how long it's been for them, though. And I thought we had to worry about rescuing them, but now . . .

Elliott: Now what?

T.K.: Now I'm worried they're choosing to stay.

I talk a lot of shit, but honestly? Being with Zeri felt like fate. Like everything I ever wanted the future to be.

They'd known I was there, they told me, on the other side of the portal.

"So, the hair ties were messages?" I teased, wishing I'd brought their rings to slide back onto their slender fingers.

The person I'd crashed into—their roommate, Eka, apparently—had vacated the premises, probably because of how obnoxiously Zeri and I were flirting.

"Oh, a lot of times we're just losing stuff." Zeri laughed, tugging at the tie holding up their thick black hair. They had an accent I'd never heard before, and used a translator when we got stuck on phrases that weren't mutually intelligible across time periods. "Things fall through the cracks. But I've been getting better at figuring out how to send what I want to you, and the fact that you want to receive it—that seems to make it easier to get things through. You got my note, right?"

I nodded, taking a step closer. "I tried to write to you."

"Doesn't work that way. You'd have to leave something for me to find back in your present, and let the world wait."

I examined the smile on their face. "Did I?"

"Can't tell you," Zeri said. "Might've, though."

"I missed you," I said, though that made no sense at all. But they seemed to get what I meant, closing the gap between us like it had never been there.

"Missed you too."

Zeri kissed like a summer storm—slick, hot, leaving me parched despite the onslaught of rain. The first time we fucked I wanted to crawl inside them, live there through every season, watch cloudbursts come and sunsets settle then wake up to do it over again in a freshly made world. God, I wanted them like I wanted no one else, no one in the past-present-whatever, and it made my hands shake, my breath stutter. It made me shy, and I was never shy. When they laid me out on their bed, I threw up one arm like a damsel, hiding my face in the crook of my elbow while they mouthed me apart, each pinprick of their teeth and slow slide of their tongue imprinting a message across the bounds of time. *You and me*, it read, despite the impossibilities, despite how my head ached when I tried to work out the Gordian knot of our recursive temporalities. *Me inside you.*

We fucked in simulators, too, in virtual environments without pop-up ads or creepy tracking or clickable porn categories that felt like ordering off the grossest deli menu. These weren't made to sell you anything, but to tap into the human imagination's full potential: for sex, for art, for science, whatever. You could summon up impossible spaces, shapeshift, create feedback loops of pleasure and pain, act out whole scenarios seemingly having nothing to do with orgasm but which got you there anyway. We turned into galaxies, merging, falling apart, experiencing the truth of each other when we contained a hundred billion stars, and sinking back into our ordinary bodies to touch and arch, still thrumming with celestial power.

Zeri had modifications, like the lavender reptilian skin they threw on some days and the swirling tattoos they sported on others, but they were the same kind of human I was. On those first mornings when we woke up together it didn't seem to matter when we were—2198; 2029; 1993; the dawn of time. The futurekin weren't fundamentally different. I remained sure of that, even as I tried to wrap my mind around the simplest facts of the era I'd found myself in.

Future histories didn't make sense to me. I didn't know what the Zed Accords were, or why 2044 was a turning point in climate technology, or why Astren Pelas was the last president of what used to be the US. Zeri explained, but the effects that created Zeri's world—the cataclysms averted, and the disasters that happened; the good, the bad, the thrilling, the boring—didn't stick with me, because it wasn't my history. I was too into it being my future.

Zeri, in the meantime, wanted to know all about my present past. I caught them up on Reyhurn and his attempts to freeze time. "But the future's amazing!" I said. We were bathed in the violet light of a floating gallery, gently rising on hovering platforms to take in the exhibition while adjustable anti-grav cushioned my hips. "Look at this. Who could give this up?"

That made them sad, I could tell. I didn't know why. 2198 was paradise compared to 2029, and I wanted to dwell there with Zeri for as long as I could. I was sure T.K. was freaking out; they'd surely mobilized the collective. I should have tried to send reassurances, but I couldn't fathom what to say. What if I was always meant to end up in the future? What if that's what the portals were *for*? Maybe they were escape hatches from time, not cabinets to rifle through for trinkets.

Zeri didn't want to talk about the portals.

"I don't want to mess with them too much, or tell you anything that might . . ." They sighed. "It doesn't matter. Let's focus on the time we have before you go home."

I should have pushed. Said what I'd been thinking for a week: *What if I don't go back?* But I was high on 2198. Nothing could bring me down in the heady early days, despite the ways I felt out of place. I kept looking for reference points between our eras, but they were rare. It took me six hours of watching *Bruce the Vengeful Pterodactyl* to realize it was a *Batman* remake. "Oh, yeah," said Zeri, plugging into the episode I was viewing. "He's been a pterodactyl since my grandma was a kid."

Other conversations made me feel even more alien, like when Zeri told me about the vibrational technology that parted walls, allowing anyone to walk through them. That wasn't its main purpose—the primary use was rearranging matter for construction and renovation, which had made housing easy to obtain and infinitely adaptable—but the development of the technology meant anyone could permeate physical barriers with a relatively affordable device.

I couldn't wrap my head around it, and hated the way that made me feel ancient, like some relic that couldn't get with the program. I'd dreamed of the liberated future—no cops, no borders—but *this*? Locked doors had kept me secure in countless situations, especially when someone was trying to kick them in. How were you supposed to keep yourself safe—your people safe—without the ability to protect your home?

I blabbered as much to Zeri.

"It's not like that here," they said. "There's a theoretical threat, but people don't violate that boundary as much as I think they . . . did. Say someone does come into your house. The question is why, you know? They can replicate most necessary items, so if they're trying to take something of yours—what's that about, exactly? It's usually down to some kind of loss or trauma, so a mediator talks it through. And if they're looking to mess with your privacy—that's about control, or shame, or something they don't want other people to see, so they're turning the spotlight on you. Violent intent— that's the hardest, and that's what the time-locks are for. They make someone unable to move for up to an hour. They're not deployed often, and we're trying to work through better solutions, because even in those situations, we'd rather not remove someone's auton- omy. How you get past it, I don't know." They smiled, a little, and I couldn't take my eyes off their expressions, the way I saw complex thoughts flitting across their face. They hadn't had to hide them, not like T.K. and I had, so vigilant from childhood about protecting our inner lives. "Maybe that's the question for another future."

Samara to T.K.: Hey, I know everybody's freaked about Kinsey, but did you see this Reyhurn shit? "It's sickness. It may well be a mental disorder, this hallucinating about the future. We need to stop it before it spreads farther, and I—not my op- ponent—know how to stop it at the source."

T.K.: Fuck. Get everyone prepped for possible raids. Also got another letter from Kinz—I think they're in trouble. I don't know why else "Step 3" would be—

UNFUCKING THE FUTURE, STEP #3: FUCK THE FUTURE. FOR GOOD.

No, Tony! You can't fuck the future! The future fucks you.

My dad used to say that: a line from Saturday Night Fever. *Thing is—he's still out there, saying it, even though his teeth are dust where I am now, and he said his last words—"Take care of yourself, kid"—four years ago, back where I came from. It's happening at once, the now, the then, the yet to come. My personal walls of time are collapsing. It's what I wanted. It's what I didn't want. The paradox of simultaneity, see? You can live to see the future you longed to manifest and hate it and love it at once. You're straddling too many lines, decades out of sync with where you thought you belonged. No—you thought you belonged here.*

But you were wrong, kid. You were so wrong.

"There's something I haven't told you," Zeri said to me on my sixteenth day in 2198. We were sitting at a café on a bustling street corner, the sun casting amber rays across the planes of Zeri's face. "It's about the others who have come through the portal."

They had only mentioned them in passing—the time travelers before me, or after me depending on how you accounted for timelines. Eka's partner's partner was from 2054, but I had only met her briefly at the house. "Yeah? Lana seems fine. Is there something I should know?"

The newness of the future was wearing thin. I'd started feeling weary, trying not to notice how Zeri's melancholy grew by the day. "Most of them don't fare well, not after the first month. I hate it, but you can't stay, Kinsey. You'll get sick."

"So what?" Sick didn't scare me off: I'd been sick. Sick was a typical state of being under capitalism in the 2020s. "I can manage it."

"It's not only the sickness. When you leave the past, your present . . ." They paused. I swallowed my last bite of dessert, a syrup-soaked pastry that had turned unappealing on my tongue. "It makes holes in time. Lacunae in the world, and you never know what'll get in. Some people, they come through and they belong here, like Lana. It's not as if there's some perfect fit. But when someone gets here and they're meant to stay, you *know*."

My gut twisted. "So I'm not good enough for the future. That's what you're telling me."

"No, not at all." They leaned forward, slipping their hand over mine. "You *make* the future. You were trying to find a way to stop Reyhurn when you came to me, right? Who do you think is going to see that through if you don't?"

"T.K."

"And T.K.'s depending on you."

"They're—" I longed to argue, but it was true. I'd put everything into motion with Reyhurn, and T.K. and the collective were paying the price. Yet this place proved things worked out okay: that one day people like us could thrive.

"It'll stop feeling real for you," Zeri said softly. "If it's not right, you'll start to see something else. Other possible realities. I don't know if they're truly out there. I can only tell you what people have told me. Or what they've—" They went silent a moment, their throat clicking. "They've left things behind. Records of what they felt. They stop being able to see this time, this place, and what's there instead—it's—I don't want to show you. I want you to keep seeing the future you love."

"Zeri, please." They didn't get it. They couldn't, because this was their present. "I don't want to be dead by the time this future comes."

They reached out, pulling me half-across the table in an embrace. But they didn't offer words of comfort. What could they say? Zeri hadn't convinced me. I'd been mapping the contours of the future through the portals since I was twelve. Who could belong here more than me?

Lana, for one. I ran into her at the house after I told Zeri I needed to clear my head, and blew up at her, though I wasn't proud of it. Time was a squeezing vice, and I wanted out. How had she done it, and why couldn't I do the same?

"Are you done?" she said after I accosted her. "Because you don't know me. You don't know that I'd give anything to belong in the time I came from—except my life, which is what it would cost. I didn't *want* to leave. I think I'm meant to be here, but there were costs, Kinsey. I lost everything and everyone I loved. They're gone."

When Zeri returned to the house, I reached for them, letting present and future grief pour into me. "Two weeks," I whispered. "You said a month, so I've got two weeks. I don't want to go back without solving the Reyhurn problem—but I've got an idea, if you're willing to help me."

Zeri pulled me in, their voice soft in my ear. "Sounds good, babe. Come to bed first, though. Right now, we've got all the time in the world."

KINSEY, 2029

I arrived home on a Tuesday morning feeling like I had the world's worst hangover and craving sweet, nostalgic sustenance, like the Goo Goo Clusters I had stashed at the house. When I got there, though, Elliott told me—after exclaiming over my return—that Quiche had eaten them all.

"Who the fuck is Quiche?" I said, before the rest of the collective walked into the house and the place exploded into pandemonium.

I'd tried to send instructions: plans for battle, so T.K. could set things in motion before I got there. Turns out only my rough drafts made it through, though, the ones that were diary entries as much as anything else. I cursed the fickleness of the portals, but couldn't dwell. I had to get the whole Future Collective on board.

"We blow it up."

"What?" T.K. blinked as everyone else murmured.

"There's too much coming through to hide. Hiding shouldn't be the goal anyway. So we don't." I scanned the faces in the room, fighting the pang of guilt that arose at the thought I'd left them to fend Reyhurn and his people off alone. "Zeri—my contact on the other side—is going to flood the pipeline. They and everyone they know will send as much through as they can. And us—we need to make the present the future."

I don't know how long the news articles and broadcasts about what happened will endure. Reyhurn's viral tantrum when he lost the election probably has a longer half-life than anything else, and the reporting on the rest was confused if anything. All the authorities could figure out was that their methods for discerning the present from the future were failing as public opinion swiftly turned against them.

It was us: the Future Collective, planting bits of pocket futures everywhere we could and mashing up present objects with past, modifying and hacking, collaging them together, distributing them as widely as we could to show others what the future could be—to make them want it, the way that Zeri suggested we needed to for more portals to appear. The scanners Reyhurn's people had devised to determine temporal origins had never worked right, and they went haywire when confronted with a coat stitching together parts of 2038, 2126, and 2023. The anti-futurists didn't know what to do with the cutting-edge assistive tech that Samara patented, legally attaching it to 2029. They didn't know what to do with us, not once we came out of the shadows.

"Could this material exist?" asked a lawyer in a court hearing that became infamous, holding up a piece of fabric from our anachronistic coat, the patch that warmed its wearer through no method they could understand.

The textiles expert on the stand regarded them steadily. "I don't understand the question. It does exist—right here, right now."

Like I wrote: fruitful chaos. We had worked out the methods to incite it, Zeri and I, in those last days, though I suspected they'd known what was coming all along.

"I didn't," they promised. "Not totally. But it's true I knew you. There are bits of your future that are my past. That's all I want to say about it, babe, because I don't want to mess things up."

We'd done it out of order. I knew that for sure once I got back. Zeri's sensory films had faded, only the faintest hints of light and taste and sound left on them, but I recognized the scenes and filled the details out in my mind. The café. The gallery we'd visited. The stars we'd seen; the stars we'd been.

I didn't know how I answered them, how I seeded myself through time so they could know me in the first place. But I had a lifetime to figure it out.

"Think Reyhurn was right about one thing?" T.K. asked one June night, sitting on the front porch. "That it really could be us that did it—made the portals pop up by scheming with the futurekin to make a mess of time?"

I leaned back in my chair. "Zeri thought it was possible. They said the ripple effects might affect the years around the flooding of the conduit, and it might have been what punched holes in the walls. But I don't know." I shrugged. "I'm not sure I want to know."

They smiled, glancing out at the sunset. "Thought you wanted to be sure of the future. Get all the answers."

"I did," I said, and then didn't say anything more.

We watched the sky turn red, Quiche snoozing at our feet. They hadn't been pregnant: they'd been twelve segmented beings who preferred to move around as one. "The queerest shit I've ever heard," said Marley, declaring them the house mascot. Above us the stars started to surface in the sky, casting light across time.

"You can thrive there, too," Zeri told me. "I promise you. It's how you get us here."

T.K. and I rocked in our chairs like old men we'd known in our youth, the moment stretching into eternity. Past, present, future: it didn't matter. We were here; here was everywhere.

Bang Bang

by Meg Elison

YOU WON'T EVEN SEE the sign until you're past Phobos, and even then only if your nav system is calibrated to pick it up. It transmits on an old frequency; the sound is faded. It'll give you the directions, and from there it's just fifteen AU to the Love Shack, baby.

You'll be heading down the route past Hanny's Voorwerp. There was a quasar event there that left those bright, glittering fields when a little galaxy winked out. See what remains when something bright and beautiful collapses into a field of glamorous debris with a black hole for a heart. That's basically me out there.

Me? You're probably seeing me on viz by now. I've got me a Kreisler M345. It's old, handles like a whale. But it still moves fast and silent. She berths about twenty. So when I found out the Love Shack was open again, I sent out an encrypted message: Be ready to launch tomorrow, and bring alloy chips to pay the musicians. Do not bring alliance credits; nobody will accept.

It used to be on Europa, you know. Sounds like a myth but I swear to gods. I used to go there when I was a beautiful young thing. Just me in my putt-putt Vespa SoloMio. My parents didn't know, and when it was in the solar system I could sneak back in before dawn and they'd never know I was gone.

My viz from then looks incredibly dated now, but we were all so young. When I was twenty-two, everybody was wearing those retro shiny onesies. In viz, they reflect all colors of light. Hot as an oven in there. Here, look at this one. See Manny's thighs? You can see the reflection of the shooter. He was in the airlock for a long time, psyching himself up. And then he just stood there and watched a while.

Manny didn't make it. Yeah, I was there. The Love Shack closed after that for an Earth year or two. Or it was open somewhere and nobody told me. We used to joke that survivors were bad luck charms. And then there were so many of us they couldn't keep that going anymore.

You found the sign! It has that warning to stay away—that's to keep fools from trying it when they're not ready to take the risk. You said you're ready, right? That's what I thought. They've got better security than ever now. I've been four times, at this location. I remember when it was in the Kuiper Belt for a hot second. That was a funky little rock. Sat way back in the middle of the dynamically cold field, and we could watch centaurs coming and going as we partied.

Love rules at the Love Shack. That's the purpose. No speeches about our rights, or how many have to fall. No memorial buoys droning the names of the dead. It's literally just . . . yes. Those are important. No, nobody is forgotten. Kid, listen to me. It's literally just a place to dance and kiss and hug without looking around first. In that outfit you're afraid to wear. Yes. The music will be loud. They play stuff from before the bans, when we could still publish. No, not the stuff that will make you cry. If Lil Nas X makes you cry, that's on you.

The glitter effect. You'll be able to see it as soon as you're in visual range. Girl, on everything. No I—I'm sorry. It was different for us. We were all girls. No, I understand. I'm not one of those. Do you have a preferred—boi? Thank you, my boi. You'll see it as soon as you're in range, because they put it on fucking everything. It used to be a seasonal thing, and then they just hosed the place down with the stuff. It's on the main port, sprayed all over the transmitter array. Even on the mattresses inside. There's synth g. Of course there is—you ever try to have an orgy in zero g? Oh, you haven't. Never? This will be your first . . . sweet Selena. No. No, honey boi, I am so happy for you. You're gonna remember this night for the rest of your life. Yes, it's safe. Well, the sex is.

It's a little old place where people like us can get together. You won't believe what it's like inside. The crowd is one living organism. Rooms writhe and spin around and around, like a single animal that's in love with itself. Everybody is so kind to one another. There is no wrong body. I promise, baby boi. They're not invited. Yes, the whole Shack shimmies. We are all quaking organelles in a sweet and salty body, passing the energy from one to the next, making and sharing everything we need in that place with each other. Nobody else can make it. It has to be from us, to us. For us, made by us. We have to love us.

Of course there's a signal. There's been a signal since the last time it happened on Earth. The secret knock—you've got it down? Who taught you? Your brother! Is he on this trip too? Let me talk to—oh. I'm so sorry to hear that. Ceres. Yeah, I was there for that one, too. A lot of brave people died that night. He was one of the ones to run toward the device? Most of the rest of us made it out. Travis. Twenty-five, wow. The most beautiful ones are always the first to go. Me too, kid. Maybe that's the secret.

You mean a signal if shit is going sideways? Honey, you'll know. I don't keep a count. Two dozen, maybe. Everyone on my ship. We're all geezers, baby boi. There are always survivors. The ones who are left are too mean to kill.

Your brother teach you the password? Let me hear it. You're what? No, it's tin. Tin? A cheap soft metal mined on Earth a long time ago. The Love Shack accepts it in alloy chips, but only at a small percentage. Yes, corrosion. Caused by moisture—or bacteria in the moisture, maybe? Eats your alloys. No, I've never seen rust. I'm not that fucking old, kid. It only comes up in songs and stories. It was red. No idea, but those are the words. Let me hear you say it again. You're what?

Perfect. You're perfect.

It might be. I don't know. You have to know somebody to find out about this one, like you heard about it from your brother. There might well be another one somewhere, but we don't know anybody who can clue us in. I hope so, too. No, not really. It might be the last. But as long as there's one. Yeah, me too.

I'm about to dock. Folks in all kinds of ships lined up outside, just to get down. I'll stay on the comm with you. You have the pattern? Hit it. What frequency are you on? Turn that up. Knock a little louder, sugar. I can't hear you, so they definitely can't hear you. Again. Bang on that door, baby. Again. They're clearing me to come in now. Hit it. Hit it like you mean it. Bang bang! Bang bang! That's it. That's it, my brave boi. I'll see you inside. Let me know when you're leaving. Last call? Good to be young. Yes, commlink me then. Let me know you're safe. You too, baby boi. You too.

Contributor Bios

ESTHER ALTER (she/her) is a trans anti-Zionist Jewish short story writer, game designer, and open source software engineer. Her fiction has been published in *Baffling Magazine*, khōréō, and the anthology *Luminescent Machinations*. Her games are available at https://subalterngames.itch.io. Her software can be found at https://github.com/subalterngames. Follow her on Mastodon @ esther_alter@mastodon.social

BENDI BARRETT (he/him) is a speculative fiction writer, game designer, and alleged grown-up living in Chicago. He's published interactive novels through Choice of Games, and his novella *Empire of the Feast* was a 2023 Ignyte Best Novella finalist. He also writes gay erotic fiction as Benji Bright and runs a Patreon for the thirsty masses. He can be found at Benmakesstuff.com and occasionally on twitter/x as @bendied and blue sky as @bendibarrett.bsky.social.

TA-WEI CHI 紀大偉 (author), with a PhD in Comparative Literature at UCLA, is associate professor of Taiwanese literature at National

Chengchi University in Taipei, where he teaches LGBT studies and disability studies. His academic monograph discusses a history of queer literature in Taiwan from the 1960s to the new millennium. His queer science fiction novel *The Membranes*, originally published in Chinese, is available in Japanese, French, Korean, Italian, Danish, and English. His story collection, *The Pearls*, is available in French. Visit him at taweichi.com.

ARIEL CHU (she/they) is a PhD student in Creative Writing and Literature at the University of Southern California. She received an MFA in Creative Writing from Syracuse University, where she was awarded the Shirley Jackson Prize in Fiction. Ariel has been published by *The Rumpus*, *Black Warrior Review*, and *The Common*, among others. Her works have been nominated for the Pushcart Prize, Best of the Net Award, and Best Short Fictions Anthology, and she has received support from Kundiman, the Steinbeck Fellowship, the Luce Scholars Program, and the P.D. Soros Fellowship for New Americans.

CD COVINGTON has MAs in German and linguistics. She is an alumna of Viable Paradise, an associate member of SFWA, and a member of Codex. Her website is at cdcovington.com.

COLIN DEAN is a writer, and he is also the pseudonym of an award-winning children's book author. This is Colin's first published work.

MAYA DEANE (she/her) first retold the *Iliad* at the age of six. Athena was the protagonist; all six pages were typed up on a Commodore 64; there were many spelling errors. (She has only doubled down since then.) A graduate of the University of

Maryland and the Rutgers-Camden MFA, Maya lives with her fiancée of many years, their dear friend, and two cats named after gods. She is a trans woman, bisexual, and fond of spears, books, and jewelry. Aphrodite smiles upon her.

DOMINIQUE DICKEY is a speculative fiction writer and game designer. As the creative director of Sly Robot Games, they've created *Plant Girl Game* and *Tomorrow on Revelation III*. They contributed to the Nebula Award-winning *Thirsty Sword Lesbians*, and the ENNIE Award-winning *Journeys Through the Radiant Citadel*. Their novella *Redundancies & Potentials* was published by Neon Hemlock in 2024. Their short fiction has appeared in venues including *Fantasy Magazine*, *Lightspeed Magazine*, and *Nightmare Magazine*. They live in the DC area, where they're always on the hunt for their next idea. You can find their work at dominiquedickey.com.

KATHARINE DUCKETT (she/her/they/them) is the award-winning author of *Miranda in Milan*, the Shakespearean fantasy novella debut that NPR calls "intriguing, adept, inventive, and sexy." Her short fiction has appeared on Tor.com and in *Uncanny*, *Apex*, *PseudoPod*, and *Interzone*, as well as various anthologies including *Disabled People Destroy Science Fiction*, *Wilde Stories 2015: The Year's Best Gay Speculative Fiction*, *Some of the Best from Tor.com 2020*, *Rebuilding Tomorrow: Anthology of Life After the Apocalypse*, and *Greater Than His Nature*. She served as the guest fiction editor for Uncanny's *Disabled People Destroy Fantasy* issue, and is an Advisory Board member for the Octavia Project, a Brooklyn nonprofit offering free summer programs that use the creative power of science fiction and community to inspire young women and trans and nonbinary youth to envision bold new futures. Originally from East Tennessee, she now lives with her wife in New York.

MEG ELISON (she/they) is a Hugo, Philip K. Dick and Locus award winning author, as well as a Nebula, Sturgeon, and Otherwise awards finalist. A prolific short story writer and essayist, Elison has been published in *Scientific American*, *McSweeney's*, *Fantasy & Science Fiction*, *Fangoria*, and *Best American Science Fiction and Fantasy*. Elison is a high school dropout and a graduate of UC Berkeley. She lives in Brooklyn. megelison.com

PAUL EVANBY (he/him) is a Dutch writer living in the Netherlands. Among his novels are the critically acclaimed *De scrypturist* and *Een rivier van goden*. His shorter work has appeared in a variety of Dutch publications, and in two collections: *Gödel Slam* and *Systems of Romance*. English-language stories have also appeared in *Strange Horizons*, *Interzone*, *Harrington Gay Men's Literary Quarterly*, *The Elastic Book of Numbers*, and other venues. He is online at www.metromantyck.net, and on social media.

AYSHA U. FARAH is a science fiction writer and game dev from the American South. You can find her work in *Uncanny Magazine*, *FORESHADOW Anthology*, and Magic the Gathering. She lives with her wife and large cat, languishing in the humidity.

SARAH GAILEY (they/them) is a Hugo Award Winning and Bestselling author of speculative fiction, short stories, and essays. Their nonfiction has been published by dozens of venues internationally. Their fiction has been published in over seven different languages. Their most recent novel, *Just Like Home*, and most recent original comic book series with BOOM! Studios, *Know Your Station* are available now. You can find links to their work at sarahgailey.com.

ASH HUANG'S (she/her) fiction appears in *Apparition Literary Magazine, Orion's Belt,* and *Alien Magazine*. Her novel-in-progress, *Rogue Mother,* won the 2022 Diverse Worlds Grant from the Speculative Literature Foundation. She is an alum of the Roots. Wounds. Words. speculative fiction workshop, the Tin House Workshop for short fiction, and the Periplus Fellowship. Find her at https://ashsmash.com/ or on Twitter and Instagram @ ashsmash.

MARGARET KILLJOY (she/they) is a transfeminine author and musician living in the Appalachian mountains with her dog. She is the author of *A Country of Ghosts* as well as the Danielle Cain series of novellas; she plays piano, synth, and harp in the feminist black metal band Feminazgûl; and she is the host of the community and individual preparedness podcast Live Like the World is Dying and the history podcast Cool People Who Did Cool Stuff.

WEN-YI LEE is a Clarion West Workshop alum whose short fiction has appeared in venues like *Lightspeed, Uncanny,* and *Strange Horizons,* as well as in various anthologies, National Gallery Singapore, and a national future thinking project. She likes writing about girls with bite, feral nature, and ghosts. She is the author of YA horror *The Dark We Know* and is also working on an adult historical fantasy set in postcolonial Singapore. Find her on socials @wenyilee__ and otherwise at wenyileewrites.com.

EWEN MA (they/he) writes fiction and poetry, devises theatre, and is a lapsed visual cultures scholar made in Hong Kong. Ewen's work has been published in venues including *Uncanny, The Deadlands, Fusion Fragment, Anathema Spec,* and *Voice & Verse,* as well as shortlisted for the Future Worlds Prize in 2020. A graduate of both Clarion West and Tin House, Ewen currently divides his time between Hong Kong, Taiwan, and the UK. Catch Ewen online at http://ewenma.com or @awenigma.

JAMIE MCGHEE (any pronouns) is a novelist who aspires to build, through language, interactive spaces of resistance and experimentation. She is the author of several books, including *You Mean It Or You Don't: James Baldwin's Radical Challenge* (co-authored with Dr. Adam Hollowell of Duke University) and the forthcoming graphic novel *Not Light, But Fire*.

SAM J. MILLER'S books have been called "must reads" and "bests of the year" by *USA Today, Entertainment Weekly, NPR,* and *O: The Oprah Magazine*, among others. He is the Nebula-Award-winning author of *Blackfish City*, which has been translated into six languages and won the hopefully-soon-to-be-renamed John W. Campbell Memorial Award. Sam's short stories have been nominated for the World Fantasy, Theodore Sturgeon, and Locus Awards, and reprinted in dozens of anthologies. He's also the last in a long line of butchers. He lives in New York City, and at samjmiller.com

AIKI MIRA (they/them) is an author of essays, short fiction and novels. Their short fiction has received significant recognition, including the German Science Fiction Award in both 2022 and 2023, as well as the Kurd Laßwitz Preis in 2022, and is being translated into English, French and Chinese. In 2023, Aiki was honored with the Chrysalis Award from the European Science Fiction Society. Aikis debut *Titans Kinder* was nominated for major awards and the novels, *Neongrau* and *Neurobiest*, each received the prestigious Kurd

Laßwitz Preis for Best Novel. *Neongrau* is currently being produced into a drama series for radio. Beyond their writing, Aiki co-hosts the science fiction podcast *Das war morgen*.

SUNNY MORAINE is—among many other things—the author of the novella *Your Shadow Half Remains*, published by Tor Nightfire. Their debut short fiction collection *Singing With All My Skin and Bone* was released in 2016 and their short stories have been published in Tor.com, *Uncanny*, *Clarkesworld*, *Strange Horizons*, *Lightspeed*, and *Nightmare*. An occasional podcaster/narrator/voice actor, they are the writer, producer, and lead actor of the serial horror drama podcast Gone, which wrapped up its first season in January 2018 and released a second season in 2022.

NAT X RAY (he/they) is a trans writer originally from Austin, Texas, and currently based in Brooklyn. "Trans World Takeover" is his first literary publication.

NEON YANG (they/them) is the author of the Tensorate series of novellas from Tor.Com Publishing (*The Red Threads of Fortune*, *The Black Tides of Heaven*, *The Descent of Monsters* and *The Ascent to Godhood*). Their work has been shortlisted for the Hugo, Nebula, and World Fantasy Awards, Their debut novel, *The Genesis of Misery*, will be published by Tor in September 2022. Neon is queer, non-binary, and lives in the UK. Find them on Instagram as @its-neonyang, and otherwise at http://neonyang.com.

RAMEZ YOAKEIM (he/him)—born in Egypt, raised in Australia, and now living with his husband in the United States—spent his whole life adapting. A one-time engineer and educator, Ramez writes mostly about hope, including "More Than Trinkets," named one of Tor.com's Must-Read Speculative Short Fiction. You'll find more of his stories in Flame Tree Press and Little Blue Marble anthologies, podcasts from Metaphorosis and StarShipSofa, and online in Translunar Travelers Lounge, UtopiaSF, Sci Phi Journal, among others. Discover more on his website, yoakeim.com.

Acknowledgments

Let me first thank all the people whose friendship, care, and affection keeps me going. From the groupchats to the dinner companions; from the daily texters to the ones who check in at just the right time; from the local pals who take afternoon walks with me to the folks I have to fly cross-country(s) to see . . . every one of you contributes to the fullness of my life. Salute to the problem children and the sexy fun queer media we share—plus all our favorite boys. Juggling writing a dissertation for a PhD in Gender Studies, which has been successfully completed as of the publication of this book, while editing an anthology at the same time wasn't the easiest thing . . . but having good friends to commiserate with lightened the load. Without you all, there probably wouldn't be any books to my name.

Thank you to the late José Esteban Muñoz, whose philosophy both undergirds this book and keeps me going on the hard days—but who I never once met. Thank you also to the other artists whose work buoyed me through the lengthy process of crafting and editing an anthology, which from start to finish took a couple of years. To name a handful of pieces that kept me company while I was gnawing on the concept "stories of queer futurity": an inspirational run of queer Thai series including but not limited to *The Eclipse*, *Not Me*, and *Moonlight Chicken*; the 4k restorations of Gregg Araki's *Teenage Apocalypse* trilogy and also Jane Schoenbrun's *I Saw the TV Glow*; the second season of *Interview with the Vampire*; the *D-Day* album by Agust D (a.k.a. Min Yoongi); and novels like Dolki Min's *Walking Practice*, Vajra Chandrasekera's *The Saint of Bright Doors*, and Justin Torres's *Blackouts*. (There's a hundred more, of course. And then another hundred after that.)

I must also thank the entire team behind the creation of *Amplitudes*. Firstly my gratitude to Tara Gilbert, the agent who sold this project, and to Kate McKean, who currently represents my work. The entire Erewhon team deserves my thanks as well— Cassandra Farrin, Kelsy Thompson, Rayne Stone, Adrian James, Noah Camp, Shannon Gray-Winter, and Kasie Griffitts—with with a special shout-out to those I worked closest with: Diana Pho, Viengsamai Fetters, and Martin Cahill. Thanks also to all the folks at Kensington, and to the Penguin Random House sales team. Then, of course, a triple-strength thank you to all the writers and translators without whose work this book literally wouldn't exist. I am so grateful that you trusted me with your stories. It was an honor to bring them into conversation with one another, and an honor to collaborate with you all.

Lastly, thanks as always to the readers: you make this possible.

Discussion Questions

These suggested questions are to spark conversation and enhance your reading of *Amplitudes: Stories of Queer and Trans Futurity*.

1. Lee Mandelo writes in the Introduction, "I see the process of editing an anthology to be more akin to curating a conversation . . . rather than staking any authoritative claim on representing a given theme." What kind of conversations did this anthology spark for you?

2. What are some of the many different ways queerness and-or transness appear, intersect, and are understood as well as lived out by the characters in these stories? How do these sometimes widely varying approaches toward what it means to be queer and-or trans—as both an identity and a cultural/material experience—come into conversation with one each other?

3. The word "amplitudes" has a few different definitions. According to the Merriam-Webster dictionary, amplitudes can mean the "extent or range of a quality, property, process." It is also defined as "extent of dignity, excellence, or splendor." Does the impact of this anthology and its exploration of queerness and transness fit either or both definitions, literally and artistically? How so?

4. Many stories in *Amplitudes* take place in near- and far-future dystopias and address the radical ways people survive inside a dystopian world. Which stories with this theme stood out to you the most? Why?

5. How do you think these stories portray political organizing? In your opinion, are some methods more plausible than others? How did certain characters or groups in these stories work together despite holding different perspectives or coming from various backgrounds?

6. Faith and religion play a role in several of these stories. How do these queer and trans characters incorporate faith into their lives? Or, how did they reject or resist certain religious beliefs and practices?

7. Punks, vagabonds, mercenaries, lumberjacks, drug-runners, spies: many of these protagonists live life on the social margins. Do you think there is a thematic link between the queerness of these characters and their occupations and/or other subcultural identities? Why or why not?

8. Found family and alternate forms of community are a common theme throughout. Some found families are based on cooperation and trust; others are built out of fear and necessity. From these stories, what are the challenges in trying to create and sustain found family and community?

9. What kinds of ideas about "futurity," or possible ways of imagining our collective futures, did you find most compelling? What about the most realistic, or most hopeful? Were those ideas the same or different?

10. Were there any stories that made you consider a political or social concept in a new light? How would you say a certain story helped expand your perspective, and were there any other reoccurring themes that stood out to you across several stories?

11. Why do you think the editor arranged the stories in this order? What connections do you see between the first story and the last story? Additionally, several stories use experimental structures or prose styles—how do these contribute to and shape the experience of reading the anthology?

12. Lastly, taken as a whole, what messages or emotional responses do you think this anthology wants to convey to the reader—and how would you describe it to another reader interested in exploring more queer and trans fiction?